SHIFTER SCHOOL

A WYRDOS UNIVERSE NOVEL

GWENDOLYN DRUYOR

SHIFTER SCHOOL BOOK ONE

Get your Bonus Wyrdos Book!

Want to know more about the Wyrdos world? Visit my website below and subscribe to get your complimentary copy of *Doug vs. The Boogeyman*!

Wyrdos.net

Enjoy!
Gwendolyn

v25116

1

Normal fourteen-year-olds don't wake up thinking about death. But Laylea wasn't anything close to normal. She woke up composing a letter to her adopted parents telling them all the things she'd never get the chance to say in person. Sometimes she thought of writing a letter to her brother, Bailey. Some mornings she imagined leaving a letter for her birth mother too, in case they ever found her. Laylea had been composing the morning letters ever since she'd gone to a veterinarian's office on a case last summer. Waiting in the lobby for the tech she was following, she'd read every pamphlet the clinic had. Including one that said the average lifespan for a twelve-pound terrier was thirteen to fifteen years.

She'd been fourteen for eight weeks now.

"Lee!" Bailey's voice sliced through her morbid thoughts.

They lived in a basement studio apartment. He didn't need to yell.

Laylea whined back at him and stretched all four paws against the bedsheets. She rolled to her side and tucked her nose under her tail. She loved her tail. She'd probably spend more time in her human shape if she could keep her tail. Not that she really had a choice in the matter, as Bailey constantly reminded her.

"Laylea Hillen." Bailey could sound an awful lot like their mother when he wanted to.

Laylea missed Sher and all her rules. She missed Clark even more, if she were honest. After three years apart, the aching loss had dulled a bit, but now, with fifteen looming on the horizon, Laylea found herself getting a little desperate to see her parents again before she died.

An uncommon scent drifted over the bed. Her tail, with no permission, popped out and thumped against the mattress. Laylea poked just the tip of her pale muzzle between folds of the tangled sheets and sniffed the air. The familiar, soapy musk of her brother and the tang of his computers were muted by the joyful smell of a peanut butter oatmeal tuna muffin. Laylea barked. She wriggled out of the sheets, stupid tail throwing her balance all over the place.

She was thrown even more off balance by Bailey's shout. "Lee Woodford! The solar panels are blocked and Madam Hu's grow lamps are dimming."

She stared at him for another moment. He'd used her alias. Though unusual, that wasn't so terribly surprising. After three years in hiding, she was used to answering to the name, just not used to him using it. But she stared at him because he looked like his natural self. His hair lay in black curls over his light-brown face.

When they ran to Chicago, Laylea and Bailey needed to hide as best they could from the Consortium. It was easy for Laylea to live under the radar. But Bailey had been accepted to DePaul as Bailey Hillen. There were public records pointing straight to him. He couldn't change his name. So he changed his face.

He changed his entire appearance, actually, to look like Laylea's blood-brother. It was the only magic he did these days, and since he never changed back, Laylea had almost forgotten how different he really looked. Where she was tiny as a human, he was big. He had wide shoulders, a preternaturally muscled torso, and perfectly monstrous thighs. Where she was pale as a Swedish shut-in, he could have won a tanning contest in Belize.

He leaned out of their galley kitchen, holding onto the post with one thick forearm, blue eyes sparking and sharp features setting off the cleft chin, which was one of the few innocuous genetic traits he'd inherited from Clark. One hand held the walkie-talkie their landlady had given them when she offered to lower their rent in exchange for handyman help. His other large hand held a plate with her adoption-versary muffin.

He lifted the muffin to his lips. "If you don't get out of bed and up to the roof, I'm going to eat your breakfast."

Laylea wriggled out of the sheets and leaped to the cushioned barstool Bailey used as a bedside table. She used the back of the stool to help her spring up to the empty shelf on the brick and 2x4 bookshelf they used as a headboard. The window was open a crack, which made it easy for Laylea to push it with her head and paws until it was wide enough for her to squeeze out into the little wooden crawlspace under the front porch.

"Don't forget your—" Bailey's admonition was lost as the dust under the porch tickled Laylea's nose.

She gave one sharp sneeze, blowing the dirt around and dusting the stash of emergency sundresses she kept piled in the corner. She never wore them for long anyway. She took a peek through the latticework to check for witnesses before pushing through the loose slat on one side of the crawlspace and out to the front steps.

Laylea shook the last of her sleepiness away and took a breath of the crisp air. The low sun was awfully bright for May in Chicago but clouds warned of rain later. She hopped up the stairs and ran out to relieve herself by her favorite tree on the devil strip. Out of habit she grabbed a quick sniff at the base of the tree for any new dogs in the neighborhood. Smelled like Nemo was still on prednisone, poor Shepherd.

Laylea pushed her dog instincts to the side and head-butted her way through the rarely latched gate to their side alley. Near the back of the house, she trotted up the ramp on an old shoe-shine stand Madam Hu used as a table for the food she put out for area strays. Lee jumped from the base up to the faded and torn bench seat and from there to the fence between Madam Hu's backyard and the apartment building next door. She tight-rope walked along the fence for three feet before she could leap up to the back porch of the second-floor west apartment. A nice lady named Sue lived there.

Laylea took the rickety wooden porch steps up to the third floor. This was the tricky maneuver. She backed up the entire length of the porch the top two units shared and raced like an airplane down a runway. She leaped to the railing at the last second and vaulted into the sky, aiming for the slightly higher rooftop of Madam Hu's house.

Halfway through her death-defying leap, Laylea remembered to retract her claws. This distracted her just enough that she twisted as she landed on the slick, tilted solar panels. Her little body slammed sideways into the smart-glass surface and she tumbled down, hurtling toward a thirty-foot drop.

Even as her heart clawed its way up to choke her, Laylea diagnosed the problem with Madam Hu's power. The neighbors had erected a projection screen on their roof that was blocking two-thirds of the solar panels.

The edge of the solar panels slid past and Laylea tensed. She prepped her dad-like reflexes. By the time she hit the wide gutter surrounding the roof, instead of bouncing off and falling thirty feet to her demise, she was ready to launch herself back over the divide to the apartment roof. Her normally sharp internal sensors were kind of dizzy by the time her paws hit the gravelly tar paper of the apartment building's unfinished roof deck. If she fought her momentum, she might just tumble backwards off the roof, so she just tried to keep on her feet as she barreled forward on all fours.

The makeshift movie screen was just a white sheet hung from a hastily-erected PVC frame, and Laylea's trajectory sent her smack into the base. The entire structure collapsed.

When the tumbling and crashing quieted and the sheet finished billowing down over her, Laylea gave herself a moment to breathe.

Bailey could have gotten to the rooftop, too. And he could have opened doors and climbed the inside stairs to get there safely. Why had he sent her instead? Was there some reason he needed to get her out of the apartment on this very special day? Were Clark and Sher hiding around the corner just waiting for her to leave so they could sneak in?

No. They could have snuck in while she was sleeping and woken her up with Bailey like they did back home.

Was he kicking her out like he'd threatened to if she couldn't control her shifting between human and dog? She really was trying. She just didn't have anyone to help her. The only other shapeshifter she knew was Captain Morioka, and the dragon-lady's advice hadn't been particularly helpful since she'd learned how to shapeshift literally eons ago. Laylea might as well ask her to explain how she blinked.

Laylea tried to not blink, but the white sheet didn't really block much sun, so she gave up.

Sher said that certain people, most people, were wired to respond. If you said blink, they would blink. It was a basic principle of operant conditioning. Maybe she could condition herself; think *shift* or ring a bell like Pavlov every time she changed shape.

She felt a pressure deep in her mouth, right back where it turned into throat. The birth of a yawn. As soon as she thought the word, the pressure rolled forward, up through her face bones and down along her lower jaw. The pressure rolled her long, pink tongue right out of her mouth and squeezed a squeak from her. Yawns happened naturally. But she could also make herself yawn. Just thinking the word again did it. She yawned.

Maybe shifting was like that.

She tried to feel the tingling burn that started in her stomach when she shifted naturally. But all she dredged up was a gurgle of hunger and a memory of the delicious muffin waiting for her downstairs.

Today was her adoptionversary!

She scrabbled her way out of the sheet and scattered frame. Right on time, someone on the third-floor porch pulled down the hatch with hidden stairs. Laylea scampered over behind the trash-barrel keg on the far side of the roof. Anyone coming up would be drawn to the disaster that used to be a cool private movie theater. They'd be looking away from the keg.

"Is someone up here?" The guy's eyes were so quickly drawn to the mess that he almost fell up the last couple of steps. "What the hell?"

Laylea didn't wait. She raced out from behind the barrel and glided as silently as she could down the skinny steps. Once on the porch, she gave up all caution and galloped to the ground level. Jumping the fence would be faster, but she was done with fantastic leaps for a few hours at least. She scrambled through the neighbors' out-of-control azalea bush and wiggled through the tunnel she'd dug under the fence a year ago. It came up behind Madam Hu's tomato plot. She ran back along the alley and then down the stairs, into the crawlspace, and smack into a closed window.

2

Laylea fell back into the dirt under the porch. Bailey had closed the window. She stuck her nose beside the frame and pushed. It didn't budge. She tried to use her paws and had no better luck. He'd locked the window, too.

She pawed at the glass and whimpered. She could see her brother, sitting at his desk, facing the three giant ultra-private monitors attached to his computer. She couldn't tell if he was working on some class report or his own personal research. But what did it matter? She'd been gone ten minutes and he'd locked the window and gone back to work.

Maybe he really was kicking her out. Maybe he'd finally decided her shifting issues were too likely to get them discovered. But she really was trying. She bit back another whimper.

Bailey never did anything but study. Every day he drowned himself a little more in learning everything his teachers and the vast interwebs could teach him about biology. He never spent time any more practicing magic. He knew how hard it was to get magic right and how much he'd learned during those few years when the mom was giving him lessons. So why was he so hard on Laylea for not figuring out her own magic when she'd never had anyone but a Pre-

Cambrian Era dragon-demon to teach her? He had to see what a double standard that was.

Plus, if he kicked her out, Sher and Clark would kill him. Wouldn't they?

Laylea spotted her peanut butter oatmeal tuna muffin sitting on the desk beside him. He hadn't eaten it. Why would he have even made it if he was kicking her out?

She barked.

Bailey swept his screens blank as he spun around. He pointed at the door and raised his eyebrows. She raised her eyebrows and lifted one thumb-less paw. He held up the muffin. She showed her teeth.

Was he trying to force her to shift? A shift-or-you-don't-get-the-muffin kind of thing?

Laylea tried again to think of the burning spark in her belly. Then she realized she was in a three-foot-tall crawlspace with a half-foot-wide exit and stopped.

Inside, Bailey was holding something up in his other hand. She pressed her nose against the glass to see better.

It was a standard brass door key with a green sleeve over the head: her house key. Even if she could shift, she still couldn't get inside.

Don't forget your key.

That's what he'd said. That's what he said pretty much every time she left the apartment. Like he never forgot his key when he was a kid. Even if she did forget to take her key now and then, their landlady, Madam Hu, always buzzed her in. Madam Hu would invite her upstairs for tea or her grand-niece would run down to sit on the porch and pet Laylea's belly for hours. That kind of reinforcement didn't really help her remember her key. One time, when she'd *had* her key, she'd scratched at the door anyway just for the belly rubs.

Laylea backed away from the window and slipped out to their door under the stairs. She made one more half-hearted attempt to shift before she started straight-up howling. She heard Bailey's chair smash into the desk inside. Bailey tripped once getting to the door and nearly ripped it off its hinges when he got there.

Laylea quietly trotted past him and hopped right back into bed.

"You have to remember your key. You can't count on Madam Hu or Fan to buzz you in. We need to be more invisible." Bailey paused for a breath. "Do you get it? Do you know what the Consortium would do to you if they found you? If they found me?"

Laylea dropped her head. She pasted her ears back against her head and sunk so far into herself that she felt like she was being swallowed up in the comforter. Today was her adoptionversary, her special day. It was the day her bio-mom saved her life by finding her the best dad and mom and big brothers in the whole world. Fourteen years ago today, six-year-old Bailey had found her on the front porch; a tiny fawn-colored puppy with a white triangle over her eyes, tucked in an old Easter basket.

Today was supposed to be the best day of the whole year.

"Happy Adoptionversary, Lee." Bailey said it with a sigh in his voice. He didn't mean it. She wasn't his beloved puppy or sister anymore. She was just a burden.

He sat on the edge of the bed. "It's just that they're counting on me, you know? To keep you safe."

Laylea looked up. He took the muffin off the plate and held it out. As he reached toward her, the hair on his hand turned blue. He made the blue wash up his arm to his elbow.

Laylea dropped her jaw in a grin. He was doing magic. She barked through a mouthful of muffin and her brother smiled.

He scratched her ears for a bit as she ate. Then his mind went back to his own day. "I've got a meeting with Dr. Palmer after class, so I don't think I'm gonna make it to your barbecue at The Office."

She pouted up at him.

He wiped a chunk of tuna off her nose. "Oh, you won't miss me. Every time I meet you at The Office, you and your Team Wyrdos run off to save the world or rescue a nest of fledgling imps or something."

Laylea stopped licking her paws to stare at him like he was crazy.

He glared back. "Every time."

He stood and Laylea leapt up to lick the last bits of muffin from his blue hand. He took the plate to the kitchen while she stuck her butt up in the air in her first good, long, morning Downward Dog.

Laylea spun around at a sudden clank from the ancient claw-foot radiator. She felt that spark in her belly that she'd been trying to ignite. If she could tamp it down and stop the change, that would be something. But she couldn't. She barely had time to think the thought before the spark blazed up into her chest and filled her whole body with electric pain. She shifted. In a flash she went from cuddly fuzzbucket stretching on the side of the bed to awkward, stick-shaped girl losing a wrestling match with the sheets. Laylea yelped as she tumbled off the bed. She landed on her left hip and yelled, her human vocal chords unable to imitate the canine cry she heard in her head.

Bailey swept all the dishes into the sink with a clatter. His sigh could have been heard in outer space. "You're hopeless, Laylea."

Even though she agreed, she coughed out an objection. "Be nice. It's my adoptionversary."

Talking was always difficult right after she shifted. Her stubby tongue felt awkward and fat. She loved the thumbs that came with being human. But speech was overrated.

"Hey!" Laylea hustled to grab her green robe from its hook over the bed. She had a whole list of things she needed to do while she had thumbs, and she couldn't be sure how long she'd have them. First on the list, a request Bailey was guaranteed to deny. "Could you make my hair purple? As my gift. I saw a girl at the library with purple streaks and she looked so cool."

Bailey did not deny the request. He ignored it. From the doorway to the bathroom he asked, "Your hip okay?"

It was nice to hear his concern. Most of the time he was too preoccupied with his studies to worry about his little sister.

"Yeah. It never bothers me as a human." She grabbed her water bowl from its spot on the floor by the radiator and hustled over to the kitchen to rinse it and refill it with cool water. "Not since Mom woogied it."

Bailey had invented the word *woogie* to describe magic. The bathroom door clicked shut. Apparently, he was done talking about it for the day. Laylea sighed. She worried about him. Sher had said if he didn't practice, he'd be dangerous. Bailey was her son so he got half his genetic makeup from her crazy-powerful witch family. But he was also Clark's son, and Sher had genetically modified Clark for the Consortium. Sure, they knew Bailey was strong. He had heightened hearing and pattern recognition skills rivaling a computer's. But what else had he inherited from Clark? And how was that affected by his magical side? They had no answers and the mom and dad had only just begun testing him when the Consortium found the family and they all had to run.

Laylea took a deep breath and tilted the bowl up for a drink as she crossed back to replace it on the floor.

She'd covered their cement floor with layers of rugs other, more discerning, Chicagoans had thrown out. One of the more recent acquisitions still smelled a little like the explosion that had left its former owner not needing rugs anymore. She couldn't even cajole Bailey into woogiing the gas smell away, as easy as that would be.

She knee-walked her way over the rugs to one of the six packed bookshelves that insulated their walls. Her hardcover copy of *The Call of the Wild* was tucked in behind a row of must-reads Bailey would never voluntarily pick up. Plus, it was on the bottom shelf, which was, historically, her domain. Listening to the shower start up, Laylea opened Jack London's illustrated classic to reveal a hollow center filled with cash.

Laylea didn't exist as far as the United States government was concerned. This meant she couldn't open a bank account. The whole hiding-from-a-team-of-evil-scientists also precluded leaving a money trail. But since she couldn't go to school, Laylea worked.

Laylea solved problems. Mostly she hired herself out as a Private Investigator specializing in Paranormal Mysteries. She couldn't call herself that, though, for two reasons. First, her cop friends wouldn't let her call herself a PI because she wasn't licensed. Detective Kyle Nellwin had said she could call herself a PUPPI, a Preternatural Underage Person Pursuing Information. Though, mostly she didn't, since her clients wouldn't get the joke. Second, most of her clients didn't realize their mysteries were paranormal. Most of her clients were thumpers, natural humans, and most thumpers had no clue about the supernatural world all around them. Laylea had only ever known of one thumper in the know, and Kyle wasn't a thumper anymore. All her friends knew he was dead, but that wasn't the whole truth.

When Laylea did spend money, it was usually on clothing. She wasn't a fashionista or anything, she just lost a lot of clothes. She only wished there were more size one homeless girls in Chicago to benefit. Well, she didn't really wish there were more homeless at all. But she did keep caches of clothing all over the north side for shifting emergencies. Their friend Amal's grandson ran a clothing warehouse and provided her with size one sweats, t-shirts, and sundresses in bulk.

Amal and his brownie friends Orin and Lucio had worked with a Renn Faire artisan to create a wide fabric collar for Laylea. The yellow polka dotted collar featured several zippered pockets and elastic all around so it would fit both her dog and human neck. The tag read *Lee* since that was the name the boys knew her by. It was Laylea's most prized possession. The only other thing she'd ever really owned was the stuffed lizard Sher had made for her out of a patchwork of fabrics. Laylea'd had to leave the lizard behind when they ran away. She still missed it on sad nights.

She unzipped one of the pockets on her collar and wrestled out a folded wad of bills. She smoothed them on one knee and added the cash to the hidden stash in her book. Laylea didn't hold on to much money herself. She mostly ate kibble since she couldn't count on turning human at meal times, and Amal got her a killer discount on the bulk clothing orders. She didn't have an El pass since there was nowhere to hide on a public train or bus and lots of loud, surprising noises that might make her shift. She couldn't fit a cell phone in her collar and couldn't risk carrying around a GPS tracker anyway. So her costs were pretty minimal.

But there was the rent. Bailey's full-ride scholarship had included room and board, but they'd had to find a new place to live after Bailey had been kicked out of the dorms for hiding a pet.

Clark and Sher sent cash when they could, but they'd not sent any money or letters in months. And as sparsely as the Hillen kids lived,

Laylea worried that Bailey wouldn't be able to survive on his own after she died. So she hid most of what she earned in Jack London's masterpiece. She'd have to mention it in her letter to Bailey, when she finally got around to writing it.

The back door slammed outside. Laylea pulled a few bills out of the book and then slipped it back onto the shelf behind the novels their parents sent for them to use as ciphers. Laylea had read all of them. Bailey never read anything but textbooks and scientific journals.

Laylea headed over to the desk and reached up to twitch aside the heavy brocade curtain on the window. Madam Hu was rolling a wheelbarrow along the path between patches of her vegetable garden. Madam Hu's garden was her pride and joy. She spent hours working over it in all weather. She even had a small herb garden inside her apartment for deep winter, and she loaded Laylea down with herbs each time she succumbed to the old woman's entreaties to join her for tea.

Madam Hu was a dream landlady. She'd bought the converted three-flat just days after Bailey and Laylea had applied for the apartment. She lived on the top floor with her grand-niece, Fan, who always carried liver treats in her pocket.

Laylea took Bailey's wallet from his backpack and slipped the bills inside. Then she grabbed the envelope sitting in the empty ashtray designated to hold *her* things and hollered to Bailey, "I'm running out to pay the rent. Think about the purple. I'd look so cute!"

The door was already closing behind her when she realized what Bailey had yelled back, "Don't forget your house key!"

She spun, but the door latched behind her.

"Shit."

3

Laylea glanced over at the latticework hiding the crawlspace under the porch but there was no way she could squeeze through that window in human form, even as piddly as she was. Without thinking, she tried the doorknob because, though she knew the door locked automatically, she persisted in hoping that her brother would magically unlock it for her. Nothing. Well, she didn't really need to get back inside right now, anyway.

She turned in the little alcove under the front steps and jogged up the side stairs. Glancing out at the wet street, she pulled open the old wrought iron gate blocking the little alley. The latch had long been broken on the old gate. Bailey had offered to fix it, and Madam Hu's response had put her permanently on Laylea's Good Girl list.

The old woman had raised her heavily painted eyebrows and said, "No, dear. That alley is a perfect shelter for neighborhood dogs to hide out from the weather."

Laylea jogged down the poorly weeded passageway to the back yard. She squeezed by the shoeshine stand instead of trying to vault over it. That hadn't gone well last time. Her puppy parkour skills did not translate to her human form. Which was odd since she always felt the dog inside trying to take over. Three years as an occasional human and she still had to fight to keep her arms from twitching when she ran upright. Walking was okay. But anything faster and she wanted four paws and a tail.

"Top o' the morning, Madam Hu," Laylea called out as she rounded the building onto the brick pathway winding through the immaculately weeded gardens.

Madam Hu emptied her shovel into the wheelbarrow before she turned. "Good morning, Wai-Sun."

Laylea had no idea what that meant. She called Bailey Mr. Woodford, but Laylea was always Wai-Sun. Her grand-niece, Fan, also called Laylea Wai-Sun, and it made the puppy-girl smile every time.

Their landlady wiped a hand on the apron covering her purple Northwestern sweatshirt. "Have you come to help me spread compost?"

Laylea crinkled her nose, thankful she wasn't a dog at that moment. She had a preternaturally good sense of smell as a human, but it didn't even compare to the sensitivity of her canine sniffer. "Aw, man, poop day, and I'm all booked up with other plans."

The old woman laughed. As usual, her face was covered with extensive, stylized makeup. She always painted her face ghostly white, sometimes leaving a clean border to give herself a pointy chin or widows peak. Everything else was constantly changing. Today she had tiny pink lips and red shadow brushed over and under her bright eyes, but no liner. She tilted her head in a slight bow. Laylea responded with a lower bow.

"Sorry, Madam Hu. Just bringing the rent." She held out the envelope.

Madam Hu took it and tucked the money away in the deep pocket of her apron. "Never apologize for giving me cash. But do you know you're ten days early?"

Laylea bounced over to the gardening shed and grabbed a shovel. "Fan said you might be going out of town, and I didn't want to be late." She dug into the rich black dirt tumbling out of the bottom of the wooden composter and scooped a little into the wheelbarrow.

Madam Hu leaned on her pitchfork. "I don't understand why

people complain that teenagers are so irresponsible these days. You are a very good girl."

Laylea ducked her head to hide the blush burning up her cheeks. She felt her psychic tail wagging at the magic words. Good Girl was even better than Wai-Sun. She shoveled more compost into the wheelbarrow. "Thank you, ma'am. Wish I could stay. I've got to get back inside before Bails leaves for class."

"You forget your house key again?"

Laylea glanced up. One black eyebrow rose high into Madam Hu's pale-painted forehead, and Laylea unconsciously raised a hand to the pale diamond on her own forehead. If she ever learned to keep human form she'd have to try that makeup trick. The white would cover her birthmark perfectly.

"Yes, ma'am."

"Do you need me to buzz you in?"

Laylea looked up so sharply, she spilled most of her shovelful before she even reached the wheel barrow. "Wouldn't you have to go all the way upstairs to do that?"

The woman didn't move. "Yes."

"That's silly." Laylea dashed over to return the shovel to its hook inside the shed. "I'll just run around and knock. Bailey has to be out of the shower by now."

"Okay."

"Thanks, though."

Madam Hu nodded. "Anytime."

Laylea waved as she tripped through the carrot patch, heading for the alley.

She'd just turned the corner when Madam Hu quietly called, "Oh, Lee?"

She flipped around and leaned past the corner. "Yes, ma'am?"

"Happy Adoptionversary."

Laylea felt the tingle in her belly just in time. She ducked back into the alley as the spark rose to ignite behind her heart. She fell to the ground in a pile of green flannel. Her tail wagged in circles even as she sighed in frustration. So, happy surprises could make her shift now. She allowed herself a moment of joy at Madam Hu's recognition of her special day. Then she grabbed her robe in her tiny terrier teeth and galloped up to the unlocked front gate. It took a little maneuvering to get her robe through untorn, but she managed. It took more effort to scratch at the front door. She dreaded Bailey's reproach.

Sure enough, he shoved the door open so fast he almost hit her. Laylea had to leap back and then, of course, she tripped on the twisted fabric of her robe. Bailey grabbed the robe, searching the limited view to the street for any passersby. Laylea rolled to her paws and slipped inside.

Bailey barely waited until he'd closed the door to start lecturing her. "You have to learn to control yourself. What happens to Mom and Dad if you get caught? They can't protect you and fight the Consortium at the same time. Really, Laylea, you know better."

As if knowing better made any difference. Bailey could choose not to do magic, as stupid as that choice was, but she didn't have that option. She was a dog. And sometimes her body wanted to be a human. The only people who had any clue why were an evil scientist named Walter and her birth mother who had abandoned Laylea and her brothers to hide them from Walter.

"You know why I won't turn your hair purple?"

Bailey wouldn't even use the word woogie.

"Even if I turned your hair purple, it would just reset to blonde seconds later when the radiator scared you."

On cue, the radiator clanked. Laylea sucked in her breath and fought to hold her shape. When no tickle wriggled through her insides, she sat up and raised an eyebrow at her brother.

"That was luck. You have no control and no discipline and thank goodness we were kicked out of the dorms before anyone saw. I shouldn't let you out of this apartment."

Laylea sucked in her breath again, but Bailey's threat was negated as he pushed open the crawlspace window over the bed. When she saw him going for his backpack, she dashed into the kitchen to scarf down the kibble he'd put out for her. If she were human, she could scold him right back for holding in his magic and risking a blow up. He had a social security number and a school ID and an email address. There were a dozen ways the Consortium could track him. Legally, she didn't exist. She was born a puppy. There was no way she'd ever have an honest-to-goodness PI license, since she'd never have a legal name to register under unless she stole it or bought it on the black market. She could disappear into the mist and nobody would ever notice. Most of the time, Bailey didn't even notice her. Despite fourteen years and eight weeks on this Earth, three of them partially as a human, the world would just keep on spinning when she died.

But she wouldn't tell him any of that if she were human. Because he already knew it. And she had to keep him calm. She was the only one around who knew what he was, the only one who could keep him from busting through his own self-control. And if he ever lost it, the fallout would be way worse than if some thumper learned shapeshifters were real.

"Are you ready to go?"

Laylea looked up to see Bailey waiting by the door. She dashed over to the radiator for another drink.

"Busy day?" he asked as he tucked an umbrella in his backpack.

Like he'd use it. Bailey adored rainy days. It reminded them both of home in the Pacific Northwest where rain either became a close friend or drove you bat shit.

Laylea had a very busy day planned. She wanted to check out a couple possible locations for the illegal drug lab the Wyrdos Team had been trying to find. The drug, N, was giving thumpers wyrdo-like abilities and frying natural and supernatural brain cells equally. She also needed to run some research at the surveyor's office if she could go human while Chad was working the front desk. She'd get some bonus info on her client's project while she was there and then run by his mom's house to double-check the results.

Then, of course, she had to run all the way south to Common Electronics to actually meet with the client, which was sure to be a blast. He was such an open-minded and engaging guy. Not.

She just nodded at Bailey in answer, dripping water all the way over to his side by the door. He wasn't even looking at her.

In fact, he avoided her eyes while he pulled his key ring from the hook by the door. "Have fun at The Office barbecue."

Laylea whimpered.

"I've got a lot of work to do and the library closes early."

Laylea noticed that was a different excuse than he'd used earlier.

He lowered his voice as he turned the knob. "If there's anything at school from Mom and Dad, I'll bring it by."

Laylea stood up on the door before Bailey could open it.

"I promise."

She barked and shook her head vigorously, flapping her ears in the move Clark had called 'helicoptering' since it sounded like thwapping rotors.

Bailey's brow wrinkled and he shook his head a little in unconscious imitation. It took him a good few seconds before he caught on. His hands flew up in front of him. The left was still covered with blue hair.

"Right." The blush was barely visible under his dark skin. "It's nice to look like me."

He stared at his hands for another moment. Then he shook his head to spur the wave of transformation from his hair down through his whole body. His skin paled, his eyes shifted from blue to brown, and his curls straightened into a dirty-blond mop that exactly matched the color of Laylea's fur. His muscled chest sunk in and the stretched fabric of his pants and sleeves relaxed. He grinned down at Laylea while, just for an instant, he sported what looked like a white scar or birthmark between his eyes in imitation of the mark on her forehead. Laylea sang out and the white faded away, as did the blue hair on his hand.

"All good?" he asked.

Laylea checked him out. He looked just like her, if she were a boy, and human. She bobbed her head.

Bailey opened the door and let her go out ahead of him. "Do me a favor and be safe with whatever PI job you're doing." He bent down to scratch between her ears. "And don't get killed rescuing a kitten from a tree."

Laylea *pffd* between her lips. As if she'd do any favors for a cat. Please.

It wasn't until he'd locked the deadbolt and was headed up the stairs that Laylea realized she still didn't have her house key.

4

Laylea had been trying to shift for twenty minutes in the alley behind Common Electronics when a bat fell out of the sky and onto her head. She and the bat rolled in opposite directions. It hit the crackled cement with a thud and a plink. The plink caught her attention. Why would a bat go *plink*?

She leapt from the muddy puddle it had knocked her into and, not really looking where she was going, slammed into the alley wall. She spun around to growl at the tiny winged rat, but as soon as she'd gotten herself straightened out enough to bare her teeth, the bat blinded her with a flash of brilliant light. Her fierce growl petered out as she blinked the sparkling dots from her eyes.

As the light show cleared, she realized she knew the tall black man who stood where the bat had fallen. He didn't stand solidly. Laylea cowered back between the wall and the crate holding her hidden sundress and sandals while Kyle teetered and tested his balance. He failed.

As a dog, she could only watch all the gangly limbs of her vampire friend flail as he tumbled to the cracked and muddy ground of the alley. Despite his utter lack of grace, one of Kyle's hands managed to land squarely on top of the finely wrought mortise key that had plinked when he hit Laylea.

Laylea knew that key. She was the one who'd hung it around Kyle's neck. She couldn't see the key through his ashy hand, but the silver chain that held it snaked out between his fingers. That key had almost brought about Armageddon. It *had* brought Armageddon if you believed Amal's version of events.

"Hey, Lee. How's tricks?" Kyle's long, sharp face brightened in a smile.

Laylea barked a reply and raised her eyebrows.

"Same old, same old," he replied. "You know."

She looked pointedly from his washed-out eyes to his smoking hand. He followed her gaze.

"Hard habit to quit." Kyle kept his tone light, but he lifted his smoldering hand an inch off the iron mortise key.

He paused for a bit, watching her as if he expected the twelve-pound terrier to continue the conversation. He was always polite like that. Even back when he was a thumper cop running around with Dee solving murders. It wasn't just that he treated Laylea the dog like a person, he treated Laylea the teen like a real person.

"So, I've got some news," he finally continued.

Laylea blew air through her lips in her canine version of *duh.*

"Turns out I can turn into a bat."

Laylea dashed in to nip at his pants leg, her jealousy plain in the stiffness of her ears and tail.

"Yeah. My clothes shift with me. Sandals, wedding ring, everything in my pockets. But not the key." He pulled a handkerchief from his back pocket and wrapped it around the rapidly healing burn on his hand. "The cursed thing just dangles around my tiny bat neck, weighing me down. Flying is hard enough to begin with. I tried to leave the key in the apartment, but I never made it more than a block away before I *had* to go back to it."

When Kyle said *cursed,* he wasn't being metaphorical. His maker had been cursed by some überpowerful vampire muckety-mucks to carry this key and keep it away from its lock. Somehow, possibly because his maker had died during the process, she'd passed her curse on to Kyle in making him. Laylea had carried the key for less than 12 hours and Kyle had unknowingly followed her the whole time, while turning from a human homicide detective into a blood-sucking demon. Good times.

Kyle gathered up the key and its chain. "I need to get better at flying, kid. And I need to figure out what to do with the key when I shift."

Laylea had plenty of ideas on that. The key was tiny. They'd just have to find him a necklace with elastics, like her collar, that would shrink when he shifted to bat.

But Kyle went on. "So I've come up with a temporary solution." He pulled Laylea into his lap before she knew what was happening. "I trust you. I'm going to give you the key until I've got a better grip on this flying thing. You don't mind, right?"

She did mind. Laylea didn't want anything to do with that cursed key. She struggled against his hold, stunned that he'd do this after everything she'd done for him. She'd helped him survive the turning. She hadn't told anyone he was still alive—well, still around. She even checked in on his wife and daughter regularly without him asking.

Her struggling did no good. He was bigger than her and he had vampire strength. He fumbled with a zipper on her collar, barely shoving the key in before he dropped her back to the alley floor and stumbled to his feet.

"I'm sorry." The worthless apology scratched from his throat as he ran away.

She chased him. She'd almost caught up when he slammed into a metal dumpster. He flashed and her chest exploded in a white-hot pain.

Then, her human knees slammed into the broken cement, and she barely got her hands out to save her face from smashing down, too. Kyle the bat stuttered through the air and away.

Laylea blew on her bloody hands and knees for just a moment before she dashed back to the crate and her spare clothes. She was already ten minutes late for her appointment, and, since she couldn't fly, she might as well address the problem in front of her. The scrapes were bad but they'd heal as soon as she shifted again, so she hustled down the alley to the back door of Common Electronics, brushing the dirt and rubble from her bloody palms.

An argument had been raging in the back room of the store since she'd arrived. One reason she scheduled meets at CE was because they kept the back door cracked, but today it was a little embarrassing. Even though their distraction meant it would be easier for her to slip in, she actually considered going around to the front like a real customer.

"Karly Carlotta, you listen to your father. We know what's best for you, and you are going to the compound."

That was Mrs. Delcampo, one of the owners. Laylea never asked her for help finding things in the shop since the woman generally assumed anyone other than her was an idiot.

Laylea paused outside while the daughter yelled, "You are such liars!"

"Watch your tone." Mrs. Delcampo kept her voice low or maybe she was looking out at the floor to see if any customers had overheard.

"Kitten cat," a male voice cajoled. Mr. Delcampo worked the register and didn't mind bargaining if Laylea was buying in bulk. But even though she'd been in the store a dozen times, he never remembered her. She had the feeling this retail thing hadn't been his original life plan.

"You said if I came up with the tuition on my own I could go to L.P."

"LPSS is a school for losers and failures who don't have the family connections you have." It sounded like Mrs. Delcampo had slid the office door shut because her voice was suddenly much quieter. "You're going to—"

"I am not going to the compound. I am not going to spend the next six years being bullied by my brainwashed cousins."

Laylea slipped through the door. The back hallway was stacked with boxes and open containers holding customers' equipment and appliances waiting to be repaired. She took a second to adjust to the dimmer lighting and strange smells inside. Her senses always focused on the deep, unexpectedly musky scent underlying the eye-watering tang of electrical equipment and metal. Her human brain couldn't quite isolate the confusing combination, and it made her a little wary.

"Your great-grandfather is—"

"The smallest-minded bully of them all. I earned the money, Mom. I already sent it in and got a spot in LPSS. All you have to do is take me there."

There was a hopeful pause before Mr. Delcampo put his foot down. "We won't do it."

"I'm your kid. Parents are supposed to love their kids and want them to be happy."

Laylea decided her eyes and nose had adjusted enough. She felt creepy listening in to this fight. And, to be honest, it made her miss her parents. Sure, they made mistakes but they loved her and Bailey, and definitely wanted them to be safe and happy. So why hadn't they sent her any message for her adoptionversary? Or any message at all for months now?

Before the tears could come, Laylea tiptoed past the office door, around the repair cubby, and under the front counter into the retail section of the electronics shop. She looked up at the security mirrors in the corners. Her client was, as she'd expected, staring out the front door. Despite the warm sun, he stood bundled up in a trench coat and scarf with a Sox cap pulled low over his greasy hair.

Durant Felzer had been referred to her by a previous client. All her clients were referrals. Advertising didn't really work since she had no contact information. She met with her clients in person and that was the only communication she had with them. Usually she met them first at Seb's bar, The Office. It was *the* supernatural hangout in Chicago, and she could count on Seb and the regulars to get her back if ever a meet went south.

She'd met Felzer at a law office on Canal. He'd wanted her to have their second meeting at his mother's new house so he could watch Laylea examine the place. It had taken some convincing to get him to understand her process and agree to meet here for the results. Even then, she'd had to stake the house out for a few days before she found a time to get in when Felzer wasn't there.

Frankly, the mother was probably safer with her ghosts than she was with her overbearing son. She didn't seem bothered by the dead family at all, and the ghosts didn't mind her living in their home. They really didn't like her son, though.

"We want you to be successful. You belong with the pack in Montana." Mr. Delcampo's voice was muffled enough that neither of the customers browsing near the counter could hear. It was just Laylea's special abilities that allowed her to eavesdrop on this family drama.

"I'm not going to Montana. I'm going to LP."

The girl's tone had shifted. Laylea heard a decision in her voice that hadn't been there before. She quietly cheered for her even as she headed down the right aisle to surprise Felzer.

Mrs. Delcampo's ultimatum froze her in her tracks for a moment. "Then you're on your own, Karly Carlotta. Don't expect us to take you back in."

"What?" The shock in the daughter's voice matched the fire Laylea felt in her heart for the girl.

"I'm sorry, kitten cat, but your mother is right. If you want to live under our roof, you have to follow our rules."

"I *am* following your rules. You told me if I paid the tuition, I could go." There was steel in Karly's voice that her parents clearly didn't hear.

The office door slammed open as Mrs. Delcampo dismissed the whole discussion. "Your imagination is going to get you into trouble, young lady."

"I'm not making it up. Dad, you know I'm not making it up. You said—"

"You're getting on a plane tonight for Montana and that's it." Mr. Delcampo had the decency to whisper but that made no difference to Laylea's hearing.

The entire Delcampo family came out of the side office and turned as one to check if any customers had heard their argument. Laylea dropped to the ground. Every nerve in her body sparked, terrified they'd seen her. Every nerve, but especially in her belly. Laylea slapped her hands over her gut. She had nowhere to hide. The back door was blocked by the Delcampos, and the front was blocked by Durant Felzer. If she shifted now, everyone would see. Slowly, the tingling burn rose to her chest.

5

Laylea held her breath. She forced her mind to her happy place like Captain Morioka had suggested. Though she kept her human eyes glued to the well-worn carpet under the pass-through counter, her mind's eye focused on the image of fluffy clouds beyond the cockpit window and Clark's concentrated face. She heard him singing his stay-calm song.

I will not kill another soul today.

What a dumb song. She'd never thought of it before. But how did reminding himself he was a killer calm him down? And what made her think that remembering flying with her dad when she hadn't seen him in three years and probably would never see him again because she was going to die any day now would calm *her* down? This was all just some stupid floofy, woo-woo, mumbo-jumbo when what she needed were real, solid answers to how to shift and not-shift on command. She couldn't be the only shifter in the world besides a brand-new bat who got to keep his clothes and an eons-old dragon. And she wasn't. She had a mother and four biological brothers out there in the world somewhere. If she could find her mother, she could learn how to shift.

"Can I help you?" Karly Carlotta used both hands to help her lean over the counter. A thick, brown, double ponytail dangled over one shoulder. She looked about the same age as Laylea, and her voice held a challenge. She knew Laylea had heard something and was daring her to say something. Though her eyes were puffy and red, a spark of defiance still lit her up.

Laylea grinned up at her. She'd managed to keep from shifting, but she couldn't keep the blood from flooding her pale face. "I'm . . . looking at these old thumb drives." She tapped the glass display case. "Not many people use these anymore, huh?"

"Nobody uses them." Karly Carlotta frowned at her. "USB has been dead for like a decade."

"So . . . it would be good for passing secrets." Laylea untangled her limbs and pulled herself up.

The darker girl seemed to forget her parents and their fight while she considered the idea. "If you both have ancient technology, yeah. But better to go with codex-encrypted dibs drives."

"Those little quarter-sized drives you set on the CPU?"

The girl held up her arm to show Laylea a charmband resting above her elbow. "I've got some you can just set on any connected device."

Laylea leaned in to look at the three attached drives pressing little circles into Karly Carlotta's upper arm. She whispered, "You okay?"

The girl's eyes flashed with anger and Laylea cowered back. But then an intense sadness softened Karly's face for just an instant.

She nodded and an evil grin bubbled through. "I can make you a real good deal on a pack of these dibs drives right now. Just got them in today."

"I'll take them." Laylea looked down the aisle at Felzer who was still staring daggers at the front door. "Be right back."

Karly pulled a set of keys from the wall of cool tools behind her head. "I'll get your drives."

Laylea headed down the aisle to meet her client. She lifted a package of cabling off the end cap as she passed.

"Mr. Felzer? I didn't notice you come in. Why don't you walk with me? I need to get a couple of those new dibs drives for my dad."

Felzer spun around. Laylea barely controlled her inner joy at making him jump.

"I was expecting you a half hour ago."

"I'm sorry. I've been comparing cables in the far aisle. Maybe I was crouched down when you looked around the shop for me."

The shadow that crossed his eyes confirmed her suspicion that he'd gotten here early and taken up his post at the door just to call her out on being late. He'd never even thought to look for her inside.

"Well, we're both here now and I've got news for you if you've got cash for me." She strolled up the aisle as she spoke, picking up different data storage devices and examining them as she moved away from the front door. Felzer followed.

"Is it haunted or not?" He whispered the question, looking over his shoulder as he did. He didn't look up at the mirror where he would have seen Karly Carlotta watching from the checkout counter.

She whispered back, "Yes."

Suddenly Felzer was over the discreet game. He yelled, "I knew you were a fraud."

He turned as if he were going to storm off. Laylea grabbed the belt of his trench coat.

"You owe me the rest of my fee."

"I don't pay liars." He smacked her hand then tried to pry open her fist.

"You wouldn't have given me half upfront if you didn't believe in me."

Felzer raised his hand like he was going to hit Laylea. She'd never had a client get violent before and was regretting all the times she'd chickened out of asking Dee for self-defense advice.

All she could do was throw an arm in front of her face, tamp down on that burny place in her belly, and keep talking. "I'm sorry you don't like the answer, but it's the truth. There's nothing I can do."

"Except . . ." Karly Carlotta Delcampo was suddenly standing behind Felzer.

The man wrenched his neck turning to look at her. He used his raised hand to adjust his ball cap like he hadn't just been about to hit a fourteen-year-old girl in a public store.

Karly Carlotta stood solidly. All five-foot-two of her in purple plaid capris and a yellow Common Electronics tee planted between Felzer and the exit.

She flashed a look at the security mirror in the corner, pointing it out to Felzer, and then conspicuously lowered her voice. "Except we called an exorcist. Should I cancel the exorcist, Lee? The exorcist that you had me hire for Mr. Felzer? For the haunted house?"

Laylea gawked at the girl. How did she know the client's name? They were too far away from the counter for her to have heard Laylea say it. How did she know Laylea's name? Felzer hadn't exactly greeted her. And how did she know about the haunting? A million questions buzzed through her mind before she grasped the relevant fact that Karly Carlotta was saving her butt.

"Yeah." She released Felzer's belt and resisted flexing the sore fingers. "Definitely cancel the exorcist since Mr. Felzer is refusing to settle his bill. Can you call Captain Morioka, too? If he's refusing to pay us, I'd bet he's done this before."

Karly Carlotta was already tapping and swiping away on her wrist pad. "I'll just shoot a note to Dr. Rishmurthy at Public Health, too."

"The psychiatric specialist?" Laylea asked. "Yeah, make it a public bulletin. I think all the docs on the city net will want to know that a purportedly healthy stock analyst believes ghosts are real. Good idea . . ." Laylea knew it would be easy enough for a smart guy to figure out who worked at Common Electronics, but Felzer didn't seem like a really smart guy, so she quickly changed what she was going to say. "Good idea, KC."

A grin flashed across Karly Carlotta's face and disappeared. Sweat dripped down Felzer's forehead. Could have been because he was swathed in clothing in a pretty hot store, but Laylea didn't think so.

"No," he hissed. "Hold up your armpadd, I'll credit you the rest."

"Cash only, sir." Karly held her fingers poised over her wrist. "I've got the police captain on Urgent Message. What should I tell her?"

Laylea paused for a second to give Felzer a chance. When he didn't speak, she said, "Start with our location—"

"Fine." Felzer pulled a hand from his coat pocket and threw a stack of bills in Laylea's face. She let most of them flutter to the worn carpet.

"I think you've overpaid, here." She tried to count the bills then gave up and bent to scrape it all up.

"Call off the police. Don't you post on the public bulletin." He held a claw over Karly Carlotta's wrist like he would peel the armpadd from her skin. "And," he remembered to whisper again, "don't cancel the exorcist."

Karly Carlotta shook her wrist to cancel out of all apps. She smiled at Felzer. "There's no exorcist. But I've got a top-of-the-line night vision camera hidden in this crystal cat that might help you confirm Lee's conclusions. Since you don't believe her." She reached over without looking and scanned a box on the shelf to her right. "You seem like a cat lover."

Laylea wasn't certain but she thought Karly Carlotta meant that as an insult.

"And the store does take credit." Karly held up her wrist with the glowing invoice.

Felzer looked around the store for help, but there were no adults in sight. Unless you looked in the security mirrors, which he didn't. He slapped his wrist and then held the exchange chip on the back up to Karly's invoice. Both devices chirped. Felzer tore the box from the shelf and shoved Karly Carlotta aside to storm out of the store. The bells over the door didn't so much jingle as crash against the frame.

Laylea goggled at Karly Carlotta. She'd never met a girl her own age with such chutzpah. But even as she stared in awe, the girl seemed to shrink in on herself. Her eyes flashed to the mirror in the corner just as Laylea saw Mr. Delcampo lift the pass-through on the counter.

"Sorry!" Laylea trilled out the apology while she bounced to the front of the store. "Karly Carlotta told me you were getting the latest dibs drives in today. Do you have them?"

"Oh. Yes." Mr. Delcampo physically backed away from her enthusiasm. "And how do you know my daughter?"

She'd been in the store at least a dozen times. She'd bought nearly all of Bailey's computer equipment here.

"She's a friend from school, Dad." Karly pulled one of her ponytails forward and wrapped it around a finger. "I talk about her all the time."

"Oh. It's nice to meet you. Wrap this up quick, kitten cat. You have to pack."

Laylea could feel the heat coming off Karly Carlotta. She pretended not to see the tear that sizzled down the girl's cheek as her father brushed a hand down her hair and wandered out to the floor to help an adult customer.

Karly Carlotta ducked under the counter to the register tablet. She pulled a short stack of plastic wrapped dibs drives from a pocket. "You want me to cut off the tag so they'll fit in your necklace?

Laylea nodded until she found her voice. "Thanks."

Karly Carlotta shrugged a shoulder. "You're a good customer." She sliced the cardboard tag off with a box knife and resealed the plastic with some sort of squeezy heat gun she pulled from the wall of cool tools.

"How did you know my name?"

The other girl raised one expressive eyebrow and tilted her head. Then she pointed. "It's on your necklace."

Laylea blushed again. "Right."

Before she could gather her wits to ask how she knew everything else, Karly Carlotta asked, "Did he really overpay you?"

Laylea glanced down at the bills in her hands. "Yeah. Hey, you need —" She'd almost blurted out *cab fare* but that would have revealed how much she'd heard of the argument. "Here." She held out the whole stack. "Your collection fee."

Karly Carlotta glanced at the mirrors before she selected three of the bills. "Oh." She took a fourth. "For your dibs drives. Do you really want that cable?"

Laylea shook her head. "It was just a prop." She turned to hang it back on the end cap display. "Good luck."

"Don't forget your dibs." Karly Carlotta held out the small package.

Mrs. Delcampo stormed in through the back door. Her hair and clothes were damp and she shook herself as she made her way up to the front counter. The way she did it put Laylea in mind of herself in dog form and she almost smiled until the woman glanced around for witnesses and apparently decided Laylea didn't count.

"Karly Carlotta Delcampo, you get right upstairs and pack. You will not be late for that flight."

Laylea pulled another bill from the stack and set it on the counter before taking the pack of dibs. "Always a pleasure doing business with you."

Mrs. Delcampo completely ignored her. "Young lady, do not ignore me. It is nearly five o'clock."

"What?" Laylea freaked. "Really? Shit, I'm supposed to be at the bar." She winked at Karly Carlotta and ran down the aisle to the front door and its jingle bells.

6

Come the end times, Seb's bar was where all the wyrdos would gather. In fact, it's exactly where they did gather when Onioka destroyed the world. Now, Laylea's adoptionversary wasn't exactly the end of the world, but with only three people in the bar, it sure felt like it.

Laylea had a brief, crazy hope that once her eyes adjusted, the bar would miraculously turn out to be filled with friends come to celebrate with her. It was perpetually gloomy in The Office. The windows looked filthy, but really Seb had sprayed them dark so it always felt late in the little 1920's style pub. As her eyes adjusted she confirmed that the only other people in the bar were Ned at his customary two-top and Seb, changing a keg behind the bar.

Ned always sat in the farthest, darkest corner from the front door. He nodded at Laylea but quickly turned his eyes back down to the chunky cable afghan he was knitting. He wasn't concerned about a fourteen-year-old in the bar.

Laylea stepped away from the new digital jukebox to shake the rain from her hair. The downpour had begun in earnest when she was still three miles from The Office, and she couldn't move very fast as a pixie-sized human.

The Office wasn't really the kind of bar you'd expect to feature an app-driven jukebox. But after last October, the regulars couldn't really face his antique quarter-driven machine anymore. So Seb had relegated it to Brown's Resale and Consignment across the street and replaced it with this slick modern contraption. Now you could play a song on the thing from anywhere in the world.

The door opened. A gangly white guy in his early twenties with untamable brownish blond hair backed in shaking the rain from his umbrella. Junior had put some meat on his bones since they'd first met last October, but not much. He still looked like his jeans were a couple sizes too large and his pea coat was too heavy for his lanky frame. The smile was a nice new addition.

He flung his arms wide as soon as he spotted her. "Happy Birthday, Lee!"

She disappeared in the boogeyman's embrace.

Technically, Junior was just the boogeyman's bastard son, but he'd adjusted to that unpleasant fact enough to accept the inherited title, if not all the preconceptions that went with it. And he didn't know that Laylea was adopted. Or that her real name was Laylea.

She was in hiding, even from her friends. The only wyrdo who knew the truth, or at least some of it, was Orin Morton, one of the three brownies that owned Brown's Resale and Consignment. He'd dated her mom decades ago when they were in college together back East. Now he was the only other one around to keep an eye out for Walter. He might have told his sister but Laylea couldn't really tell. Detective Dee Morton had always been a hard woman to read.

"Lee?" Junior asked the question with Laylea's face still smooshed against his chest.

"Mmm hm?

"You couldn't have told me you're soaking wet before I hugged you?"

Laylea stepped away to see a her-shaped wet mark up and down Junior's coat. "You didn't really give me a chance. I just got here. Why didn't you come through the closet?"

As the boogeyman's son, Junior had the ability to travel to any bedroom closet in the world from any bedroom closet in the world. Since Laylea regularly napped in The Office's supply room, Junior usually came to the bar through the supply room closet.

"I did. I was on time. Just had to run out to pick something up." Junior dug through the canvas satchel he always wore across his sunken chest. "I'm surprised you're late for your own party."

"Like it matters. No one else is here either."

"Really? Think maybe they're all out back since this is a barbecue party?"

"In the rain?"

He pulled a three-inch-long, one-inch-wide brown paper package from a pocket of his bag and looked around the nearly empty bar before slipping it to her. "Happy birthday. Beef flavored. Do not eat that all at one sitting."

Laylea felt a glow wash over her whole body and the tail she could only imagine right now wagged wildly in her mind. She could tell without even unwrapping it, he'd gotten her a rawhide bone with a knot at either end. Laylea loved rawhide. The beef flavoring only lasted a few licks but since the rawhide was rolled you kept finding new bits of flavor. And it felt so good to chew it down into slobbery, slimy strips of textured goodness. Bailey never let her have rawhide just because it made her gums bleed and she sometimes threw up.

Junior pointed at the hallway beyond the long mahogany bar and its row of padded stools. "Go hide it and change into something dry. Seb?"

The Office's owner and bartender finally looked over. He nodded at them both and greeted them in his charming Scottish accent. "Scarecrow. Happy day, Lee."

As far as anyone knew, Seb had been born right here in Chicago. Possibly right here in the bar. But it was a nice accent and added even more character to the dark pub atmosphere so Laylea never questioned him. Laylea had never even asked him what kind of wyrdo he was. It wasn't really a polite thing to ask. Either you were told what a person was or you assumed they were a thumper. Seb knew way too much about the wyrdo world and the many creatures who hid amongst natural humans to not be supernatural.

Seb looked like he could be Scottish with his rugged, handsome face and thick hair. But he also looked like a wyrdo, standing barely four-foot-five in his stocking feet with muscles that would put a professional wrestler to shame.

"Everyone's out back. The boys rigged a tarp over the courtyard."

Junior hopped up on a stool as Laylea picked her way around the tables to the back hall.

She heard him ask Seb, "What am I drinking tonight?"

"Something without much alcohol if you're bright," came Seb's reply.

As soon as she passed the archway between the bar and the hallway that led to the restrooms, storeroom, and back courtyard, she heard the party. Although most of the conversations weren't very casual.

"It's either Starwood or Wacker Valley labs." That was Dee.

Amal's deep voice answered her. "How did you eliminate the one out in Oak Park?"

"Narcotics raided them yesterday. They're just cooking herointin."

Laylea peeked around the doorframe. Someone had propped it open with a cinder block, which was also holding up a bamboo citronella torch. Once upon a time, the barbecue courtyard had been a muddy recess for the bar's dumpster. Then Amal had built a flap into the door so Laylea could get in and out. Then bit by bit, the brownies had transformed the rest of the wasted space into a classy outdoor lounge where patrons could smoke, if they wanted to be shamed mercilessly by Lucio.

The ground was now covered with well-tended faux grass while the cement walls were hidden with lattice walls attached to a redwood frame. All the wood was woven with ivy and so-called *fairy* lights. They must have attached the tarp to the top of the frame just today. It looked like canvas but the rain sounded like it was pattering on plastic.

Laylea leaned her head on the door with a sigh. Almost all her friends had come to her party.

Amal and Dee sat on the edge of the fountain cobbled together from found rocks, old bike parts, and a tuba.

Dee, the banshee and homicide detective, wore her usual; crisp slacks with sneakers and a button-down hidden by a hoodie and jacket combo. She carried three guns and a fairly comprehensive first aid kit somewhere under all those clothes as well. Amal, the tall brownie, kept reaching over to run one black hand over the fine red fuzz on Dee's head that had been wild curls yesterday. She cut her hair off every year and let it grow back until it bothered her too much. Amal was the only one who could get away with touching it because he allowed Dee the same favor each time he shaved his head, though in his case it was a more regular event. Neither of them had much use for style. For the celebration today, the brownie was wearing camouflage cargo shorts with a purple t-shirt reading "Team Thumpers."

It was clear they were really in the party spirit with their intense discussion of the N drug lab search.

The other two brownies, Lucio and Orin, manned the barbecue pit while little Diejuste helped from her comfy seat in one of the few tall chairs scattered about the courtyard. Lucio stepped behind the cross-legged girl as Orin flipped a couple racks of ribs and slathered them with Seb's bourbon barbecue sauce.

"Whadju do, Lucio?" Diejuste asked in her piping voice.

Diejuste made it look like Laylea had a friend her own age. But that was only because Laylea looked eleven and Diejuste was a centuries-old voudon loa inhabiting a ten-year-old girl. She was cool but she was also kind of a god.

"What do you mean, *what did I do*?" Lucio swept his tweed vest clean and checked the marcel wave of his hair as he stepped back to his beer.

"Your karma keep da sauce off ya clothes, yeah?" she pointed out. "If ya haven't done no bad ting."

Lucio retorted, "My karma's just fine, little girl. The universe knows I went to the black market for good reasons. Sometimes you need to get help. Many heads are better than less than many."

Orin spun toward Lucio like the black market was new news. "You got a bead on who's buying up sligh nuts?"

Sligh nuts were one of the few elements they'd been able to isolate in the N recipe.

"Dude!"

Orin hadn't put down the sauce brush. Bourbon-honey goodness flicked across Lucio and Diejuste. The loa laughed and licked the sauce from her arm.

Lucio pulled a snazzy, mustard-colored handkerchief from his pocket and started dabbing at the stains. "Turns out sligh nuts are legal. They're not dangerous to thumpers. They call them seabat seeds."

Laylea perked up. She'd seen a truck with those words on it when she'd been staking out the Starwood labs building earlier. It was a Healthy-T Snacks semi. The sides were plastered with images of their products and the rear sliding door listed products. Seabat seeds had been on that list. She'd heard the door guard direct the driver to the sleep lab and guessed it was just a delivery of snacks for the machines, but maybe it was more than that. A semi-trailer's worth of snacks would be a bit of overkill for a private sleep lab, wouldn't it?

"What else did ya buy on da black market, brownie?" Diejuste leaned forward to wipe some barbecue sauce from Lucio's sleeve, giggling.

"What? I didn't . . ." Lucio spluttered.

"Your karma did not protect you," she said.

Orin set down the brush and snapped at Lucio. No magic leaped out to clean the sharp-dressed brownie's vest. Orin raised one eyebrow.

Lucio reached into his waistcoat pocket and pulled out a gold ring set with a series of purple stones. "It's the most exquisite efflorescence-cut amethyst. Clearly somebody loved it very much. I'm hoping they'll come looking for it at the shop."

"You plan to put that on our consignment shelves?" Orin asked.

"Obviously."

Orin snapped his fingers in front of Lucio again. The sauce remained. Diejuste giggled.

Lucio stuffed the gem back into his pocket. "Well, I do now."

Orin snapped. The sauce splatters disappeared.

"You're still wet."

Laylea turned to see Junior coming down the hall from the bar. Captain Yaksha Morioka followed at her own pace.

Junior mussed Laylea's sopping hair as he rushed past her into the courtyard. "Hey guys, it's confirmed. They're cooking the N at Starwood Labs."

Laylea heard his announcement but she kept her eyes glued to Captain Morioka. The ancient demon followed slowly behind Junior. She was a tiny Japanese-looking woman who'd been alive longer than humanity had existed. She rarely rushed. Right now, she seemed to be gliding and her black pupils had swallowed up all the white in her eyes. She nodded once at Laylea as she hid her eyes with mirrored sunglasses. When she passed, Laylea sucked her breath in. Folded wings glowed almost invisibly against the back of Morioka's taupe trench coat.

Laylea stayed in the doorway as Morioka stepped out into the courtyard. She imagined the fairy lights dimmed and clouds wafted in to block the pale sun.

All the bright conversations died as well.

Dee rushed the captain. She was the only wyrdo in the courtyard who didn't seem to sense the power rolling off Morioka. "You got him to talk?"

Morioka crossed to rinse a hand in the fountain. "He did not talk. I picked his brain."

There was a pause as every wyrdo in the courtyard decided they did not want to know what that meant.

Morioka wiped her hands on the handkerchief Lucio handed her. "Starwood is the site. And his boss has a meeting there at seven tonight, with the man in charge."

"Hey," All heads turned toward Laylea as she grinned. "I know how we can get in!"

7

Laylea's heartbeat competed with the patter of the rain on the tarp for the loudest sound in the courtyard. All eyes turned from Morioka to her.

Junior nodded his head gingerly. "Yes. We're going to use the brownies' cunning and karma to get us past the guards like we usually do."

"We'll split up into three groups." Dee turned to the others like Laylea hadn't even spoken. "One to find out where that meeting is happening and figure out who the boss man is. One to scout the building and identify a means of thwarting production and/or legally shutting down the ring. And one to hang nearby as backup. Okay?"

Amal was tapping on his armpadd as Dee planned. He held it up and projected a series of pictures onto the uneven wooden wall of the courtyard. "There's a public playground a block away, so Diejuste and I could run the bathroom ruse to get in the front, then scout the building. I think Morioka, Lee, and Orin should hold back. So, the question is, how do we get Dee, Lucio, and Junior in?"

"They get their sligh nut deliveries through a small door in the back," Laylea chimed in.

The others went on planning, flipping through to pictures of the rear entrance. Dee took two steps to close the distance between her and Laylea.

She lowered her voice to a hiss. "You knew they were getting sligh nuts? Morioka only ate that guy because we needed proof. And you had the proof all along?"

Laylea looked down at her wet uggs. She bristled at the accusation but she didn't dare look in Dee's eyes.

For one, Dee could see when people were going to die and she had a pretty bad poker face. Knowing she was going to die soon was one thing. Laylea did not want to know she was going to die today.

For another, she had the irrational feeling that if she let Dee look her in the eye, the detective would be able to tell that Laylea was keeping a secret from her. And if Dee found out that Kyle was still alive, or at least still around, Kyle would kill Laylea. Possibly literally.

So she looked at the ground as she defended herself. "I saw the delivery this morning. I didn't know seabat seeds were the same thing till just now. Look, when I was there, I saw—" Laylea started to explain about the sleep study but Dee dismissed her.

"I vote for the health inspector ruse." Orin raised the grill fork.

Dee shook her head. "Offering sealed snacks doesn't count as serving food."

"Really?" Lucio gagged a little. "They don't have to follow sanitary rules?"

Orin gestured to Lucio with the fork as proof to his argument. "And if Lucio doesn't know that, you think an underpaid rent-a-cop stuck with the night shift is gonna know it?"

Amal waved his hand at the boys and lights flashed across everyone's faces until he refocused on the wall. "It's too risky."

Laylea watched the others arguing. There was no way for her to help her parents fight the Consortium. But she could help Team Wyrdos and they weren't listening. Her frustration boiled over into a sudden flash behind her breastbone and she found herself on the ground, crushing the drenched uggs with her puppy belly. She howled and just as suddenly she was human again, her dress wildly askew.

She had their attention. Before they could dismiss her again, she blurted out her idea. "The fourth floor of the building houses an experimental sleep lab and there's a supply closet indicated on the blueprints. Junior can take Dee and Lucio in, but I think I should go with them since I can sniff out the seabat seeds."

Junior looked back at Diejuste who had travelled with him most often, "Think I can take three people?"

"Take Lee and Dee. I'll hang with my girl, Morioka." Lucio flashed the captain his charming grin.

Orin set down his sauce brush and fork and started damping the fire. "I'll run the *Sneakers*' messenger routine to help Amal and Diejuste." Orin was a huge heist movie fan.

Dee slid her car's starter ring from her finger and tossed it to Amal. "I'm parked a block north. You and Diejuste get going. Everybody who's got a padd, attach your patch and keep your audio links open." She peeled the patch from her own armpadd as she spoke and rubbed it in place under her ear.

Just like that, they were in motion.

So, of course, that's when Bailey showed up.

"Hey, Bails." Amal slid a palm along Bailey's hastily proffered hand as they passed in the doorway. "Catch you on the flip."

"Try da ribs. You need meat on ya bones, boy." Diejuste grinned as she trotted after the brownie.

Laylea blanched. "I'm so sorry, Bailey."

Orin hollered from the exit to the alley where he was grabbing his helmet and messenger bag from a secret cubby behind the wooden frame. "You got stellar timing, Bill Bailey."

He waved over his shoulder and hopped on his classic cruiser.

Lucio didn't even acknowledge Bailey. He was too busy wheedling Morioka to let him drive. They left via the alley as well. Dee nodded her chin at Bailey but stepped away from the fountain to start testing that everyone had their ears on.

Bailey looked at Junior. "You don't have to go?"

Junior adjusted some invented issue with his satchel. He cleared his throat before he said, "I do. But I'm taking her. You want to come with us? You know what Lucio always says, *many heads are better than less than many."*

Bailey raised an eyebrow at that.

Junior stammered, "Or you could wait here in case we need your pre-med skills. Not that we're doing anything dangerous. We're totally not. No one's gonna get hurt. Especially not your sister." He physically reached up to put a hand over his own mouth to stop talking. "Awkward." The boogeyman sidled toward the door. "I'll go wait in the closet."

They watched him slink out and around the doorframe like a goof.

"He's cheered up considerably," Bailey said when he was gone.

"He still has down days. He's kinda unpredictable." Laylea hugged her brother. "Thanks for coming."

"Sure." He started to say more but Dee tapped her wrist as she headed in to the bar, too.

"You should have some ribs." Laylea looked back at the still smoking pit. "And maybe put the fire out some more if you don't mind."

Bailey pulled something from his pocket. "I brought you this."

Laylea held out a hand, suddenly nervous he'd see the rawhide bone that she'd dropped during her quick shift earlier. A spark drew her attention back to now. Her house key, complete with its green plastic hood, lay glowing in her hand. She blinked her eyes a few times and the glow disappeared.

He hadn't really come to celebrate. He'd just brought her house key. Laylea stuttered in a breath and then held it to keep from crying. She kept her eyes down as she slipped the key into her collar beside the roll of dibs drives. She made sure it wasn't in the same pocket as the mortise key.

"Thanks. I'll try not to forget it."

"You can't forget it anymore." Bailey gave her a half-hug to soften the ultimatum. Then he scratched behind her ear and whispered, "Happy Adoptionversary, Laylea."

He walked inside with her. Laylea headed for the supply closet. She watched her brother stroll down to the bar where business had picked up in the last fifteen minutes. She saw that he didn't even turn around when he yelled, "Be safe."

"Kid!" Dee stood in the closet of the storeroom, beside Junior. "It's your plan. Let's go."

Dee had been kinder before she lost Kyle. Laylea dropped her eyes at the thought and hurried over to the closet. She slipped behind the door and kneeled on her red corduroy dog bed to grab a dry pair of knock-off uggs from the shelf holding a stash of her clothing.

Her feet felt so much more ready for an adventure when she stepped in and took Junior's hand. She didn't know how this travel-by-bedroom-closet thing worked but Diejuste said Junior had made leaps and bounds in accuracy, actually getting to the closet he wanted to visit most of the time. She trusted him. Though she and Bailey had nailed their closet shut just in case. So maybe she didn't trust Junior quite as much as she thought. They could really end up anywhere. They could end up in a bedroom closet on fire or in a flood or in Reno.

Laylea jerked from where she waited, calmly holding the boogeyman's hand. But Dee pulled the door shut before she could escape.

8

Junior opened the door into a cold, sterile dorm. Laylea wrinkled her nose. Her eyes watered. How could anyone sleep in here? A sickly sour scent permeated the room. Someone had made the smell worse by trying to mask it with alcohol and industrial solvents. The door fell open all the way and the three saw two rows of beds made up with crisp, white linens. The dim lighting and utter lack of windows made it seem as if the room went on forever, all white and clean and precisely arranged, though there were only about twenty-five beds in each row. Everything looked perfect. The beds were so professionally made that the many tubes and cables and tie-downs coming out of the people didn't even wrinkle the sheets.

The room was too cold, too clinical for comfort. Laylea felt a strange memory tug at her mind. It took her a second before she pegged it. This room reminded her of the lab where she was born.

Junior whispered, "Are they alive?"

Dee asked, "Do you hear the beeping?"

The heart monitors didn't beep as loudly as in the movies. It was more of a dull chorus of low, even beats, not one quite in sync with another.

Laylea breathed in the warm musk of *live creature* lurking beneath the chemicals. They were alive but they were out cold and some of them had been out for a long time. Laylea moved into the room, sniffing the air to catch more detail. She wished they'd thought to get some seabat seeds for her to reference. Still, she didn't smell anything like food. The flavorless Gatorade flowing through their IVs did not count. A sound, though, led her over to the crack of a white door that blended almost perfectly with the wall. She jumped at the sound of voices right outside.

Laylea skittered back to where Dee was pacing down the row, looking into each of the sleeping faces. She grabbed the banshee's wrist and whisper-yelled at the padd screen, "Hide!"

Junior looked over from his examination of the chart at the foot of one bed. Laylea pointed wildly at the door even as she dove under a bed. Dee did the same, and Junior dove back into the closet just as they heard a buzz. A pair of burnt-tan brogues tapped into the room, ushering a pair of dull, black Oxfords ahead of him.

"Bertram, you can see they continue to thrive."

Laylea stretched her neck to grab a better look at the men.

Brogues had a face to match his shoes. He was a well-proportioned man with a fighter's stance and professionally designed facial hair. His shiny ponytail hung down to his shoulder blades over the white lab coat that covered his bespoke suit. He wore a nametag opposite the breast pocket but Laylea couldn't read it from where she was.

The man called Bertram barely glanced around the room filled with unconscious people before he turned to face the beard model. "Adrien." The older man emphasized the name distastefully. "What more do you need from me?"

Laylea caught the impression of a constipated pug dog in the brief instant she saw Bertram's face. The rear view didn't do much to alter the image. Though his voice came out more like a bulldog's on a particularly drooly day.

"I stand ready to help the cause."

Adrien twisted the end of his handlebar mustache into a tighter flip. "Mr. Durrah has been more than generous with biological materials. What our researchers really need is more data."

"Biomedical readings?"

"Everything, really. Behavioral analysis, test scores, shift patterns, and pheromone tracers if you can track them.

Bertram spluttered, "You're asking for a lot. I'll have to set up readers around the entire facility without anyone but our people knowing what they are."

Adrien crossed to the bed Dee was currently hiding under. Laylea sucked in her breath as he bent to straighten a tube that was barely kinked. "I'll send you some help."

Laylea read the hot one's name tag, *Adrien Denier, Top Dog*. Then he straightened and turned to face the approaching Bertram.

"Yes, good, a great challenge. Anything else?" Bertram's Oxfords stopped just before they would have blocked Laylea's view of Dee's face, Dee's tortured face.

Her eyes had glazed over and her skin was paler than usual, even the freckles. As Laylea watched, the banshee's buzz cut grew. At first it was red hair tumbling across her face but white soaked in from the ends, chasing the red back up to her scalp. Dee's entire body trembled. She slid one shaking hand up to cover her clenched lips, and Laylea could see the tension in her jaw as she held back her need to keen.

Someone had died.

Bertram heard the monitor flatline at the same time Laylea did, but he didn't recognize the changed sound. "What's that noise?"

Dee's hand slid from her mouth to her com-patch. Still struggling against her gift, she shook her head. She couldn't speak.

A crash sounded from the closet and both men turned away from the flatlining patient. Laylea rolled over and crouched. As soon as their feet passed the bed she was under, she scurried over to Dee and shoved her out the far side. Laylea peeked over the bed to see the men approaching the closet. She hoped Junior had the sense to travel away before they opened it.

She looked down at the trembling Dee, who had one hand on her mouth and one hand on the gun at her side. Dee jerked her head at the door. Laylea nodded.

They headed for the exit, neither one making any noise. They were there, Laylea's hand on the handle, when Dee's head jerked and the keen suddenly burst through her control.

Thunder crashed through the room. Lightning flashed in the high corners, setting off alarms and stunning the high-tech equipment. A violent wind slammed Laylea back against the door with Dee's thick, white hair blinding her.

Junior chose that moment to burst from the closet. He rode on top of a rolling cart that sailed between the two men. Adrien scrambled to one side while Bertram fell over a bed. Laylea pulled off an ugg to protect her hand and directed Dee's sparking hair to the doorpadd. The lock shorted out and the door popped open. Junior hopped off the cart as it rolled close. He tackled Dee from the front and pushed her out with Laylea hot on their heels.

Dee's keens quieted when the door shut, but only for an instant. Laylea fell to the ground as Dee let out one last piercing cry, punctuated by a crack of lightning and the fizzle of a frying electronic door lock.

Laylea scrambled to her feet, surprised to find herself still human. She sucked in a series of breaths and turned south. "I smell sligh nuts this way. And blood."

She would have run toward the smell, but Dee grabbed the back of her sundress just as they heard the sleep lab's door handle jiggle.

Dee hissed, "We've seen enough, kid. We're getting out of here."

Laylea didn't like it, but she capitulated pretty quickly when a body threw itself against the other side of the door. Dee pushed her ahead as Junior ran on to find a way out.

"Stairs!" He mouthed the word, more for those on coms than Dee and Laylea.

Laylea just had to trust her lip-reading skills. She ran with Dee and dashed into the fancy, carpeted stairwell. They both tripped down a couple when red lights began flashing. An alarm blared one growling blast.

A smooth, calm voice with a twisty mustache said, "Guards to floor three. Guards on alert report to floor three. We have intruders. Staff with training, secure your departments. Freeze the elevators and lock down the stairwells. We have intruders in the building."

Junior passed the first floor door as four guards burst in at the ground level. He spun and crashed into Dee. Laylea slowed her speed by grabbing the stairwell door handle and all three squeezed out nearly at once. Dee stared at her wrist as they ran. Laylea saw she'd pulled up a rough building schematic on her armpadd. They dashed around three corners, two rights and a left, barely keeping ahead of the guards.

Then, the thin hallway opened onto an elevator plaza with an open set of stairs leading down to the front doors. Laylea pushed her human legs even harder. She soared past Junior, her heart pumping so hard it threatened to burst from her chest. He gave her a push as he grabbed the railing. She thought he might vault right down all the steps but he used the fulcrum to push Dee, too, giving them all a little extra momentum down the stairs. Still his crazy legs passed them both as he leapt the last four steps to the bottom. He dragged Dee with him and shoved her ahead again.

Laylea saw the front door just beyond them. She had half a dozen steps to go and she'd be out. There were guards running from the various elevator banks, but Orin stood behind the desk instead of any uniform. He did vault the counter and dashed out the Guards Only door right there as soon as he saw Junior, Dee, and Laylea.

A shot cracked through the air. Laylea felt heat and sparks on her face. For an instant she couldn't hear anything but a distant ringing. Then, her hearing flooded back and the tiny burns healed as her flesh turned to fur. She rolled a few steps and skated along on the marble floor. Two of the guards skidded to a stop, eyes wide, hands now going to their guns as they watched a person turn into a dog right before their eyes. One of them screamed.

Junior glanced over his shoulder. He ran back to scoop Laylea into his arms.

He was turning into the door, Laylea could see out into the rainy dusk, when a second shot rang out.

Junior spun. His face slammed into the door in a spray of red. The door opened a crack and blood splashed over Laylea as she flew out of Junior's arms into open air. She tumbled to the ground an instant before Junior slid down the door and crushed her.

9

Laylea's fur sopped up the rain from the soaking ground and the blood from the dying boogeyman on top of her. She lapped at his face even as she struggled to breathe beneath him. He didn't respond. His weight shifted and she yelped as something sharp in his satchel dug into her ribs. Junior's eyes shot open.

Laylea trilled a desperate song at him, begging him to be okay. But his eyes fell shut again even as his body lifted off her. Orin and Dee stood over them, struggling to pull the lanky young man to his feet.

"Retreat. Everyone back to The Office." Dee's voice stayed calm on the com. But she growled when she glared down at Laylea. "Go."

Laylea ran. She circled the building in time to see Amal helping Diejuste climb into Dee's unmarked sedan. The car pulled away from the curb, stopping at the light where Lucio slipped into the back. The light turned green but Amal stayed put. Laylea started toward them until she saw Morioka's car peel through the intersection. Amal peeled through after, heading in a different direction. Soon, both dark cars had disappeared in the distance.

Laylea followed the car carrying Junior.

At first, she ran as fast as she could and almost caught up with the car at two red lights and a stop sign. But her heart couldn't keep it up and her pace slowed even as her thoughts sped into overdrive.

Was Dee's hair white? Was it white? It was, wasn't it? Junior's dying, and it's all my fault. If I'd only been faster. If I'd shifted earlier, I could have kept up.

A car swerved left around a corner, not even slowing for the red light and Laylea splayed her claws and reversed all her muscles to keep from being hit. It almost wasn't enough. Debris littered the sidewalk, slick from hours of rain. Laylea skidded along even after she stopped running. She tried to dig her claws into the cement. One caught on a seam in the sidewalk and the nail flipped back. Blood splattered everywhere but Laylea barely felt the sharp pain as she fell into the gutter just behind the racing car's rear tires.

The car hit a pothole as it sped off. Laylea took the brunt of the splash.

Afraid to lay there in the street, Laylea limped across to the far sidewalk. She watched Morioka's taillights vanish into the gloom as she dripped and bled there on the Chicago streets.

A shadow passed across a streetlamp. Laylea realized she'd been seeing this shadow since she'd left Starwood labs. She bit at her bleeding nail to try to at least set it straight on the paw and then set off at a lope. She had to stop again to chew a piece of glass from the pad of one front paw. The shadow swooped down low.

Laylea leapt to her paws and ran. She focused on the pain to keep her going. Junior had to be in even more pain. Unless he wasn't in any pain at all anymore. The thought spurred her to run faster.

Her legs fell into a rhythm and her mind focused on the goal. She heard sirens in the distance, dogs barking challenges down residential streets, and rain pattering down on everything. Screeching tires were par for the course in the city, and Laylea didn't worry about them unless she heard them behind her. She slowly noticed a new smell creeping up over the expected raw symphony of garbage, sauerkraut, gasoline, and her own terrified sweat. A musky scent that pushed her more than the screeching tires or swooping shadow.

She tripped over an abandoned shoe because her senses were more focused on the imagined dangers chasing behind than the reality right in front of her. She hit the ground hard and rolled sideways to slam into a brick building. The aggressive musk exploded in her senses and she instinctually rolled into a protective ball, ears pasted back and her tail curled up into her belly. But the shadow swooped down into the sodium glare of the building's security lights and Laylea recognized her stalker as her newly shifting vampire friend, Detective Kyle Nellwin. The little bat soared down through the light, over Laylea, and out into the darkness down the street.

His scream shifted in pitch as he flew away, and Laylea watched, entranced until the scream cut off. The whole world hung still for an instant, filled only with the echo of a vampire's haunting cry and the paralyzing musk of a hunting pack. Then the world erupted in a crash that sounded like a heavy body slamming into a parked car. The roars and howls of a pack of dogs shocked Laylea to her feet. Forgetting the pain of her flensed paw and displaced nail, Laylea bared her teeth. The fur in the center of her back from her ears all the way down to the tip of her tail stood at attention.

The street lit up with a flash and the howls changed pitch.

"Run!" The pitch of Kyle's voice, the raw grind of his tone, spurred Laylea more effectively than the word.

She'd seen him feed before.

She turned tail and ran.

Twenty minutes later the rain had effectively washed all the blood from her fur: hers and Junior's. She was desperate to shift to relieve her many pains but needed her canine speed to get back to The Office. Once she spotted the flickering sign of the panaderia down the street from The Office, she started trying to stoke that spark in her belly or behind her heart. But her heart was too full and her belly too sore to feel anything but her grief. She tripped down the side street to the alley that led to the barbecue courtyard. It took two tries for her to get through the doggy door into the hallway.

Inside was pandemonium. Some Marion Hill remixed remix played from the digital jukebox under the murmur of a dozen people trying to be quiet. Fear was the only smell of consequence. It handily overwhelmed the usual dark aura of musty beer and liquor. Laylea darted backwards as Lucio raced from the supply room, his arms filled with linens, one hand gripping a bottle of grain alcohol and the other holding Laylea's rawhide. He didn't even see Laylea follow him to the bar.

Seb had a few guests in the bar, mostly regulars. They hung back against the far wall, most holding forgotten drinks. A young couple Laylea couldn't name held each other close, not looking at the chaos in the middle of the room. Ned sat in his dark corner looking oddly incomplete without his knitting needles. Seb stood behind his bar filling a pitcher with the water gun while cleaning out a bloody glass in the sink.

Team Wyrdos surrounded Junior. They'd cleared away a space and laid down some tablecloths to set him on. The afghan Ned had been working on earlier was folded up under Junior's head. Orin knelt on one edge of the afghan, a hand on either side of the boogeyman's face. Morioka knelt similarly at his feet. She'd pushed up his jeans' legs and a faint glow suffused his skin where her hands gripped the skinny man's bare ankles. Lucio tossed napkins and towels to the ground and used some to soak up the bloody mess around Junior's body. Dee stood between the team and the bar. She grabbed the full pitcher from Seb and delivered it to Amal, who soaked a napkin and wiped away what blood he could as Diejuste dug her tiny fingers into her friend's shoulder.

She said something so softly, Amal had to lean in to hear her. He turned to Dee.

"Do you have tweezers in your kit?"

Lucio dug into an inner pocket of his vest. "I've got serrated diamond tweezers." He held out a long set of tweezers with a gear on one side. "Will these work?"

"Ya done good fa once, Brownie." Diejuste smiled her nothing-rattles-me smile but Laylea thought she saw a little doubt in the goddess's eyes.

Amal took the tweezers and dunked them in a pint glass filled with clear liquid. He swirled them a few times and held them out to Diejuste.

The loa wrapped her tiny fingers around the stainless steel and lowered the tips into the hole in Junior's chest. Marion Hill asked, *Are you down diddy down diddy down diddy down down down?* on the jukebox as blood poured out around Lucio's gem tweezers. Laylea caught Morioka's icy gaze.

Plink. Diejuste dropped the bullet into a waiting shot glass. Dee took the glass and poured the bullet into a plastic evidence pouch she pulled from her jacket. Amal dove in with a handful of clean napkins to put pressure on the wound. And everyone breathed. Some of the watching regulars cheered. Laylea couldn't help herself. She joined them with a singing trill.

A few faces on the team turned her way. Their smiles faded. The rest kept their eyes on Junior's wound or Dee's face.

Orin muttered, "You know better, Lee."

But when he looked back up to Dee, she was shaking her head at him. "There was never any doubt, Orin. He never had a pallor."

He never had a pallor. That meant she never saw death coming for him. Dee's was a strange gift.

Everyone's eyes spun back to Junior as the man coughed. Nobody seemed to know what to say.

"Hey man, if it hurts too much, you can chew on this." Lucio held up the rawhide Junior had given Laylea for her "birthday."

Junior grinned weakly. He muttered something inaudible and shut his eyes. Orin breathed out half a sigh, half a laugh.

"What? What did he say?" Lucio asked.

Orin looked up. "He said *ew*."

"Hey, Lee." Seb gestured her around to the side.

Nobody seemed to need her around the man she'd gotten shot, so Laylea slunk over to the far curve of the bar. The mahogany top continued all the way around to meet the backing mirror. The bar had a counter flip top on hinges, but Seb never bothered to use it. He'd built a ramp down from the elevated floor behind the bar. Laylea found Seb sitting on the raised floor, his feet dangling beside the ramp. He had a little white box in his hand. Laylea trotted up the ramp to sit with him.

"This showed up about a month ago." He tilted the box. It read *5/5* in her mom's handwriting.

Laylea nosed at it. She flipped the lid off. It looked like the box was filled with a scrap of Clark's favorite paisley bandana. But then Seb tilted it into his hand. Sher had sewn pieces of the dad's bandanna into the shape of a lizard's foot. It could have come right off the patchwork lizard she'd sewn for Laylea when she was just a puppy. Laylea stuck her nose against the fabric. She could smell where Sher had poked herself with her needle and bled on the little stuffed foot. Clark's scents were embedded in the fabric.

Seb tugged a well-folded note from the bottom of the box, and Laylea sniffed that too. She could smell their friend Jay Doe on the note. But it was the dad's handwriting.

Fair winds, LG. Keep Lizard with you always. Burn this note.

Laylea's eyes welled up. She read the note again, then took it gently from Seb's hand and chewed it up. It tasted pretty gross.

Seb held up a threaded needle. "I thought we could sew it right on so there's no chance you'll lose it."

Laylea stood up on Seb's barrel chest and tilted her head away. In moments he'd attached the lizard to her collar. She'd only be able to see it in the mirror, but when she was human, she'd be able to feel it too.

Her parents hadn't forgotten. Her parents weren't dead. A weight she hadn't really been aware of fell from her shoulders.

And just as her heart lightened, it was stomped on again.

"Lee Woodford." Morioka stood just on the other side of the bar.

Laylea licked Seb's cheek. Then she turned to face the dragon demon.

"Lee Woodford, you shifted in front of natural humans."

Orin yelled from all the way over by Junior, "Again."

The brownies laughed. Morioka didn't even twitch.

"This behavior has put our team in danger in the past and now your lack of control has risked one of our lives." She picked Laylea up for the first time in their entire association. "You are under arrest. I'm taking you to juvie where you will have plenty of private time to practice shifting."

Amal almost stood but remembered he was holding pressure on Junior's chest. "What are you arresting her for?"

Morioka reached into the pocket of her taupe trench coat and pulled out a pressed powder cross. It was N. Laylea turned her nose away, afraid to inhale the drug accidentally.

"I am arresting Lee Woodford for drug possession. Our mayor has very little tolerance for illegal drug use." Morioka didn't wait to hear any objections. She tucked Laylea under her arm and strode past Junior, down the length of the bar to the front door. "Dee, I'll take your unmarked. Please tell Bailey his sister is not going to be coming home tonight."

As the door fell shut behind them, Laylea didn't hear a single voice speak up for her.

10

The vinyl of Dee's backseat was clearly not designed for puppy paws. The demon's driving didn't help. Morioka took a left. Laylea slammed into the passenger-side door and tumbled to the floor.

Her sliced paw slipped in something squishy, and Laylea leapt back up to the seat. It smelled like Lucio had thrown up after they saw Junior get shot. And now Laylea had sick all over her front paws.

She trailed the bile across the seat as Morioka took a right.

Dee's car normally smelled overwhelmingly like pine. Kyle had bought the obnoxious air fresheners in bulk, and Dee kept a box of them under the passenger seat. It wasn't helping much right now.

They turned again and Laylea extended her claws, only to be sharply reminded of the one she'd half torn off on her race back to The Office. She wondered if Captain Morioka was trying to physically beat her into shifting because she couldn't very well walk into a police station and process a dog, no matter how much of a legend she was on the force.

If she could only explain to Morioka that things had just been worse lately because her parents hadn't written in months, because

Bailey was increasingly isolating himself, because she was going to die this year. It was a lot of stress.

Morioka took two quick turns and killed the engine. Laylea hopped back up to the seat again and stood her front paws on the shiny black grate separating the front and back seats. Morioka was messaging someone on her armpadd. Laylea couldn't see who.

She had to convince Morioka to let her go. It would be better to live out the rest of her life in the apartment than to die in prison. She'd stay in dog form and promise never to go farther than the backyard. She might be able to use Sher's operant conditioning techniques on the captain. Layer in a little of the grunt magic she'd learned to enforce it. She did it all the time with clients. She could do it with Morioka.

Except that to condition anyone, you needed to touch them, speak to them in a low voice, and look into their eyes. That could prove a challenge as she was currently a dog in the back seat of a cop car. So, no speaking, no touching. Plus, there was the small point that Morioka was a dragon-shaped demon who could flame her to ash faster than Laylea could catch her eyes.

Those black eyes turned to her, not at all surprised to find her peeking into the front. "Stay."

Morioka left the car.

Sher always said it was better to address a problem than worry about it. So Laylea pushed off the grating and sat quietly on the barf-painted vinyl, focusing on finding the spark in her belly. All she could find was nausea as the crack of two shots rang in her memory and an ice-cold knot of fear of what bat-Kyle had attacked in the darkness.

After a while, the back door opened and Morioka shoved a kid inside. She kept a hand on his head, though the kid wasn't nearly tall enough to bang the frame.

Angry silver-gray eyes sparked out of a Black face just shedding the roundness of baby fat. He had the kind of build that made adults say he was shaping up to be tall one day, but right now, he just looked like a DIY bookshelf assembled without the instructions. Though he wore all black, the kilted shorts and snare-snap hoodie screamed fashion. It was like he'd studied videos to see what criminals wore and then did the best he could with the shops in his posh neighborhood. Laylea smelled expensive body wash ruined by beer and vomit, which meant he wasn't much of a drinker. She sniffed closer and jerked away. He smelled like N. If he was being taken in for drug possession, too, why hadn't Morioka taken the drugs off of him?

Morioka put the car in gear. Laylea saw a sign for the Evanston South PD as they pulled out of the parking lot. What was going on? What was Morioka doing? Collecting juvenile offenders from all over Chicagoland?

"Hey." The kid knocked on the black grating. "Ma'am?"

Ma'am. Yeah, a real threat to society.

"There's a dog back here."

Morioka didn't reply. She turned right and the kid scrambled for his seat belt. Laylea caught herself on the driver's side door, partly to keep her bum left hip from hitting it again and partly to see if the pain of smacking her flensed paw pad into the glass would shock her into shifting. It didn't work.

Probably for the best. Teenage boys weren't really equipped to handle naked teenage girls. And she was already in trouble for shifting in front of thumpers. She hunkered down behind the seat belt strap and cleaned off her front paws. She focused on the tang of her own blood because she really didn't want to think about what Lucio had been drinking before she sent them all off to infiltrate the Starwood labs.

Lights flashed by overhead. Morioka wasn't running the siren or the wig-wags but she was still driving faster than most of the cars on the road. They splashed through puddles, spraying the other cars as she weaved through the traffic.

She banged a left through a pink traffic light. Laylea slammed into the kid's remarkably muscled thigh and tumbled over his lap to look out the window at the headlights of the car sliding toward them. Laylea felt the kid's arm wrap around her in the last second before the car crossed the center line behind Dee's rear bumper.

The kid hissed. He did a great imitation of a spitting mad street cat. Laylea looked up in admiration. He seemed to realize he was holding her and set her back over on her side of the car.

"Cats and dogs living together," he said.

Mass hysteria. Laylea thought the end of the quote. Ghostbusters had been a regular in the movie night lineup back home in Foothills. She dropped her jaw in a smile, but the kid was staring fixedly out his side of the car. He gripped the door handle as if for life. Laylea didn't blame him.

She looked out her side and noticed that Captain Morioka had pulled onto Lake Shore Drive. They were headed south at serious speeds now. All that *Frogger* nonsense on the surface streets was over. This was real driving. Laylea hated it.

She slunk back down on the vinyl and shut her eyes. She opened them again when all she saw was Ned's bloody afghan. Instead, she watched the shifting patterns of the muddy mess on the back floor.

Morioka had to slow down to get off the LSD. Laylea and the kid both tensed up but almost as soon as they'd exited the Drive, Morioka took an easy left. She stopped to hold her arm out the window. A pattern of lights flashed from her armpadd and the double barriers in front of them lifted.

"You screwed up." Morioka started talking as she pulled into the long, deserted parking lot beyond the gate. "I have determined you are a danger to Chicago. But if you can change, you could be a benefit to our city. I am giving you one last chance."

The car almost stopped by the entrance to the Lincoln Park Zoo. But it didn't. Laylea and the kid were thrown back. Laylea landed in his lap again when the captain spun the car one hundred and forty-five degrees and slammed to a stop in the grass at the end of the lot, a figure pinned in the headlights. The girl hitched her heavy backpack higher and held up a hand to shield her eyes.

Morioka turned to the back seat. "If you fail, I'll turn you over to the Enforcer."

Then she got out of the car and called out, "You're looking for LPSS."

The girl nodded. Her voice squeaked, like she'd actually been hit by the car rather than just its lights. "I . . . I can't find the entrance."

"Come here." It was a tone that brooked no objections, and the girl approached.

She kept her eyes shielded from the lights until she thought to step out of the beam. Laylea could only see the overstuffed backpack and two dark brown ponytails hanging down on a yellow shirt as the girl spoke with Morioka.

"I'm supposed to be here."

"Your letter has instructions." Morioka tilted her head in the way that Laylea knew meant she was analyzing the girl. "Where is your letter?"

"I didn't get a letter. Maybe my—" The girl cut off what she was going to say.

"If you don't have a letter—"

"Really, I'm supposed to be here." The girl choked up. "I saved for so long."

"You cannot attend LPSS without an invitation." Morioka stepped back to the car, and Laylea got a good look at the girl's face.

Tears streamed down Karly Carlotta Delcampo's pudgy cheeks. Laylea barked. She hopped out of the rich kid's lap and stood up on the grate to get Morioka's attention.

Morioka ignored her. "What's your name?"

"Kar . . . KC."

Morioka nodded and Laylea heard her tone shift. "You are trespassing on private property, KC. I am pressing you into LPSS. Get in the car."

The newly dubbed KC took a step back. "You work for the Enforcer?"

Morioka glowed a little. Laylea saw the outline of her ridges but not her wings. "I don't work for anybody."

KC relaxed. How bad was this Enforcer?

Laylea bounded to the open door and sang. The girl walked over, if only to see what was making all the noise.

"What is wrong with you, dog?" The rich kid wiped her fur off his lap. "I mean other than being a dog."

With another glance at Morioka, KC shoved her pack on the floor and got in the car. She picked Laylea up and set her on her lap before reaching to close the door. Morioka spun the car and cruised back to the Lincoln Park Zoo entrance.

"Is that *your* barf?" KC asked the kid as she got a whiff of the inside. "Or . . ." She lifted Laylea in the most embarrassing move humans had ever invented. "Or hers?"

The kid declined to answer. KC wouldn't have heard him anyway. She'd caught sight of Laylea's collar.

"Lee?"

Laylea barked.

Morioka looked at the three in the rear view. "I'll need a last name, KC."

"It's . . . Dells."

The rich kid scoffed. "Like the Wisconsin Dells? You're named after a sand dune?"

KC bristled. "That would be pretty impressive, wouldn't it?"

Morioka popped the doors with a button up front. Laylea hopped out of KC's lap. She watched the kid swing a leg out.

"Sure, mad impressive." He waggled an eyebrow at KC as he got out and shut the door.

Laylea scrabbled at the handle and then bounded over to KC's side as she wrestled her backpack out. Laylea hopped out and followed her around to the zoo side of the car.

KC's scorn came through loud and clear. "What's your last name?"

He turned a shit-eating grin on her. "My last name is Luke." He held out a hand. "Oscar Luke. Nice to meet you."

KC inhaled sharply. Laylea had never heard the name before but it clearly meant something to KC. She scoffed and started to retort, but instead she took a second breath and muttered, "Oh, guess I'll get down on my belly now and grovel, your majesty."

"We don't stand on formality." Oscar said. "You can just call me Oscar."

Morioka slammed the trunk. A clicking screech up among the dull stars drew her eyes for a moment. Laylea followed the dragon-shifter over to the Zoo's iconic lion statue where the captain set a pair of uggs and a sundress on the low stone plinth.

Then, she exploded into the sky. Green and gray leather wings twenty feet across beat bitter air over the kids. Debris washed past them to stick against the zoo's stone wall and gate. Morioka grew to triple her size. Her eyes didn't change at all in a face that suddenly featured a long muzzle with two rows of razor sharp teeth and an undulating forked tongue. She threw that head back and screamed up at the tiny black figure flapping across the cloud-covered moon. Her tail lashed out, striking a chime from the thorny metal archway over the zoo gates.

The tone rang on as tiny Captain Morioka appeared before them again. Those unchanging eyes looked down at the sundress and back up at Laylea.

Laylea hadn't even noticed herself shift. She held her hands up in front of her face. The nails were all in place. She felt no pain from slicing open her paw earlier and the stinging in her hip had vanished. She was so overwhelmed with relief from the pain that it didn't even occur to her to be embarrassed about standing there naked beside two strangers and the captain.

"Dress," Morioka ordered as she passed the kids to climb up to face the lion.

Laylea scurried to get into her dress but kept her eyes on Morioka. Oscar put a hand out to keep her from falling when she tripped putting on the second boot.

He muttered, "Guess we know why you're here."

Morioka reached out one non-scaly human hand and stroked the metal lion's nose three times. "Once for pride, twice for pack, thrice so the phoenix will never come back."

The ground trembled beneath their feet, shuddering as the great lion pivoted aside. As one, the kids stepped forward and peered down a stairway of cobblestones leading into darkness.

"This is where I leave you. Oscar Luke, Lee Woodford, and KC

Dells." Morioka looked at each of them in turn. "Welcome to Lincoln Park Shifter School. Your last chance."

With that she strode back to Dee's car and drove away.

11

"The Enforcer lets dragon shifters run around the city?" The rich kid, Oscar Luke, stared after Morioka's departing car.

"The Enforcer doesn't decide who lives in Chicago." KC peered down into the dark hole beneath them.

Laylea peered up, trying to see the screeching figure Morioka had screamed at. She could have sworn it was Kyle. "Morioka isn't a shifter. She's a demon. And it's just her."

"If she shifts, she's a shifter," Oscar told her, not kindly. "There's no such thing as demons."

Laylea didn't see the point in arguing. She couldn't exactly tell him the tiny black figure in the sky was a vampire bat.

Oscar didn't seem to care if she had a response anyway. He poked KC. "Go on. You're the one who wants to be here. You scared?"

KC took a breath to respond, but didn't. Instead, she stepped onto the first stair. Laylea followed close on her heels. They'd only descended three steps when Oscar caught up.

"What? It's this or prison for me," he said when Laylea glanced up at him.

"Isn't this just prison for wyrdos?"

The other two stopped walking to ask, "For what?"

"Wyrdos, supernaturals," Laylea explained. Didn't they know the word wyrdos? "People like us. This is a prison for us."

Oscar started down again. "It's a school. If it were a prison, do you think the dragon would have just let us decide for ourselves if we wanted to come down?"

The steps shuddered and all three put their hands out to hold on to the walls. KC cried out and flailed. There was no wall on the far side. Laylea and Oscar both grabbed for her and caught parts of her enormous backpack. They held her steady as the entrance swung closed above them, leaving the three in near perfect darkness. Oscar was the first to start moving again.

KC hissed, "Careful, Luke. We don't want to have to scrape you off the floor."

"It's Oscar," he whispered back. "And I'm a leopard. I can see well enough. Would you like to hold my hand?"

He made the offer in a mocking tone, but Laylea stumbled forward to take him up on it before he moved too far out of sight. "Come on, KC. Just until our eyes adjust."

KC put a hand on Oscar's shoulder and kept the other on the wall.

Laylea worried that the rich kid might shake them off, but he moved slowly and his hand felt just as clammy as Laylea's entire body. The blackness didn't seem to be getting any thinner as they descended. She felt her heart in her stomach and while she tried not to fall, she also focused on staying in girl form. She had to stay human.

"So, Lee," Oscar asked. "Why have you been pressed to shifter prison?"

A flash of the gunfire, rain, and the smell of Junior's blood spiked through her senses. "I almost killed someone."

KC choked out a laugh.

"Attempted murder?" Oscar laughed too. "You, puppy?"

"No." She remembered what Morioka had said in The Office. "I'm here because I shifted in front of thumpers."

Both of them gasped this time. Killing someone meant little to them but shifting in front of thumpers shocked them. Laylea hurried to turn the conversation away from herself. "What about you?"

"I stole a six-pack of crappy beer," he admitted. "But my daddy is rich, so I get to come here."

"If you're rich, why did you steal it?" Laylea felt his hand grow a little warm in hers when she asked this.

"For fun."

She didn't believe him.

KC wasn't even listening. "I see light."

Laylea peered down and she saw it too. A small yellow glow bounced along far below them. She sped up.

"You don't think we're rushing toward a dungeon?" Oscar teased.

Laylea ignored him even before KC said, "Ignore him. This is a school. They wouldn't put us in a dungeon at a school."

Laylea noticed that despite his teasing and the light, Oscar hadn't let go of her and he wasn't shaking KC's hand off his shoulder. None of this seemed exactly *right*, but at least she wasn't heading into it alone.

"I've never been to school," Laylea said. "But I didn't imagine you had to whisper a password, go through a secret lion door, and descend a deadly stairway to get there."

"This is all just so we'll look forward to the tests," Oscar whispered.

KC snorted.

A flaming torch illuminated a female figure, draping her in waving shadows like feathers. She stood just a few feet from the bottom of the stairway. The torch she held projected the shadow of a raven onto the wall behind and above the figure. Laylea spotted the bird itself roosting on a ledge high on the stone wall.

"Come now, don't dawdle. It's already quite late," the woman called out to them. She wore a loose, linen jumpsuit, tied at the waist with blue fabric. Her dark hair hung over one shoulder in a neat braid. The flicker of the flame in her glasses hid her eyes but she had a kind smile and cheekbones to die for.

"Come, come. Watch the last step. It's a doozy." She reached out her hand, seconds too late with the warning as all three tripped off the shortened last step.

Laylea caught herself against the wall. The raven spread its wings in alarm so she waved to show she was okay. KC caught the woman's hand to save herself.

"There's a bit of a doozie farther up, too," KC muttered.

"This is the oldest section of the school, pre-electric lights." The woman gestured with the torch. "Good thing we still have these around. Come. This way."

She turned to lead them into a musty tunnel with a ceiling so low, they could see the scorch marks from previous torches. Laylea kept her eyes on the ground in case any more doozies showed up in the stonework.

"My name is Ms. Crow. I am your intake coordinator, which means I'm here to help you get settled in today, of course, but you should also come to me if you ever need something in the future. I work as the librarian and help out maintaining the gardens, although we all do some of that. Now, Oscar," she looked over her shoulder at him and he nearly ran into her as she turned right at a junction.

"Yes, ma'am?"

Yeah, big tough beer thief.

"You're werepanthera obviously. A leopard, I believe?"

KC scoffed. "He's a Luke. They're all leopards."

Oscar shoved her. "What are you? A gazelle?"

He spit the word out like an insult but Laylea thought it was an odd choice to use to put someone down. Gazelles were sleek and beautiful and she could totally see KC as a gazelle.

"Captain Morioka," Ms. Crow glanced over her shoulder at KC, "didn't tell us much about you, KC. Lee is a werecanid. Canus Familiarus. The first I've ever met." She nodded at Lee with a smile. "And what creature do you transform into, KC Dells?"

She stopped at a doorway to face them. KC looked at the floor and fingered her dibs drive charmband. "I'm a dog, too. Coyote."

Laylea could see KC was lying, but Ms. Crow let it pass.

"Very good. And did you get much instruction at home in shifting?"

"No." KC looked up at Ms. Crow as she lied. "I'm an orphan."

Ms. Crow didn't even blink. "You're not alone. A lot of us are."

She pushed the pocket door open and ushered the three inside what Laylea thought could be a giant ring box. The plush velvet carpet that had probably been green at some point stopped several inches before the doorways at either end of the narrow room. The raven soared in and settled itself on one of the swirly decorations on top of the ornate cabinet that took up most of the room, while Ms. Crow set her torch in a sconce beside the door. Scalloped metal handles like upside-down candlesticks hung from the cabinet's highly worn, marbled mahogany.

Ms. Crow grasped these handles and braced herself. The thick cabinet doors opened to reveal dozens of cubbies. Each of the doors was made up of cubbies as well, and, opened as far as they could go, the doors would have doubled the cabinet's width. Ms. Crow only opened them wide enough for all of them to see that the cabinet was filled with clothes, all more or less the same shade of blue.

Ms. Crow pulled a few bundles from a couple of different cubbies along the same shelf. "Here you go, Oscar. We don't often stand on modesty here at LPSS, but some orphans and wanderers are new to shifter customs. We try to ease them into the amount of nudity you experience when many young shifters live together."

"We've already experienced some," Oscar said.

"And I'm sure, as a legacy student, you demonstrated the appropriate respect. Thank you, Oscar. You'll change in the gents." She pointed him toward the door on the left. "I lit a torch in there earlier. If the suits don't fit, you're welcome to return and find another size. You'll notice we have several different styles of jumpsuits, as well. Some students choose the same style regularly, some mix it up. Some find a particular fashion fits them best." She crouched down and rummaged through the lower shelves, handing jumpsuits to KC and Laylea. "We have clothes closets throughout the facility and you'll either quickly learn how to control your shifting or learn where all the closets are. Sizes are organized from bottom to top, styles from oldest on the right to newest in the leftmost cubbies. You are to do your best to be clothed when you are human. Go on, Oscar. I'm sure you've been warned about all of this. Leave all of your belongings in the changing room for tonight. Dr. Fenn should be here any minute to help you. Ladies, with me."

KC and the raven followed Ms. Crow into the *Ladies* changing room. Laylea glanced back to see Oscar returning to the cabinet. He sneered at her and she hurried after the others.

12

The changing room was smaller than Laylea had expected. There was a sort of double-sided bank of four open lockers down the center of the room with a bench on either side.

Ms. Crow led KC to the right as she gently pushed Laylea to the left. "Lee, you get yourself set over on that side. I'll be right there."

Laylea caught KC's eyes for a moment before the other girl turned to follow Ms. Crow. She wanted to ask why she'd lied about her parents and her name but a part of her already knew. She thought back to the argument she'd overheard earlier that day. Karly Carlotta's parents did not want her to be here. If she could get away with the fake name, the school wouldn't be able to reach out to her parents and send them reports. And if Karly Carlotta Delcampo wasn't in LPSS the Delcampos couldn't make her leave. Laylea might not want to be here, but KC had fought to come. Laylea wasn't going to give her away.

Her eyes adjusted to the thin light trickling over the divider until Ms. Crow set the torch in the far wall, beside a second door. Laylea set her pile of jumpsuits on the bench and separated the three options. All three looked too big, but Laylea had seen her take them from the bottom shelf so she didn't bother going back out. The bluest of the three had no sleeves and she was already shivering in her sundress and uggs. She reached for the next version of the uniform but the raven swooped down and grabbed the palest version. It dropped the suit on Laylea's head.

"Thanks."

"I'll be with you in a minute, Lee." Ms. Crow called from the other side. She went back to murmuring with KC so Laylea didn't answer.

The fabric of this suit was as soft as Lucio's first-date shirt. It slid through Laylea's fingers like silk but without the coldness. She stepped out of her uggs and pulled the pants of the suit on under her dress. She sat to pull the dress over her head. It felt strange. She couldn't remember the last time she'd taken her clothes off. She couldn't really remember ever taking her clothes off except at her once-a-year sizing appointment with Amal. They usually just fell off when she shifted.

Ms. Crow came around the corner as Laylea was zipping up the front of the soft jumpsuit. The legs puddled around her feet and the long arms hid her hands completely. But otherwise, it was comfortable. She liked the pockets on the thighs and the easy elastic at her waist. The top zipped up to a neck so high, Laylea could tuck her face in all the way up to her eyes.

"Look at me." She glanced from side to side and then popped her head up out of the neck. "I'm a wereturtle."

The raven hopped up and down along the bench, cawing. Ms. Crow walked right by it, hiding her amusement.

"Don't let Benny see you do that. He's a little sensitive." She looked Laylea up and down. "It looks like it was made for you."

Laylea waved her flapping sleeves. "Really, Ms. Crow?"

"Yes, really, Ms. Woodford." She took the end of Laylea's sleeve and crisply folded it up in increments until her hand showed. Then she reached up inside the sleeve and pulled out a tab that snapped to the outside. "The legs work the same way." She bent to roll up one of the legs while Laylea did her second arm.

"As you grow up, you're going to need bras and underwear. We've got closets for those in the girls' dorms. Hopefully you'll have mastered shifting by that point." She sat back, leaning against one of the locker dividers.

Laylea kept her eyes down. Ms. Crow couldn't know that Laylea wasn't ever going to grow up. At least, as long as she was trapped here underground, it was unlikely Walter would ever find her. That was an upside to this madness.

Ms. Crow fussed with the buttons of her blue sweater as she asked, "Now, is there anything that I need to know about you, Lee? Every student who ends up at LPSS is a special case, no matter how you arrived. I know you have trouble shifting at will and your family isn't in the picture." Ms. Crow let her voice trail off like she'd asked a question.

"When can I leave?"

Ms. Crow coughed. The raven croaked, laughing again. "Well, Captain Morioka has determined that your inability to shift at will just yet makes you a danger to the shifter community. You simply have to prove to our shifting master's satisfaction that you can control your animal. The faculty will report on your progress and you'll have to pass a specific test. Then you could leave. But I hope that you'll enjoy LPSS perhaps more than your last school. We are a little different."

Laylea had always wanted to go to school. She'd been fiercely jealous of Bailey. But now, with less than a year to live, it seemed like it was too late. She realized she'd been wasting her time before. She needed to find her parents and just hug them before she died. After finding out why Kyle had followed her to the school. The only way she was going to do any of that was to learn how to shift.

Ms. Crow was still looking at her, hopefully.

Laylea admitted, "I've never been to school before."

"Don't worry about that. We'll test you for placement in classes and we'll get tutors to help you. Do you have any food allergies?"

Laylea shook her head. She didn't care for Brussels sprouts but that wasn't an allergy.

"Are you on any medications?"

She shook her head again but added, "My hip aches in certain weather. I just take carprofen when I need it."

Ms. Crow laughed. "We'll stick with human medications. Dosing is easier and frankly animal medications don't get the same rigorous testing."

Laylea wanted to point out that her hip didn't hurt when she was human, but Ms. Crow was already leading the way to the far end of the room.

"Are you ready, KC?"

Laylea scooped up her dress and boots. "Do I put these in a locker?"

"Just leave it. I'll collect everything in a minute."

Laylea set her things down and joined Ms. Crow and KC as they headed through another pocket door to a tiny, gray, Victorian version of the Starwood sleeping lab. Three cots lined each wall, minus all the beeping medical equipment. Each low cot featured a white pillow, white sheet, and grey wool blanket hanging to the floor. Instead of a heart monitor beside each bed, short tables held ewers and bowls. The stony ground was covered with an immense rag rug that might once have been shades of blue. Laylea's toes impulsively dug into the knots of the odd carpet.

The raven soared in behind them and circled Oscar where he stood with a short man in his forties. Neither of them ducked or paid the bird any attention. It finally settled on one of the empty sconces beside a rough wooden door on the far wall. It looked like it had to crouch to fit. The ceiling definitely hung lower than Laylea was used to. Even the short stranger had to hold his flaming torch by his waist to keep from hitting the ceiling.

His face broke into a wide smirk under his mountain-man beard when he spotted Ms. Crow. "Sorry to be late, Elizabeth. I was just explaining to Oscar here how the founders designed this room to keep new students in their natural form."

"Although it wasn't originally intended for students." Ms. Crow avoided his smile by turning to the girls. "This is Dr. Fenn."

The doctor wasn't much taller than Oscar but Laylea doubted that she and Oscar together could reach around the man's thick chest. Something about the man put Laylea on edge. He had a nice smile and was rocking the tweed vest but her psychic tail drooped when she met his icy eyes.

"You'll visit him tomorrow for an intake physical."

Laylea raised her hand.

Ms. Crow tucked her hands into her sweater. "Yes, Lee?"

Dr. Fenn said, "Trouble already."

"I'm not sure what—" She took a breath. With less than a year to live, she really didn't have time to hem and haw. "What is this place?"

"Holding." Oscar rolled his eyes.

"No." Laylea focused on Ms. Crow's sad, kind eyes. "Is this a prison or a school?"

Ms. Crow shushed Oscar's laughter. "LPSS is an elite academy for shifter kids. It's just like any other school except we don't have to hide what we are down here."

The crow croaked and flapped its wings. Nobody paid it any mind.

"You'll attend classes in math, science, language, and the arts as well as the practical aspects of shifting. Tomorrow's Testing will determine your placement in these classes. It may feel like prison because you and KC are required to attend, but other than your chores, your life at LPSS will differ in no way from the paying students. Our mission is to form students into thoughtful, well-educated citizens who will be a benefit to both human and shifter society."

Laylea hadn't really heard much beyond the word 'Testing.' She'd never been to school before but Bailey had moaned and bitched about tests. He'd played sick and once woogied himself blue to get out of tests. Laylea suddenly felt like she shouldn't have picked the long-sleeved jumpsuit. Maybe she could go pick another. She wiped her hands on the pants and unzipped the turtleneck down to her collarbone. The cowl felt kind of like a little cape hanging off her shoulders and her psychic tail perked up.

The adults perked up too.

Dr. Fenn shook a finger at her "No belongings in Holding."

Ms. Crow explained, "You have to leave everything in the anteroom tonight, Lee."

Laylea's hand shot up to her collar. She ran her fingers over the new lizard foot.

"You can have it back in the morning." Ms. Crow looked at the others. "You each get to keep one item. Everything else will go into storage until you leave school." She returned to Laylea. "I can take that for you."

"Sorry." Laylea reached to undo the clasp at the back of her neck. She only ever took the collar off to clean it, but one night with a naked neck would be fine. She'd never worn a collar to bed before the brownies gave her this one.

She finally got her nervous fingers to work the clasp and handed her collar with her cash, notes, dibs drives, and the keys over to Ms. Crow.

Pain shot through her core as her fingers left the collar. She yelped as the fabric of her new jumpsuit floated down around her furry form.

"Oh my phoenix." Ms. Crow slapped a hand over her mouth.

"Are you hurt?" Dr. Fenn crouched at Laylea's side.

Laylea shook her head. She was just surprised.

"I'll take her to the infirmary."

"Sydney," Ms. Crow pulled on his arm.

The two stepped to a side and whispered.

Oscar wandered off to look into each of the ewers. "Looks like you broke Holding, Lee. Nice."

"What are you looking for?" KC asked.

"Water." Oscar tilted one of the pitchers to his lips. "Three of them have water. Pick one of the beds with a toothbrush on the stand."

KC looked horrified. "There's no bathroom?"

Ms. Crow came back to them. Dr. Fenn left through the *Gents* changing room door without another word. He left his torch in a sconce by the door.

"Of course there's a bathroom, KC. It's right there." Ms. Crow pointed at the wooden door.

Oscar stage whispered, "It's a hole in the ground. No running water."

"That is true," Ms. Crow confirmed. "There was no running water when this section was built. Now you should all wash up and get to bed. I'll be coming to get you early tomorrow morning. The torch will burn down quickly." She stepped over to the *Gents* door to shut it and then over to the *Ladies.* She smiled at each of the kids though her brow furrowed when she looked down at Laylea. Then she stepped through and closed the *Ladies* door.

The three watched the door for a moment as if they expected Ms. Crow to come back. But it eventually dawned on each of them that they were stuck here for the night.

Laylea wished they'd talk. She felt a strange pull towards the changing room, like she had to go get her house key, which was a strange thought since she couldn't go home. She was scared by the way Dr. Fenn and Ms. Crow had looked at her. Oscar and KC both knew more about shifters and the school than she did. They could tell her what was wrong. But they didn't. They each turned away to a bedside and started brushing their teeth and getting ready for bed.

She looked around for the raven but it was gone. She hadn't seen it leave.

Laylea hopped up onto the bed closest to KC's chosen cot. She dug at the blanket and shoved it and the sheet around until she had the perfect nest. She circled four times clockwise and twice counterclockwise. With a sigh, she dropped into a ball. It had been a long day.

"You done, puppy?" Oscar's question startled Laylea.

She'd popped up to sitting and tilted her head before she realized he was mocking her.

KC was staring too. "You really did fall asleep that fast, didn't you?"

What could Laylea say? She fixed her nest, pulled the pillow closer, and circled again. She couldn't find the right spot this time. She tried and circled several more times before she gave up. She just crashed against the pillow, trying to imagine it was Bailey. This time, she didn't drop right into sleep. This time her mind filled with Bailey's disappointment, Morioka's anger, and Junior's blood. She felt the whimper in her throat before it broke the heavy silence in the room.

Neither Oscar nor KC said anything. Laylea peeked through half-closed eyes to watch them get into their own beds. She saw KC bury her face in her pillow and for a while she could tell Oscar was holding his breath. When their breathing settled, Laylea sang out a good night.

"Good night, Lee." KC rolled over to face her and called over to the other row, "Good night, Oscar."

After a big sigh, Oscar said, "Go to sleep. We're perfectly safe in here."

KC rolled her eyes. Laylea dropped her jaw in a grin. They both shut their eyes and Laylea felt the warm weight of sleep falling over them. She sighed and let unconsciousness wash her away.

She'd just slipped into a dream of flying with Clark, Kyle soaring along beside them, when the howling started. Laylea and KC stared at each other as dozens of cries echoed through the cold stone walls. Laylea's blood ran cold but her fear was nothing compared to the terror in KC's eyes.

Oscar whispered, "It's not a full moon. Why are they Wilding?"

"They're not." KC barely breathed her reply. "They're looking for something."

Laylea had the strange idea that KC thought they were looking for her.

It was hours before any of them fell asleep again.

13

"You are a strange one, aren't you?" Dr. Fenn set down the little rust-colored reflex hammer.

Laylea had shifted when he tapped her puppy knee. Sher had never hit her so hard during exams. Maybe she'd been gentle because she was Laylea's mother. Or maybe Dr. Fenn was just a jerk.

Dr. Fenn was the only one who reacted to her sitting there naked on the exam table. Not standing from his stool, the doctor rolled over to open the door to the infirmary. "There's a clothes closet just down the hall in the alcove."

She felt a little odd heading out into the hallway naked, but on her way out the door, Laylea was distracted by Ms. Crow admonishing Dr. Fenn.

"I've explained that every student here is unique."

"There's unique and then there's—" Dr. Fenn stopped himself. So Laylea, who had paused to listen, headed on down the hall to the closet.

They'd seen half a dozen of these on their way from Holding. Not many in the low, dark tunnels of that older section, but once they hit the wider corridors of what Ms. Crow called the modern school, they saw a closet after every turning. The closets were mostly enormous wardrobes that had been retrofitted with shelves or cubbies. Some of the closets held flip-flops and cheap sneakers for kids who wanted shoes, like KC. Laylea loved going barefoot.

No two of the closets they'd seen so far matched. The one in the Medical Wing was the most modern closet yet. It was a line of black-brown Ikea bookcases with opaque doors on each of the thin towers. The bookcases fit perfectly against the back wall of a small alcove featuring a stiff couch and one over-stuffed chair.

Laylea picked one tower at random and dropped to her knees to pull a jumpsuit from the bottom level. The material was a bit stiffer than the one the raven had picked for her. But she kind of liked the high waist and loose short sleeves.

She hadn't seen the raven today. Ms. Crow had fetched them from Holding and had them pick which item they wanted to keep before they packed the rest of their belongings in boxes. Laylea chose her collar. But when Ms. Crow took everything out of it first, she almost changed her mind. She felt a strange need to keep her house key near though that made no sense. She'd have to carry it and she couldn't when she was a dog. Once she had her collar on, the need went away. The three had paraded with the boxes and Ms. Crow all the way through the ancient tunnels to the modern school and through to the Medical Wing where they'd left the boxes in the hall beside the infirmary door, across from a door to what Ms. Crow called ST.

She hadn't noticed on her way to the closet, but now Laylea saw that their boxes were gone. Neither she nor Oscar had much; just their clothes and the contents of their pockets. KC seemed to have brought everything she owned. She'd kept the dibs drive charmband she'd shown off to Laylea at Common Electronics. Everything else was now in LPSS storage. She wondered briefly where that was.

Laylea slipped back into the infirmary just as Dr. Fenn was finishing up KC's medical history. It didn't take long since she was claiming to be an orphan.

He'd started the intake exam by inoculating each of them against shifter-specific diseases. Then each of them got an individual physical and medical history quiz, even Oscar, whose pediatrician was sending over his records. Laylea hadn't found Dr. Fenn's veterinary skills to be anything to write home about, except that Sher had worked as a vet, and if she knew where to send the letter, she'd love to write home about anything.

Ms. Crow hustled KC off the exam table while Dr. Fenn ran a sanitizing wand over it. "We just have time for a quick tour before you all need to be at Testing."

"Hold on there, Elizabeth. Now that she can speak, I'd need to get a more thorough health history from the girl."

Laylea glanced at the notepad on Dr. Fenn's desk. She'd written out her answers for him. "I don't have anything to add."

"Did you know what you were writing, Lee?" Dr. Fenn asked, like she'd been in a trance rather than just in her other form.

Did he think shifters were like mental patients with multiple personality disorder? Was that what shifting was like for him?

If it was, Laylea didn't think it was common based on the looks Oscar and KC, and even Ms. Crow, were giving him.

She just reanswered his questions. "I don't know any of my biological family and I have no history of illness."

She had a history of injury, but he hadn't seemed interested in her bum hip when she'd mentioned it the night before, so she didn't see any point in mentioning it again. Since Sher had done it at the same time as the surgery on her hip, Laylea didn't think to tell him that she'd been spayed.

"Alright." Ms. Crow held the door. "Thank you, Sydney."

Oscar was already waiting in the hall. KC pulled Laylea past him to whisper, "He wanted to do blood work and stuff because you shifted in Holding."

"Really?"

"Yeah." She glanced over her shoulder but Oscar was keeping Ms. Crow distracted. "He was insisting but then Ms. Crow asked him if he really wanted to send you to Dr. Durrah and Fenn got really upset."

Laylea whispered back, "Who's Dr. Durrah?"

"No idea."

Something about the name caught in Laylea's brain. She'd heard that name before. Before she could place it, Ms. Crow and Oscar caught up and they were rushing off out of the Medical Wing.

Ms. Crow pointed out about one in every ten doors. The doors had as much variety as the closets and none of them was labeled. A set of heavily carved oaken doors that looked like they'd been stolen off a church led to what Ms. Crow called the Executive Wing. She said they'd hopefully never have to go there and they weren't to go in unless escorted by a faculty member.

"Dean Gorse will want to meet each of you. He likes to get to know all of the students, but he is a very busy man. Just keep in mind that at LPSS his word trumps the Enforcer's."

"Could we be released on his say-so?" Laylea asked.

Ms. Crow looked so sad, Laylea had to look away. "Only if you pass the shifting test."

One of the oaken doors burst open and Laylea caught sight of a pair of dull black oxfords before the figure spun around and let the door fall shut on his words.

"Mr. Benniker, you admit that the wolves were on these grounds. Good. Well, do we allow any non-faculty, non-students on grounds after curfew?" The guttural voice wasn't hindered by the door, though they couldn't hear Mr. Benniker's responses at all. "That's right. So what made you think I had approved a hunting party to trample all over our grounds after curfew for the first time ever? Oh? I'm supposed to reward you for keeping them out of the tunnels? The tunnels handle that themselves, Mr. Benniker. No, Mr. Benniker, there are no such things as vampires. They are a legend, a myth, a bedtime story for unruly pups. Do you see a wolf here? Do I care what they prefer their young to be called? Are you telling me my job, Mr. Benniker?"

The voice faded away as a paradiddle of footsteps echoed out of the Executive Wing.

Were the wolves hunting Kyle? Laylea peeked at KC. The girl had blanched.

Ms. Crow pulled her light-blue sweater tighter around her shoulders. "Just do what Dean Gorse says and you'll be fine."

They headed up and down several hallways and cul-de-sac-like wings, which Ms. Crow identified as Biology Row, Physics Square, Musician Central, and the ModTech Corridor. She let them stick their heads in a few classrooms and took them past the enormous smoked-glass doors of the cafeteria, only to take them into a place called the night kitchen, via a small, red panel door. Most of LPSS was cold but the night kitchen was a sauna. Ms. Crow showed them where to get bowls from a stack and sent them to the three cauldrons hanging over an open fire. She directed them to use a wooden handle to pull the leftmost cauldron away from the fire. They used a wooden spoon hung near the handle to scoop out some kind of spicy porridge.

"You'll want to shut your eyes as you go through here."

Ms. Crow's advice seemed crazy until they'd pushed through the swinging metal door into blinding light. The door led into the grandest room Laylea had ever seen. But she couldn't see it right away because she'd grown accustomed to the dimness of the hallways and classrooms in the rest of the school. Even the wash of white lights in the infirmary couldn't compare with this. Sunlight shone down from multiple archways of glass far overhead. Long, thin shadows made by the metal frame of the ceiling traced spiderwebs of darkness across the long wooden dining tables filling the room.

"Come, sit."

Laylea swung her eyes away from the sky to find Ms. Crow sitting at the end of the closest of ten heavy tables. A couple dozen kids were spread out among the tables. A few sat studying by themselves, but most sat in groups, laughing and goofing around. One girl lay on a table in a ray of sunlight, her hair draped out like a halo and falling off the edge of the old wood.

Laylea slid onto the bench on the far side of the table from Ms. Crow. Oscar sat beside her. The tables were long. They could probably seat twenty-five students to a side. But they weren't as wide as you'd expect, maybe a meter across.

"Go on, eat up."

Laylea wasn't the only one who'd forgotten her food. She dug in. It was a mix of oatmeal and barley and some grain she'd never had before, overly-spiced with cinnamon.

Ms. Crow brought them water from a four-foot tall bronze silo at the end of the table. Laylea made a note of the giant dog bowl positioned beneath the nozzle. It was the first concession she'd seen to shifters who preferred animal form, or, more likely, got stuck in animal form.

"You can get porridge or soup in the night kitchen any time you need. And the keg is always filled with fresh water. Chef Tod is a caffeine addict. Since caffeine interferes with calcium absorption, we don't permit it in the school. So, you'll find that his night kitchen offerings feature a healthy dose of stimulating spices. You won't have much free time, but this is one of the places in school where you are welcome at any time." She looked around. "Everyone feels different and lonely sometimes. I encourage you to reach out. Make friends and try to get along. It's not that hard to fit in."

KC scraped the bottom of her bowl. "Sure, if you're a paying student. But is it so easy if you're pressed into enrollment?"

"It really doesn't make much of a difference," Ms. Crow said. "Nobody can tell from looking at you whether you're paying or pressed."

Emboldened by KC, Laylea licked her bowl clean. She asked, "What's that mean? Paying or pressed?"

"Some of the students here have paid for the privilege of attending, while others have been given a recommendation."

Oscar laughed. "The dragon gave you and KC a *recommendation,* AKA you both got *pressed* into enrollment because you did something bad."

KC turned on Oscar. "You were in the back of the cop car, too."

"That was just transportation. I had to get here somehow. I'm a paying student."

Laylea tilted her head. "Did your parents pay to keep you out of juvie?"

Oscar glared at her. He pushed out the bench, nearly making her fall off, and snatched his bowl from the table. KC followed him to a hatch Laylea hadn't seen. They both tossed their bowls inside. She hopped up to do the same and heard KC cackle, "They were pressed into paying."

Ms. Crow stood when Laylea returned from the dish hatch. "I was pressed. This school changed my life. You're going to learn many things. Don't start out with a closed mind about how anyone got here."

The trio followed her between the tables to the great glass double doors. Ms. Crow paused at the reflection and for a moment it seemed like she was reaching out to touch her own face. Oscar and KC were too busy bickering to see. But then she pushed the door aside and strode out into the dark corridor.

She didn't speak again until they reached a pair of Craftsman-style doors, each with a grid of smoked glass windows.

"We've got one more stop before I take you to Testing."

A stocky, acne-cursed boy pushed out of the door on the left, hugging a stack of books to his chest. He blinked at seeing all of them but when he recognized Ms. Crow, he smiled up at her and then ducked his chin behind his books.

"Good to see you, Benny," Ms. Crow called after him as she led the way into the room.

Laylea watched the boy scurry off. When she turned to see where Ms. Crow had brought them, she froze.

14

Laylea would swear up and down for the rest of her life that the air filled with a chorus of angels when she first walked into the LPSS library. It was the most magical place she had ever seen. Most libraries featured rows and rows of shelves lined with books, and that was pretty magical itself for a dog who loved to read. But Ms. Crow's eight-foot-tall shelves curved around the room like some giant's domino art. Just like Laylea and Bailey's apartment, layer after layer of area rugs covered the floor. The rough rock and daub walls that weren't hidden by wooden shelves featured enormous tapestries in rich colors. Countless nooks had been created throughout the room with heavy tables, couches, comfy chairs, and piles of pillows. Somehow, filtered sunlight shone through a row of thin windows high on the far wall though it couldn't possibly reach the sky.

Ms. Crow stepped to the side as they came in the doors. She slipped behind a tall counter made of the same rich wood and in the same classic style as the shelves. The counter created a little closed off area that featured another set of smoked-glass doors, shelves, and an old roll top desk. Ms. Crow paid no mind to the raven, which stood on the top of the desk, diligently cleaning one wing.

Ms. Crow placed one palm on the countertop and then typed a password into the inset deskpadd. "This is where you'll find me most of the time." She tapped a particular rhythm on the countertop with her middle finger and a clear screen slid up. "I know that it's all the rage to use the desktop screens, but that is very bad for your spine. All the Personal Access Device Desktops in the library and in the dorm pods have elevated options. I highly recommend you use them."

She swiped and typed for a minute. "There we go. Oscar, can I have your handprint, please?"

She set a flat device that looked like a mobile padd on the public side of the counter. Oscar spread one hand and set it on top like he'd done this before.

"This is for our internal systems. Your files will be stored in the primary mainframe and you'll be able to log in and access them from any padd throughout the school." She came out from behind the counter and set the mobile padd on the carpets. "If you'll just shift please."

Oscar scoffed. "Why would I need to log in if I'm in animal form?"

"You will be required to attend certain classes in animal form, Oscar. And you cannot access certain areas without paw print clearance."

Oscar rolled up his sleeves and the legs of his pants. For an instant, his face lost its permanent sneer and he looked as content as Laylea had seen him. Then the visual field around him shuddered. His face lengthened. His eyes grew. His legs shortened while his elbows reversed. Oscar fell to all fours. He whipped back to growl at his backside, still trapped in the now ill-fitting jumpsuit. When he looked back, Laylea gasped. Oscar was gorgeous. Laylea wasn't into cats but she'd never seen anything like him. He was a leopard, like KC had said he'd be. But instead of orange circles and swirls, Oscar's sleek form was all black. He had swirls and circles. But the patterns were black on black. He set one paw on the padd and opened his mouth wide in a snarl.

"That's got it. Thank you, Oscar."

The next instant, Oscar the boy stood in front of them again, straightening his jumpsuit and unrolling the legs; a sinuous rolling of his neck the only hint he'd been a cat a moment ago.

Ms. Crow looked at the girls. "Next."

"This is just internal, right?" KC asked.

"Yes. For safety purposes we keep our internal systems carefully segregated from all external file structures. It's the way the school is built. We can get web access and files can be transferred in, but the only way to send any information off grounds is to print it or transfer it to an external drive and walk it out."

KC nodded and stepped up to the padd. She knelt to put her hand on it. That made Ms. Crow laugh. "I would have put it on the counter for you. That's good. Now, please shift."

KC stood. She rolled up her sleeves like Oscar had. She made faces like she was trying to change. She strained, scrunching her eyes and clenching her fists. After a minute, she looked up at Ms. Crow.

"I'm sorry. I'm no good at shifting under pressure."

Oscar choked. Ms. Crow didn't notice.

"That's okay. You probably won't be placed in any of the restricted access classes in that case anyway. Lee?"

Laylea searched for the burny place in her gut. She closed her eyes and tried to hear the clunk of their radiator or a car backfiring or a dragon screaming into the dark night. She opened her eyes when she felt Ms. Crow put a hand on her shoulder.

"It's okay, Lee. You're here to learn how to shift. I'll just take your handprint for now." There was a deep sadness in Ms. Crow's eyes. The blue of her irises faded away as Laylea watched and she thought Ms. Crow might shift. The raven flew from the desk to the edge of the counter right beside Ms. Crow. It leaned in closely to peer at the librarian and had to leap backward when Ms. Crow shook herself awake and set the padd on the counter for Laylea.

"You are officially checked in. Step two, Testing."

"Hey." Oscar played with the buttons on his jumpsuit. "Is the testing gonna be like general testing, like science stuff or specific, like biology stuff?"

Ms. Crow said, "You'll start with general questions and they'll become specific. So, yes, you'll have to answer biology stuff. Are you worried?"

"No. I'm fine."

He clearly wasn't, but Ms. Crow accepted the answer and led the way out of the library.

"Hey, Oscar." Laylea reached out to take his hand from the buttons. When he looked at her, she enclosed his hand in both of hers. She lowered her voice as Sher always did when conditioning people. "You'll remember everything you ever learned about biology, Oscar. It will be easy. Easy." She slid her hands away but held his eyes until he blinked.

"What was that?" Oscar wigged out. He looked at KC and Ms. Crow to see if they thought it was weird, too. That was okay. The odder he felt, the more his subconscious would cling to the memory and the stronger the conditioning would imprint.

"Operant conditioning. I help my brother with his tests all the time. He hates tests."

Which was true. But the conditioning didn't work well on Bailey since he knew exactly what she was doing. Sher could have done it and used real magic to boost the effect, but she called that cheating. The best Laylea could do for a boost was a little grunt magic push on the memory catalyst in his hippocampus.

Oscar followed Ms. Crow out the door. KC giggled at Laylea before she left, too.

Laylea trailed after the others. She gazed longingly over her shoulder at the books, vowing to return as soon as she could, then wiggled her fingers at the raven, which took another hop back before it launched itself into the air and swooped out the door ahead of Laylea.

The raven soared ahead and then turned on its wing and swooped low over their heads, down the way they'd come. Laylea raised her hands into the air, like a goalpost and the bird folded her wings to slip between them, before jerking sideways to avoid running into Ms. Crow.

KC and Oscar followed behind Ms. Crow quietly, ignoring each other.

"We'll just cut through the Fields real quick. Keep up now. Watch out for the gym class. Just don't get in the way of any balls flying around." Ms. Crow said this as she pushed through a heavy steel door.

All three kids traipsed through after her and then slowed to stare at the forest around them. Ms. Crow had led them into what could only be described as an underground jungle. Laylea couldn't see the ceiling because it was either too high, or the trees obscured it, or both. The wall holding the door featured rows of cubbies on either side. But then it quickly disappeared behind bushes and flowers and climbing vines.

The overwhelming scent of old throughout the rest of the school was replaced with bright, new, fresh, green, moist, living, growing outsideness. A river flowed by somewhere near that they could hear but not see. And this was punctuated by the sound of screaming kids, howling wolves, croaking birds, and the gruff, distant voice of a teacher yelling, "Get the lead out. You're gonna let Reginald keep that ball? This is gym class, not hibernation! Move it!"

"Come on. Come on" Ms. Crow urged. "You don't want to be late to Testing."

Laylea didn't give a fig about being late for Testing. She wanted to shift and run around in here. She wanted to get the ball from Reginald. Bailey had never liked gym class but Laylea couldn't wait. The raven circled her and she noticed that Ms. Crow and the others were almost out of sight.

She caught up with them by the river. Three sleek forms cavorted under the water. She couldn't see very clearly what they were until one of them leapt out of the water with a volleyball balanced on its nose. The dolphin tossed the ball up and smacked it down, diving after it all in one smooth motion. When he sailed under the water, Laylea saw that the river seemed to end at the base of a mountain that rose up, covered with ferns and more greenery.

She spotted the tiger just as it dove from the mountainside into the water and disappeared under the cliff. She ran ahead through a little tunnel in the rock wall to find herself in a wide-open garden and orchard. Food plants abounded and Oscar picked a handful of strawberries from a thicket beside the river, which had popped back up aboveground.

A gorilla on the far shore yelled, "Hey Reggie! I'm open!"

The tiger flew through the water, its front paws grasping a sailfish's fin. As Laylea tried to follow Ms. Crow along the narrow path, she watched the sailfish leap into the air. The tiger launched itself with an assist from the fish's tail just as the dolphin with the ball came up.

"Reggie!" The gorilla danced around, hollering in a human voice, "Over here, Reggie!"

The tiger swiped the ball to the gorilla, who caught it and disappeared into a stand of apple trees.

A chorus of cheers and bleats and squeals went up from students all around, most of whom Laylea couldn't even see. Taunting and grunts wafted from the grove where the gorilla had vanished. Laylea had no idea what game they were playing but it seemed like the tiger-gorilla-sailfish team was winning.

The path led Laylea away from the apple trees and the game. It wound through a variety of gardens and curved back to a bridge that led over a swampy area beyond where the river had disappeared. Here, Laylea could see a great glass ceiling like in the dining hall glimmering far above. There were two levels of glass. First, a flat plane that had people walking on it and watery roots dangling from dark patches. Then, above that, a great vaulted series of glass panels welded together. All of it shimmered with the golden glow of residual magic.

"Is that the Chicago Conservatory?" Laylea asked out loud, even though she was nowhere near Ms. Crow and the others. She ran again to catch up.

The laughing voices and animal chatter fell behind as Laylea ducked into a tightly woven grove. The branches hung so low she had to weave her way through to the other side where the trees changed and spread out. Every kind of willow filled the sky overhead and roots obscured most of the paths winding among a dozen lakes. She vaulted over logs and boulders and cut through some bushes she didn't expect to be so thorny, catching up to KC, Oscar, and Ms. Crow at a dead run.

"Whoa." Ms. Crow caught Laylea and pulled her back from the edge of a marvelous waterfall.

The water from the lakes came together to flow over the side of a high cliff, just to splash down into rocky terrain featuring more cave openings than Laylea could count.

Ms. Crow had to yell to be heard over the roaring falls. "You'd climb down through the rocks." She pointed out a pathway that crossed under the great waterfall and between the many caves. "And exit through that vault door over there to get out of the Fields and back to the library corridor."

Oscar nodded but Laylea couldn't see any vault door.

"Follow me." Ms. Crow led them away from the waterfall, back through the lake land to a fancy white door that would fit well on a Southern mansion. Cubbies framed either side of this entrance as well. A few of them had folded clothes inside.

When the door shut behind them, the brilliance of smells and colors and light cut off too harshly. Laylea sighed and followed Ms. Crow's brisk progress down the cold stone corridor dimly lit from recesses along the ceiling. She looked back to see KC pull the Fields door open and peek back inside. The raven flew out over her head like she'd been trapped. KC didn't look at the bird. She sighed. When she caught Laylea watching her, they both grinned.

The next door Ms. Crow opened led them into an ornate room that could have been a polar opposite to the Fields if it had tried just a little harder. Velvet-cushioned benches lined rough, turn-of-the-last-century school desks, all facing a stone podium raised on a dais. The raven settled on the podium. Its beady, searching gaze added to the gothic mood. The room resembled nothing so much as an Episcopalian chapel in everything except the leafy green Linden tree leaning on one of the tall desks in the back row of the classroom.

About two dozen kids waited on the velvet benches. A few more stood in groups around the room talking with adults. A grey-haired man sporting a plaid bow tie excused himself from a gaggle of equally well-dressed boys.

"Ms. Crow, has your morning gone smoothly?"

"It has Mr. Bianchi. These are our new students, KC, Lee, and Oscar."

Ms. Crow nodded encouragingly at the three as Mr. Bianchi shook each of their hands. "I'll see you at dinner." The raven followed Ms. Crow to the door and then circled the room before it returned to the dais.

"Ah, Oscar. I knew your father well. He was an excellent addition to the choir. Did you inherit his voice?"

"I don't think so."

"We will have to find out." Mr. Bianchi finally released Oscar's hand. "But later, later. Today we find out where your scholastic skills lie." He raised his voice to reach everyone in the room. "Please, find yourselves a seat."

"Excuse me, Mr. Bianchi." Laylea said. "Why are they all here?"

"Anyone can come to an optional Testing Day. New students and transfers must endure Testing so we can place you in the appropriate classes. Current students can test at any time to change classes or in a bid to graduate."

"Oh."

"Just place your hand on the padd to palm in and answer the questions as best you can." He addressed his directions to all three of them. "Go on and find a seat now."

The three headed for the nearest bench.

"Ah, separately please. You've grown accustomed to each other, but we'd like you to spread out for the Testing. No talking allowed anyway, you understand."

Laylea touched Oscar's arm and reinforced her conditioning. "Easy."

He rolled his eyes and crossed the room to a girl with colorful braids who waved him over.

"Hey, Oscar."

"Hey, Julia."

"It's *hulia*. Get it right." The older girl straightened his jumpsuit.

"I know, Julia." Oscar leaned on the aitch sound.

She flipped her braids over one shoulder. "Never thought we'd see you here."

They sat, still chatting.

KC shrugged at Laylea and turned to the padd inset in the desk she'd chosen.

Laylea looked around as the kids who'd been chatting all picked seats. Nobody seemed to be going for the standing desks in the back, so that's where Laylea headed. She picked a spot under a branch of the Linden and, though she had to stand on her tiptoes to reach the deskpadd, she didn't mind. Her heart was racing. She had to wipe her sweaty palm before signing in to the padd. After years of home-schooling and reading every book she could get her paws on, she was nervous to find out how much she knew after all. The tree relaxed her.

Until the trunk twisted toward her and whispered, "Breathe. It's gonna be okay."

Laylea whipped around when Mr. Bianchi called to her from the podium. "Lee, could you please move a little farther from Caliban, please?"

15

Laylea meant to step away from the tree. She meant to slide down a couple of spaces and be cool. Instead that tickling burning exploded from her belly to her heart, and she dropped into a pile of jumpsuit. She couldn't see from where she stood but it sounded like everyone else in the room laughed at her. She heard Mr. Bianchi's footsteps striding toward her.

"It's okay, Mr. Bianchi," The tree's wispy tone conveyed unshakeable confidence and calm. "I'll help her."

The footsteps stopped. Laylea looked up to see the tree reach two branches to the desk high above Laylea's head. The great head of leaves shook like Sher changing her hair color and a wash of change flowed down the tree to her roots. A thin olive-skinned girl popped the deskpadd out and knelt to set it on the floor beside Laylea. She was the girl Laylea had seen lying on one of the dining tables earlier. Her hair draped like willow fronds down past her waist. It brushed over Laylea as she swiped through to the settings on the padd.

"I'm Caliban Meilissene. I'm a fourth year." Caliban adjusted the display until the multiple choice boxes were large enough for Laylea's paws. "Don't worry about what you don't know."

Caliban helped Laylea wriggle out of the jumpsuit. She puddled it on the cold floor beside the padd, and then stood up to palm into her own deskpadd. Laylea nosed the padd over a few inches and settled herself on the jumpsuit. The Testing started with questions about her past schooling. Since none wasn't an available choice for *How many years of schooling have you completed,* she chose *one.*

A half an hour later she looked up to see that everyone else was standing, stretching and getting water. She was the only one still tapping on her padd. The questions were all incredibly basic but they covered a wide range of topics at random. Laylea had stalled at a math question when she saw two answers that could be correct. Mr. Bianchi was pouring himself a glass of water from a carafe over by three padded doors on the far side of the room. Laylea wondered if she should bark or just go over to him. A question mark popped up on her screen, followed by two options: *Need help* and *Continue.* She tapped on *Need help.*

Mr. Bianchi looked down at his armpadd and then over toward the rear table. He turned back to the water carafe for a moment and then approached Laylea with a silver bowl. He set it beside her as he sat cross-legged on the floor.

"Thinking is thirsty work," he said. "How can I help? Oh!"

He accompanied the last exclamation with complicated swiping and tapping on her paddscreen. A notepad program came up. Laylea tilted her paw to try to isolate one nail. She managed to tap the button that released a stylus pen from the top of the padd and gripped the pen gently in her teeth.

She wrote *assume base ten?*

"What do you mean?"

Can't tell if question is on math or music. If she were writing to Bailey she would have drawn a treble clef. They'd invented their own shorthand when she was growing up since writing with a pencil in your teeth isn't easy for anyone.

"Are you a musician?" Mr. Bianchi asked this as an aside while he swiped through information on his armpadd.

Not practical. I studied theory and comp.

Mr. Bianchi glanced at her answer and did a double take. He

tapped a few items on his wrist and then swiped her screen back to the question application.

"Let's try starting you a little differently." He set the padd back down in front of her. "Call out if you need me."

Instead of asking about her schooling history, the app this time invited her to choose the kinds of math, science, and languages she'd studied. It asked her to fill in the last five books she'd read, what her favorite pieces of art were, and what kinds of music she listened to. These questions were more fun even if there was a series where she had to select *Do not understand* several times.

There was a pause after this series before the padd got back to the random subject quizzing. This time some of the questions challenged her and she loved it. It was probably an hour later that the screen blinked three times before displaying the full screen message *Take a Break.*

Caliban was no longer standing beside her. She wasn't even in the room. There seemed to be several kids missing. Some of the ones still around were, like her, Testing at the desks. Some were getting water and wandering around aimlessly. A few waited by the three padded doors. Laylea lapped up some water from the silver bowl. It was good to move. She hadn't realized how stiff she'd gotten standing over the padd for so long. Looking around to be sure nobody was watching, she galloped up to the front of the room and back. She stood up against the leg of the tall desk to stretch her back and then ran through her morning yoga moves.

"Arrrgggh!"

The kid who yelled was sitting near the back, hunched over, even though he'd elevated the screen as Ms. Crow had suggested. His hair stood up in all directions and, as she watched, he popped out of his human form, spread a pair of wings wider than the benches and soared over everyone's heads to the front of the room. His feathers coruscated through shades of green and blue with red tips. At the front of the room, he beat his wings down once and a clap of thunder echoed off the stone. He popped into a rich brown-skinned boy with panic in his eyes when he turned. His face flushed and he popped back into the magnificent bird to fly back to his seat where he shifted and groaned again, more quietly.

"Arrgh."

"Mr. Ahanu." Mr. Bianchi intoned this as a warning but Laylea could hear a laugh hidden deep in the words.

She went to stand from her upward dog pose and only then realized she'd shifted herself. She hadn't felt any burning or pain. Or maybe she'd just been so distracted by Ahanu that she hadn't noticed. If she could negate the pain factor, maybe her subconscious would be more willing to shift on command. It was something to think about.

Caliban came back into the room from one of the padded doors as Laylea was pulling her jumpsuit on. She smiled and looked back to her padd. When Laylea picked up her padd to set it on the desk, she saw that the message had changed.

It now read *Room 3.*

Laylea looked around for Mr. Bianchi. He was sitting on a desk beside a small white-haired girl with a fierce overbite. Room three had to be one of the padded doors. She just had to figure out which one. The middle door opened as she approached. KC came out. Laylea caught her eye and smiled, but KC looked like she was going to cry and dropped the gaze to shuffle back to her seat. Laylea would have followed her, but a woman with the crinkliest face she'd ever seen stepped out and crooked a finger at her.

"Room three?" Laylea whispered.

The old Black woman stepped aside to usher her in.

A single chair sat just inside the door facing a vast triangle of open space. Laylea only realized how green the lighting in the main room was, now that she saw the cool blue rising from recesses in the walls here. Ms. Crow had called them light troughs.

"When you are ready."

Laylea turned to see the teacher settled in the chair, one leg crossed elegantly over the other. The padd still read *Room 3.* It was no help. She looked around at the tapestries hung on the stone walls to see if they offered any clue.

"Shift, girl."

"Oh." Laylea turned to face the woman. She shut her eyes and then opened them again to set the deskpadd on the ground. She searched for the burning in her gut but she thought about how she had just shifted without knowing it. So maybe the burning wasn't the key. Maybe that wasn't how she should chase the Change. She thought about being a dog, focused on her tail, which never left her mind even if nobody could see it wagging. But her mental tail right now was tucked firmly under her belly, protecting her from that woman's coldness. She scolded her tail.

The woman wasn't dangerous. She wasn't a dragon-demon or a vampire or a drug-lab goon. Nobody ever got hurt from being judged, she thought, and then immediately regretted it. People got hurt all the time from being judged. Especially dogs. Nobody was ever afraid of her because she was a cute little blonde terrier with impossibly adorable floppy ears. But there was a pit mix that lived two doors down who hung out in her front yard, desperate for her dad to come home, and people would cross the street in fear. Sammy was the sweetest, most loving slobber monster Laylea had ever known. But people were afraid. Someone had even tried to rescue Laylea from Sammy's yard once when she'd gone over to play. The world really wasn't very fair sometimes.

"Ms. Woodford."

Laylea's eyes popped open. She was still standing in front of the cold teacher. She was still human.

"Sorry. If you throw something, I would probably change. Scaring me usually does it."

"Despite what you may have heard about the extreme measures we will take if necessary, I am not in the habit of throwing things at my students." The woman swiped her armpadd. Then she stood and floated to the door. "You will not be my student though, so I shall consider your suggestion." She held the door open.

Laylea thought that might be a joke, but she couldn't tell from the teacher's face. She bobbed her head at the woman as she left. "Thank you. Sorry."

She was halfway back to her desk when she remembered she'd left her padd on the floor. When she spun around, the old woman hadn't moved. Laylea dashed in past her. It took her three tries to get a grip on the thin glass padd and by the time she got it, her fingers were so sweaty, she gripped it with both hands till she was out of the room.

"Sorry, thank you, sorry."

This time when she left the room, the door was firmly closed behind her.

When she could, Laylea peeked up to see if anyone had seen her double-exit. KC was grinning madly at her. They shared a sigh before a gentle voice interrupted.

"Lee Woodford?"

Laylea turned to see a white-haired man sporting a handlebar mustache and braided goatee raising his out-of-control eyebrows at her. "Lee?"

"Yes. Hi. Sorry."

Half a grin twinkled in the man's eyes and he twitched his fancy mustache. "I'm Mr. Vronumraju. It appears you're interested in physics and mechanical engineering. Come talk with me."

Laylea glanced back at KC before she headed into the second room. "Aeronautical engineering, actually."

One of the eyebrows rose.

"I flew a lot as a puppy."

After a long conversation with Mr. Vronumraju, Laylea was ushered into the third room, *Room 1,* for an only slightly shorter conversation with a socially awkward teacher who introduced herself as "Madame, with the French pronunciation." Madame covered languages, reading comprehension, musical skills, dance, and artistic ability. When Laylea expressed an interest in Capoeira, Madame informed her that was more a martial art than a dance, although it was debatable due to its dynamic inception, and transitioned into a conversation about sociology and history. Laylea hung in there pretty well with the human society questions but she clearly disappointed Madame with her utter dearth of education on shifter history and politics.

She dismissed Laylea to lunch, which consisted of sandwiches and fruit delivered to the Testing room by a Shetland pony. A few kids gathered around the basket of food were gossiping about a pack of wolves being attacked by a vampire bat somewhere up in the city. One of them asked KC if she'd seen anything. She rolled her eyes at them and took her apple back to her desk. Laylea returned to her own desk before they could question her. She wanted to ask them if the vampire had hurt anyone. She never considered that Kyle could have been injured.

Following lunch, Laylea's padd resumed the random quizzing, though there were fewer multiple choice questions in this round. After one more break for stretching and water, the padd announced *Last Question* and asked what subjects she most wished to study. She found it an impossible question. It took her twenty-five minutes to complete her answer. Twenty minutes in, she realized that she didn't have the time to learn everything she wanted to learn. She wanted to study the history of flight but with less than a year to live, her time would be better spent either learning how to shift, if they could teach her, so she could get out and see her parents or finding a way to extend her lifespan, which seemed a bit ambitious.

When she finished, she found that she was nearly alone in the Testing chapel. Mr. Bianchi was sitting on the base of the dais with headphones on, directing an invisible choir or orchestra. Laylea watched him for a moment to see if she could figure out which. Caliban had returned to her tree form and had one root dipped into the silver bowl of water that still sat on the floor. The raven perched in her branches and seemed to be sleeping.

Everybody else was either gone or in two of the triangle rooms. The door to the third was ajar.

Mr. Bianchi suddenly looked at his wrist and then up at Laylea. "Well done, Lee. Well done." He folded his earphones down and tucked them away in an inner pocket of his vest. "We aren't supposed to say so, but well done. For a girl with no formal education, you have certainly put our Testing algorithms through the paces today. I know that you're going to need to focus on shifter sociology and history but

I do hope you'll make time for music. For now, Caliban will take you to dinner."

He gestured behind her where Caliban the girl stood now. When she looked back, he was already hustling back to the padded doors where the raven waited on the water table.

"You'll have to tell me if I walk too quickly for you, Lee. You are very small and I like moving swiftly when I'm not a Linden."

Caliban did lead the way quickly through the corridors. She seemed to glide on her long legs and Laylea tripped twice before she admitted it was too fast.

"If I could shift, I'd love to race you," she panted. "But I'm not very graceful as a human."

Caliban slowed. "When I first shifted, I drank dew off my sisters' leaves and ate the grasses at my feet and what nuts blew into our grove. I didn't realize my trunk had bifurcated into legs. I didn't walk until an elder sister journeyed through the grove. She had to tell me what I was." Caliban's breathy laugh put Laylea in mind of a winter breeze. "I gain two legs when I'm human. You lose two."

"Are there a lot of orphans like us here?" Laylea asked.

"I'm not an orphan. All trees are my sisters and brothers. And I'm welcome to rejoin my grove. I just think there's great responsibility in being sentient and expressive and I want to learn everything I can to protect my grove from humans."

"My parents were humans." It hurt Laylea to speak of them in the past tense. It always did. It felt like she was tempting fate.

Really?" Caliban stopped walking for a moment. "What a strange childhood that must have been."

Laylea fell silent and they walked most of the way to the dining hall each contemplating her own thoughts. When they reached the hallway that ended in the great glass doors, Caliban apologized for her silence.

"I sometimes forget I have a voice," she murmured.

Laylea grinned up at her. "I'm a dog. I don't talk much either."

Caliban smiled at that. Then she reached out one too-long, yet still-graceful arm to pull open the dining hall doors and they were assaulted by hundreds of voices. Of course, Laylea shifted.

16

According to legend, a guy named Noah once packed animals of every species onto a boat. Laylea couldn't swim very well. She hadn't had much opportunity. But she decided there, at the hell mouth of the dining hall, that she would have jumped overboard.

The glowing room was in riot. Nearly three hundred kids and animals jockeyed for seats at the long tables and the room wasn't even close to full. There were more than enough seats, but everybody wanted to sit at the same five tables, and the bear, tiger, wolves, and goat took up extra room.

"Britny." A strident voice cut through the din from a raised platform on the northeast corner of the room. Several adults sat at this table, including Dr. Fenn.

The goat sparkled into a girl with a deep blue, long-sleeve jumpsuit and the most stunning afro. "Sorry, Ms. Davies."

"Certain animal forms have been banned from the dining hall," Caliban explained as she scooped up Laylea's jumpsuit and moved to toss it into a bin just beside the doors.

A scrawny boy caught the jumpsuit and spun Caliban around to pass her. "It's not fair. Eating is so much more fun as the monkey."

"Harper." Caliban draped the suit over his neck so it wasn't dragging on the ground.

Harper darted his way through the crowds to a short line against the far wall. A lion pounced on him and they tussled for an instant before the lion dropped to the ground and shuddered into a pile of fur and then into a blonde girl. She struggled into Laylea's jumpsuit and smacked Harper for the too-short arms.

"That's where we pick up our meals at breakfast and dinnertime." Caliban seemed perfectly comfortable to wait in the doorway, though Laylea knew they'd have to go in at some point.

"Thank you, Caliban." Ms. Crow appeared at the doorway. She held a crumpled cloth napkin in her hands and twisted it as she led them over to the service line. "If at all possible, you are to retain human form when dining, Lee. It's considered polite," she explained. "If you get stuck in dog, you'll have to get someone to help you with your tray. Now, Caliban, can you help her with that today?" She paused while the weretree nodded. "Thank you. After dinner you, KC, and Oscar will be assigned to your dorms."

Laylea wanted to ask about the Testing results but she was a dog and she didn't have any pen or paper handy. Ms. Crow stopped to talk with a few other students as she made her way past the long empty tables back to the raised area in the northwest corner.

"Many teachers eat in the faculty dining room on the far side of Chef Tod's kitchen. Some are assigned to eat in here on occasion to oversee. And some like to eat in here. Ms. Crow always eats with us."

Caliban gathered two prepared plates onto a tray and took a variety of sides, telling Laylea what they were as she did.

Back out in the dining room, they found space among a bunch of girls from Caliban's dorm. The girls squeezed together to make room for the tree shifter. Even though it felt rude, Laylea stood her front paws up on the table so that she could see everyone and her food. Caliban introduced her around the table but Laylea only caught a few of their names.

When the skinny, black-haired girl to her right introduced herself as Ali, a hawk, Laylea nosed the tribal-style tattoos running up her arm. Ali said her grandmother had given them to her to exorcise the demon she carried inside.

Across the table, a plump girl named Carrie blurted out, "You're p ... p ... possessed?"

As far as Laylea knew, Morioka did not suffer other demons to live in Chicago. That was the very reason she spent so much time helping Kyle hide from her.

The girls laughed.

"No." Ali rolled her eyes. "They thought hawk-me was a demon."

Everyone else laughed again like this was hilarious. But Carrie looked as shocked as Laylea felt. "Y ... you have a l ... lot of tattoos."

A little blonde girl Laylea recognized from Testing asked, "How did you get here, Ali?"

"Well, Milly." Ali put on a tone like she was telling kids a bedtime story. "When I started fighting back against the tatts, my family locked me in a shed out on the fallow lands. It took a week for my grandfather to man up and let me out. I think he robbed a bank or something on the way here from Kentucky. Told Gorse to keep me till the money ran out."

Laylea swallowed against a sudden change in air pressure. Where Carrie had been sitting, stealing food from everyone's plates even as she stared in horror at Ali's story, a small tawny wolf appeared. It fell off the bench and the air popped again.

Carrie the human crawled back up to her seat gawking at the Ali. "He n ... never told your g ... grandmother that he was a shifter?"

"Never told any of them. Made me swear I'd never tell either." She snorted. "Like I'm ever going back there."

Laylea put a paw on Ali's thigh. When the girl looked down, Laylea blew air through her teeth.

Ali shrugged but Laylea insisted, "*Pfff.*"

A smile ghosted Ali's lips. "Thanks."

"Hey!" A girl with purple hair smacked Carrie's hand. "That's my food!"

In a rather ironic response, the other girls at the table pelted the werewolf with bread roll pellets.

"I'm Milly, a weremouse." The blonde girl from Testing bounced on the other side of the table. "Did you really get to spend the night in Holding with Oscar Luke?"

She looked like she might faint when Laylea nodded.

The girls mocked Milly. They called her boy-crazy and threw pellets at her. Laylea picked the chicken cutlet off her plate and sat back on the bench to eat it. The other tables were all just as raucous. A huddle of half a dozen boys broke up with howls of laughter. They all looked over at a group of students who had books open on the table as they ate. The geeks had no idea the boys were talking about them. She spotted Oscar near the glass doors, sitting beside Julia with an H. She'd piled the braids on her head like a crown. A Latino boy sporting a patch of fuzz he probably thought was a goatee sat on Oscar's other side, looking awfully chummy. A lot of kids were talking about the vampire attack up in the city. The rumor was that the bat got away unscathed but none of the wolves had been bitten. Laylea knew how much to trust rumor.

A quiet caw drew her attention upwards. The raven stood on the edge of the table, looking down at her. Laylea swallowed. She bit off a chunk of chicken and tossed it beside her on the cushion. The raven tilted its head. Laylea nosed the chicken and backed away. She backed into Ali and the pierced girl looked down. Laylea shrugged in her way and glanced meaningfully at the raven and then back to Ali.

The girl looked at the table over Laylea's head like there was nothing there. She rolled her eyes and turned back to the discussion of Reggie Betts; hottie or nottie?

Laylea wondered if they were talking about Reginald, the tiger she'd seen playing in the Fields. If so, she'd vote hottie. She also wondered how she was ever going to remember everybody's names. She'd only met about a million people today.

The raven hopped down to the bench and Laylea bumped into Ali again. She kept her eyes on her chicken cutlet until Ali looked away. The raven kicked its bite of chicken at Laylea. It had carved a D into the meat. Laylea traced LEE into the nap of the velvet cushion. The letters actually stayed and the raven hopped around, croaking. It had trouble isolating one claw so the writing wasn't as precise but when she was done, Laylea could read, *Dizzy*. Laylea dipped her head and put a paw up in *shake*. The raven, Dizzy, touched her beak to Laylea's paw.

"Hey, got room?" KC stood behind Caliban.

The raven snagged the D morsel and flew off.

KC leaned in. "Are you feeling dizzy, Lee?"

The raven's scratching stood out bright on the maroon velvet. Laylea shook her head and scratched at the cushion to make it more comfortable.

"Whoa, hey, stop that, Fido." Brenda, a werepython if Laylea remembered right, spilled her water leaning over the table. "You're gonna get us in trouble. Stop her."

KC set her tray down. "She's not a real dog. She knows what you're saying."

"Really? I thought it was our new mascot," Brenda said.

A girl so white Laylea wondered if she'd been born down here hollered, "For all those games we play against MSC and NESS?"

"Yeah, Emerald, because I hadn't noticed I'm stuck looking at the same ugly faces everywhere I go." Brenda sneered through a mouthful of cherry cobbler. "I mean Mer's new mascot."

Emerald looked like she'd melt in a light drizzle, but her voice had the force of a hurricane. She had braided her white-blonde hair into a thick twist that smacked Carrie in the face when she whipped around to sneer back at Brenda, "I spent a year at the New England Shifter School."

"I'm not insulting NESS. I'm insulting the new kid who can't change out of her dog costume to come to dinner."

Brenda and Emerald seemed to enjoy arguing. Laylea didn't really listen. She hadn't noticed there was cherry cobbler. She climbed over KC's lap as soon as the girl finally sat down. Caliban saw her coming and set the cobbler at the edge of the table. Laylea dove in.

"Do we really play against the Montana Shifter Collective?" KC asked Caliban in a whisper.

Ali overheard her. "Yeah, and New England, because the tuition is so high it covers regularly traveling a thousand miles to play soccer."

"Five minutes." A few kids looked over at the raised dais where Mr. Bianchi repeated himself into a cone connected to a cable that twisted up into the rafters. His sonorous voice echoed through the room. "Five minutes."

A bunch of the kids around them hurried to finish eating.

"The tuition here is pretty steep," KC pointed out.

"How would you know, Presser?" Brenda cackled with a mouth full of cobbler.

Ms. Crow had said it didn't make any difference if you were paid or pressed. But it mattered to these girls. Laylea suddenly felt like she'd eaten too much. KC was scraping her own plate, so Laylea nosed the rest of her cobbler under her friend's fork.

Emerald asked, "How would you know she's pressed?"

Brenda shot a withering look her way. "I work in the Wing, Em."

Emerald shot back, "Like there's anyone who doesn't know that, Bren."

Ali explained, "The Executive Wing."

"Yeah," Brenda lowered her voice, "and I know we were supposed to get two paids yesterday but only one showed up."

The girls all leaned into Brenda's end of the table at this. She ate it up. "Fido and her bodyguard are both pressed. Oscar is paid. So where's number four?"

"Do you know?" Milly, the weremouse with the hots for Oscar, started piling dishes and stacking trays. Brenda left them in suspense while other girls slid their plates and silverware down to Milly.

Ali lowered her head and muttered, "Of course I do," in a snarky voice.

Laylea's tail smacked between KC and Caliban when Brenda, in the exact same tone, said, "Of course I do."

KC choked a little on the last of Laylea's cobbler. Her face flushed bright red as she stacked the empty plate on her own tray.

"Her name was Delcampo."

The whole table erupted. Some jeered. Some laughed. Every one of them recognized KC's real last name.

Milly said, "No way. There are no Delcampo girls."

While an older girl asked, "Why would a Delcampo ever come here?"

"Listen up!" A teacher decked out in White Sox gear joined Mr. Bianchi on the dais. This tall white guy didn't bother to use the microphone. "New students, front and center."

The girls didn't pay him any attention but kids around them started rushing their trays back to the kitchen.

"It *was* a girl. Her name's Charlene," Brenda said, getting KC's real name totally wrong. "Obviously, their people sent her tuition here when it was supposed to go to Montana."

More jeers rang down the table accompanied by shouts of, "No way" and "Delcampos don't pay."

Ali said, "Grandpa Delcampo would never make his own blood pay tuition."

"All hail, King Werewolf." Emerald whispered this and still the rest of the girls shushed her.

A bunch of them shot glances over at the table where Oscar had been sitting. Laylea wondered if they were talking about KC's grandfather. Back at Common Electronics she'd called her great-grandfather "The smallest-minded bully of them all." Who were the Delcampos in the shifter world?

Brenda hissed at Emerald, "You don't want the werewolves to hear you call him that."

From the far end Carrie stuttered, "I . . . I'm a werewolf."

Several girls told her, "You don't count."

"Can you imagine if she came here?" Emerald asked quietly. "The wolf boys would be all over her."

"Yeah, but at least she'd get to date." Milly stood with her overpiled stack of trays. "Out there, she'd be *related* to all of them."

KC stood, too, and ran smack into Oscar's chest. Leftover mashed potatoes and green beans flew. Laylea leaped to get out of the way of the stack of trays tumbling down on her. Sparkling pain shot through her torso and she landed on the velvet bench with two human feet.

All conversation in the room stopped. Laylea stood in all her flat-chested glory, on a bench, in front of the entire school. She felt the blush start. It washed from her pale hair, down her face and kept going all the way down to her toes. Every single face in the room was looking at her. And then every single person in the room was laughing at her. Loudly.

She barely heard Ali mumble, "Nice balance, freak."

17

Laylea had a good view of the student body from her perch on the velvet bench. A good two-fifty to three hundred faces laughed back at her. Even the howler monkey laughed. And a lynx pawed the stone floor with a distinct attitude.

"Get down," KC hissed.

She reached a hand up and Laylea grabbed it. Her knees were so wobbly she would have fallen if KC hadn't helped her off the bench.

Oscar kept his hands to himself. He futzed with his zipper and laughed along with everyone else. "You're such a thumper. Can't you try to be normal?" He said it loud enough that the crowd of guys he'd been sitting with could hear. Which meant that everyone could hear.

Laylea was hemmed in by Oscar on one side, KC on the other and the table right behind her. She was too big to dash under the table, weave through the legs, and escape like she was dreaming. Of course, the great glass door was shut so there was no way she'd get out of the room as a dog. She was dreaming of melting into mist and felt a tingle of possibility in her stomach that maybe she actually could. But then she realized that tingle was nausea and swallowed against it.

"Earth to puppy." Oscar got her attention. "Take it."

She automatically took the jumpsuit he was handing her, just realizing he was naked in the instant that he went leopard. A collective gasp went up from the girls behind her. She was sure Milly was ready to faint. Instead of looking, she climbed into the way-too-big jumpsuit. KC helped her roll up the sleeves.

"New kids!" The white guy hollered again. "You may have had to hide at your old schools, but there is no hiding at LPSS."

He paused for a general cheer and some shouts of loyalty.

"Get up here so we can assign your dorms."

"Sphinx rule!"

"Sphincters drool, Centaurs rule!"

"Mers desperately want to see the sun!" The girls at their table howled their approval of this odd cheer.

Mr. Bianchi took the microphone. "And we all want to know if any of today's Testers passed, right?"

A smattering of students laughed. Some of the girls at the Mer table wished Caliban luck and Laylea hoped the tree wasn't going to leave. The giggle in her head at the pun lent her the strength to pull up the legs of Oscar's jumpsuit and follow the other two to the teacher's platform.

"Oscar, could you please join us in the furless flesh." Mr. Bianchi raised his voice even though he still held the microphone. "Could someone grab a uniform for Mr. Luke? Jase?"

The Latino boy Laylea had seen sitting beside Oscar and Julia, the one with the sad facial hair, was already striding in through the glass doors with a deep blue jumpsuit held over his head. He strutted like a peacock, but the girls had implied that Julia and Jase and everyone at that table except for Oscar was a werewolf. Something about him made KC drift behind Laylea.

"Here I come to save the day."

"Thank you, Jase."

Jase bowed before the assembly while Oscar shifted and pulled on the new jumpsuit. Laylea rolled her pant legs up while he was changing. KC kept her head down.

"Now," Mr. Bianchi began. "Welcome to Lincoln Park Shifter School."

Some cheers. Some catcalls.

He went on, unperturbed. "After careful consideration of your backgrounds, your particular needs, and your class schedules — yes, you have been placed in classes already — the faculty have chosen to reward Sphinx dorm with your deeply unique presence, Oscar Luke."

Jase and the rest of that table cheered. Oscar waved like he'd won a spelling bee and headed for the table.

"Mr. Oscar, please wait." Mr. Bianchi himself waited until Oscar returned to his place at the front. "Our two new ladies will be sticking together for the time being and I hope you will all be as helpful as Mr. Jase if you see them shift in the halls."

He hadn't announced a dorm, but the ladies of Mer and pockets of boys around the room cheered as though he had.

"Thank you, Mer. Yes, you are going to enjoy Ms. KC's computer expertise. I'll tell you right now, Ms. KC, we keep test scores and class assignments on a special faculty server separate from the student accessible drives, so don't pay attention to anyone asking you to hack in. You cannot do it from student padds."

There was murmuring throughout the room and Oscar even gave KC a new once-over.

"Yes," Mr. Bianchi confirmed. "She is that good. Ms. Lee will be the girl to go to for help in nearly every other subject. We have never before had a first year student place into so many fifth level courses. Now, for our hopeful Testers."

The kind interrogator from Testing ushered KC, Oscar, and Laylea out the glass doors. "Let's have a word about your electives."

Mr. Vronumraju handed each of them a small card showing their Testing levels and required courses. He listed only a few suggested electives for Oscar and KC. They both chose choir and then each tried to back out.

"No, no, no. Choir is a perfect choice for both of you. You each need to pick one more. Now, Lee." He turned to her as the other two scanned their cards. "You have a wider option of electives. If I may though, I strongly suggest you take the sociology symposium."

He went on for some time, explaining why she should know more about the shifter community. Laylea zoned out. At any other time the courses he was describing would have thrilled her. But she was tired and she was surrounded by strangers. All she wanted to learn right then was how to shift and leave.

The glass doors hit Laylea in the butt.

Mr. Vronumraju hustled them to the side as students poured into the corridor. "Do you have any questions?"

Laylea shook her head even though she had a million. KC hid a grin behind her usual guarded expression as she shook her head. Oscar pointed at a line on his card.

"Are you sure about this score?"

Mr. Vronumraju checked the card against his armpadd. "Yes, that is correct. Well done. Biology levels five through seven meet together twice a week so you and Lee will have class together. Very well done, both of you. You will get your Pressed assignments on your podpadds and I will see you, KC, tomorrow in History of Coding."

He shook her hand and then swam upstream through the kids to get back into the dining hall.

"Luke!" The Jase guy stood in the middle of the corridor, not worried about all the people having to push around him.

Oscar looked up, anger flashing in his eyes, but when he saw Jase he just waved and hollered, "Keep your skin on."

KC tried to look at his card. "What's wrong with your biology level?"

"I got a five."

"Wow," KC said. "I got a three."

Oscar tried to question Laylea, but Ali and Caliban waded through to gather KC and Laylea into the stream heading right, down past the night kitchen.

"Mer dorm, this way!" Ali yelled. She pulled a face at Oscar. "Shoo, Sphinx!"

Milly tripped along behind the energetic girls. She wiggled her fingers at Oscar and squeaked out a small, "Hi" as she passed him.

Eighty people tried to introduce themselves at once and deliver the secrets of Mer dorm as they all stampeded down a diminishing stone corridor. The melee stopped at a low-ceilinged indoor courtyard of real grass surrounding two pools. A mix of couches, comfy chairs, and trees created half a dozen nooks. The trough lights glowed with a warm orange tone that felt like dusk.

A boy, almost as short as Laylea, bumped into her and looked for a second like he would run away. Without breathing once, he said, "No peeing on the furniture. They want us to use the stone around the pool or the trees. The pressed crew can clean those so it doesn't get stinky. I'm Peter." He stuck his fist out.

Laylea brushed his knuckles with hers. "I'm Lee."

"And she's a girl. She doesn't pee on things, Peter." Ali pulled Laylea toward a door on the far side of the freshwater pool. "Boys over there. Girls over here."

The thunderbird boy from Testing, Ahanu, popped up in front of KC. "So, Lee's a dog," he started.

Other boys cackled and one shouted from the far side of the saltwater pool, "*You're* a dog, Ahanu."

Ahanu flipped the bird at the guy. "You're a loser, Conner."

Conner and a small crew around him howled.

"Fucking wolf pack." The girl with purple hair high-fived Ahanu. She ran at one pool and leapt into the air at the last second, diving into the water as an iridescent orange koi.

Ahanu never took his eyes off of KC. "Lee's a dog. What are you?"

KC tore her eyes from the fish. She spit out, "I'm a coyote."

"Okay, okay. Just asking. I'm Ahanu, the thunderbird. If you're a coyote, you must have native in you?"

It was a question, but Ali left Laylea to grab KC away before she could answer. "Ew, Ahanu. Nobody wants your little native in them."

Laylea had a second to hitch up her too-long pant legs before Ali was hustling her away from another approaching boy and toward the girls' door. "The courtyard is Mer's special treat because we get all the sucky shifters."

"And cuz we don't get any classes upstairs," Brenda threw in.

Harper, the boy who'd taken Laylea's jumpsuit for his lion friend leaned by the girls' door. He explained, "Upstairs means outside."

"Bug off, Harper." Brenda feinted a hitch kick at the boy and landed with the nails of one flat hand an inch from his eyes.

Harper's body lost focus and reformed at their feet in the form of a rhesus monkey. He wove through Brenda's legs and knuckled over to the pack of wolf boys.

Emerald squeezed past them through the door. "We don't get to go outside because they don't trust us not to shift in front of thumpers."

The small room on the other side of the sliding door held rows and rows of built-in cubbies separated by five archways hung with colorful beaded curtains. The beads clattered against one another as girls pushed in and out. It sounded like rain on an airplane's wings.

Laylea realized Emerald had implied that some kids had classes outside. She asked, "We have classes with humans?"

Again, everyone laughed at Laylea.

"Some classes convene outside in the zoo or along the marina." Caliban stood by the beaded curtain. She gestured for KC and Lee to join her. "I'll take them, Ali."

"Thanks, Cal." Ali flipped around and performed some kind of complicated handshake with Emerald before she stripped down and threw her jumpsuit into the white bin. She spread her arms and the tattoos glowed against her skin for an instant before she sparked into her hawk form, circled Emerald's head, and flew back out to the courtyard.

Emerald put her palm up against one of the cubby doors. The door glowed around her hand and then popped open. The tense lines around the white girl's eyes smoothed as she pulled a bundle of sleek, grey fur from the locker. She shoved her jumpsuit in as she wrapped the fur around her shoulders. She approached a low stone well in one corner of the room. With a leap and a twist, Emerald fit into the fur and cut smoothly into the water.

"Emerald can't sleep in her human skin." Caliban murmured. "Many Mer students sleep in our courtyard. If you ever see me out there when I should be in class, please wake me up. Don't ever wake Ali. She's not a morning bird."

The tree-shifter led KC and Laylea through the beaded curtain to a room unlike anywhere else they'd been in the underground school. The walls and floor were made of wide panels of wood. Long, colorful tapestries, corners attached but drooping low in the middle, hid the stone ceiling. Caliban led them past a couple of curtained beds to an open space along the left side.

"Like this." She stooped to place her palm against a darker panel in the floor by the wall.

A section of the wall cracked open. Caliban pulled on a handle that tilted out as the section leaned forward. A Murphy bed folded down, draped in rich curtains.

Caliban pointed across to the opposite wall. Someone had stuck two post-it notes up beside the tucked away handles. They read *Lee* and *KC*.

The girls found the dark readers in the floor and placed their palms down. Nothing happened. Laylea tried again. Nothing. She looked up when KC leaned over to put her hand on Lee's reader. The bed clicked open.

Caliban helped KC fold it down as Laylea released her own bed.

"These are your private pods. The padd has a small local drive, which can only be accessed by you. It also connects to the shared student drives, the net, and shifterweb. The bathroom is through that door. You're free to roam anywhere in the dorm except the boys' side. Lights out is at nine. If you can't find what you need, ask. We've all been new."

"Thank you, Caliban," Laylea put her fist out, but a broad-shouldered girl with a thousand-yard stare walked right between them.

KC leaned out of her curtains. "What's wrong with her? Zombie-shifter?"

The girl hadn't spoken to anyone else and other girls were avoiding her as she walked to a space and lowered a pod. Her pupils were so blown out, you couldn't see what color her eyes were.

"She was in ST," Caliban said. "Special Testing."

"Like what we did today? Cuz that is definitely how I felt after that last interview with Madame-with-the-French-pronunciation."

Four voices echoed, "with the French pronunciation" and laughed.

Milly stuck her head out of her curtains. "Nice, KC." She glanced at the zombie-girl and her smile faded. She ducked back into her pod.

Caliban stepped closer to KC and Laylea so she could lower her voice. "Special Testing is not academic. It's medical." She looked like she would say more, but all she added was, "Don't worry. Dove will be all right tomorrow."

Up and down the row, girls joined each other in their pods. Some took their padds and headed out through the beaded curtains. Some headed for the bathroom. Laylea was too tired to think. The little pod held a bed and a slide-out desk where she found a nested padd. When she logged in, her schedule for the next day came up with detailed directions on how to get to each class. A blinking M popped up as she was looking over the long list of electives she'd been approved to take. She tapped the M and a message window popped up from *KC Dells*.

Did you find your toothbrush?

Laylea looked around the little pod again. She spotted a dark palm reader in the wood of the wall. It opened a drawer holding a top-of-the-line sonic wave toothbrush, a nail file, and a wide-tooth comb.

She clicked on the circling *Reply* icon. *Just found it.*

Wanna explore with me?

Yeah. She yawned and added, *But I'm really tired.*

Maybe we just explore the bathroom, then.

Laylea grabbed her toothbrush. She slid out of the pod and knocked on the wall beside KC's curtain. The two met a dozen new girls and animals in the bathroom. Carrie, the food stealer from dinner, shifted into wolf even as she tried to stutter her way through an offer to take KC to her first class. KC asked if she'd take them to breakfast, too, and the little wolf barked a happy yes. Her tail untucked for a quick wag before she trotted between some jeering girls over to the patch of grass, sand, and dirt to one side of the toilet stalls. Laylea's own psychic tail flipped up at the sight of the grass.

When they got back to their beds, Laylea asked, "What's your pod like?"

She knew it was a stupid question the moment she asked but KC swept her curtain back.

"Come see."

Laylea tossed her wave brush on the shelf in her pod and hopped up onto KC's bed. Her pod looked exactly like Laylea's except that KC had stowed and locked her padd.

"It's a really nice bed." KC stowed her brush in the drawer. "Better than what I have at home."

"I share with my brother at home." It didn't even occur to Laylea that this was weird.

"Wow. Your parents can't afford two beds even? I have three brothers. We all had our own rooms."

"I have my own bed." Laylea didn't mention it lived in the back room of a bar. "I've just slept in Bailey's bed since I was a puppy."

"Is Bailey a weredog too?" She quickly added, "No offense. I just know sometimes it doesn't pass down to everyone."

Laylea shook her head. "I'm adopted. My family is human."

"Whoa." KC's pupils widened almost as much as zombie-girl's. "You were raised by thumpers? Did they know?"

Laylea had never talked to anyone about this stuff before. She'd never had anyone to talk about it with. "*I* didn't even know. We only found out when I shifted three years ago. Did you always know you were a—" Laylea almost said coyote. But it was so obviously not the truth and she didn't want KC to have to lie to her. So instead she said, "a shifter?"

The girl with a million secrets looked away as she slowly nodded. "I can't even imagine being raised by thumpers."

The tone of her voice was so horrified and disgusted, Laylea couldn't interrupt her fast enough. "I love my family. My mom and dad and big brother are the best humans in the world. I miss them like crazy and I think I'm the luckiest dog in the world that I got to grow up with them and my dog brother, Woodford."

Laylea realized her error when KC started to ask, "Isn't your last name—"

The awkward silence stretched on a bit too long.

"Hey, KC?"

"Yeah?"

Laylea knelt up and whispered in KC's ear, "Why don't you tell them you paid?"

KC futzed with her charmband. Tears started to well in her eyes but she frowned them away.

Finally she said, "Because my family isn't like yours and this is the first time I've ever had the chance to be judged for who I am." She added, "I'm kinda tired, Lee."

"Okay. Good night." Laylea wanted to apologize but she wasn't sure what for.

"Yeah, good night. Hope you can sleep without Bailey."

"I did last night."

"Yeah." KC reached back to pull her hair out of its ponytails. "But you cried for hours first."

Laylea didn't answer. She couldn't. The thought of curling up with her big brother had ignited that spark in her core and she shifted.

"It's okay, Lee. It's gonna be okay." KC caressed one of her velvet ears and Laylea pushed her head into her hand before she wriggled out of Oscar's too-big jumpsuit and hopped down and over to her own sleeping pod.

She dragged the plush blanket around with her teeth and dug at the crisp sheets until she had a sad nest. When she finally dropped into a curl, she stuck her head under the pillow to cry.

Ten minutes later, KC climbed in through the curtains and curled up around her.

18

"Yeah, I get *that.*" Laylea banged her head again on the corduroy cushion of the bolster bench in their favorite library nook. She'd been in school over a month and still couldn't grasp concepts shifter kids took for granted. She still couldn't shift at will either.

It turned out that shifting was more of an art than a teachable skill. Shifters of the same species tended to shift in the same way; werewolves tended to pop between forms with little fanfare and they got to keep their clothes. Birds typically sparked into a shift and their clothes did not shift with them. Selkies shifted like they were going outside in winter. They'd put on or take off their seal skin to change form. Ms. Syperek's Beginner Shifting class was all about theory and watching the Intermediate Shifting class practice. Laylea asked every successful shifter she met *how* they did it. They gave pretty much the same answer; they imagined themselves in their other form and, boom, they shifted. They all had different answers, though, for why they stayed in school even after they mastered shifting. Most stayed because they didn't have a reason to leave. She discovered that a lot of students, like KC, had never had trouble shifting.

KC wanted to help Laylea with the shifting but, for her, it was like walking: she'd almost always been able to do it and couldn't remember how she'd learned. She wouldn't demonstrate to Laylea for fear of being seen in wolf form. KC didn't miss her wolf shape and she couldn't explain that either. Laylea thought being trapped as a human would be worse than dying at fifteen.

She had wondered if she could beat her canine lifespan by staying human, but it just wasn't an option. What was the point of living if she couldn't be herself?

While they'd given up on the shifting tutoring, KC continued to battle Laylea's horrendous ignorance of the shifter world. A month in, and she was trying, again, to get Laylea up to speed on their sociology homework. And Laylea was, again, asking her questions so basic Mr. Barrett didn't even cover them in level one.

Laylea moaned, "You can't call them human because we're human some of the time. But why *thumpers*? I don't get it."

"Really, Fido?"

Laylea and KC looked up to see Ali at the mouth of the library's bright nook. She pulled a book from the shelves before rolling her eyes and leaving.

Laylea tamped down the burning. She'd started shifting every time she was embarrassed and that was all the time. Although, she considered, the stupid sociology symposium was much easier to take as a dog. The symposium was just students discussing their ideas and when she was furry, nobody expected her to engage in the conversation. But the burning sparkle was tamped. She stayed human.

"Ali thinks I'm an idiot."

"No," KC corrected her. "Ali knows you're an idiot. They're called thumpers because they just are."

Dizzy croaked. The raven perched on the back of the French changing-room chair that blocked the entrance to this little nook. It happened to be the one spot pinpointed with sunlight. The bird shook its head at KC.

Laylea could almost count on seeing Dizzy in the library. Sometimes the bird would show up in a classroom and she was always in the dining hall for dinner. Dizzy hadn't scratched in the velvet again and Laylea had been on a hunt for an etch-a-sketch. She'd learned how to write on the quick-wipe toys when her family first discovered she was smart. They'd had them all over the house and even in the dad's airplane.

Nobody else ever talked to the raven. Nobody else paid any attention at all to the raven. Laylea had asked Ali to be sure it *was* a raven and not a crow. But Ali had rolled her eyes and informed Laylea she was a *hawk,* not a raven or a crow. So Laylea didn't talk to people about Dizzy.

"*Thumpers* is pejorative." Ms. Crow leaned around the end of the bookshelf.

Dizzy croaked again and flew away. Laylea popped into dog and back, undoing the braids KC had worked into her short hair during Animal Lit. KC choked on her water.

When she could breathe, she said, "Didn't see you there, Ms. Crow."

"*It just is* is not an acceptable answer in my library, KC." The librarian pulled her sweater tighter around her shoulders. This sweater matched the faded blue of the oldest student jumpsuits. "Back in the 1920s superstitious folks would say *rabbit, rabbit, rabbit* for good luck. Some shifters in Europe started calling them thumpers in code and when Felix Salten's *Bambi* came out, the slur became popular worldwide. The phrase mocked humans for being superstitious when they should have been afraid."

"Why should they have been afraid?" Laylea asked.

"Lee!" KC groaned her you-are-so-dumb groan.

"This was before the first Ten Percent Plan. Right before. When Stanis started hosting his cleansing speeches in public venues. It's not a nice word."

Laylea made notes. She could search the shifterweb later. Surfing the shifterweb was dangerous. It was like having access to this whole secret world that nobody else knew about, except all the shifters who had always known about it. She found a lot of misleading articles about non-shifting humans. But because the school was isolated from outside access, she couldn't update the articles or comment on them. The best she could do was correct KC's misunderstandings. And most of the time, KC didn't believe her. The werewolf couldn't let go of the idea that thumpers only kept pets because of some devious shifter plot to justify veterinarians.

"The bell is about to ring. Shouldn't you two be getting to class?"

"Yes, Ms. Crow."

"Yes, Ms. Crow."

Laylea shoved the notepaper and golf pencil into her collar. KC stuffed the history books she'd picked out into the knapsack Mr. Vronumraju had loaned her. Ms. Crow moved the chair aside so they could get out and they hurried by her to the library doors.

An old guy in a crinkled button-down and corduroy pants waited by the front desk. He perked up as KC and Laylea walked by.

"Lee?" He held out a hand.

Laylea and KC both stopped.

"You go on ahead to class, dear. Go on." The man said this to KC as he took Laylea's hand. "Lee, I'm Dr. Durrah. I heard about your shifting incident in Holding last month, and I've been trying to find the time to meet you. Dr. Fenn wants you to come to ST for a quick examination."

"I have class right now." Laylea looked longingly at the door swinging shut behind KC.

"Oh, don't worry about that. I can give you a note to excuse you from any class."

"Dr. Durrah, we don't see you in the library very often." Ms. Crow slipped up behind the old man, buttoning a light orange cardigan. "Lee, get to class."

Laylea nodded and tried to go, but Dr. Durrah was still holding her hand.

He barely looked over his shoulder at Ms. Crow. "Dr. Fenn wants Lee to come chat with me in ST."

"Lee can't afford to miss her symposium, David. They've got a pop quiz and you know Mr. Barrett's point system."

Laylea's heart sped up at the word quiz. She didn't have a chance on any quiz in Sociology. She didn't know they would even have quizzes in Sociology.

"Symposium is a chat class. Lee can miss it." He doubled down on the forced hand-holding by covering her knuckles with his other hand.

The one-minute bell rang overhead. Laylea instinctually took a step for the door. Dr. Durrah didn't give an inch.

"It's not a chat class for Lee." Ms. Crow glanced over at the shelves and the high window in a way that reminded Laylea of Sher practicing behavioral conditioning. So she wasn't surprised when Dr. Durrah looked over at the window himself.

Ms. Crow turned back and caught his eyes to say, "I would think you'd be too busy with the full moon tonight."

Dr. Durrah glanced down at his armpadd. He chuckled. "Elizabeth, you're a wonder. I don't know what Dr. Fenn was thinking. Yes. Yes, I'm sorry, Lee, we'll have to have our chat another time. I can't have a puppy in the clinic with a hundred itching werewolves pacing the place. Shoot me a message and let me know what class you'd like to get out of."

Laylea didn't want to miss any of her classes. She'd never been able to learn so much from just books. Books couldn't respond. But teachers had answers right away. She still hadn't gotten a good answer for why human blood was so different from animal blood or why DNA could rearrange to accommodate shifting. But she'd learned that shifter blood donors had to match in animal and human blood type and that there was a whole coded language used by shifter first responders in an emergency to alert shifter doctors. Laylea could never have learned that from a book.

She wanted to run to Sociology, but Dr. Durrah still had her hand. Although it was so sweaty now she thought she might be able to slip out of his grip, if only that weren't rude. She didn't want to be late for a quiz.

"Sure, Dr. Durrah. Only I have to go now."

Ms. Crow explained, "The bell means she has a minute to get to class."

"Oh, go." He let go and waved her away. "No need to upset old Ferret-face."

"Mr. Barrett," Ms. Crow corrected.

Laylea bobbed a weird curtsy as Dr. Durrah turned away from her to Ms. Crow. "Now, Elizab— Elizabeth? Where. . ."

Laylea didn't hear the rest of his sentence. She ran from the library, wiping her hand on her jumpsuit before she raised it to trace her lizard-foot with shaking fingers. She reached the Socio-History Hall as the final bell rang. When she burst through the door, twenty pairs of eyes turned to her. KC waved her over. She'd saved a seat on a couch tucked back a ways.

Mr. Barrett, the sociology guru who taught both the symposium and her Intro to Basic Shifter History course, shut the door. "Glad to see you, Lee. KC had us concerned that you'd rather open a vein than discuss shifter socio-political history."

Oscar's friend, the awkwardly-bearded Jase, muttered, "I know I would."

While the rest of the class laughed over that, KC whispered, "How'd you get away?"

"Durrah has to see all the werewolves today because of the full moon or something. Ms. Crow reminded him. Did I miss anything?"

She reached over KC to grab one of the deskpadds that were kept scattered around the casual classroom. KC had gone white as a polar bear.

"What's wrong?"

"Tonight's a full moon?" She fidgeted with her charmband.

"That's what Ms. Crow said." Laylea wanted to focus on her friend but the class discussion caught her attention, for once.

"Yeah, let the vampire bleed you dry, Jase." Dove murmured. She didn't care for Jase too much. Laylea thought that showed good taste. Dove had recovered from Special Testing by the morning as Caliban had said she would. When they weren't blown out, her eyes were the same gorgeous emerald green as her brother, hottie Reggie Betts. Like him, she was a weretiger and a scholarship student.

The Mer selkie, Emerald, stood to smack Dove on the back of the head. "Oh my phoenix, there's no such thing as vampire bats."

"Thumper myth," Brenda added.

Carrie, the werewolf girl from Mer dorm stuttered, "Y... you're an idiot if you d... don't b... b... believe."

"Why is that?" Emerald asked.

Carrie took an enormous breath, sweat beading on her forehead. But Big Mo, a werewolf from Centaur, answered for her. "You may have heard, Emerald, that the vampire attacked a pack of wolves last month. It ripped them to shreds."

The whole school had been arguing about whether this was true or not. Supposedly it happened the night Oscar, KC, and Laylea arrived and kids kept asking if they'd seen anything, like upstairs wasn't a city of three million people. She'd heard so many different versions of the story, Laylea had no idea whether Kyle had really killed any werewolves or not. She definitely didn't believe that he'd ripped them to shreds. Kyle wasn't that kind of guy. Her real worry was if he was drinking fresh blood. She was pretty sure that would tip him over the edge into evil territory.

A weight-lifter from Sphinx dorm said, "My dad says it's the start of the second Ten Percent Plan."

"Really, Dustin, your dad says? Ooooh." Dove mocked him but stopped short at the look on Dustin's face.

"Even if it is real, it's not gonna survive long in Chicago," the most beautiful girl in school, Raederie, said from her place curled up in a comfy chair. "Demons never do."

Laylea wondered if she was talking about Captain Morioka. Morioka always said she kept her city demon-free. Kyle's maker was the first demon Laylea had ever met, other than Morioka. And she had trouble thinking of Kyle as a demon. He'd managed to hide from Morioka for seven months so far. But that was with Laylea's help. Now she was trapped in here and he was on his own.

Carrie's theory cut into her worried thoughts. "M ... maybe that's why it w ... wants to get into the school."

"The vampire is trying to get into the school?" Laylea forgot her self-imposed vow of silence. As expected, the other kids laughed at her.

Mr. Barret must have heard the panic in her voice. He rarely interrupted the discussion, but now he stood and circled to the couch. "Lee, there are no such things as vampires. An orphaned bat has found its way to the zoo and is living in the trees upstairs. You have nothing to worry about. Especially in Mer dorm. Now let's relate everyone's fascination to reality. Jase Batka." He turned to Jase. "What was Rico Stanis's intention with the Ten Percent Plan?"

There were some groans from around the room. Jase rolled his eyes. "Public or private?"

"His true goal." Mr. Barrett leaned against the back of a desk.

"Scientific theory said that—" Jase began.

Emerald shouted, "He made it up!"

"Commentary later, Emerald. Go on, Jase."

"The scientific theory is that if you decimate a species' primary breeding population, you effectively end the species."

"Clarify your terms, please."

Jase rolled his eyes like this was an old argument. "Decimate literally, as in kill off ten percent, not figuratively, as in destroy utterly. Although that would probably have worked better."

"What results did the theory in action garner?"

Laylea couldn't parse the question and Mr. Barrett must have seen that on her face. He translated himself. "What did Stanis learn?"

Everyone in the class had an answer.

"Th … thumpers aren't so d … dumb after all."

Emerald said, "Go for the women" at the same time Ali said, "Women and children first." They fist-bumped.

Raederie murmured, "Payback is a bitch."

"Thumpers are monsters." Dustin glared at Carrie.

"Werewolves rule." Jase shot a clawed hand into the air. Four other students, including Big Mo and Dustin, followed suit. Carrie's automatically went up but she pulled it back down very quickly.

Mr. Barrett gestured for the others to put their hands down. "How do you come to your conclusion, Jase?"

Jase leaned back and threw an arm over the back of Dustin's chair. "Fewer than one percent of the wolf population died from the thumper poisons compared to the twenty percent of shifters overall. Wolves are biologically stronger."

Emerald stood again. "The wolves survived because they ran and hid. We fought."

"What about the other supernaturals?" Laylea asked.

The class went dead silent. Even Mr. Barrett looked around for someone else to respond.

Finally Jase asked, "What are you talking about, Fido?"

She ignored the insult. She was getting used to it. "The other fae, the brownies and goblins and fairies and . . ." she trailed off at the look in KC's eyes. But she had to know. "What side were they on? How many of them died?"

"Oh my phoenix, freak. Those are just stories." Brenda informed her. "It's fiction. Made-up?"

Dove won points with Laylea by objecting, "Bren."

Emerald explained, "Superstitious humans created those kinds of monsters to keep their children in line. Fairies aren't real."

"Lee thinks the boogeyman is hiding under her pod," Dustin laughed. "He's gonna decimate Mer dorm."

"Okay, okay. Calm down, class." Mr. Barrett strode over to pick up a padd from his desk. "Lee, maybe we can talk before Basic tomorrow. Why don't you try to get here early?"

Brenda risked Mr. Barrett's wrath for one more dig. "But what if the dungeon troll eats her tonight?"

Laylea felt her face going red and that was okay. Her hair would glow and the other kids would just have more ammunition. But she also felt the heat rising in her belly, and hard as she tried to tamp it down, it rose to her heart and she shifted. Her padd clattered on the bare floor making sure that anyone who might have missed her change to dog, noticed now.

Even Mr. Barrett chuckled. "It's okay, Lee. We know you come from a strange background."

That was code for *raised by thumpers*. She hadn't realized she should keep that a secret, even after KC's reaction. But she wasn't really raised by thumpers. Her mom and Bailey were as supernatural as anyone in the school. They were witches. And her dad was genetically altered to be a super soldier. What was normal-human about that? Most of her friends in Chicago were wyrdos. How did none of these shifters know about that world? They were as blind as the thumpers they mocked for not seeing shifters all around them.

"So, Dustin," Mr. Barrett said, demanding everyone's attention. "Your father says that this *vampire,*" Mr. Barret did air quotes, "is the start of the second TPP."

"Yeah."

"So then, why did the vampire attack a pack of werewolves?"

Dustin sat up straighter. "The werewolves were our strongest defenders in the first Plan. The thumpers are targeting them first."

"You believe this vampire is a human weapon? So this is the human's Ten Percent Plan."

"Yeah." Dustin should have stopped there. He didn't. "But it's a stupid name, Mr. Barrett. The thumpers killed twenty percent of us, so why call it the Ten Percent Plan?"

Laylea breathed a sigh of relief as the general class disbelief and scorn turned to Dustin. Mr. Barrett tried to address his misapprehension gently.

He began, "The TPP was—"

The class bell blurted three aborted rings. Jase and the six other werewolves in class leapt to their feet. Carrie stumbled over her own feet and fell into her werewolf form. She followed the others to the door with her tail tucked under.

"Hold on." Mr. Barrett interrupted their exit. "I want a paper from each of you on the results of Mr. Stanis' war on humans. Pick one specific aspect of your life that was directly shaped by his attempted decimation. Post it to the server by ten a.m. Thursday."

"That's the day after tomorrow," Jase complained. "We're Wilding tonight and we'll be in ST all tomorrow morning."

Big Mo added, "That's not fair, Mr. Barrett."

"I have faith that you can do it, Mo. Werewolves rule." Mr. Barrett held his hand up in the claw sign the wolves had thrown earlier.

Jase made a face at Mr. Barrett's back. "Don't talk about us while we're gone."

"Hey," Emerald shouted. "If you guys are so much stronger than everyone else, you should hunt down that bat tonight."

"Your wish is my command, Em. One dead vampire coming up." Jase howled and it wasn't only werewolves who joined in.

19

Every full moon the wolves went to ST and then upstairs to run wild. It was nearly the only indication of passing time. It certainly couldn't be marked by any improvement in Laylea's shifting. Classes were scheduled seven days a week with lots of time set aside for electives and free study. Pressers had daily chores. But they shuffled around so you could try different chores until you found one you liked, like Brenda working in the Wing, or if you just couldn't stand doing the same thing week after week, like Brian. He shifted his chore section every chance he got.

Nobody ever went home and parents never visited. Every day was different. The trough lights brightened and dimmed to indicate the time of day. Upstairs classes got to experience spring move into summer. But except for the few werewolves in their dorm, Mers never got upstairs. They got sun in the dining hall and the Fields but no true fresh air. No seasons. No sense of time passing.

Laylea spent most of her free time in the library searching the stacks for any clues that might help her shift. She lived for the sunlight that filtered into the bright nook Dizzy favored. KC fell in love with the nook in moonlight. After dinner, if neither had any Presser chores to do, she would search Laylea out and drag her to the bright nook. There, they worked on homework or just read; KC sprawled in the pillows piled on the floor in the corner, and Laylea stretched out on the corduroy cushions of the wide wooden bench built against the wall.

KC had stumbled upon a mention of Special Testing in her research for history class. Ever since, they'd both been devouring any books they could find about Lincoln Park Shifter School. KC hoped to figure out what ST was before they had to go there while Laylea was looking for a way to get upstairs without knowing how to shift.

"Excuse me." Ms. Crow alternated sneaking up and telegraphing her approach, much as she alternated her sweaters. Laylea thought of them as mood sweaters because the librarian always seemed to be wearing orange when she was happy and blue when she was pensive and distant. She usually wore blue.

This time she was in orange and she set the book down at Laylea's front paws before KC even sat up.

Laylea barked.

"Hey, where'd the book come from?" KC asked, ignoring Ms. Crow.

Laylea barked again but KC was already scanning the index.

Ms. Crow laughed. "I was never here." She put a finger to her lips and disappeared into the stacks.

KC flipped to the middle of the book and, instead of turning the book so they could both see it, read aloud. She sometimes forgot Laylea the dog was just as smart and capable as Laylea the human.

"In the years following the Phoenix Event, the surviving students began claiming they were seeing ghosts of their former classmates. The new staff at first attributed these reports to survivor's guilt and the stresses of living entirely without sunlight. But when one departing faculty member admitted he was leaving because of the ghosts, LPSS hired a staff psychotherapist and instituted regular special testing for students and faculty."

She looked up at Laylea. "So ST started as mental health checks."

"It's still a mental health check." Oscar stood where Ms. Crow had been a moment before. "You're mental if you volunteer."

"Don't let your friends, the wolves, hear you say that."

He ignored KC. "You freaks want some fresh air?"

Laylea sat up. KC slammed the book shut. They both tilted their heads in a silent demand for more information.

"Come on. One of my wolf friends knows how to get upstairs without a teacher."

Laylea leapt from the bench. Oscar barely realized what was going on in time to catch her. KC stuffed the book into her backpack and tucked it behind the pile of pillows.

"Won't the upstairs classes see us?" KC whispered as they tried to stroll casually out of the library.

"Mendenkov took the archery team to an old abandoned warehouse he uses out in Oak Grove and Advanced Astronomy is on the lake all night. The zoo is ours."

Laylea trembled with excitement. If she could get upstairs, she could find Kyle and then, maybe, go find her parents. Her tail thwacked Oscar in the chest until he moved her to one arm where her tail could wag freely behind them.

The three met up with other students as Oscar led them to a section of the underground tunnels neither Laylea nor KC had ever seen. He gestured at a curtained archway where several more kids joined them.

"Sphinx dorm."

They'd only gone a few more feet when he took a turn and most of the kids stopped.

"What's the joke, Oscar?" KC looked mad.

The corridor thinned down to a low archway about two meters tall and four meters wide. Laylea couldn't see anything in the darkness beyond because the school's ubiquitous trough lighting stopped at the mouth of this tunnel.

"Trust me, KC." Oscar set Laylea on the floor and greeted the newest arrivals: Jase and the top dog in the school's werewolf circles. Patrick DelValle, as handsome as he was egotistical, strode over to one side of the fancily carved arch. He set a palm against the stone. When it glowed, he tapped in a rhythm. The open archway sparked and the light reached farther in as if some kind of curtain had been removed.

Patrick looked back at the dozen shifters watching him. He made a flourish with one arm and reached into the tunnel. All the younger kids around Laylea gasped. The older ones laughed and ran forward.

The tunnel entrance sparked as each one passed through. The younger kids followed tentatively. They reached out like they expected to feel something solid, like they had to push through a door, but their hands passed through as easily as Patrick's. Oscar came back out to encourage KC and Laylea. KC seemed frightened so Laylea stayed by her side. When they got to the archway, KC squeezed her eyes shut and Oscar had to grab her hand to pull her through.

"The cave wall is an illusion. With the force field down, it's perfectly safe. Come on. The gems aren't real either."

In the tunnel, kids ran their hands along the rough stone walls, marveling and stopping to stare at sections. Laylea trotted over to Ali and Emerald but she couldn't see why they were agog. Eventually everyone reached the second archway. Again the new kids slowed and stopped like they were afraid to go through.

The older kids all shifted into animal form. Those who, like Laylea, couldn't keep their clothes when they shifted, wriggled out of their jumpsuits and dragged them along. Ali followed suit, grabbing her jumpsuit in her talons to carry it through the archway.

Patrick kept his voice low as he called out, "Second gate, second form. You have to shift to get through."

Laylea trotted right through. Emerald, Carrie, and surprisingly, Kara, a bird from Centaur dorm all stood in the darkness, trying desperately to shift. KC froze. Laylea sniffed the little river running along the side of the tunnel. She followed it back through to where Raederie Rivers was trading her jumpsuit for the seal skin she pulled reverently from a bag on her shoulder. She shoved her jumpsuit in the bag and handed it to Oscar.

"You don't mind?"

"Nah, I'll meet you at the next gate." He raised his voice to add, "You only have to shift long enough to get through this gate."

"I know, Oscar. I've been in Sphinx for three years." Raederie leapt into the tiny pool of water and shot along the little river.

Oscar turned to take Em's bag and jumpsuit. She took her seal skin out and wrapped it around her shoulders, but neither she nor Carrie nor Kara changed. Laylea bounded over and voiced a series of the high-pitched *alert alert alert* barks that had been banned back home. All three girls shifted. Emerald fell into the little river and a little nightingale buzzed Laylea with a series of scolding chirps before she flew after Carrie's bounding wolf.

Only Oscar, KC, and Laylea remained. Oscar looked around, both hands shielding his eyes as if he couldn't see.

He called out, "Anyone else here? KC? Puppy? I can't see anything in this darkness."

Then he dropped into his gorgeous black panther and duck-walked his way through the archway. The arms and legs of his jump-suit dragged beneath his paws, nearly tripping him up, while Raederie and Emerald's bags bumped along the ground under his belly. He looked like a clown. Laylea bounded after him, tamping down on her singing laughter.

She felt a change in the air behind her and then a soft paw thwacked her in the side, sending her rolling over the rough stone. Before she could recover, a white wolf with black markings and ginger tufts behind her ears pounced on her. She slobbered one long lick up Laylea's muzzle. Then KC shifted back into a giggling girl and they raced past Oscar to the third gate. Oscar shifted and ran after them. He nearly beat them to it.

"You must be in your natural state to get through the third gate!"

Laylea heard Patrick's yell after she'd already run through. She dashed around the others' human legs as they all slowed and ducked to get out of the zoo's replica of a natural environment. Laylea turned around to see the other kids climbing out of the opening at the base of a molded-cement tree. The older kids pushed on out of the double doors of the building. The newer kids stopped to stare at the sleeping gorillas in the transparent cage opposite the fake tree.

Oscar hustled KC and Laylea out the door and down a curving path beside an enormous outdoor play area that made Laylea feel better for the poor apes. The kids ran and shifted and vaulted over fences and into roped-off areas, roughhousing in a way that made Laylea feel both grateful for all her first-aid training growing up and sad that she was kind of afraid to join in with the bigger kids and animals.

Then she saw the grass. All rational thought abandoned her. She galloped under the chain, past the sign clearly saying to *Keep Off the Grass* and dove ear first into the rich, rough green. She ground the earthy goodness into her fur and reveled in the tickling of the turf on her back. Ali, in hawk form, dive-bombed her. Laylea didn't care. It had been so long since she'd smelled fresh grass and fresh air and actual outdoors. She heard kids up ahead yelling about her and some ran back to laugh. Carrie dove over the barrier in human form and landed on four paws in the most deliberate shift she'd ever achieved. The scrawny, tawny wolf nearly crushed Laylea with her own joy at rolling in the grass.

She wasn't even bothered when Oscar and Jase ran by. Oscar yelled, "Puppy, try to be normal for once."

Jase yelled, "Heel, Fido!"

Laylea would have stayed there forever, but KC grabbed her up and ran after everybody. "Oscar says we have to go meet the depressed bear. Come on, Carrie."

They ran on down paths and through enclosures. Oscar pointed out some pavilion where they might take classes someday if they ever learned to control their shift and then they were beyond it, sneaking through an enormous bamboo door, dodging mechanical equipment and then jumping another set of chains to get to a quaint path in front of a long low building.

"Guard!" A voice hissed at them from a copse of trees on the far side of the path. "Hide!"

20

Oscar and Jase, halfway across the path, threw themselves into the trees. KC hissed the warning back at Carrie who dropped behind an air conditioning unit. KC dodged right and hid with Laylea by a low metal sculpture.

Thick cloud cover shaded the area from starlight and a new moon contributed to the darkness. Laylea held her breath all the same when footsteps drew close. The guard whistled as he strolled. He stopped right beside them.

"Hey, Nick."

The radio squawked. "Yeah, Beta?"

"Dude, don't call me that. All clear, here. I thought I saw the bat by the depressed bear's cage but there's nothing out here."

Laylea's tail sprang to life. KC held it still.

"Copy that, Beta."

The guard hit the button like he was going to say something else, but he didn't. It took forever for his footsteps to fade out of hearing. Even then, kids came out of the trees whispering and shushing each other as they ran down the path the guard had come up.

KC waited till everyone else was ahead, even Carrie, before she sat up and let Laylea out from under her. She slapped the sculpture in front of her. Then she whispered in Laylea's ear, "Pee on him."

Laylea looked up at her friend. She twitched her ears towards her.

"You heard me." KC skootched back and pointed at another sculpture a few feet away.

There were three frozen, metal wolves standing in a small clearing. With one last look at her friend, Laylea trotted past the howling wolf they'd hidden behind and peed right at the nose of the wolf sculpture sniffing the ground. KC applauded. She picked Laylea up again when she returned to her. "My uncle."

Laylea woofed.

They found the older kids scrounging wood from the man-made forest and stacking it in the center of a clearing surrounded by low log-benches. A huge section of transparent plastic, like the cages in the ape house bordered one side of the clearing. The other border featured formal public benches and a giant, hollow tree trunk kids could climb on. Laylea hopped up in it.

She ran out again when a cry went up.

"Toby!"

The kids ran to the plastic wall. On the far side, an enormous black bear ambled out of the trees. It stared at the kids. Laylea could barely see him. It took her a moment to realize the white spot above his face was the bear's left ear.

A memory popped into her head. She'd lived in a cage for the first six weeks of her life with her four brothers. Rhemy, the biggest, was fuzzy black all over except for one white ear. Laylea remembered chewing on it. He always smelled like milk bones and she'd thought maybe he tasted like one too. Where was Rhemy now? Where were any of her brothers? Had Walter caught any of them?

"Toby, my man!" Jase held a palm up against the clear cage like he expected Toby to come high-five him but the bear stayed in the trees. "Cheer up! Life's good."

Jase held up a silver flask as if offering it to the bear. The bear didn't move so Jase unscrewed the cap and took a long drink himself.

"We have fire!"

Everyone turned or ran over to see Patrick standing over a tiny fire. Brian, the weregorilla from Laylea and Oscar's biology class, fanned the flame and added grasses to it while Patrick pounded himself on the chest.

Ali hollered, "You teach him that, Brian?"

"No. He must have bought the online course, *How to Look as Cool as a Gorilla in Twelve Easy Lessons.*" Brian pounded his own chest and shifted as he did.

A bunch of kids danced around the fire with him, pounding their chests and waddling like an ape.

"Mers desperately want to see the sun and the moon!" Ali hollered this up at the dark sky and all the other Mers cheered.

KC set Laylea down to take a flask from Raederie. She sipped from it, choked, and passed it on to a Sphinx werewolf. Laylea turned away from the party at the fire.

As her eyes adjusted to the dim starlight, she could see why Toby was called the depressed bear. He stood with slumped shoulders, his head hanging low. Plus the corners of his muzzle turned down and the shading around his eyes made it seem like he was about to cry. Laylea trotted to the wall to get a closer look.

Toby straightened up when he caught sight of her. He stumbled away from the tree line towards her. But Ali and Emerald shouted to the others that the sad, old man had moved. He stopped. He dropped to his butt in the dirt and hid his head. Laylea set a paw on the Plexiglas. She barked. But he didn't look up again.

"Ahwoooo," Brian flung his gorilla head back and howled up to the stars.

The werewolves around the fire all mocked him and some dropped into wolf to show him how it was done. Emerald and Raederie, both sea creatures, howled in human form.

Laylea tapped the barrier again and sang out a short howl at Toby. Then she bounded across the path, leapt onto a log-bench, and launched herself onto Carrie's wolf back. Before Carrie could react, she leapt to Brian's wide shoulders, pushed off his head and landed atop the giant hollow trunk.

"Ahwoooooooooooo." Her howl couldn't compete with the chest rumbling depth of the wolves' howls but Patrick shifted to human just to praise her effort.

"Nice job, Lee!" He spotted KC picking her way over to the trunk. "Hey, aren't you a coyote? Give us a howl!"

KC blanched.

Oscar tossed back a shot from the flask. He offered it to KC. "Yeah, Dells, shift and show everyone that huge scar on your butt."

Most of the kids laughed. Emerald didn't.

"Oh my phoenix, KC, you shifted?" Carrie stopped howling. "No one's ever seen you shift."

"I saw her go through the second gate," Oscar said. "Her ass is messed up."

"What's the story, KC?" Jase grabbed the flask from KC's limp fingers. "You get caught by a wolf?"

"Or a vampire?" Dustin yelled.

"Vampires bite your neck, not your butt, Dustin."

Emerald tossed the flask to Patrick. "Vampires are imaginary, Ali."

"Thumper myth," Raederie added.

"Then what's that bat doing up there?" Ali asked.

Everybody looked up. The sky was empty. They all piled on Ali.

Laylea leapt from the trunk into KC's arms. She licked her face.

"Look at the bear."

Laylea looked over. Toby was staring up. He was following something in the sky with his eyes.

"I think there is a bat up there," KC muttered.

If it was Kyle, he flew away when Emerald leapt onto a bench. She pursed her lips and whistled a long crescendo that cut through all the chatter. She followed that with a trilling run from an impossibly high note all the way down to her lowest note. Somewhere in the run, Ali joined in with a sweet, clear human voice. The two sang a high duet, their tones floating up into the clouds, and it was heart stopping. Until a husky, breathy voice picked up the melody two octaves down, and Laylea's heart beat hard enough to burst out of her chest. Raederie lounged against a log bench, singing like it was nothing. But her voice clearly destroyed the boys around her, and Laylea felt no differently. She was ready to follow the selkie anywhere.

The song ended. The last notes floated away. But nobody moved except for Carrie, who never stopped braiding Raederie's hair. She glanced over at Brian after several long breaths and broke into her own song. Her stutter was gone.

Brian blushed and jumped in with a harmony that wove through the tune. Patrick dropped into wolf and howled out a bass line. Oscar laughed quietly and joined in with a high harmony. Carrie grinned approvingly.

One by one, each of the kids joined in the tune like it was an old favorite. Even KC joined with an enchanting, breathy voice Laylea would not have expected from her.

The song ratcheted up each time they got to the chorus and by the third time through, Laylea felt safe barking along with the shouted lines. She looked over to see how the depressed bear was enjoying it. He was staring up the path.

Then Patrick was staring up the path. "Scatter!"

They heard the guard's radio before they heard him. "Students in the zoo! Freeze!"

Not one of them obeyed. Ali and two other birds flew off over Beta's head. They distracted him just long enough for three wolves and a midnight-black feline to kick dirt over the fire and then scramble through the brush towards the reptile house. The guard chased them, leaving everyone else free to dash back down the path.

KC followed the crowd until Laylea barked at her. The fire was still smoking. It wasn't fully out.

"Come on, he's never gonna catch them in that brush. He's gonna come back."

Laylea barked again. She had not been raised to burn down a forest. Or a zoo. She turned her back on the fire and kicked more dirt over it, but leaves got scattered in too and they caught the small remaining flames. Her tail got singed and her feet burned but she kept kicking. She focused on kicking and breathing. She would heal when she shifted. She would heal when she shifted.

Chanting the mantra loudly in her head, she charged through the little bonfire. Logs scattered and some small flames flared up with the new oxygen. Laylea turned to charge again.

"You idiot," KC dropped on top of her and rolled her over in the dirt. "You're on fire."

Laylea squirmed out of her arms and ran into the smoking mess. KC sighed and stomped on the glowing bits. Laylea aimed the best she could, being a girl, and peed on everything putting off heat.

They still heard the guard's yells moving farther away when they were satisfied.

KC looked at Laylea. "I have no idea how to get back."

Laylea wagged her tail unhelpfully and faced the bear cage to get her bearings. Toby was still sitting. But he was watching them now. KC walked toward the Plexiglas. Laylea followed. Once on the path, they looked both ways. There was only one way to go unless they wanted to shove through brush like the wolves and Oscar.

"What do you think, Toby?" KC asked.

The bear looked up.

KC laughed. "We can't fly. I guess we'll have to go back the way we came." She and Laylea turned and jogged back down the path. They reached an unfamiliar crossing pretty quickly and realized they were already lost.

"We came through the primate house. All we have to do is find a map." KC sounded a little more panicked than her words implied. "Map!"

They raced across an open area to a display board beside the Kovler Seal Pool. KC was so focused on her search for the *You Are Here* indicator, she didn't hear the first squawk of the radio. She had a finger pinned to the board. Laylea hated to interrupt, but both of them heard the second squawk and Beta's triumphant yell.

"I've got two of them!"

KC took off, Laylea racing ahead. "Right past the lion house!"

Laylea saw three lions strolling on some rocks up ahead. She tore past them and stopped dead. The only things there were a path up to a carousel and the front gate. No primate enclosure right past the lion house. She turned around.

"GO RIGHT!" KC repeated the breathless order as she pumped her arms.

Laylea spun and dashed right into the guard's legs.

"Hah! Got you."

"Lee!"

Her claws couldn't get enough purchase for Laylea to scramble back fast enough. Beta caught her by her neck. He lifted her into the air, his fingers pushing into her windpipe and cutting off her yelps.

Then she was falling, terrified of landing on her messed up left hip again. Panic sparked the heat in her chest and she landed like a skilled primate, on her two human feet, crouched, and ready to spring away.

"Lee!" KC cried in her ear, "Run!"

KC grabbed her arm and dragged her away from the guard. Laylea had no choice but to trip after her. But she heard the guard's screaming. It followed them down the wide zoo entrance and under a sharp archway.

"It's the lion!" Laylea pointed at the back of the lion sculpture Morioka had moved to get them into the school. "How do we open it?"

KC scrambled up the plinth and slid over the lion. She stroked its nose and Laylea heard her mumbling.

"Once for pride. Twice for pack. Thrice so the phoenix will never come back."

A long, shrill scream drew Laylea back into the zoo. The guard who didn't want to be called Beta was backing away from a tall black man in jeans, a button-down, and Fox sandals.

"Kyle!" Laylea screamed his name even as she heard KC screaming hers. "Kyle! You're a good man! Think of Jeannie and KJ!"

The vampire looked her way. His wedding ring glinted as he twisted it. His familiar, affable smile appeared and he waved at her. "We're just gonna have a talk. Get back to school, you reprobate."

Then the smile melted away as though it had never been and Kyle stalked out of sight.

"Lee, come on." KC yanked her out the entrance.

"No," She tried to pull away but KC was strong. "I have to help him."

"No one can help that guy now."

Tears poured down Laylea's face. KC was right. If Kyle had already killed a pack of werewolves, Laylea wasn't going to be able to stop him from killing one guard. She didn't even know what kind of shifter not-Beta was.

But she had to try. She hadn't spent the last seven months hiding him from Dee and Morioka and everyone else just to give up on Kyle now. "I can."

She yanked her arm out of KC's grip and they both fell on the uneven steps of the plinth.

"I can," she insisted, more to herself than to KC. "If I don't, Morioka's gonna get him."

KC held her hands up, palms open, like she was saying she wasn't going to force Laylea anymore. But the terror in her eyes was enough.

"Lee." Her voice broke. "Morioka is going to hand you and I both over to the Enforcer if we don't get back into that school." A tear spilled down her cheek. "And you don't want to meet Adrien Denier. Ever. Please come with me."

Laylea couldn't hear anything from the zoo. She thought of her brother and her parents, off fighting for her freedom. She thought of herself. And she nodded.

21

Laylea was finding it hard to trust her teachers when they all kept insisting there were no such things as vampires. It had been over a month since the bonfire. The werewolves had reported that the bat was still haunting the zoo. Nobody knew what had happened to Benniker.

"There are no such things as vampires." Dr. Fenn slammed his beloved pointing stick down on the lab table. "And for the last time, his name is Mr. Benniker. Not Beta. He was not *bat food*. He had to leave the school to attend to a family matter."

Dizzy took off at Dr. Fenn's display of violence. She attended most of Laylea's biology classes, watching from the stone podium, standard even in this room, though the rest of the furniture was cold, sterilized metal: long cold lab tables with tall stools which made class torture when Laylea was a dog. If Carrie was stuck in wolf, the two of them would curl up together under Brian's desk. Even when he wasn't a gorilla, Brian let off a lot of heat. The biology classroom's sterility allowed for no rugs or wall hangings to warm it up. Dr. Fenn kept warm by constantly strolling around the room, like a shark. Maybe he was a shark. Laylea had yet to find out.

Dr. Fenn spent a lot of time sharing others' private information but he never talked about himself.

". . . because we have enough to study in ourselves. For instance, why Lee's white birthmark appears on her canine form while none of her other coloring does." Dr. Fenn actually stopped in front of Lee and stared at her face. Which meant the rest of the class stared at her face as well. Or, the back of her head since she was in the front row.

Apparently nobody else had a cross-form feature like that. Some kids had similar coloring to their animal, like Oscar's leopard. But that seemed like coincidence since apparently his parents, both Black humans as well, turned into normal brown and yellow leopards, and he didn't know of any living relatives with his particular melatonin issue.

"We have to study empirically because so many of us, like Lee, are orphans and can provide no genetic history. Is the mark an indication of some internal breakdown when she shifts from form to form? Is it a scar of some sort? Is it the reason her papers are always so much more intriguing than any of yours?" He scanned every other face in the room, and Laylea silently thanked him again for making them hate her.

"Speaking of papers."

Everyone groaned.

"Pick a trait you have that you only share with a small subsection, preferably something unique to you alone. Hypothesize on the reason you possess this trait and outline how you would conduct research to prove your hypothesis."

The end of class bell rang the short, sweet sound of freedom. Nobody stuck around after Dr. Fenn's class. Brian was out the door before the bell died away. Dr. Fenn had used him to address the physics of volume change last Tuesday. Sure, he was a big gorilla, but he was also a big guy. Laylea was more intrigued by tiny Chloe turning into a Moose.

"Oscar." Dr. Fenn pulled he and Laylea aside. "Lee and you both have free study right now. She's going to help you review chapters seven and eight as you have failed to grasp the details and differences between the subclasses of Canidae."

"Why do I need to know canine biology? I'm a cat."

"Oscar, this is Practical Biology. You should think of this as a class in what to do if one of your friends gets hurt. All your best friends are werewolves, right?" He didn't wait for a response. "Good. Thank you."

Laylea didn't bother to object. Dr. Fenn never listened to Pressers anyway.

Dizzy flew out of the room overhead. She soared down the halls, completely ignored by all the other kids rushing to their classes. Even the other birds made her get out of their way. It was like she wasn't even there.

The warmer, lower lights of the corridor helped settle Laylea's mental hackles and her feet took her, without much conscious thought, toward the library. Oscar kept pace with her, probably smoothing his own hackles at Dr. Fenn's oversharing. The teachers never asked if she'd like to tutor someone. They assumed she would because she knew so much already; surely she'd want to share it rather than spend her time learning more. Or possibly researching how to increase a twelve-pound terrier's lifespan.

Pounding footsteps in the library/Fields corridor startled them both. Jase Batka bared his upper teeth and dodged at a girl, pretending to bite her neck. She laughed and shoved him off.

"Luke, the pack is—" Jase caught up and pushed Laylea. "Shoo, Fido." He laughed with Oscar before finally getting to his point. "We're playing slap in the commons. Come on."

"Sorry, man. Fenn assigned me a tutoring hour. You know he'll monitor if I go to the library or not."

"Dude!" Jase slapped his palm against Oscar's forearm and held on. "Just tell him you were studying in the commons."

"You'll be there all night. I'll catch up." Oscar returned Jase's grip and they performed some elaborate non-hug before Jase took off, casually harassing a civet girl he passed.

KC came out of the library just in time to see Jase pull his vampire act on Dove. She pretended to barf. "Ew."

"Want to study with us?" Laylea pushed the door open.

KC looked away as the one-minute warning rang. "Can't. I've got Historical Languages."

"See you at dinner, then."

Oscar pulled one of KC's ponytails. "Hi, KC."

KC smacked his hand away. "Bye, Oscar. Bye, Lee!"

"Oh, Oscar." Ms. Crow set a stack of books on the front counter and slipped behind to draw a small, red envelope from her desk. "You have mail."

Oscar reached out like she was handing him cake, but then held the envelope like it might bite him.

Bailey used to treat letters from his friend Davis like that. Laylea had learned to give him space while he read them and then hang nearby afterward in case he wanted to talk. "I'll grab some books and padds and meet you in the Cube, okay?"

Oscar nodded. He was already tearing open the envelope as he headed between two stacks towards the most private study nook in the library. Laylea grabbed a physical copy of their textbook and Bio Two to Four's textbook as well. It didn't take long. All the textbooks were shelved together. So she waited outside the Cube and watched Dizzy try to annoy Benny at the central table until Oscar was ready for her.

Benny was easily flustered most days. Today he didn't even react when Dizzy managed to knock a book right off the table. His eyes were aimed at the book open in front of him, but Laylea didn't see him turn a single page in the whole time she watched him.

After she failed with the book, Dizzy spotted Laylea and soared over. Together, they watched Benny doing nothing.

After a while, Laylea asked, "ST?"

The bird nodded.

"Is that your story, too?" she asked. "Did something happen to you in ST?"

The raven hopped far enough away that she could look up at Laylea. She tilted her head and then shook it slowly.

"Does nobody else talk to you because of some shifter tradition I've never heard of?"

Dizzy shook her head. She hopped toward Benny and cawed at him. Then looked back at Laylea.

"Did Timmy fall down the well?"

Now Laylea knew how her family had felt before she learned how to write.

Dizzy rolled on the ground, croaking. She hopped back to her claws when Laylea fell backwards into the Cube.

"Let's get out of here, puppy." Oscar barely whispered. "I have to get out of here. You're obsessed with that bat. Let's go. I'll help you catch it."

A million responses overloaded Laylea's brain. She nodded at Dizzy. She knew better now than to speak to her in front of others. Then she shut the bookshelf that served as the Cube's secret entrance and faced Oscar.

Anything she might have said fled when she caught a whiff of the letter.

"Did somebody send you N? Oscar, you can't do N again. It's really, really dangerous. Wyrdos die on the stuff."

"I would never touch N." Oscar slammed a chair into the small table in the nook. The red letter, the only thing on the table, shivered.

Laylea hissed, "You had some on you in Morioka's car."

"No, I didn't."

"Yeah, you did. I smelled it on you, just like I can smell it on that letter." Laylea stood her ground. "You didn't get busted for beer. You got busted for N."

Oscar shook his head. He sank to the only chair he hadn't thrown around yet. "I stole the beer so they couldn't kill me for stealing the N." Oscar crumpled the red note in his hand. "My mom's dealer owns a liquor store. I couldn't get my mom to stop doing N so I thought if her dealer didn't have any to sell, she couldn't get it. But he caught me. He and this other guy were herding me into the open, trying to get a clean shot. I grabbed a forty." He pronounced the r. "I broke it so I'd have some kind of weapon."

"A broken bottle against guns?"

"It was the only idea I had!" Oscar took a deep breath. "Until I saw the loss prevention tag on the cap."

"What's a loss prevention tag?"

"Stores can tag their merch so that if it passes a certain barrier, an alarm sounds." He shrugged. "I thought that would draw out the neighbors and give me a chance to get away. I grabbed a six-pack and ran out the door. I didn't know their tags were linked to the local police."

A grim smile ghosted his face. "This prowler pulls up before I'm a block from the store. The dealer and his friend are hot on my heels but not shooting because it's a decent neighborhood, the kind of place people call in things like gunshots. They tried to talk the cops out of arresting me. Said I was just a dumb kid. So I trash talked at the cops. Called them pigs and said they were bad at their jobs and stuff. I was so scared they weren't gonna take me. I threw up right there in front of Giordano's Pizza. They almost let me go then so they wouldn't have to clean their car. But the one guy was a wolf and he'd heard of my father. He convinced his partner they needed to take me in to teach me a lesson."

"They never frisked you?"

"I dropped the six-pack when I was running away. They figured there was nothing to search for."

"And they were a little afraid of your dad?" Laylea guessed.

"The werewolf was. Dad's lawyer got to the station before we did. That's really why I'm here."

"Why didn't you just tell your dad you were trying to help your mom?"

"Didn't you hear me? Dad's lawyer showed up. Not Dad. And he doesn't care. It keeps her out of his way." He stood and started pacing. "I didn't help her anyway. She's still doing it."

"How do you know?" Laylea asked.

Oscar stalked to the table. He flattened the red letter and shoved it under Laylea's nose. "Because this letter is from her."

The fancy red stationary was nearly covered with a series of paw prints the size of her palm. On the very bottom, in handwriting that rivaled Laylea's very first attempts at writing, his mother had written, *Love you, kitten.*

Oscar snatched it and crumpled it again. He threw it into a corner. "She needs me. There's nobody else to look out for her, to tell her to stop. I have to get out of here."

He pulled his chair over right next to Laylea's. "Tomorrow is a full moon. It's the perfect time to sneak out. I'll just tell the guys we're going to make out at the marina. They'll hide us from the staff wolves. Come with me. Come save your bat."

"Morioka said she'd turn us over to the Enforcer."

Oscar waved the objection away. "She'd have to catch us first."

"KC says the Enforcer is a really, really bad guy."

"Which is why we're not gonna meet him. Besides, I'm a cat. You're a house pet. He doesn't care about us. He more concerned about the bat taking out *his* people, werewolves."

"The shifter Enforcer believes in the vampire?" Laylea sat up.

"Yeah. Before the vamp got him, Beta Benniker was planning to let the high Chicago pack in again to trap it."

"Again?"

"Yeah. According to Brenda, Dean Gorse really lit into Benniker for letting them into the zoo our first night here."

"But if he's gone, then the high pack can't get in."

"Sure, but Lee," Oscar said. "A bunch of the wolves from Sphinx are taking it into their own paws. They're planning to hunt down the bat tomorrow night. If you want to save it, you have to come with me."

"His name is Kyle." Laylea stood.

"What?" Oscar asked with a glint in his eye. He knew he had her.

"The bat's name is Kyle. And I'm the only friend he has. I'm in."

22

The monthly bells calling all wolves to ST rang just after Laylea and Oscar found KC in the bright nook the next day. She sat on a pile of pillows using the bench as a desk. The sound startled a cry from her and tears welled in her eyes again.

"That is the dumbest plan I've ever heard." She wiped her face with the arm of her jumpsuit and turned away from them. Dizzy nodded her agreement from where she stood, just behind KC's screen.

Laylea wanted to ask KC why she'd been crying but Oscar just barreled on with his single-minded plea.

"You don't have to come with us. Just hack into the faculty server and give me palm access to the first gate." Oscar offered KC a red handkerchief from his back pocket. Did he really not care why KC was upset?

She used the handkerchief and threw it back at him. "Of course I'm not going with you. I *want* to be here. And Lee, you *need* to be here. You almost got your friend killed because you can't shift right."

"Don't worry about it, KC." Oscar's scathing tone belied his easy words. "My mom's gonna die and vampire Kyle will kill more wolves if we don't get out there, but if you can't hack into the faculty system, I get it."

Doubting her wouldn't work. KC had hacked into the faculty server their second week in school to reassign Laylea and herself to the same Presser chores. And she wasn't the kind of girl to put up with such blatant manipulation. Not to mention, she and Oscar still didn't know what she'd been crying about before they asked for her help.

Oscar had woken up realizing they wouldn't be able to sneak through the gates at the same time as the actual wolves so he'd devised this plan of asking for KC's help. Laylea hadn't even considered that leaving LPSS meant leaving KC.

She didn't want to lose the first girlfriend she'd ever had.

KC rolled her eyes at Oscar and turned back to her screen. "Your mom is an addict. There isn't anything you can do about that. Are you gonna rob her supplier again?" She typed furiously. Dizzy peeked over the top of the screen, but from their angle, Laylea and Oscar couldn't see what she was working on. Laylea suspected the typing was all for show.

Oscar had told KC about his mom in the hopes that his sob story would convince her to hack the system. Laylea could have told him that KC didn't need a good reason to hack into anything.

"Lee, Kyle has evaded every Wilding so far. What magical skills do you think the Sphinx werewolves have that you imagine they're going to succeed where the religiously-trained high pack failed?" Her voice cracked and she snatched Oscar's handkerchief back.

Laylea knelt beside her. "What's wrong?"

"You're leaving me."

Dizzy croaked her opinion of that answer.

Laylea agreed. "You were crying before we told you that."

Heartless Oscar pushed on. "KC, they need us."

"No." A ray of sun caught her shifting yellow eyes as she turned on them. "They don't. They're adults. They can take care of themselves. That's what makes them adults. We're kids. We're idiots. That's why we're in school, to learn how to be slightly less stupid."

Oscar bristled, "I'm not stupid."

KC goggled at that. She growled deep in a shifting throat before she regained control of herself. "You're a cat running with wolves."

"I don't care about things like species."

"Well, that's great, kitten. But they do." KC hadn't seen the note. She couldn't know why the endearment pissed off Oscar.

He hissed at her. "I'm friends with them because it's smart to align yourself with the strongest group."

"This isn't prison."

"Maybe not for you."

Dizzy watched the two fight like it was a ping-pong match. Laylea looked back at the stacks, afraid that Ms. Crow was going to hear. But Ms. Crow was busy rounding up werewolves. KC lowered her voice. Tears leaked through her anger and the strain in her voice made her barely audible, even to them.

"You know why there are more werewolves than any other shifters, why they're the strongest?" she asked. "Because they hid when they should have been fighting to save all the other species. Your family was still in Africa then, Oscar. You don't know."

"Where was your family?" Oscar threw it back in her face. He didn't expect her honest answer.

"Hiding."

The word came out as a croak. Dizzy echoed her quietly.

It was the first time KC had openly admitted she was a werewolf. She folded in on herself, silent tears darkening the blue of her jumpsuit. Her body shook and Laylea skootched in to hold her, but KC sat up. She flung her arms out, knocking Dizzy right off her perch. The top of the bench slid out of place, though no one paid attention when the raven knocked it back into place with her head.

"I'm still hiding," she whispered. "I don't want anyone to know what I am. I don't want anyone to know who I am. I don't want to be slotted into the right place in the pecking order so the pack can control me." She caught her breath and when she looked up again, her wolf eyes glowed. "But I want to Wild. I want to stare down the full moon and dare her to catch me. I want to hunt and chase and howl and run with a—" She threw her head back and stared up at the sunlight. White fur framed her features. "They go Wilding because the pack leaders have declared it's unhealthy to deny the call of the moon. But it's really because Wilding the best way to reinforce pack structure. It's the best way to remind everyone how the wolves are on one team."

The class bell blurted its second call. KC started to stand and fell back to her knees with a wet laugh. From the front counter, Ms. Crow called out, "All werewolves to ST. Dr. Fenn will be coming through to make sure nobody skips this time, so you'd better close up your books and go."

KC wiped her eyes again for all the good it did and held her hands to her heart like she was keeping it inside her chest with the pressure. "I don't want to run with this pack. But I don't want to be alone."

Oscar wrapped himself around her back. Dizzy rubbed her head against KC's knees.

"Please don't leave me." Her eyes faded to brown again as she looked at Laylea. "What could you really do for Kyle? He's probably just here for the key and you don't have it. It's in storage."

Laylea hadn't considered that. KC was probably right. Kyle hadn't followed her to LPSS to protect her. He'd followed the key because he was cursed to follow it. And if he'd already drunk from those wolves, how much could she do to turn him from evil?

KC broke out of Oscar's hug. She took his hand in her furry one. "And you can't help your mom, Oscar. You know you can't."

"My mom loves me."

"Of course she does. She loves you. But so does my mom. And so do Lee's, both of them. They all still gave us up."

"Any wolves back here?" Ms. Crow called down the stacks.

Oscar leapt to his feet. He pushed past the French chair, "Just KC and Lee gossiping back here, Ms. Crow. I'll go check the Fields for you if you want."

"That would be nice of you, Oscar. Thank you." Their voices receded.

"Hey, Emerald." Oscar's footsteps stopped. "Emerald?"

Dizzy spread her wings and hopped up to the back of the French chair, looking out.

"Go on, Oscar." Ms. Crow sounded tired. "Emerald just came out of ST. She just needs a minute."

"Are you sure? She doesn't look good."

At that, Dizzy soared away.

"It was her second visit in as many months. I never handle that well, either. Go on, now."

KC lunged forward to hug Laylea. She whispered in her ear, "Please don't leave me. You two are the only friends I have."

Laylea crinkled her human face. "Oscar isn't much of a friend. He just ran away. And remember upstairs, when he made fun of your scars?"

"Yeah, he mocked me so hard I couldn't shift without everyone making fun of me. He gave me an out."

"But he told everyone about your scars."

"Lee." Now KC laughed. "I don't have any scars. I have a fabulous ass."

"Really?"

KC grinned. "Ahwooooo."

"Is it really hard for you when they all go Wilding?" Laylea asked.

KC's smile faded. The strain came back into her face. "It's the full moon more than the Wilding. I can feel its pull even from all the way down here and it's hard to stay human. If you *see* a full moon? Game over. The wolf takes charge no matter what the human wants."

"You talk about it like you're two different people." Laylea had heard other shifters talk like that, too.

"I kind of am. And both of us want to go Wilding. Even more because neither of us can."

Laylea pulled her into a hug.

"Why can't she?" Ms. Crow stood behind the French chair. Laylea held her breath, wondering how much she'd overheard. "She wants to run and hunt and chase with a pack. I'd bet a lot of non-wolves do, too. It sounds fun to me." She raised her eyebrows at Laylea. "Isn't there a war game human kids play? Capture the Flag?"

Laylea knew the game. She nodded her chin against KC's back. "Yeah, Bailey's band played Capture the Flag every year against Elmdale High's band."

"There are no classes scheduled in the Fields for the rest of the day." Ms. Crow took off her orange sweater and laid it on the back of the chair. "Here's a flag."

Laylea started to object, but before she could get any words out Ms. Crow said, "You know I have others."

"Good. We need two. What do you say, KC?" She pushed back from the hug. "We don't need wolves or a moon. Let's have our own Wilding!"

KC looked at her like she was crazy. "You can't Wild with two people."

"Then let's go recruit some more!" Laylea hit the button to shut down KC's padd and dragged her out of the nook. She meant to thank Ms. Crow but the librarian was gone. Dizzy perched on the back of the chair, a blue sweater in her beak. When Laylea grabbed the sweater, the raven leaped from the chair and led the way to the big study table where Emerald sat alone.

"Emerald!" Laylea started to invite her.

KC pulled Laylea away. "She looks like she's drugged."

Laylea followed KC, but she kept looking back at Dizzy rubbing her feathered head against Emerald's cheek. She knew that focused gaze. Another glance and she had it.

"She's got that look my dad used to get when he was trying to remember something."

KC pushed out into the corridor. "Your dad went zombie?"

Laylea turned in the direction of the dining room. "Doctors messed with his brain. He didn't have memories of anything from before he met my mother."

"No wonder ST bothers you so much."

"It doesn't bother you?" Laylea stopped just past a fire door that led into the ModTech Corridor.

"As long as it's voluntary, no."

She pulled Laylea away as the fire door slammed open against the stone wall. Big Mo, a werewolf from Centaur dorm tripped out. Dr. Fenn followed him. Big Mo turned left. Dr. Fenn grabbed the back of his jumpsuit and pulled him around to face the other way. "You cannot join the Wilding if you don't go to ST first. Go."

As the door fell shut, he spotted Laylea and KC huddled against the wall. Laylea hid the sweaters behind her back.

"Girls, if you see any werewolves, please remind them they are due in ST."

Big Mo rolled his eyes over Dr. Fenn's shoulder, but when the doctor turned, he spun and hastened down the corridor in the direction of the Medical Wing.

Laylea looked over at KC. "Does that seem voluntary?"

KC shook her head. The door opened again. This time it moved reasonably for how heavy it was. Ali came out. She flipped the bird at the departing figures before she noticed her dorm mates.

"Fenn is an ass."

"You look like you need some fun time."

Ali stared at Laylea for a very long time before she said, "You are a freak."

"Shut up." KC grabbed her hand and pulled her along. "We're going to the Fields. You're coming."

"The Fields are that way, weirdos."

Ali let herself be dragged into the dining hall. She stood by the door with her arms crossed while KC and Laylea bounded up to each of three small groups and dragged them away from their snacks and studies. Caliban lay, in her usual fashion, spread out on one of the rarely used tables, her hair draping off the edge. She didn't wait for them to approach. She rolled herself off the table and joined Ali at the door.

About twenty kids joined them. Some came reluctantly but most of them caught Laylea's excitement and by the time they got to the Jungle door, they'd conscripted a dozen more kids from the halls.

"Alright, Fido. What's going on?" Brenda bust through the small crowd. She was glistening with sweat and threw a punch at Brian when he complained about her shoving. "I'm trying to get a workout."

"You're in luck! I pick you for Jungle Team." Laylea tossed Brenda Ms. Crow's orange sweater. You're in charge of hiding our flag. Oscar!" She spotted him prowling around the back of the group. "You pick for Cave team," she yelled, holding out the blue sweater.

"No way. I don't want to be a captain." He ducked behind Brian to avoid her gaze.

KC yelled, "Don't go. You don't have to be captain. Just," she repeated her plea with a question in her tone. "Don't go?"

Brian jumped sideways, revealing black panther Oscar wriggling out of his jumpsuit. The cat paced around the blue jumpsuited legs between himself and the girls. He looked at KC and then at Laylea. They held their breath.

Some kids stepped away as he licked a paw and then rolled his neck. His lips curled back and he cracked his jaw with a growling roar. When he was done with all this posturing, he rubbed against KC's shins.

Laylea put an arm around her friend to keep her upright. "I'm staying too."

"You'd better stay." The weremonkey Harper looked at his neighbors for support. "You're the one who dragged us here."

"Yeah, Lee," Milly asked, "What's going on?"

Laylea grinned. "Do you know what the wolves do on the full moon?"

"Yeah." To everyone's surprise, Benny answered with more than a hint of jealousy in his voice. "They go Wilding upstairs."

"Well, we can't go upstairs," she said. "But we can go Wilding."

The little group exploded in an uproar. Some cheered. Others objected, jeering and shaking their heads.

Brenda shut them all up. "Wilding is a wolf thing. They'd kill us."

Everybody started yelling again, most of them agreeing with Brenda.

Laylea looked at KC who was closing in on herself again. She watched as her friend's hands curled into fists. It broke her heart.

Laylea turned very carefully until she couldn't see KC. She took a deep breath and said, "Well, Brenda, I don't see any wolves here, do you?"

Everybody seemed to hold their breath.

Brenda didn't respond, so Laylea asked, "Are you gonna tell them?"

Before anybody else could say anything, Ali pushed through to the front. She grabbed the blue sweater out of Laylea's hand. "Fido, you really are crazy. I pick Oscar for Blue team." She tossed the sweater on his head. "Go hide our flag."

23

The game took a dark turn after the sun went down. Literally, the rooms got darker. And figuratively, several players discovered they too had a Wilding instinct in the light of the full moon.

They'd ended up with seventeen players on each team after they harried Emerald and the koi from Mer dorm, who rarely took human shape, into playing. The koi, Merrilynne, shifted to human when a crowd leaped into the lake to convince her to join in.

"The hell?" Her jumpsuit clung to her as she stalked out of the river.

"We're Wilding." Ali tagged her. "You're on my team, Blue team. We've got to steal the orange sweater from the Jungle and get it to our Alpha, Oscar. Orange team has to get the blue sweater to Brenda."

Merrilynne stopped wringing out her purple hair and stared at Ali like she was pranking her. She looked around at the others. They all nodded.

She cackled and threw her head back. "Ahwoooooooo."

The rest of Blue team joined in.

KC had named the flag-bearers Alphas and suggested the captains choose a Beta who would know where their Alpha hid but could still run around. The Betas had also become the collectors of lost jumpsuits.

Laylea didn't think the game would last so long but she hadn't really grasped the size of the Fields and she hadn't expected the moon to turn the game vicious.

Milly got knocked into the river during a battle over the blue sweater and nearly drowned. After shifting into mouse form when a fox shifter leapt at her, she'd scampered back and been swept from the bank by a spray of water from the fierce battle between Emerald and Merrilynne.

The fox quickly came to his senses. He shifted back to human and dove for the tiny white figure under the waves. But while the fox tried to help, Brian knuckled over to grab the dropped sweater from the riverbank. He stared for a moment at the chaos in the little river. Then, instead of helping, Gorilla Brian stared up at the moon and roared.

It was too much for the peaceful tree-shifter. Caliban waded across the river from the apple grove, both arms lengthening as she reached for Brian's ankle and scooped the little mouse out of the water. Caliban grew into her tree form. Brian dangled from a high branch while Milly coughed up water on a low one. Caliban spread her upper branches, growing thick leaves to block the moon.

Laylea leapt from the bridge to the handrail to an elephant's back and barely caught herself on Cal's lowest branch. The familiar fire burst in her chest and she shifted just in time to grab at the branch with human hands. Once she got herself atop the branch, she checked to be sure Milly was okay. Laylea found the little mouse safely inside an open knot in Caliban's trunk, giggling.

A massive splash drenched Laylea. Caliban had dropped Brian and the blue sweater into to the river. It was exactly the right move to break the growing intensity of the game.

While nearly everybody in sight laughed, Laylea saw Benny edging his way toward the tunnel between the Farm and Jungle. She tapped at Caliban's trunk to draw her attention to it. Benny was on the other team. What did he know? Caliban twisted and bent to let Laylea down close to Benny.

But the turtle shifter saw and he ran. Laylea leaped from Caliban. She landed and rolled, then burst forward as smoothly as if she were in dog form. Benny tripped alongside the river, tracking Brian swimming upstream underwater. Benny was so focused, he didn't see green-eyed Dove crouched in the brush up ahead where the river turned.

Water sprayed out at that turn as Brian broke the surface. He threw the sweater into the air and Benny leapt just before Dove did. For an instant, a part of Laylea hoped that Benny would get to it first. The kid didn't have a lot of confidence. But it was a fleeting thought and she cheered when Dove snatched the blue sweater in her tiger teeth and rolled safely on the opposite bank.

Benny shifted the instant he hit the water. He was not one of the lucky shifters who took their clothes with them in the change. The poor turtle didn't so much flounder as immediately sink as the jumpsuit soaked up river. Brian saw it, too. He swam upstream till he could scoop Benny and his clothes out of the current and onto shore. He found the neckline of the jumpsuit and held it up so Benny could walk out.

The little turtle's head twisted and looked at Laylea. Brian looked over, too, and that's when Laylea noticed the horde of kids stampeding through the tunnel. A flash of orange caught her attention and she forgot about Benny. Their flag!

The horde centered around Harper. The monkey held the orange sweater in his teeth like it was worth his life. His face scrunched up around a permanent hiss. All four paws gripped the sweater and he'd curled himself tightly around it. The other kids were fighting over him like he was the flag because they couldn't get it away from him.

"He hates water!"

Harper's eyes shot open as his very good, dear friend Brian sold him out.

In seconds, Harper was sailing through the air at the river. Laylea got there second. She shoved a log into the river for Harper to grab and as he lunged at it for dear life, she dove for the sweater.

The water was colder than she'd expected but, by this point in the game, she didn't even pause when she noticed the sharp, sparkling pain shooting through her. She calmly shoved the sweater into her mouth and kicked for a rocky overhang. By the time she reached it, she was doggy paddling. She came up on the far side of the overhang and tried to stay low through the rocky shoreline.

A cry went up behind her. It wasn't a *we won* cry, so she kept making her stealthy way towards an exit from the Jungle. She made it a few more inches before she felt a tug on her upper back fur that sent her emotions in a tailspin. An old memory flashed through her mind. The warmth of her mama's breath washing over her head, driving away the frightening licorice smell of Walter.

Then she was back in the Jungle and flying. She twisted but couldn't see who'd grabbed her up.

"Ali! Be careful." Ms. Crow yelled from over by the cubbies.

Laylea could see the librarian poised, ready to help. She'd found another orange sweater to wear.

One reward for the pain of flying in Ali's claws was that Laylea could see everything from up so high. Down in the deep grass, Dove had the blue sweater. Somehow, she'd shaken off her pursuers and now she had the sweater in her tiger teeth and was crawling, just as Laylea had been doing, towards KC and Brenda, the Orange team Alpha.

KC had calculated that she was least likely to see the full moon in the thick tree cover of the Jungle. So when night fell, she had assigned herself to guard Brenda. KC had acquired a stack of pussy willows and to judge from the number of Blue team members covered in yellow fluff, she'd been whacking anyone who got close.

She stood with her back to the opening in a tight arrangement of trees, vines, and rocks, like she was protecting it. But Brenda wasn't hiding behind KC. She had wrapped her python form around one of the vines over KC's head. She was so still Laylea would never have seen her if KC hadn't peeked up.

Three or four leaps as a tiger and Dove could win the game for Orange team. But she was aiming behind KC, not at Brenda. Laylea had to tell them. She reached for the spark in her chest and shifted. She was so concentrated on the game that she didn't even realize that she'd just shifted at will.

She yelled, "Dove, look—" but didn't get any further.

Laylea the human was too heavy for Ali the hawk. They fell. When Ali released her, Laylea fell faster. A hammock of vines slowed her fall and she caught herself with her gut. The breath was knocked out of her and her lunch almost followed. The orange sweater did follow. It fluttered down to the craggy rocks below.

Even falling, she had a great view of Dove leaping out of hiding at last. She had a perfect line of sight to catch Oscar tackling the tiger and ripping the blue sweater from her teeth. She also saw Merrilynne reaching to grab it right out of Oscar's hand.

Then the vine creaked and she slipped. She managed to swing herself into a new trajectory, sending her tumbling through the air toward a great mossy boulder. The fall made her shift and her paws hit the boulder rather than her human butt. She pushed off that one to the next, lower rock, and finally she leapt right into Brian's broad chest. He stumbled back a few steps but neither fell.

A small figure dashed by them as Brian regained his balance. Benny had the orange flag. Laylea barked.

"No worries, Lee. Merrilynne's right there."

Brian stepped around a tree to see Merrilynne holding the blue sweater high over her head at a swirling, shifting half-python, half-human Brenda. Their Alpha had almost formed an arm to reach down. Then she had. And she reached for the sweater.

But too late.

A cry went up back in the tangle of tiger Dove and human Oscar. Benny had trotted over and put the orange sweater in Oscar's still-outstretched hand.

Laylea growled and found the reaction morphing into a huge human laugh as she realized she'd shifted yet again. She nearly sprang out of Brian's arms yelling, "Blue team wins the Wilding!"

"Hold on." Ali shifted before she'd finished landing and Brian dashed over to keep her from falling. "Oscar isn't in the Caves, Benny."

Benny pulled his hands up into his sleeves. "Was that a rule?"

Everyone looked around at KC who'd ended up calling out the rules.

"Get the blue to Brenda or the orange to Oscar. Those were the only rules." KC grinned. "Blue team wins! Good job, Blue team. Ahwoooooooo!"

"Ahwooooooo!"

Every single kid from both teams joined in the howl. Their voices overlapped, echoing through the Jungle and ringing off the high glass roof. Brenda howled when she spun KC and Merrilynne in a hug. Emerald howled from the water as she slipped out of her seal skin. Harper howled as he helped Dove to her feet. All of Blue team howled as they lifted Benny to their shoulders and paraded him to the cubbies where Ms. Crow stood howling through a giant grin.

"WHAT DO YOU THINK YOU'RE DOING?"

No one had seen Dr. Fenn come through the Jungle door.

"If Mr. Mendenkov caught you in here mocking the werewolves, your lives wouldn't be worth the tuition your parents pay. Every one of you Pressers would be shipped off to the Montana Collective. What do you think you're doing?" He tore jumpsuits from the cubbies at random and threw them at the few naked students. "You are not permitted to gather in here without faculty supervision. What if somebody got hurt? What if one of the wolves couldn't go upstairs and caught you? Answer me, what do you think you were doing?"

"We were just—" Emerald started to answer his question but Dr. Fenn interrupted her.

"I don't want to know." He held the door open. "Get to your dorms. Lights out was an hour ago."

"Not for the wolves."

Dr. Fenn spun back to see who'd said that but nobody fessed up and everybody very carefully did not look at Benny. A few brave souls howled a quick, "Awhoo."

"Out!"

The kids filed through the door, not the least bit repentant, though a few played at it. Laylea headed toward Oscar with the jumpsuit she'd gotten for him. KC was already helping him into one. So she looked for Ms. Crow to ask why she didn't stand up for them, but the librarian had gone.

"Lee," Ali grabbed the back of Laylea's 1980's jumpsuit and popped the collar. "Don't let Fenn get you down. This was the best night ever." She jogged past Laylea to join Emerald and Merrilynne. They whispered to her and she turned back. "Oh, hey, don't know when you plan on giving Ms. Crow her sweaters back, but we'd like to be there."

24

Nobody ever admitted to it, of course. But somebody who was at the non-wolf Wilding told somebody who wasn't. And eventually one of them told a wolf who told the rest of them. Mostly, they didn't take it well.

When Mer dorm's only girl wolf, Carrie, found out, she crawled into Laylea's pod to tell her and KC she'd rather go to their Wilding. Then she'd tucked herself under the sheets and gone to sleep. In the morning she swore up and down she'd gone to sleep in her own pod.

The wolves had assumed it was Emerald's idea to mock them until Monday evening's Orchestra recital. Laylea arrived late, and tripped over the threshold when she did get there. Naturally, she shifted to dog. Instead of fretting, she walked right out of her jumpsuit, hopped up onto a chair and from there to the back of a sofa. Brian lifted her over to where KC was saving her a seat in a wide comfy chair with a clear view so they could record the recital for Oscar's mom.

Brian ahwooed a tiny howl as he swung her over. Ali heard and she repeated it more loudly. Then everyone in the room who'd been at their Wilding and several non-wolves who weren't joined in.

"Lee. Lee. Lee. Lee." The chant was cut off when Mr. Bianchi come out to introduce Mr. Cahill and the orchestra. But when the curtains parted, Oscar winked at her from behind his oboe and Benny held his hand up in an L until he needed it for his xylophone.

Lee wanted to credit KC. KC wanted to be invisible. So Lee got all the love and howling. And she adored it. She had friends. She fit in. She belonged.

A week after the Wilding, Carrie tanked a Bio test she should have passed easily. She told Laylea it was because of an anti-anxiety medication Dr. Fenn gave her after the post-moon ST. She just couldn't focus. On the upside, she wasn't shifting as often, she'd added.

Laylea decided enough was enough. Her parents hadn't raised her to sit by and let people get hurt. She was supposed to learn from their mistakes. And while Clark couldn't remember any of his life before the Consortium messed with him, Sher could remember everything she'd done. She'd run a lab just like Dr. Fenn did. She'd altered her subjects' genetic structure and screwed up their brains. She'd stolen a lot of memories, not just Clark's.

Laylea didn't believe Dr. Fenn thought he was doing anything that bad. But he didn't see the kids after they left. Maybe he didn't know he was making temporary zombies. And whatever was going on in ST, it was clear that Dr. Fenn was messing with people's brains.

Perhaps if she talked to him about it, he'd stop. Like Sher had. She made her mind up then and there.

She left Carrie to hunt down Dr. Fenn.

"Lee!" Merrilynne reverse-fived her in the corridor. "Three weeks till the next full moon, Bitch."

"Merri." Both of her Centaur friends looked horrified.

"She's a female dog."

One of them said, "That's your excuse for calling wolves that."

Merrilynne stopped walking away. "That's no good. Hey Lee, what should I call you?"

"An insulting but secretly affectionate nickname?"

Her feline friend laughed. "Exactly."

"Well, lots of people call me Fido."

Merrilynne's friends came back to reverse-five Laylea but Merrilynne just called back, "I think I'll go with Captain. Peace out, Captain."

Laylea pretty much skipped the rest of the way to the Medical Wing. She ran smack into Ali as she swung around the sharp corner that led down to ST, the Infirmary, and the waiting room alcove.

"Whoa. Where you going so fast?"

"The infirmary," Laylea said. "I've gotta talk to Dr. Fenn."

"Hey, Lee." Ali looked back to make sure they were alone. "Don't go in there if you don't have to. Fenn's in a mood. He's out to get everyone who was at our Wilding. And he just kicked me out to go fetch some drives for him from ModTech while he and Durrah yell at each other."

"What are they arguing about?"

"My guess?" Ali headed on down the hall as she said, "Their mutual crush on our Ms. Crow."

Laylea considered following Ali but the infirmary door opened and Dr. Durrah backed out of the room, saying, "I'm thinking of the children, Sydney. Where does your concern lie?"

She stepped back behind the corner when Dr. Fenn followed the older man out into the hall. "My concern lies in the supposition that your theory is right. If it would help the students, then, yes, we should test all the kids who Wild and compare that data with the wolves. I'd do the data work myself, David."

Laylea couldn't hear Dr. Durrah's response as the door closed in Dr. Fenn's face. She leaned in to hear and forgot that she was hiding.

"Lee Woodford?" Dr. Fenn's tone flipped from anger to concern. "Are you feeling all right? I heard you shifted a lot on Thursday. Maybe you're actually learning something in Ms. Syperek's class. I fear you learn nothing new from me."

He walked all the way down the hall and escorted Laylea by the arm to the infirmary.

"I don't get to do anything in Shifting Studies. I watch other kids shift and talk about what it feels like for them." Laylea liked Ms.

Syperek. She didn't want Dr. Fenn to think she was dissing her. "Ms. Syperek says I'm a special challenge since there's nobody else like me. I'm the only werecanid anybody here has ever heard of. But I am getting better at dealing with the shifting when it happens."

Dr. Fenn sat Laylea in one of the two chairs in front of the desk in his office. He took the other. "I notice you haven't said anything about my class." Dr. Fenn leaned forward in his chair and pasted on a charming grin.

"Actually, I'm here about Bio," she lied. "I'm a little bored. I was hoping I could do a paper on the Special Testing program."

"Really?"

Laylea felt the temperature drop. She smelled rank sweat on Dr. Fenn. "Specifically, I'd like to learn more about why the wolves go to ST before and after every full moon."

"I think, Ms. Woodford, that you should be more concerned with your inability to shift. You could expand your research to the many boys and girls in Mer dorm who cannot seem to control themselves either. Your friend, KC, for example. I have never seen her in coyote form." He scanned through something on his armpadd. "Nor has any other faculty member. I think it would be a good idea for you to focus on your immediate issues rather than on the wolves' Special Testing."

Laylea picked at her jumpsuit legs. "I just thought, since I've studied advanced genetics already, that if you told me why—" She stopped as he tapped on his padd.

"Now that you've reminded me, I should have KC come in for ST. Taking her genetic measure might help her past this shifting problem."

"But she's not that bad. I've seen her shift. She shifts in the dorm all the time. She's a gorgeous coyote. Lots of fur."

The outer door burst open.

"Fenn. We have an emergency." Mr. Mendenkov's voice blasted through the infirmary. "Fenn!"

Laylea followed Dr. Fenn through the curtain to see Mendenkov setting Big Mo on the exam table. Both had blood smeared over their clothes. Big Mo's typically dark face had paled to gray and his eyes fluttered like he was desperately trying to stay conscious. He held Mendenkov's beloved Sox hat in one bloody hand.

"Shift." Laylea wondered why he didn't just shift. Big Mo wasn't Mer so why didn't he just shift and heal?

"Fido," Mendenkov swirled to spit at her. "Out."

Fenn never took his eyes off the gash in Big Mo's big leg. "Go, Lee."

Laylea backed away. She wasn't afraid of blood. She'd helped at Sher's veterinary clinic enough to be inured to most wounds. But Mendenkov's face wasn't entirely human and that did scare her.

She should have paid as much attention to where she was going as to what she was leaving. She backed right out the door and into Dustin.

"Sorry." She flipped around.

"Are you?" Dustin stepped closer to her.

Ten sweaty, worked-up werewolves blocked the hallway. Some, who had been headed away, turned at Patrick DelValle's call.

"Hey, look who it is. Hey, Fido."

"Hey, Fido." Jase shoved her.

Another werewolf got in her face. "Hey, Fido."

Laylea backed away into the little alcove with the clothing closet. "Hey, guys. Big Mo is in good hands. His leg is gonna be fine."

"And if it's not," Patrick asked, "will you invite him to your guppy Wilding, Fido?"

Laylea forced a smile. "We were just playing Capture the Flag."

"And howling," the Sphinx wolf named Julia (pronounced hulia) said. She tied her braids back and rolled up her sleeves.

"Imitation is the highest form of flattery."

"Why are you backing away then, Fido?" Dustin followed her.

Patrick threw back his head and howled. Nobody else took their eyes off Laylea.

"Go on." Jase smiled at her. If he weren't human she would have said he was baring his teeth. It had the same effect. "Imitate him, Fido."

"Why are you upset? We weren't mocking you." She talked fast as the wolves kept moving in, howling in turns. "We were jealous. You get to go upstairs. We hear you howling at the moon. It sounds like fun."

The door to the infirmary cracked open. Dr. Fenn leaned out. He looked over the kids crowded into the alcove and Laylea breathed a little easier.

"Conner." He pointed at the Mer wolf Laylea hadn't seen past the wide shoulders of the body-builders backing her into the Ikea shelves. "You're O neg/DEA 7, right?"

"Yeah." Conner looked to Patrick as he confirmed his blood types.

"We need you in here."

Conner left only after Patrick nodded his permission. Dr. Fenn didn't say another word.

"No Blue team to get your back now, huh, Fido?" Julia turned back to her the instant the door fell shut.

"Howl for us now, Fido." Dustin wrapped one hand all the way around her collar. She could feel the round, metal dog tag pressing into her windpipe and a pointy plastic knob from the clothes closet poking into her spine.

Patrick nodded and a wolf Laylea knew only by his vicious reputation pushed through the others. "Show us how you love us now." He raised a fist. "Fido."

She whimpered.

"Isn't Post Edict five point three known as the Denier Addendum?" KC asked from behind the pack.

Laylea could have cried at the sound of KC's voice. Then she almost did cry at the thought of KC giving herself away to save her.

"It's okay, KC. I'm fine. We're just talking," she croaked. "I was telling them about Capture the Flag."

"And I'm telling them I know about their secret code." KC barely glanced at Laylea.

"Let her go, you shitheads." Ali pounded on the infirmary door, not taking her eyes from the wolf pack.

"If I hacked into your secure site, do you imagine I would hesitate to message Enforcer Denier that his hard-won Code Edict was being flagrantly ignored by Vaughn Howe, Dustin Huono, Patrick DelValle, Julia Jimenez—"

Ali snorted. "Really? Your name Julia Jimenez? Are you from La Jolla? Do you only eat jicamas and jalapenos?"

"I could even figure out how to message Delcampo."

Dustin dropped Laylea. Her knees buckled and she collapsed. The vicious wolf kicked her in the ribs before he spun at the sound of the infirmary door opening. Mendenkov, holding a dripping wet Sox hat in his hands, glared at Ali and KC. "Get to class."

KC dropped her eyes, back to hiding-as-usual.

But Ali barely blinked. "Dr. Fenn asked us to come here."

He nearly growled at her but just turned to the pack of wolves in the alcove. "Back to the weight room. Mo is spending the night here."

He strode down the hall, not waiting to see if anyone followed him. They didn't.

KC turned to Ali and casually said, "So, Enforcer Denier, he's a forgiving guy, right?"

Ali snorted again. "He once ripped a rat's arms off for stealing a pack of vapes from a wolf-owned bodega." She turned to the wolves. "Scat."

The wolves finally dispersed. Laylea didn't move until they were all out of sight.

"Thanks," she choked.

The infirmary door opened again. Dr. Fenn came out, looking into the alcove and then up the hall. He seemed to notice the girls as an afterthought.

"Oh, yes. KC. Thank you. And Ali, you have the drives?"

Ali held out a pack of third generation power drives. KC rolled her eyes at the old technology.

"Wonderful. Now, both of you. It's time we had you in Special Testing. Lee reminded me of your shifting problems, KC. I think we can help you get to the bottom of that."

"No, I didn't." Laylea sputtered.

She pushed to her feet as KC struggled to find a way out. "I don't think it's a good idea, Dr. Fenn. I'm on—" she shot Laylea a baleful look. "I mean, don't you take a lot of blood?"

"No, no. It's fine. We don't take liters. Come on now, there's no need to be nervous." Dr. Fenn put a firm hand on KC's back and pushed her into the room after Ali.

KC continued to protest. "Low iron is a problem in my family and—"

Laylea didn't hear anything else as the ST door slid firmly shut.

25

Laylea brushed her teeth before bed even though she didn't need to. Her teeth were always perfectly clean after she shifted. Sweat and dirt, scrapes, scratches, the ragged gashes Ali's claws ripped into her back in the Wilding, all of it vanished when she shifted. If she'd broken a bone through her skin like Big Mo had, she'd probably shift instinctually from the pain and when she shifted to human again, the leg would be whole.

But she brushed her teeth and washed her face because it was what the girls did before bed. Milly and Ali gossiped about a boy in Centaur dorm who'd started having shifting troubles. Brenda told them he was gay and they all sighed at the loss. And then started listing the boys in Mer he might like.

Laylea ran over her Theoretical Physics homework with Benny in the courtyard. She helped Emerald with an itch under her left flipper and then scritched behind her earholes as if she were a dog. She turned down a game of Splat with Ahanu and his crowd. As early as she could, she said goodnight to her friends and crawled into her pod.

She sat at her padd for about a lifetime trying to compose a message to KC. When the C flashed with a new chat request, she pounced on it.

But it was from Oscar. *Puppy, where's KC? She was supposed to help me tonight.*

She typed. *Help with what?*

Just something. She there?

She's in ST.

???!!

Dr. Fenn said I gave him the idea.

What did u do?

Nothing. I just asked him why the wolves go before and after Wilding and he said I should be more worried about why KC and I have trouble shifting.

He put her in ST bc u asked about wolves? Y didn't u back down?

I didn't get a chance.

Whatev. Clear your history. KC says they can read these chats.

The window closed and Lee couldn't reestablish a connection to Oscar. She couldn't even leave him a message. He'd blocked her.

She returned to her empty message to KC and typed *O is looking for you.* Then she deleted it. She typed *What are you working on with O?* And deleted it.

She didn't even realize she was singing Clark's song until Caliban knocked on her bed post.

"Where did you learn that, Lee?

Sher had written the song, at least the first verse. It was a tool for self-conditioning. She, and later Uncle Jay, had taught the song to the super-soldiers they rescued from the Consortium's genetic manipulation program. The soldiers could sing it when their old kill-kill-kill conditioning tried to take over. Laylea had grown up listening to Clark sing it. He would run his fingers through her fur and sing when life got tough or he wanted to remember. He sang it after one of the super-soldiers tried to kill her. He sang it when Walter found them and wanted to take Laylea away. He sang it a lot when Bailey hit puberty.

I will not kill another soul today. Her life is in my hands and I will not throw it away.

She told Caliban, "It's just something I picked up somewhere."

"Can I sit?"

"Sure." Laylea pushed the curtain back.

"You're worried about KC?" It took Caliban a while to fold her long legs onto the comforter. When she was settled, she adjusted again to tuck her hands into her knee pits. "I didn't know knees could get so sweaty."

"My feet get really sweaty when I have to wear shoes."

"Trees don't sweat."

"Dogs pant. It's much easier."

Caliban leaned back against the post. "ST isn't so bad, you know. They're trying to find similarities between us to keep another Ten Percent Plan from happening."

"Can they force her to shift?" The tune crescendoed in Laylea's mind.

"No."

Laylea exhaled but Caliban went on.

"There are ways to inspire some shifters to change. Engaging the fight, flight, or freeze response. Physical violence was found effective. Electric shocks." Caliban put a hand out to stop Laylea who was already sliding out of bed to go invade ST. "But that's outlawed. Unless a shifter asks to be inspired, forced shifting is strictly forbidden."

"The wolves almost beat me up today even though there's some rule forbidding fighting in school."

"Assault is illegal anywhere, Lee." Caliban reminded her. "And, of course, there are people who consider rules and laws to be beneath them. But our bodies often have reasons for preventing us from shifting. Forced shifting caused sterilization in many young shifters during the early days of the schools. It has ended pregnancies, caused strokes, heart attacks, total systemic breakdown. Forced shifting is a crime against the entire community. Even if someone asks for it, a doctor would start with the least invasive techniques, encouraging the shift to occur naturally rather than demanding the body comply, as with electric shock."

This gave Laylea a huge measure of relief. At least they couldn't force KC's secret from her. "Why do people look like zombies when they come back from ST?"

Caliban looked over at Brenda's pod where seven girls had squeezed in to play spoons. Dove huddled between Emerald and Carrie. All three were screaming and laughing and looking perfectly fine.

The Linden shifter smiled as a fight broke out over an insincere accusation of cheating. "I've heard it's like coming down from N. People like ST."

"What do they do to you, exactly?"

Caliban thought about that for a long while. She frowned. "Nobody has ever said."

"Caliban?" Laylea shut down her padd and slipped under the covers.

"Yes?"

"What do you think it means that I was never this worried about anybody else going to ST?"

"I think it means KC's lucky to have you as a friend. I think sometimes we only realize a thing bothers us until it happens to us or a friend. You told me your mother used to say something about worry. I can't remember what."

Laylea doubted that. But she told her again anyway. "If you address a problem, you won't have time to stress over it."

"Right. Someone should tell that to the poor depressed bear upstairs. He always looks so stressed." She climbed off the bed. "*I* have to address why I Tested into level 3 Applied Chemistry for the fifth time. Try to get some sleep. And go ahead and sing your creepy song if it makes you feel better."

"Night."

Caliban reached up to twitch the curtain closed.

Laylea stopped her. "Hey, isn't AppChem all about experiments? Like mixing different materials and heating them up and seeing what happens? Merrilynne calls it Bunsen Burner Bull."

Caliban chuckled. "Yes. B3."

"If I were a tree, I think I'd kind of be afraid of fire."

Caliban's gaze went distant.

"Anyway, because I shift all *willy-nilly,* as she says, Ms. Correnti makes me wear this full fire retardant suit in Metal Shop. Maybe you could borrow one for AppChem."

Caliban brushed her braid over her shoulder. She breathed back whatever memory had captured her for the moment. "Thank you, Lee. Would you like me to leave this open so you can see if KC comes back tonight?"

Laylea nodded. She laid her head down on the cushy pillow and immediately shifted. She'd gone to sleep in human form a few times. But she never woke up that way. She got up and circled until the mattress had a suitable divot, then she lay down facing the space where KC's pod should have been.

KC hadn't returned by the time she fell asleep.

I will not kill. I will not kill. I will not kill.

A thousand voices sang the beginning of Clark's song, overlapping and echoing off the walls of the arena. With every repetition the *not* diminished until the voices were chanting, *I will kill. I will kill. I will kill.*

A pack of werewolves wearing their furry heads on top of human bodies flanked the depressed bear. The wolves prodded him with six-foot long scalpels. Dustin held the end of a boat anchor chain. The other end attached to an old iron collar carved with oak leaves and tortured faces. The collar splayed the black fur around the depressed bear's neck and he clawed at until Jase flipped the bear's white ear with his scalpel.

Laylea felt the scratch it made in her white diamond birthmark. A spot of blood glowed on the tip of the bear's ear and trickled down Laylea's muzzle. The bear's roar drowned out the chanting crowd.

Laylea backed away. She ran into the bars of her cage and saw that there were bars between the bear and his tormenters, too. She felt a sudden tightening in her throat. Then an electric shock poked her spine and she darted forward.

The crowd cheered.

And they chanted. *I will kill. I will kill. I will kill.*

"Hey, Lee. I got you a present."

She looked back at the bear. He was gone. Junior stood in his place with the iron collar around his neck. Her brother tossed her a rawhide but a silver house key landed in the dirt.

"Don't lose it." Bailey growled from the bear's side.

Laylea ran to Bailey. She missed him so much her heart ached. She felt his absence like the sharp pain of a shift. She leapt to hug him.

"Why?" Clark's voice cried in her ear and she saw her own white knuckles gripped around a leather-wrapped hilt. The blade lay buried in a blue jumpsuited back: KC's back.

"Ahwooooooo." KC's howl died with her. Her wolven weight dragged Laylea down while the crowd kept on chanting in a thousand familiar voices she'd never heard.

I will not kill. I will not kill. I will not kill.

A rain of clicks and a whirr woke Laylea instantly from the dream. Dr. Fenn pulled KC's pod down with one hand. His other held an unconscious KC over one shoulder. Laylea shut her eyes quickly when he glanced her way.

She dared to peek again after she heard the curtains rattle closed. Dr. Fenn looked around the dorm. He reached up and ran a hand along the upright post of KC's pod. Then he glided down the rows and slipped out through the beaded curtain.

Laylea waited just long enough to be sure he'd left their ante-room before she wriggled out of the sheets and hopped down to the cold floor. She scratched at KC's curtain. No response. She couldn't leave it. She would want KC to comfort her if the tables were turned.

So she ducked under the bed curtain and hopped up to KC's mattress. KC lay flat on her back. Her face looked fine, not pale or drained. Her eyes were shut and her chest rose and fell with normal breathing. Laylea wanted to lick her nose but she restrained herself.

She just circled once and curled up at KC's side. KC twitched. She pulled her arm up and rolled to her side, toward the warm, sleepy ball of Laylea. Then she shoved Laylea out of her bed.

26

KC was gone the next morning when Laylea woke up. Carrie begged off going to breakfast together like they usually did. Laylea figured the other wolves were giving her a hard time so she said she had to skip breakfast anyway. She grabbed an apple from the Farm groves instead and lay on the rope bridge staring out at the sky through the magic ceiling. Up in the conservatory, a maintenance guy swept up the cobbles and collected trash and pennies from the little pools. She couldn't see the pennies but knowing humans, she guessed that's what he was doing since not everything he picked out went into his trash bin. It felt a little eerie watching him, when he had no idea what was going on beneath his feet.

Like Dizzy, the visitors to the Conservatory were yet another element of the school that apparently only she could see. Though the sun shone through them thanks to whatever magic had gone into creating this place, Laylea could see the shadows or outlines of the garden beds in the Conservatory and the fruit trees in the new Greenhouse Grove. She liked the roots hanging from the ceiling. Dizzy would fly among them and come back down with glistening wings.

To make things easier for Carrie, she managed to miss mealtimes for a few days. And with KC coming and going before and after lights out, the two didn't see each other except in class until Saturday dinner when Dizzy flew through the library to harry Laylea out and down to the dining hall.

Nearly everyone was there. Some local politician was throwing a fundraiser up in the zoo so night classes had been cancelled. A quick howl went up from some non-wolves when Laylea tripped through the door with Dizzy at her back. An answering boo from the wolves drowned them out.

Laylea picked up her food and spotted KC sitting near Oscar. The Mer dorm regulars filled the table to her left and all the wolves Laylea wanted to avoid filled the table to Oscar's right.

Jase called out to her. "Over here, Lee. Come sit with us. No hard feelings. There's room."

He made the kids across from him squeeze down so she could sit. A few of the wolves booed again and complained about Fido sitting with them.

"Hey guys, let it go," Jase said. "She explained it. They all just wish they were werewolves."

"No, we don't," Ali muttered from down on KC's left.

Merrilynne asked, "She said what?"

Laylea caught KC's eye, trying to stay out of the argument. "Hey, you survived ST."

"I got out of it," KC muttered.

"What?" Laylea felt her chest rise as if she'd just taken off a heavy coat. "That's great. How?"

"I told them I was on my period."

Laylea didn't really understand how that would excuse her from ST, but it didn't seem like dinner was the place for details. "Then where were you all afternoon?"

"Fenn made me rest in the infirmary so he could give me fluids and iron." She, almost reflexively, reached for her water.

Oscar had half-watched the whispered conversation while tracking the argument settling between the wolves and non-wolves on either side of him. When KC drank, he asked, "Why did you tell Fenn to take her to ST?"

Laylea sat up. "I didn't."

Oscar argued, "That's what he said."

"What's your problem?" Ali turned from her own private conversation with Harper and Dove to interrupt. "ST is incredible."

Dove concurred. "It's more beautiful than the waterfalls in Caves."

Ali's pupils dilated. "Ahunu says it's like N only better because you're not afraid of anything."

"Like death?" Oscar asked. "Or never being able to shift human again?"

"I'm not gonna try N. I'm not an idiot." Ali rolled her eyes at Oscar.

"Plus, there's no way to sneak any in here." Harper added.

The kids laughed and speculated on ways to get drugs into the school. Oscar, KC, and Laylea focused on their food.

"The best drug you're gonna get in here is my mom's Nut Butter Fudge." Jase tried to get in on the conversation to the left of KC. The other wolves watched like it was a show.

Dove ignored him. "Dr. Fenn only sends you to ST if he thinks it'll help you."

Laylea nodded politely at Jase, but she turned to get more details from Dove. "How does ST help? What do they do to you?"

The table went quiet as half the kids thought about it. The answers that eventually came out weren't helpful at all.

Ali seemed a little disturbed as she said, "I don't remember."

Julia scoffed, throwing her braids over her shoulder. "It's not a big deal."

"Y... y... you know," Carrie offered the most details and none at all. "W... weight and temperature and s... stuff."

"It's so beautiful." Dove scraped at her empty plate. She seemed to have left the dining hall on her own little spirit walk.

"Damn, Jase, your mom makes great fudge." Dustin's deep voice carried down the table.

"Thanks. She makes it once a year for my birthday."

Both ends of the table could get on board with a birthday. Shouts of congratulations and happy birthday garnered echoes from other tables.

"Shut up." Jase waved away the attention. "My birthday was last week. Y'all missed it already."

"We should have cake," Dustin tried to keep the cheering going.

Jase raised an eyebrow at the body-builder. "But I've got fudge."

"Oh, yeah." Dustin grinned and Julia punched him in the gut before he could say anything else.

"Lee." Jase leaned over the table and set a small, cloth bag in front of her. It held two squares of crumbly beige candy. "I'd like to apologize for that little argument we had Wednesday. No hard feelings here about your little Wilding."

From their faces, Laylea wasn't sure the other wolves agreed, but nobody argued.

"You're cool and we want everyone to get along. So take my mom's fudge as a peace offering."

"I can't take your birthday fudge." She couldn't say why but the idea of eating anything from Jase made her stomach churn.

"Of course she'd insult a peace offering."

Laylea couldn't see which wolf muttered that but all the rest got their fur up at it. They stared at her. Carrie stood.

"No, that's not. . . I mean, yes, thank you. Peace is good." Laylea took a deep breath and grabbed a piece of the fudge. "Thank you, Jase. I didn't mean to insult you." She popped it in her mouth. "It's great."

It wasn't.

It tasted like rotten peanuts mixed with salted caramel. She squeezed the bag in her hand as she chewed once and swallowed the whole thing down.

A collective gasp sucked in all the air from that side of the dining hall. Laylea knew it had because she couldn't get any oxygen into her lungs.

"It's p… p…" Carrie wasn't the only one standing anymore but she shoved past Julia and Conner and Dustin to grab Laylea and physically shove the word out. "Poison!"

Sweat instantly covered every inch of Laylea's exposed skin. Her light blue thirties-era jumpsuit sucked to her body. Her scalp itched. Kids were going wild around her but she could only hear bits and pieces through the blood rushing in her ears.

"Why did you eat it?"

"Causes hallucinations."

"Sligh nut is poisonous to shifters."

"Didn't think she'd go for it."

"How would she know? She was raised by thumpers."

"Jase, you the alpha!"

"She's gonna hurl!"

One thought crowded out the voices. Shift. She needed to shift before her insides turned to sludge. She searched for the spark in her gut and only found smoldering embers. She swiped a stack of trays to the ground but the sound did nothing. She had to shift.

Certified hottie Reggie Betts caught her as she stumbled back into the next table over. Shift. Her guts rumbled. The burning in her stomach rose but not to her heart. Kids tumbled over each other, dodging to get out of the way as Laylea's barely digested dinner splattered everywhere. Some shifted and bounded over the tables. Others shifted small and darted through the sea of legs.

Reggie flung her away from him. Harper pushed her away to keep her from slamming Dove into the table.

Shift.

She smelled burning. Was that her? Was she going to explode like LPSS' dreaded phoenix? A part of her focused on the people surrounding her. She spotted ashen-haired, willowy Caliban. Caliban was a tree. She couldn't burst into flame near Caliban.

Shiiiiiiiift.

Nothing.

She tried to back away from Caliban, to run away. But the girl reached out an arm and pulled her in. Benny lay on the table, holding a lighter out at the length of his stubby arm. Caliban, half-shifted, held a branch over it.

"Charcoal will help neutralize the gasses." Caliban held Laylea tighter. "Slow it down. Give you time to get to the infirmary."

Had someone said hallucinations?

SHIFT.

Caliban broke off a piece of her charred branch. She held it to Laylea's lips. "Eat, Lee."

Laylea didn't have much fight left. If she ate the charcoal, maybe Caliban would let her go and she could get far enough away to keep from setting the rest of the werelinden on fire. She ate. And she ran.

Caliban had mentioned the infirmary.

Laylea ran for the glass doors. Mr. Mendenkov tried to intercept her but she barfed again and he darted to the side. Impressive reflexes.

She couldn't shift. She wouldn't heal. She'd die down here and her brother would never know. Clark and Sher would never know. She definitely wouldn't make it to fifteen and she'd never get to apologize to Junior or the rest of the team. Kyle would be all alone. Bailey would have no one to help him control himself when his witch-side got out of control.

A door opened. She recoiled from the green, rotting smells of the Jungle and fell to her knees. The sharp pain sparked some sense into her. She looked at her human hands on the cold stone floor. She had to shift. Everything would be okay if she could shift. She imagined her hands as paws, tried to make the image so. She wasn't surprised it didn't work but she was surprised to find the little bag of fudge lying by her left hand. She'd grabbed it from the table and never let it go. She shoved it into her collar, smelling the fudge as she zipped the pocket up. She could taste the awful rottenness again on her tongue.

That's when she noticed her mouth was still full of Caliban's gift. Saliva had done nothing to break the charcoal down. Chewing sent shivers up her spine. Her tongue wanted to spit the crumbly mess out. But Caliban had said it would help. Caliban had sacrificed her bark for Laylea. So, Laylea swallowed. And swallowed again. She kept trying to get the charcoal down as she pushed back up to her feet and stumbled on.

Deep under the burnt wood, she could still taste the fudge. That taste would never go away. Just like Kyle could never be human again and Bailey could never be—never was—just a normal guy, she would always know that she'd died because she was a freak. Because she didn't know enough not to eat poison. Her mama gave up all her kids. Clark and Sher gave up their kids. They all sacrificed so Laylea could live. And here she'd gone and killed herself.

If only she'd learned how to shift.

Footsteps behind her. Laylea didn't dare look back at the demons chasing her from the Jungle. She ran harder. Breath didn't matter. She couldn't get any into her lungs anyway. Nothing mattered. She just had to shift.

Shift.

She saw the turn. If she could make it to that corner, she'd be in the Medical Wing. She would find the infirmary just beyond. She'd be saved. A claw reached up from the floor and grabbed for her ankle. She fell.

She didn't shift.

"Careful. Come on." KC raced down the corridor behind her. She bent to help Laylea up.

"I can't shift!" She screamed in KC's face and flung herself at the wall when she realized she was screaming. She sobbed, "I'm so sorry."

KC's face melted into a sneer. "Sorry didn't keep me from ST. I thought you were my friend but you're just like my family." Her brown eyes snapped back into place and Laylea could smell the salt in the tears falling from them. "Better than my family. You have to be okay. I forgot you wouldn't know about sligh nuts." The chunnel lighting flashed red. KC's eyes sparked. She yanked Laylea out of her cozy stone nest and threw her down the corridor. "Dr. Fenn will take care of you now just like we should have taken care of you long ago. You won't betray anyone else ever again."

Laylea fell again. She spit bile onto the rough floor. The turn into the Medical Wing was only inches away. She could make it.

"Dr. Fenn, I need you to trust that this school puts these students first." The bulldog voice shut down the chaos storming through Laylea's mind. She froze and laser-focused her lame human hearing on that voice and the four sets of footsteps coming from the Medical Wing.

"Bertram." Boo, Dr. Fenn. "I just want to know, when we start picking students to sell to the research labs, what will the criteria be?"

"It is unfair to prioritize pressers from Mer dorm." Yay, Ms. Crow. "But what else can we do with those who won't learn?"

Shift. She had to shift. She had to learn to shift or Ms. Crow would sell her to a lab and she couldn't go back to a lab. Her mama had worked so hard to get the litter out of the Consortium lab. She had to shift. She couldn't let the Consortium get her. She couldn't let Walter get her. Shift. Shift. Shift.

"I can't shift! I have to shift!"

KC pushed Laylea around the corner, right into the distorted, flying faces of Dean Gorse, Dr. Durrah, Ms. Crow, and Dr. Fenn.

"I have to shift!"

"Ah, to be a teenager again." Dean Gorse patted Laylea's head as he kept on walking past her. "Good luck with this one."

"She's really sick," KC held Laylea up. And then her voice distorted and Laylea heard the teachers laughing with her as she shoved Laylea away from her. "She needs to go to Special Testing."

Laylea tripped forward. A tractor beam of moonlight drew her into the alcove, her feet unable to get traction against a river of bloody vomit. Laughter and howls echoed in her pounding head as the walls and the shelves and the waiting room couch flew toward Laylea, choking her and crushing her into the bare stone floor of her grave.

27

A chill breeze washed the light, fishy scent of the lake over Laylea's skin. Goose bumps prickled her flesh. The gurgling in her stomach felt more like mild seasickness than the pitched ocean battle that had been raging there when she passed out. She remembered passing out.

If she wasn't dead, shouldn't her face be resting on a pillow instead of packed dirt? She opened her eyes. She lay in a patch of crushed grass and crumbling leaves. She rested at the base of a sapling, still human and still wearing a jumpsuit reeking of dried vomit. She visually checked all of her extremities since she couldn't feel them so well. She wiggled her fingers and her toes. Thumbs. As a puppy, she'd dreamed of having thumbs.

Something was wrong with her ears. She flexed her jaw and wiggled it from side to side. The wash of indistinguishable voices cleared a little.

"Lee!"

"Wake up!"

She couldn't muster much concern for them though. She closed her eyes again and melted back into the warm, musky smell of her brothers wriggling around her. Bayard kicked her in the face and she gnawed on the paw until he pulled it away. Rhemy rolled onto her, tussling with Josh. Biggest and smallest, they fought nonstop unless one of the others picked on Josh. Laylea saw Rhemy's white ear. She lunged for it and chewed until she fell back asleep.

A blast of hot air shocked her eyes open. It was like someone had thrown a fish at her, a huge, dead fish. Sound filtered in following the heat and the smell. A roar of fury drew her eyes up to the drooling, tooth-filled mouth of Toby, the depressed bear.

Great. She was still hallucinating.

The bear roared again and swiped at the tree. Bark rained down on her face.

"Lee, wake up!"

She jerked toward the voices. A dozen kids stood on the other side of a Plexiglas wall. Dr. Fenn pointed to the chain-link section.

"There's a hole here. You can get out."

So, not hallucinating. Laylea looked up at the bear again and scrambled out of his way. He might be clinically depressed but at the moment he looked pretty alive. She flung herself past him, racing for the fence.

The hole was only a foot tall. She looked up at Dr. Fenn.

He said, "Shift."

Laylea didn't know a lot of swear words. She'd learned most of hers from one of the ex-soldiers Clark and Sher helped. She ran through all of them while she scratched futilely at the dirt beneath the hole with her useless human thumbs. There was no spark in her. No spark in her belly or behind her chest. She was fully, heavily human. She couldn't even reach in to her psychic tail.

Another roar made her abandon Dr. Fenn's useless escape hole. She scrabbled along the fence, searching for the gate. She found it. But there was no way to open it from the inside. A metal tube stuck out of the gate at knob height on the outside. Even if she could reach through the fence, she couldn't reach the latch inside that tube.

She ran on, stumbling through trees and over the logs that littered the bear's enclosure. She scrambled up onto a cement zoo-designed boulder and slid down the far side. Another roar came from far away.

She planted her back against a tree to see the bear slam himself into the transparent wall. The students jumped back and their cries died for a moment.

Walter had that effect on her brothers. On her too. He'd slam a hand into the grate of their cage to shut them up when they lived in the Consortium lab. The bear slammed the wall again.

White washed over Laylea's vision as if she'd been dunked in a pool of milk. First she smelled licorice. Her stomach clenched. Slam! Her heart pounded. Walter's hand reached into the cage, fishing. Laylea cried. She yelled for him to go away. The giant fingers flicked Josh out of the way. They caught Milo's tiny tail and yanked him from her. Laylea screamed as Walter flung Milo to the bear.

Laylea nipped at her brothers. She drove them deeper into the carefully designed forest. The forest Walter knew every inch of. He plucked Josh away. Rhemy and Laylea threw themselves at the hand but he brushed them off. She tumbled over the rocks and sticks of a clearing, hit her head on the trunk of a wide oak.

The hand came back. It took Bailey next. Scooped up Bailey as he'd looked on the first day they'd met, when he was six-years-old. Laylea latched her teeth onto Walter's ring finger. When he flicked her away, she found her voice. She yelled that she knew what he did. She knew what he was doing to people. She knew and she'd tell everyone.

Her brothers, dead and living, yelled for her to shift. Bailey yelled for her to climb the tree. Laylea felt the tree at her back even as she felt Rhemy and Josh's teeth nipping at her legs, telling her to huddle with them. She pulled herself from the hallucination, forced herself to focus on the real voices yelling from the wall, the real bear coming for her, and the real tree at her back. She snapped into the present when she heard Dr. Fenn's cry.

"Get the girl."

She spun around and shimmied up the tree like Clark had done until she could reach the lowest branch. She swung up and stood to reach the next. When the milky vision washed over her again, she had her arms wrapped around the trunk with Clark's song dopplering through her mind.

This time she was alone in the cage but Walter wasn't alone. He danced with another Consortium scientist, Trask, Rhemy crushed between them, his white ear flopping as they dipped and spun around the mysterious lab equipment. She yelled for them to let him go. But they ignored her, twirling past a black SUV. Both passenger side doors opened and Clark and Sher climbed out into a ray of golden light. Laylea burst into tears. She screamed for them.

"Mom! Sher! Trask is right there! Get her. Get Walter! Dad!"

"Shut up!" The mom's eyes flashed yellow at Laylea. "Lee! Shut up!"

The voice was KC's. Laylea half woke from her vision. She turned to see her friend and the scrape of bark against her cheek brought her the rest of the way back into the real world where the bear slammed his claws into the tree. Laylea held on tight as it shuddered. She should have known that bears can climb trees.

KC pleaded with Dr. Fenn at the edge of the Plexiglas wall. Oscar ran past the other kids to join them.

"It's true," he panted. "She accidentally ate sligh nut."

Dr. Fenn turned away from them. "Don't be ridiculous. No one could accidentally eat sligh nuts. They have a very distinctive taste."

Laylea searched for a way to reach the next branch up.

"We know that," Oscar pleaded while KC abandoned the argument.

She stormed over and flung the gate open. Dr. Fenn leaped over to grab her away. He struggled to hold her and reach back to close Laylea's only way out.

Why was he doing this? Why did Dr. Fenn trap one-hundred-pound her in this cage with a two-hundred-pound bear?

As Fenn's hand grabbed the gate, Oscar shifted. The leopard managed to leap right out of his jumpsuit and land with a roar as the gate slammed shut behind him, the blue suit caught in the closure. The bear roared back. Laylea felt his hot breath on her back, the tips of those razor-sharp claws on her heels. But cold sweat washed down her body, and she felt Rhemy's hot breath, his milk teeth sinking into her ankle. She shook him off and wailed for Mama. Walter turned away from their cage. He faced off with Sher over a steely cold lab table. Clark, the dad, her Dad, lay strapped to the table. Laylea cried for him. She reached her paws through the bars, calling his name.

His eyes popped open and he saw her. He smiled. "Listen to your mother, Little Girl."

Sher looked over, "If you address the problem, Laylea, you won't have time to stress over it."

Walter sliced Sher's throat with four razor-sharp claws. Sher roared.

The tree shuddered. The bear roared again and reached down to swipe at Oscar. He missed.

Oscar danced back. His tail raised swirls of dirt as it twitched back and forth. The bear roared again and leapt from the tree. He circled with Oscar, both roaring and darting in and then away. Again and again Oscar charged, driving the bear away from Laylea's tree.

KC struggled with Dr. Fenn outside the fence. He had trouble keeping her from the fence.

Did he not see what was going on inside? Why would he let two students be killed by a bear? Why would he let other students watch?

Laylea heard an echo of Sher's voice. "Address the problem."

That's what Dr. Fenn was doing. He was getting rid of the problem. And if Oscar sacrificed himself alongside her, so be it. The other students would report that if you asked too many questions about ST, Dr. Fenn would throw you in the bear cage. Two solutions with one bear.

"No!" Dr. Fenn yelled.

The bear looked over at Dr. Fenn tripping backwards over a bonfire bench. Oscar saw his moment. No more feinting, Oscar pushed off with his powerful hind legs, aiming to take the bear down. But the bear wasn't such an easy target. One massive paw cut through the air and connected squarely with Oscar's sleek head.

"Oscar!" KC stood at the open gate. The blood drained from her face as Oscar slammed against the zoo-designed boulder in the middle of the depressed bear's enclosure.

"Get away. You can't help her." Dr. Fenn limped at the gate. He tripped on Oscar's jumpsuit and fell against the gate as he slammed it shut.

Laylea knew now that Dr. Fenn wanted her out of the way. If she didn't drop her interest in Special Testing, he was going to let all three of them die. She sucked in the deepest breath she could manage and screamed, "I won't ask you about ST anymore!"

The bear charged Laylea. He grabbed her up in his arms, squeezing the rest of the breath from her lungs as he turned and roared his own challenge.

There was some panic among the students outside the wall. For the first time, Laylea noticed the ancient, crackly-faced teacher who had demanded she shift at her intake Testing. The old woman hiked up her long skirts and pulled a gun from an ankle holster.

KC pushed away from the gate. She ran straight for Oscar and shoved two fingers against his neck. Laylea wanted to tell her she'd get a better read by checking at the source, under the cat's left front leg. But she couldn't breathe.

A gunshot cracked the air. Toby spun, his body suddenly between Laylea and the fence. His arms relaxed and she could breathe again. Then she dropped out of his grasp. She fell, her legs giving way. The bear reached for her even as he stumbled away. His black, sad eyes glazed over. He tried to roar but it came out a whimper. Laylea watched his one white ear flop bright against the dark sky and then he fell forward. A purple tipped dart stuck out of his back.

Laylea barfed all over him.

28

Laylea suffered the infirmary for thirty-three hours.

Oscar got released to his dorm the morning after he fought the bear. Apparently leopards were a hardy bunch and three broken ribs and a mild concussion were enough to require bed rest but not monitored bed rest.

Fenn had finally administered the antidote four hours after Laylea's sligh nut dosing, so he'd had to inject it directly into her blood stream and that mandated at least a day's observation. The sligh nut was the reason she didn't shift. It was one of the many reasons shifters feared it. Was that why Lucio had thought he'd find it at the black market? Was it also poisonous to other wyrdos?

She declared herself fully healed when she shifted at lights out the day after Fenn tried to kill her. She tried to get Fenn to release her then, but since he respected her even less in dog form, she had to wait until the morning. She didn't get much sleep.

The dorm hadn't been much of an improvement. She skipped all her classes that day. And the next. As punishment for her part in saving Laylea from Dr. Fenn, KC had been given double Presser duties and wouldn't be allowed to audition for any of the extracurricular choirs until next season. She spent all her free time in Sphinx dorm, with Oscar.

So Laylea slept and dreamt of everyone she loved dying over and over.

"Walter! Don't kill my mommy."

Laylea's ears twitched. That voice wasn't in her head.

"The consort is evil."

She nosed aside the bed curtain. Brenda was putting on a lunchtime show for the Mers who had nowhere better to be.

Milly cackled, "You're kidding."

"No." Brenda grabbed her hand. "Jase told me all about it."

"Everyone in Advanced Shifting saw it." Emerald confirmed.

Dove asked, "Did Oscar Luke actually attack the bear?"

"Yeah." Brenda nodded gleefully. "He shifted into that gorgeous leopard body and ran into the cage."

Milly squealed, "They're gonna kick him out of Sphinx. Oooh, I hope he gets Mer."

"Milly!"

"What? He's pretty. I don't need brains too."

"Like that bear would ever hurt anyone." Emerald picked at her nails. "Please."

"Why did she eat the fudge, anyway?" Dove asked.

Milly muttered, "Talk about no brains."

They all cackled and Brenda started doing her imitation again. Everyone jumped in, echoing the name of Laylea's nightmares. They knew about Walter.

Laylea was halfway out of her pod when she shifted to human. The girls froze for only a second before most of them started laughing even harder.

She grabbed the jumpsuit off her bed and struggled into it while her dog brain remembered how to speak with her stiff human tongue.

"You." She refused to cry. "You let me eat that fudge." They stopped laughing. "Not. . . not one of you said anything. You let Jase poison me. And you're still believing everything he tells you, Brenda."

Girls peered out of the bathroom and pushed through the beaded curtain to see what was going on. Laylea raised her voice so they could hear.

"Caliban said Mers look out for each other. She said I'd be safe here. You all had fun Wilding but not one of you stood up for me when the wolves didn't like it. You're so afraid of them, you let them try to kill me. You're sheep. You're all just sheep."

She ran from the dorm before they started laughing again. Laylea left her pod open. She didn't care. Everything she owned was either on her neck or in school storage. She'd never had friends before, she didn't need them now. She shoved through the little crowd at the curtains and didn't look into any of the faces gathered outside the girls' door. She couldn't have seen them through her tears anyway.

She wanted to shift and run. A good long run through the city would feel good. Her mind would have to focus on cars, pedestrians, uneven sidewalks, shop doors, guard dogs, and dangerous litter. She'd have no room in her head for all her worries. She wouldn't be able to think about how KC and Oscar hated her for nearly getting them killed, how if she'd run when Oscar wanted to, he wouldn't have been here to get hurt. Her mind would be focused on her own survival rather than concerns for Oscar's mom, the kids in ST, and her family's safety now that she'd spilled all their secrets in front of Jase Batka.

But she couldn't shift because she was defective. It took her eleven years to figure out she even could shift and now she was going to die without ever figuring out how. Or why. Could her brothers shift?

Her feet had taken Laylea to the Fields. Or maybe it was her stomach. She hadn't eaten since she'd snuck out to the night kitchen yesterday during first session. She could go for a long time without food. Lunch had never even been in her vocabulary until she got to shifter school. And frankly, when the first eleven years of your life feature a diet of kibble, you develop a pretty tolerant palate. So, between the night kitchen and the Farm, it was easy for Laylea to avoid the dining hall.

She ducked through the jungle to the farm's apple grove. It wouldn't be long before Seb started mixing his famous glög upstairs in The Office. Maybe he already had patrons gathering at lunchtime for the hot, cidery specialty. Seb was strict about the drinking age, even if he let Laylea and Diejuste hang out in the bar. But he'd promised to make out-of-season glög the day she turned twenty-one. Patrons half-joked about putting the date on their calendars. Laylea laughed along. But she knew she'd never make it to twenty-one. She'd never get to try Seb's famous glög.

"Lee?"

She looked up to see Ms. Crow waving her over from the other side of the river. She wore a gardening apron over her orange sweater and black jumper. Her long hair was tucked up under a floppy hat but it was so fine, strands were already falling around her face.

Laylea finished her apple and tossed it into the river as she crossed over. The fish who'd gathered around for whatever feast Ms. Crow was feeding them swarmed the core.

Ms. Crow hustled Laylea down an aisle to the tomato patch. She plucked a bright red cherry tomato off the vine and tossed it to Laylea. The fruit burst in her mouth.

"I'm picking off hornworms and stinkbugs and inviting them to learn how to swim," she said. "Help me."

Laylea crouched down. She used to help Clark spot the garden pests that hid on the undersides of leaves. Hornworms thought they blended in perfectly but they were easy to ruffle. A spritz of water or even just blowing on their leaves would make them squirm. Laylea would spot them, bark, and Clark would pick them off. She'd never actually picked any off herself, since she hadn't had thumbs back then.

"You're very thoughtful today, Lee. Near death got you thinking?"

Ms. Crow would know, so Laylea asked, "Is the bear okay?"

"Toby?"

"Is that really his name?"

"Yes. The animal control division that caught him in southern Illinois named him after a character in an ancient TV show." Ms. Crow pounced on a stinkbug. She crushed it. "Whoops. Toby's fine. He got a nice long nap. But he's back up now and moping around just like you. Whoops." She grinned at Laylea to show she wasn't making fun of her.

Laylea pinched off a leaf with a cocoon underneath. "Everyone thinks I'm an idiot."

"I don't think you're an idiot." Ms. Crow reached up to ruffle the leaves overhead as she muttered, "I think Sydney Fenn is an idiot," she sighed. "But I do think you should trust your instincts."

Laylea tilted her head.

"You didn't think it was a good idea to take that fudge from Jase, did you?"

Laylea thought about that. She hadn't wanted to eat it. But she didn't want to make the wolves angrier. She wanted them to like her.

Ms. Crow crouched beside her. She pulled something from her apron pocket and slipped it to Laylea. The blue plastic vial fit neatly in the palm of her hand. If anyone had been watching, they wouldn't have seen the hand off. Laylea peered down at white letters printed on the side of the vial. She had to hold it up close to read the words written sideways. *Drink Me.*

"Ignore that unless you get poisoned again. You would not enjoy it."

"This is a sligh nut antidote?"

"It neutralizes a few other poisons as well. Just a couple drops under your tongue and you'll be okay. It's not a magic potion. Well, it is. But it still won't work instantaneously. Our mother taught us how to make it and we have all the ingredients right here in the Fields. If you need more than this much in your lifetime, though, Lee, you're doing something wrong."

She darted a hand out and crushed another stinkbug. "Whoops."

Laylea tucked the vial into her collar beside the sligh nut fudge. "You've eaten sligh nut, Ms. Crow?"

The librarian sat back on her heels for a moment. She went a little pale before she nodded. "Yes."

"I've never been sick before." Laylea admitted. "Is that what it's like when people get colds and stuff?

She picked off some more pitted leaves and found a stripe of pest eggs while Ms. Crow explained different kinds of common illnesses. "You can feel pretty awful, but it's not like being poisoned. Unless you get a really bad fever, I guess. But you just dunk the kid in a cold bath and bye-bye hallucinations."

"Maybe being sick is like a little death to prepare you for the big one." Laylea dropped a worm into the bucket. Six green leaf eaters lay in the bottom waiting for their big death as fish food. "Maybe I don't need to prepare because I have such a short life."

"What?" Ms. Crow was interrupted by a commotion back by the bridge. "Excuse me." She grabbed the bucket and ran to the end of the aisle. "Stay here."

Laylea thought about Dee. She'd taken the banshee for granted before. Nearly every day she'd been able to look into Dee's face and see that she wasn't going to die that day. She could really have used that reassurance in the bear's cage. But what good did that reassurance do her? She was going to die soon, probably this year, and she needed to be ready.

She spotted a row of red bugs, the nymph cycle of the stinkbugs, and squished them all. "Whoops."

Their color hid them among the ripe tomatoes but it did them no favors on the stems and leaves. Oscar's mother had written to him on red paper. Was she afraid he wouldn't see her otherwise? Or was that just her thing?

Laylea stood up. Dee could check on Oscar's mother. If she met them by water she could see a person's death a long way off. Laylea could tell Dee she knew a user who might be able to lead them to some N dealers. And that way Oscar's mom would also lose her supplier. She just had to get Oscar's address. And he was in Biology right now.

She turned and walked right into Ms. Crow.

"I'm sorry Ms. Crow."

"Shouldn't you be in class, Lee?"

"Yes." She smiled as Dizzy soared over them. "Thanks."

Laylea followed the raven through to the Lakes, which had an exit door closest to the Bio Wing. She was so caught up in thoughts of how she could help Oscar, she didn't stop to wonder why Ms. Crow had changed into a blue sweater.

29

"Come in, Lee." Dr. Fenn limped over to encourage her in the door. She flinched away from him.

Oscar, in human form, sat along the next to last row of lab tables. The left side of his face had dark patches up near his hairline and he had bags under his eyes, but otherwise he looked good. She spotted a free chair behind him, beside Brian. In fact, there were a lot of free seats since Brian was the only kid sitting in the back row. All the kids were a lot more spread out than usual.

Laylea rushed over to take the seat behind Oscar before Dr. Fenn reached the door. She normally sat in the front row but she couldn't handle everyone staring at her. And she was only here to talk to Oscar anyway.

Dizzy coasted in and took up her customary perch on the podium. Some papers on the teacher's desk caught her attention. She hopped over and peered down at the notes, shuffling them with her claws.

Dr. Fenn looked back at the desk. He kept lecturing as he went to gather up the notes and secure them in his little black folder.

"Oscar." Laylea hissed at the back of his head. "Psst, Oscar."

She pulled her notepad and pencil from her collar and scratched out a quick note, addressing it to Detective Dee Morton. She just needed to add Luke's address and then get Ms. Crow to mail it to The Office for her.

Oscar waited until Dr. Fenn's back was turned before he spun around and put a hand on her table. "Look. You may already know all this stuff, but I really need to catch up."

She ran her fingers down his hand and said in a low tone, "Easy."

"Funny." He turned back around.

She looked down at a snuffling sound near her feet. Carrie bumped her head into Laylea's legs.

"Hey." Laylea leaned over to scratch behind the scrawny, tawny wolf's ears. "Thanks."

Carrie dropped her head and crawled back under Brian's chair.

"Since you have all been working very hard, I want to reward you. But life is rarely that kind, so I am going to randomly reward two of you." Dr. Fenn held up a wide-neck beaker with folded bits of paper inside. He shook it and poured them out into an open skull on the table in front of a wererabbit from Centaur dorm. "Pick two."

The girl waved her hands in the air like a magician's assistant. She darted in and snatched two slips from the skull. "And the winners are: Milly and Oscar!"

The class cheered. Until Dr. Fenn announced, "Congratulations, everyone. While Milly and Oscar are in ST, the rest of you get a pop quiz!"

Thanks to the dead silence that followed the announcement, everyone heard Laylea fall out of her chair. Her note and pencil went flying. She popped back up with her hand raised.

"Yes, Lee?"

"Sir, Oscar's missed three days of class."

"Yes, but so have you, Lee. And his absences were approved."

"Yes, sir, but." She withered in the glare of all those staring eyes, especially the unapologetic wolf eyes. "I already know all this stuff. He really needs to catch up."

Brian snorted.

Oscar breathed a sigh but then objected loudly, his eyes darting to Julia Jimenez in the second row. "Hey, you have to have all the attention?"

Laylea shot back before she could think. "Go ahead. Go to ST. I could finish the quiz and still get there before you."

A few kids laughed. None of them were wolves.

"Settle. Lee is actually right. And it's not fair that her name wasn't in the beaker. So it will be Milly and Lee."

Some more kids started to complain but Dr. Fenn interrupted them. "I understand you all want the most deserving shifters to get out of the quiz. So how about this? We'll have a quick oral quiz. Anyone who beats Lee can take her place in ST. Who's in?"

Not one hand raised.

"Alright. Raise your deskpadds. You have fifteen minutes until the bell. If you finish the quiz early, you may leave early."

Brian stood.

"If you do not answer all of the questions, you will be required to attend a special study group on game night at game time."

Brian sat.

Dr. Fenn tapped his armpadd. "Begin. Milly? Lee?"

Oscar didn't even look at Laylea as she walked past him. Dr. Fenn held the door, which was good since Laylea's palm would have left a wet handprint on it. Dizzy flew out overhead and led the way down to the Medical Wing.

For the first time, Laylea turned right instead of left and pushed through the cold Special Testing door right behind Milly.

Whatever Laylea had been expecting, this warm, carpeted reception area was nowhere in the realm of her imaginings. The room was built of actual, normal, non-stone walls. Padded benches, much like the ones in the library, lined the walls to the left. Directly opposite the door they entered through was another door. The whole wall, including the door was painted a soothing, pale green. Just a couple of feet to their right, a glass wall cut the room in half, isolating a computer tower and server-lined walls. Dr. Durrah was busy typing and swiping in this little room, his back to the door. Dr.

Fenn rapped on the glass and then palmed the door lock to lean inside.

"I've brought two for ST."

Dr. Durrah jumped at the sound. He slid a series of dibs drives from the interface padd into his lab coat pocket like he'd been caught reading a dirty novel.

Milly whispered, "I think he's a wererat."

"You don't know what he is?" Laylea whispered back.

"Nobody does."

Dizzy slipped through the cracked-open door. She swooped once around the room, gaining height. Then, as Dr. Fenn pushed the door further open, she swooped down and grabbed a beak-full of dibs drives from Durrah's pocket.

Dr. Durrah never noticed. "I was expecting five."

"I'm so sorry, David. Everyone is busy getting ready for the mandatory Testing coming up."

As Durrah brushed past them, Dr. Fenn gestured at the server room. "This isolated computer tower holds every piece of medical information collected on every student through ST since its inception." He made a point to check the door after he closed it. "This information will ensure the future safety and security of all shifters. Thanks to these records, Dr. Durrah can tell a person's shifter make-up simply by looking at their blood."

Laylea thought he was selling ST a bit too hard.

"Not always." Durrah didn't seem to care for the commercial either. "Let's get started with intake. I'm expected in the city later. Lee?" He stopped with a hand on the inner door. "I am glad you could join us. We haven't had a chance to talk about you and Holding."

Laylea didn't respond. She'd forgotten his interest in her.

"Hi." Milly stuck her hand out. "I'm Milly."

Dr. Durrah shook her hand as he slid open the door to the next room. "Yes, Milly. I've seen you dance. Do they turn off the gravity just for you?"

Milly blushed. "Nah, they turn it off for everybody. Well, not for Kara."

Dr. Fenn slid the door shut behind them and Dr. Durrah swept aside a curtain to reveal a room unlike any other in LPSS. Milly gasped and then fell silent.

Whoever had designed the intake room had either never been to a hospital or spent way too much time in one. The room was decorated in shades of brown, enhanced by soft yellow lighting. Ten stations spread at uneven intervals around the room featured leather armchairs fixed with state-of-the-art medical equipment and a rolling chair with an attached deskpadd. The only thing the decorator had missed was the smell. It looked like an old, private club. But it smelled like somebody had sprayed artificial floral scent over a mass grave. Laylea's psychic tail tucked and her hackles shot up. She expected to go dog at any second for self-comfort.

Dr. Durrah led the girls to a couple of stations at the far end of the room. He helped settle Milly in one chair while Laylea pulled her legs up on another as if she were cozying up with a book.

"Sorry." She uncrossed her legs.

"Interesting." Dr. Durrah took a blood-pressure cuff from the side of the chair and sat on one of the rolling chairs to affix it around her arm. "Are you relaxed, Lee?"

She tried to answer but found all her saliva had dried up so she just nodded.

"Better." Dr. Durrah slipped a squeezy monitor on her wrist and tapped a button on her chair. He rolled away to Milly while the cuff tightened.

A quick jangle grabbed Laylea's attention. She turned to see Dizzy ducking under the curtain. The raven flew straight to Laylea's chair and shoved her free arm off the armrest so she could perch. She'd gotten rid of the dibs drives somewhere. Laylea hoped she hadn't swallowed them.

The cuff hummed and loosened on her arm. Dr. Fenn removed it.

"Lee's pressure is a little high and her pulse rate is quick. I wonder if she's recovered enough from the incident."

Laylea clenched her teeth. If the pressure cuff has still been on, she might have busted it. Incident. Did he mean the poisoning or the bear?

Dizzy croaked and rubbed her head against Laylea's cheek. She calmed.

Durrah rolled over from Milly's side. He removed the wrist monitor and then reached behind her neck. "I'm looking forward to seeing how the sligh nut metastasized in her system. Some say it never goes away but since it's hard to find volunteers willing to take it, there haven't been many studies done beyond ours. Never with such a high dosage."

"Of course, we want her data. I'm just not sure if her psyche has recovered sufficiently to handle the memory enhancers."

"I am going to take good care of our Lee, Sydney. She's very special." Dr. Durrah disappeared.

Dizzy disappeared.

Dr. Fenn, Milly, the whole intake room disappeared.

Laylea suddenly perched in the crook of a wide tree. Sunlight rained down through the breeze-rustled leaves. Green like she'd never seen before created fractals of the sky and she felt every muscle in her body relax as the terrifying smell of the intake room was replaced with the familiar, musky scents of a forest glen. She could hear a creek trickling by somewhere far below. And a pull. She couldn't get out of the tree. It was too high, too dangerous. She was safe here in the wide nook. But she had to get out. She had to go to her house key. It was nearby and she had to get it.

She stood and shook herself from muzzle to tail to prepare for the leap.

Durrah appeared. Floating in midair, he held her down. He rubbed her ears and talked to her in that dumb-animal voice people use when they're pretending to be dog-people. She had to get her house key. It was so close.

"Cessabit. Audite me." Dr. Durrah murmured the words and the magic calmed Laylea.

Her heartbeat slowed. Her need for the key did not diminish but her panic did. She knew where the key was. That was good. That was okay. That was enough. Dr. Durrah didn't have any magic. Someone had given him the words. That was important too. But Laylea couldn't push past the calm taking over her mind to think why.

She lay down in the soft moss covering the tree. She lay without circling even once. She didn't need to. All was right. Dr. Durrah came and went. He slipped a smaller cuff on a rear leg and laid a flexible mat under her chest. She breathed in the happy smells of her puppyhood in the mountains and held tight to the comfort of her house key nearby.

When he asked, she sat up. He took away the tiny cuff and the comfy mat. He held a fabric strip against her spine, from ears to coccyx to the tip of her tail. He measured around her chest and around her neck. She had to stand so he could measure her legs.

She sat again and he was gone for a while but she didn't notice. When he was there, he was there. When he was gone he no longer existed in her world. Her world was perfect and whole and she was perfect.

Then her collar touched her fur. The intake room flashed. Dr. Durrah existed again. He flipped something over in his hands and reached up again to wrap it around her neck. The intake room appeared. Her need for the key vanished. And her panic ratcheted up to seventeen on a scale of one to ten. She jerked away and for a moment everything was okay again. She rested in the perfect nook of the perfect tree in the perfectly singular forest. Then Dr. Fenn held her still. He turned her so Dr. Durrah could see the back of her neck.

Dizzy blocked her view. The raven hopped along the arm of the chair picking at Laylea's collar. Laylea tried to nose her away. She barked. Dr. Durrah and Dr. Fenn were both focused on the clasp of her collar. Dizzy dove in again. She caught a zipper in her beak and wrenched it open. Laylea thought of putting her hand to her neck, to close the pocket, and she shifted so she could do it.

She couldn't feel her house key anymore. Her jumpsuit was wildly askew, almost backwards. She stuttered a question at Dr. Durrah and the man held her face between his hands.

"Cessabit. Audite me."

Latin. Awkward Latin. He'd been taught those words and they were laced with magic. She'd spent enough time listening in on Bailey's lessons with Sher to recognize it. But it had no effect on her. She didn't calm. She didn't have any interest in listening to him. Especially with Dizzy still poking at her collar.

Laylea instinctively reached for her adoptionversary lizard foot. When her fingers touched it, her brain cleared even more. She looked over at Milly who lay back in her chair staring at the world around her with a glow in her eyes. She reached out to touch something Laylea couldn't see.

Sher sent the lizard. Sher, who couldn't keep herself from using magic in everything she created. Sher, who thought she couldn't woogie things, had woogied the lizard to protect her canine-daughter from magic. But that didn't protect her from people.

Dr. Durrah still held her face. He squeezed and repeated, "Cessabit. Audite me."

Dizzy croaked.

Dr. Fenn put a hand on Dr. Durrah's arm to pull him away. "Let's get her inside and strap her down."

If she didn't calm, she was going into ST. And if this was just the intake room, what the phoenix went on in there?

She sank back into the chair, letting her face go slack. She tried to look off into the middle distance like she saw some gorgeous waterfall or butterfly. But she did not let go of her lizard.

"There. She's okay." Dr. Durrah released her. "Let's get Milly's mouse vitals."

He rolled away and Dizzy poked Laylea's hand. Laylea waited until Dr. Fenn followed Dr. Durrah over to Milly to zip up the pocket Dizzy had undone. It was the pocket with the sligh nut fudge. She took it out. Dizzy crowed wildly, sounding like a happy Gatling gun.

Laylea bit off a piece of the fudge, straight out of the bag. She gagged at the taste in her mouth but held it there until she had the bag safely back in her collar.

Then she swallowed. One heartbeat. Nothing. Two heartbeats. She flushed cold. Three and sweat covered her entire body. Four. The buzzing of an electric razor shot spikes of pain through her skull. She cried out. Fenn was shaving Milly. He turned to her.

"David, Lee is having a relapse."

"She's fine."

Laylea's face scrunched up. Dr. Durrah poured alcohol onto a cotton ball and wiped Milly's bare flesh clean. He wiped a needle. Laylea felt all the needles Walter had ever stuck into her puppy flesh. She threw her head back and screamed.

30

Walter shoved Rhemy aside. "You've had your liver. It's your sister's turn."

Laylea didn't care about the mushy liver Walter would let her lick off his finger after he poked her. She wanted Mama. But Mama had gone away again.

When Mama curled up and gave her belly to them, life was beautiful. You sometimes had to kick Rhemy in the face to keep him from hogging all the teats and Josh would steal all of Mama's attention if you let him. But they worked it out and everyone was safe.

Even when Mama was a human, she cuddled them and held them close and made sure Milo didn't get trapped under the towels for too long. She'd poked them all with the sharp needles too. But she squeezed their skin and slid the cold in carefully so it didn't sting so much.

Not like Walter. Nobody else in the lab ever handled the puppies. There was one lady who talked to them and sang to them while she worked. But Walter had banished her from the lab after she offered to help cuddle them.

After that, the puppies cuddled close together, as far from the bars of their cage as they could, when Mama wasn't around. They stuck their noses in each other's fur and dreamed of Mama's milk and kisses.

Walter always got them. He shoved them apart and grabbed whichever puppy he wanted by whichever limb he could capture. He took them out to the cold steel trays and left them, alone, under harsh fluorescent lights or worse; the Eye light. Sometimes he strapped them down to keep them still and if they struggled, he'd zap them with a pointy stick. Then he'd bring the Eye down and leave. Even if you squeezed your eyes tight the Eye light left you blinded. It wasn't so bad if he put you back in the cage with your brothers. But most of the time he didn't. He'd do more tests and keep shocking you if you cried.

Laylea didn't want the Eye. She didn't want the liver either. Liver was tasty when she licked it off her brothers' faces but she hated it on Walter's finger.

Walter carried her away from her brothers. Her view swung from Rhemy's white ear to the door that had swallowed up Mama. Forgetting the threat of the shocker, she struggled. Mama had gone out that door. If she could get out of Walter's hands, she could go find her.

Walter squeezed her. He held her up in front of his face. She trembled. He was going to finally eat her and Mama wasn't here to stop him.

"Hold still, you little bitch."

His breath washed over her, sweet and stinging. He was always chewing, getting his teeth ready to bite down on her little paws. But he didn't gulp her down this time. He let her slide through his fingers until she dangled by the nape of her neck. She squealed. Mama knew how to do it right. Walter hurt her.

"When I clone you, I'm going to get rid of that voice." He pulled the needle out. "Take some time to think about that."

He didn't give her any liver. He stuck her in a new cage, without her brothers. If she had any teeth yet, she would have bit him. Bayard had his milk teeth already and he'd bit Walter. Then he'd cried for hours. Mama said they shouldn't do that again. But Laylea was going to bite him. When she got teeth, she'd bite his horrid smelling liver finger. She curled in on herself and cried, alone. Josh called out to her. He wailed until Walter slammed a hand against the grate of their cage.

"Oh, Walter." Mama came back! "They'll get too cold if you leave them alone. You want them to grow up healthy, don't you?"

Mama cradled Laylea to her chest. She kissed her only girl and soothed the cold, bare, shaved spot on her leg.

"Come on, let's get you back to bed." Dr. Fenn's voice brought Laylea back to reality.

She'd been aware of him and Dr. Durrah arguing. But she didn't remember Dr. Fenn picking her up. She didn't remember him carrying her into the infirmary.

He passed the curtain that closed off the small ward she'd had to stay in the night he'd thrown her to the bear. He carried her into his private office and laid her on a cot in one corner. Laylea's stomach seized up.

"I've got you, Laylea. Mama's got you. Are you hungry?"

Mama gathered up Josh and Milo. She set them on the pile of towels where they all cuddled together.

Laylea rolled to her side. Her whole body jerked in protest to the poison in her system.

"Here you go. Just let that out." Dr. Fenn held a steel bowl up to Laylea's face. She recoiled from it but he caught her barf anyway.

"Walter, leave her alone. I'll measure them after they eat." Mama climbed into the towel nest with Bayard and Rhemy. She lay down and kissed the top of Laylea's head as she shifted.

"Laylea!" Dr. Fenn slapped her face. "Stay with me, Laylea. Can you hear me?"

Laylea squirmed.

She didn't want to lay down in the infirmary. She wanted to be alone. She needed to be alone for some reason. It was important, but her mind kept drifting back to Mama's warm milk and her brothers. Maybe if Dr. Fenn went away she would remember. She'd be safer, she knew, if Walter went away.

Not Walter. Dr. Fenn.

"Dr. Fenn." She blinked her eyes open wide. "I'm just tired."

"Of course you are. Sleep then." He stopped slapping her. He turned at a sound in the outer room. "I'm going to let you sleep here in my office so you won't be alone. I'll make sure you are never alone." Dr. Fenn said this as he left her alone in his office, closing the door until just a sliver of light cut across the tile.

Laylea fell back into the thick pile of towels and brothers. Mama nosed her in the belly. She shoved her away from her sleepy brothers until she was alone. Alone again with Walter and the Eye and his sharp needles.

A long croak echoed through the lab. Laylea's eyes popped open. She wasn't alone. Dizzy snapped at Laylea. She poked at her collar.

"Go away." Laylea rolled off the sterile cot. She hated that lonely bed. She wanted to curl up with Mama and her brothers.

Another croak. Laylea sat up. She'd fallen with the tangled sheets to the tile floor of the infirmary. Not stone but not carpeted. Three feet away, Dr. Fenn's desk and chair sat on a large rag rug. Laylea reached out but she couldn't quite touch it. She crawled after her hand. The raven flew at her, pecking incessantly at her head. Half way to half way to the desk, at which speed she would never get there at all, Laylea felt the remaining apple and tomatoes of her sad lunch take up arms against each other in her gut. She whipped around to grab the trash can that had been at the foot of the cages in Walter's lab. Here, in real life, there was nothing. She barfed an impressive lake of yellow bile all over Dr. Fenn's clean tile. It didn't smell like apple. It smelled bitter.

Like sligh nut. She'd poisoned herself.

Dizzy poked at her. Laylea opened her eyes. She lay beside her sick on the floor, no energy to sit up, fighting Walter's binds and the blazing terror of his Eye. Dizzy nipped at her fingers. Laylea dragged one hand up to her collar. Dizzy helped her unzip the right pocket. The blue vial leapt into her hand. She'd need two hands to unscrew the top. Something wrong with that design since she only had one hand.

Josh had trapped her other paw, chewing at the dried milk in her fur. She nipped at him and Rhemy nipped at her but Josh rolled off.

Laylea twisted the top off and dropped it. Dizzy nabbed the top before it rolled into her vomit. Laylea lay her head down. She tried to bury under Rhemy to block out Walter's posh tones threatening Mama. Dizzy croaked right in her face. The blue cap clattered on the tile.

Poison, Laylea thought. Antidote.

She squeezed two drops under her tongue.

The steel walls of the lab faded away with the desperate whimpers of her brothers echoing from their cage. Laylea could still hear the long-forgotten voice of her Mama pleading with Walter to let her take the puppies away, to let them all live. If he loved her at all, he'd want this for them.

Soon the pleading faded too. Laylea pushed herself up on Dr. Fenn's cold tile, extricating her hands from the tangled sheet around her. She took the cap from Dizzy and put the vial of antidote back into her collar. She started to follow the raven back to the cot but the warmth of the rag rug, so close under Dr. Fenn's desk, called to her.

She dragged the crisp sheets with her, shoved his chair out of the way, and curled up in the dark cave of the desk's footwell. She wanted to circle, but even as a tiny human, there wasn't enough room. So she collapsed and let sleep drag her away, back to her first memories while Dizzy stood guard.

"This is a priceless opportunity, Rhea." Walter looked Mama right in the eyes. "I am not giving it up for something so fleeting as love."

"These aren't opportunities, Walter." Mama kept one hand in the crate, rubbing the puppies. "They're your kids. Honor your great-grandfather and let them live normal lives."

"Nobody has shifted in my family since my great-grandfather. The medical data I gather from these specimens will help change that."

"Shifting isn't about data. It's magical. You cannot use their DNA to make yourself a shifter, Walter." She took his hand when his scent turned sour. "Just let them go home with me. I'll bring them in every day for study."

"I can't trust you anymore, Rhea."

"You don't have to. Remember I've implanted trackers in all of them. You can follow them every minute."

"If they are at your apartment, Rhea," Walter said it like she was a small child. Bayard growled and Mama put a quelling hand over his head. "If they are at your apartment, I will not be able to capture them shifting."

Rhea laughed. "We don't shift until puberty, Walter. It's going to be a few years."

"If you want more time with them, you're welcome to stay here." Walter dropped Rhemy into the cage. "In fact, I think you should. Stay here."

"I am staying here, Walter. It's time to feed them again." She lifted Rhemy and Laylea and Milo out of the cage.

Walter exhaled his sweet-sour breath on the back of her neck and all over the pups. "It's not me who'd be searching for them, Rhea. The Consortium would never stop hunting you and they have their fingers in international pies. There is nowhere you could go."

Laylea sat up. She hit her head on the bottom of the desk and suddenly Dr. Fenn's face replaced the chair.

"Don't hurt yourself," he barked. "You're very important."

Laylea had never remembered so much before. Her mother's name was Rhea. Her mother had a black diamond over her eye that stayed with her like Laylea's white diamond.

Walter was her father.

She couldn't think that too loudly. She couldn't think about how awful it was. She didn't want to know. She tamped the horror down deep and focused on the thing that really mattered.

Walter wanted data on shifters. Laylea the puppy hadn't known what that was but now she knew. Walter was willing to lock up Laylea and her brothers and Mama for the rest of their lives just for the small slice of shifter data they could offer. What would he do if he got a hold of the iso-tower in ST?

Walter, the Consortium, had found her. Mama had hidden her with the Hillens but the Consortium had found her and people had died. If they found her here, in a school filled with shifters, already trapped underground with a state-of-the-art medical facility, it wouldn't just be the Mer cry anymore. Nobody would ever see the sun again.

She had to leave LPSS.

31

Laylea slowed her heart. She had to get away from the school. But she also had to seem rational or Dr. Fenn wouldn't let her leave the infirmary. She pulled the sheets out from under his desk and folded them.

"Thank you, Dr. Fenn. I'm feeling so much better now."

"I should hope so. You slept through dinner.

That meant fewer people around. She could get to the tunnel without being seen. But then she had to get through the gates. KC and O would be at Phys Ed tonight. She was supposed to be there too. It was their one class together. She could go ask them how they got out the night Dr. Fenn tried to feed her to a bear.

"No wonder I'm so hungry. There'll be food in the Night Kitchen, right?"

Dr. Fenn's arm buzzed. He looked down and stood up. "Yes. Stay out of stressful situations. We do not want a repeat of this."

Laylea didn't reply. She took her good luck and fled. She'd barely cleared his office doorway before he answered his call.

"Yes. I've thought about it and yes." He whispered but didn't close his office door. It was like he was too distracted to think of it.

Laylea had the main door open when she heard the word 'money.'

"It's a lot of money. I couldn't say no. Plus the Enforcer would owe me a favor. Think about it in those terms, if you must." Dr. Fenn paused to listen to the other person. "I'm so glad you agree. You wouldn't hesitate to sell all the student's medical records for that, either. So I'll continue to do as Dr. Durrah asks to avoid suspicion."

Laylea's intake information would be in her medical records. Ms. Crow had said all the records were for internal use only but she couldn't have known Dr. Fenn was a traitor. If that information got out, there was no doubt the Consortium would find her, and quick.

From the other room, Dr. Fenn replied to his contact, "That means getting KC Dells into ST tonight." A pause. "Yes, I'm wondering about that too. I'll send the order now."

Did he suspect KC was really a wolf? If he got her into Special Testing, Dr. Durrah would know just by looking at her blood. She had to get to KC and then she had to get out.

Laylea ran for the Fields.

She found the class just as Mendenkov was finishing up his standard beginning of class speech.

"So you're not training just for some health benefits. You must train because someday you're going to have to fight for your very survival."

Mendenkov had no idea how soon that might come to pass if Laylea's information got out of the school. She squeezed through the kids till she found KC standing off to one side.

When Mendenkov started running through the class plan she whispered, "I need to talk to you."

KC barely glanced away from Oscar clowning around with Jase and his Sphinx wolf buddies. "If it means I can stop seeing that, sure."

Laylea's heart sped up at the sight of the guy who'd tried to save her palling around with the people who'd put her in a position where she needed to be saved. She couldn't really comprehend it. He was laughing with them. Jase caught her eye over Oscar's shoulder. The malice in his face froze her heart.

"What do you need, Lee?" KC pulled her away from the group.

Laylea led the way into Farms. "I need to get out of this school."

"Oh, so not, like, just help with sociology or something."

"How did you and Oscar get out?"

"KC Dells," Mendenkov's voice carried easily into Farms. "You're excused from class. Go see Dr. Fenn in the infirmary."

KC was already dragging Laylea farther away before she finished repeating her question. "Come on, they'll find us here. Why do you need to get out of the school this time?"

"You can't go see Dr. Fenn."

KC paused to shoot her a look. "Duh. Why do you need to leave?"

"I can't tell you." Laylea had thought about it. KC would be safer if she didn't know anything. She already knew too much and Laylea wasn't going to give her any more information for the Consortium to torture out of her. "But my being here is putting everyone in danger."

"Because of your ties to thumpers?" KC asked as she dragged Laylea through the tunnel into Lakes.

"What? No."

"Your friend Kyle has proven he can take care of himself. Oscar's mother is hanging in there."

Laylea stopped. "How do you know Oscar's mother is okay?"

KC pulled her around the far side of an old willow, into a brush of ferns. "He wrote her."

"And?"

"She replied with another red letter. Oscar got it after he left the infirmary."

"Just a paw print?"

"A letter. His family won't protect him if he leaves school without permission. So you're on your own this time."

"KC!" Several voices echoed through the tunnel.

"I don't want him to come with me. I have to go on my own. Everyone here is in danger if I stay."

"He'd have to take you as far as the first gate. Lee, do you think maybe you might still be hallucinating from the sligh nut? You ate an awfully big piece."

"I'm not. You know I have my secrets just like you have yours. And if you don't want yours revealed, you'll help me get out of here."

"Hey, KC! I know you're back here," Jase called from close by.

"KC, look at me." Laylea took KC's arm. She pushed up her sleeve and rested her fingers on the five available pulse points. KC looked down at her arm and then her eyes floated up to Laylea's.

"Sleep."

It was classic conditioning aided by a simple spell and Laylea had never tried it in practice. A grunt witch would have said the spell in Latin, like the spell someone had made for Dr. Durrah, but Sher believed most people wanted, deep down, to do what you tell them, which is why conditioning worked. Clark would be quick to point out that other people, like Sher, generally wanted to do exactly the opposite of what they were told, which is why conditioning didn't work on everyone. KC didn't speak Latin, so Laylea didn't use it. She didn't entirely expect the spell to help at all except that she was getting the idea that some witch had worked a lot of charms on the shifter school and somehow made the students more susceptible.

KC blinked four times. She took a breath to speak. And collapsed.

Laylea helped ease her to the ground among the ferns. She covered her with the ground-brushing leaves of the willow and dashed up the slope and into Jase and Oscar.

"Where's your girlfriend, Fido?" Jase stepped up into her face.

"Don't you know, Jase?" She watched Oscar backing away. "I don't have any friends, anymore. You win."

Oscar ran.

"Yeah, go get the others, Luke. We've got a rare opportunity here." Jase shoved her.

Laylea stumbled a ways back down the slope. "I said you win. I'm leaving school."

"You're a Presser, Fido," he said. "You can't leave. Morioka catches everyone. And you wouldn't be welcome in Montana, so she'd have to eat you. What do you think about that, Fido?"

Morioka wasn't going to eat Laylea. She was pretty sure of that. But she didn't plan on getting caught. She'd be far from Chicago before any of the wyrdos found out she was missing. They would be in as much danger as the students if the Consortium found Laylea. She could never see them again. Or Bailey.

Jase took her silence as fear and he loved it. "You're an orphan. You've got no family waiting for you."

Not true. She had lots of family. She just had no idea where most of them were because they'd all run away from her. She was too dangerous for anyone to keep around.

His grin widened. "Aw, the puppy cries. Might as well just kill yourself here, Fido. You're a thumper-sympathizer and there's nowhere for you to hide."

Had she pissed off all the wolves? Did they tell their parents and her name was out there already? Maybe she should just hide in here where she was at least surrounded by stone and magic. Maybe she should just let Jase kill her right now. What did it really matter? She couldn't fight the Consortium and Dr. Fenn and all the wolves. She could go back to ST, eat the rest of the sligh nut, and take off her collar. Barfing and hallucinating in a magically-induced soporific forest would beat a lot of other ways to go.

She looked up at Jase. Before she could say anything, he hauled back and punched her across the jaw. Laylea flew backwards. She landed in the ferns on fur-covered haunches and rolled all the way down the slope to the lake. Jase crunched down the hill after her.

Her jaw didn't hurt. She'd healed when she shifted. It took away all the residual nausea she hadn't even realized she was still fighting from her self-dosing. She was meant to be a dog. She liked being a dog. She'd rather just live a dog's life.

The lake rippled her reflection. She stared at her birthmark. The depressed bear didn't piss off everyone he met. She should be more like him. Then she thought of her mama's black diamond. Her mama didn't leave because she was pissed at Laylea. She left because she wouldn't put up with Walter's bullying just like Sher and Clark left her to save all the others being bullied by the Consortium. None of them gave up because life got too hard for them.

Let the wolves hate her. They had practice at it. Some of them had practice. KC wasn't one of them. Carrie was trying not to be one of them. Even Big Mo seemed like he could be a decent guy. She'd let Jase hate her. But she wouldn't let him bully her anymore. She had just conditioned her only friend into a magical sleep. Why couldn't she do the same to Jase?

She came to this conclusion at the same moment that Jase kicked her into the lake. The pain in her side was sucked in by the pain in her gut and both shot up behind her heart. She shifted.

Two strokes got her back to shallow waters. She took a moment to straighten her jumpsuit. It clung to her like Milly's in the shower, only with no curves underneath. But it gave her an idea. She brushed her hair back giving Jase a minute to look at her.

"Come on in." She tried to purr sexily. "The water's nice."

"Get out here, so I can kick your ass."

"But, Jase." She dropped her eyes like Milly did when she was talking to any boy other than Oscar. "You know I've always liked you."

She was pretty sure, from his face, that she was doing something wrong. But it didn't matter because Oscar appeared at the top of the slope, followed by the rest of the class.

"Lee! What are you doing in the water?" Mendenkov shouted as if she were in a different Field rather than just down the hill. "We're not swimming today. Jase, good on you for helping her out. KC, you're supposed to be in the infirmary."

From where she was, Laylea couldn't see KC, but the class was on the top of the rise. They could see into the deep ferns and water grasses.

"KC." Mendenkov did not like to repeat himself. "You respond to me, Coyote."

Jase pushed through the greenery. Laylea half-hoped he'd scream when he saw her.

"I saw Lee knock her unconscious, Mr. Mendenkov. She's a menace."

Oscar leapt down the bank. He shoved past Jase to kneel beside KC. "She's not bleeding. KC. KC, wake up."

Laylea knew it wouldn't work.

She got worried when Mendenkov slid down the slope to where Oscar was trying to pick KC up. "I've got her. I've got her, Luke."

The Phys Ed teacher straightened his Sox hat and then lifted KC easily. He shouted orders as he strode back up and through the kids. "Kadota, you're in charge. Run through drills until I get back from the infirmary."

"No!" Laylea yelled.

Oscar spoke over her. "I am staying with KC."

Mendenkov didn't even bother to argue. But when Laylea hustled after them, he turned on her.

"You will stay here, Lee. I don't know what part you had in this but you are trouble. You stay here."

Oscar and Mendenkov vanished through the trees with no way to know KC wouldn't wake up until Laylea told her to.

32

While everyone watched the trio marching for the Lakes' door, Laylea ran up the slope toward Caves. Kadota caught her with one long, loopy Orangutan arm before she got three steps. He folded her in to his fuzzy chest and said, "Ook" in a way that could have meant practically anything.

"She needs me." Laylea tried to fight him. Kadota didn't even notice.

He shifted something in his throat and shouted, "Line up for a single-file Caves run."

The students limped into a new grouping.

"Dude." Dustin tripped into Big Mo because he wouldn't take his eyes off Laylea. "What the hell is wrong with that Fido?"

Big Mo circled up with Jase and the other Sphinx kids, "She really hit KC?"

"I watched her do it. She hit KC and then hid her."

Raederie, the most beautiful girl in school, asked, "Why didn't you stop her?"

"Why would she hit her best friend?" Julia busted into the circle.

Laylea couldn't respond to any of the chatter. She just didn't care.

She'd failed again. KC was going straight to ST, do not pass go, and she couldn't defend herself thanks to Laylea.

"Some of you have taken geometry, right?" Kadota hadn't let her go even after she stopped fighting.

The kids half-heartedly rearranged into a clumpy line.

Gorgeous Reggie Betts defended Laylea. For an instant her heart lifted. "Hey, you know how freaked she gets about ST. She probably thought she was helping."

Dustin shoved him out of line. "KC was ordered to the infirmary, not ST."

"Does she understand the difference?" Raederie shoved in front of Dustin and pulled Reggie with her. "She's an orphan."

"And she was raised by thumpers." Reggie whispered this like it was a shameful disease.

"Whatever. She's whacked." Julia lined up in the back of the pack.

Dustin finally looked away from Laylea as he agreed. "Yeah, a total weirdo."

Laylea stood up. Kadota didn't let her go, but he let her stand up. Dumb Dustin was right. She was a Wyrdo. She was a member of Team Wyrdos because she wanted to leave the world a more just place. And as Lucio said, no matter how they tried to stop him, many heads are better than less than many.

"Run. Caves and back." Kadota covered Laylea's ears before he yelled. Then he uncovered them and told her, "I don't trust you. You and I will wait here for them to come back. Why did you hit your friend?"

Laylea thought about that. Was she acting crazy? It had been kind of crazy to spell KC to sleep when conditioning her would have been good enough. Or even just telling her to hide. She only wanted to keep KC's secret. But she wanted so many things.

"Huh?" he pressed.

She muttered, "I didn't."

He held on tighter. "You're as crazy as people say. Why would Jase make that up?"

She laughed at that but didn't answer. She wasn't getting out of

Kadota's grip, so she relaxed and tried to work things through in her head.

She had to leave LPSS so the Consortium wouldn't invade and get all the kids to experiment on. But. Dr. Fenn was selling their data to someone outside the school. Maybe he was selling to the Consortium. Maybe he was selling to Walter. Even if they didn't know Laylea was there, that would put them all in danger. Her leaving wouldn't help anybody.

To keep KC safe, to keep herself safe, to keep everyone at the Shifter School safe, she had to stop Dr. Fenn. She had to get proof and show Dean Gorse. And she couldn't do it herself. She needed a team.

KC was the hacker. She could find the proof if anyone could.

In order to save everybody, she had to save KC.

Kadota had relaxed a little. Not enough for human Laylea to wriggle out of his grasp. But canine Laylea could.

Without reaching for that burn in her stomach, without straining for her tail, Laylea popped.

She slipped right out of Kadota's arms and slithered out of her jumpsuit.

He nearly caught her tail but it proved too slippery for his long Orangutan fingers. She raced through the Lakes' swampy lowlands and hit the swinging door with her head down. She bounced off the far wall of the corridor but gained her feet with barely a pause.

The infirmary door was cracked open when she got there but there was no one in the front room. Ali burst out of one of the curtained rooms with a bandage half-wrapped around one wrist. She stared at Laylea while Laylea panted, trying to catch her breath.

"Fenn's not here."

Laylea barked.

"You looking for KC?"

She barked again and bounded between Ali and the door.

"Oscar and Mendenkov took her across the hall."

Laylea hit the closed door of ST so hard she heard her shoulder pop out of joint. She shifted even as she rolled into the alcove shelves. She slammed a door open and pulled on a new jumpsuit. Then she burst into ST, ready to argue with Dr. Fenn and Mendenkov together.

She wasn't ready to fight Oscar.

Nobody paid any attention to her.

Oscar had all their eyes. "Dr. Durrah, everyone knows you have better diagnostic equipment than the infirmary."

Oscar was holding KC on his lap on a bench. Dr. Durrah was just coming out of the server room. Dizzy barely made it out before he pulled the door shut. She hovered around him, hopping from the light trough to the ground to the bench beside KC, trying to get her beak into Dr. Durrah's pockets.

"I'm sure Dr. Fenn has all the necessary equipment in the infirmary."

Oscar persisted. "You're a doctor. She's unconscious. We don't know why."

"She's unconscious because Lee hit her over the head," Mendenkov corrected. He leaned against the wall beside Lee, his hands shoved into his shorts pockets.

"No, I didn't."

"No, she didn't." Oscar looked over at Laylea as he echoed her.

"Oscar, let's take her back to the infirmary." Laylea couldn't say too much, but if KC wasn't already in the intake room, she had a chance.

"She needs a brain scan," he insisted, his eyes a little panicked.

Dizzy poked at KC's hair. KC didn't react. The raven poked harder and Oscar reached for KC's face when she shifted in his arms. But, of course, she didn't wake up.

Dr. Durrah sighed. He wasn't wearing his lab coat and looked like he was trying to get out the door. "I'm sure she doesn't need a brain scan."

"Right," Laylea agreed. "And without a baseline scan, how much could you actually see?"

Laylea realized her mistake as soon as Dr. Durrah's interest shifted. "KC hasn't been through ST yet?" He glanced at his armpadd. "I guess we can bypass her vitals for tonight and get her settled into a bed for observation at least."

"No!" Laylea started her objection before any logical argument occurred to her.

Oscar shook his head at her. "Thank you, Dr. Durrah. Lee, go away. You're just paranoid from the sligh."

"I'm not." She knew she was fighting a losing battle. She wasn't going to be able to fight KC's way out of ST. But if KC weren't enthralled, she might be able to fight her own way out. She kept talking, giving reasons, citing all the medical knowledge she'd gained from being raised by a veterinarian/genetic scientist. She just needed to delay them long enough.

"Thank you, Lee. But I'm a doctor, you know. I'll take good care of KC." Dr. Durrah slipped KC's charmband off and handed it to Mendenkov. "She can't have this on for the scans. Can you put it in storage with the rest of her belongings?"

Laylea fumbled with the clasp on her collar. Her fingers didn't want to work right but she finally got it off and ripped at Sher's lizard foot.

Mendenkov helped Oscar lift KC, explaining he'd like to stay but he had to get back to class. Even distracted, Laylea got the feeling Mr. Mendenkov didn't want to go through the second door.

Laylea chewed at the threads holding the lizard foot on her collar. It seemed Seb was a skilled seamstress. Dizzy tilted her head at Laylea. When Oscar stood, she was pushed off the bench. She flew over and landed, awkwardly on Laylea's shoulder and snapped at the collar.

Dr. Durrah had to duck to keep KC from falling since Oscar wasn't anywhere near big enough to hold her by himself. Between the two of them, they got KC up into a fireman's carry over Dr. Durrah's shoulder.

Dizzy croaked and tried to grab the collar with her claws. She actually scratched Laylea's face. When Laylea dropped the collar, it was grabbed out of thin air by, apparently nothing. She caught it and held it up while Dizzy used her sharp beak to slice through the threads. She had the lizard foot free in seconds. Just as Oscar slid the door open.

"Dr. Durrah." He turned just enough that Laylea was able to tuck the lizard into KC's shoe, against her skin. "Let me help you."

"No, Lee. I think Oscar is right. You're still suffering from the sligh. You need to rest."

He turned away, wrenching Laylea's fingers from the lizard foot. Dizzy vanished. She couldn't even feel the raven's claws on her shoulder. She felt calmer. Like a literal weight had been lifted from her shoulders. And she felt the pull of Bailey's gifted house key.

All of those mysteries diminished beneath the joy in her heart when KC's eyes popped open. She blinked and raised her head to figure out where she was. Then she spotted Laylea and remembered. KC glared at Laylea until her eyes caught on something just to Laylea's right. Something, perhaps, perched on Laylea's right shoulder. KC's mouth dropped open as her eyes tracked up and overhead.

Then the door closed and Mendenkov shoved Laylea out into the alcove.

33

Before the outer door closed, a scream rang out from the Special Testing intake room. Laylea threw herself back at the door. Mendenkov caught her.

"I guess she's awake," he murmured.

Ms. Crow, Dr. Fenn, and Dean Gorse all hurried around the corner into the Medical Wing.

"I know what's going on." Laylea yanked out of Mendenkov's arms. She'd wanted to yell, but she couldn't work up the energy. She meant to run at Dr. Fenn but only walked. She'd confront him now in front of Dean Gorse and it would all be okay. But before she reached them, she felt the old burn in her gut. "I know why you want me—" she began but was unable to finish her accusation. She shook off her jumpsuit.

"Yes, yes, Ms. Woodford." Dean Gorse strode forward, his sturdy black Oxfords clicking on the stone. He crouched. "I know all about it. I've spoken to Jase Batka and if you'll apologize to him and the werewolf community, we can put all this nastiness behind us. Could someone tell me why I'm talking to a dog?" The dean creaked back to standing and turned his back on Laylea. "Ms. Crow, can you take her? I'll smooth things over with Denier when Durrah and I see him later.

We've already missed a fine dinner over you, girl." He said this to Laylea as Ms. Crow brought her up to human level. "That's a very nice collar. Clever. But personal items are for well-behaved students." He removed her collar and handed it to Mendenkov. "Rex, can you put that in storage for me? Dr. Fenn, your office. Let's make certain you've got the right data before we sell our souls."

Dean Gorse and Dr. Fenn cut left into the infirmary. Laylea considered her shock. She'd almost revealed that she knew about the scheme but Gorse already knew. And so did Ms. Crow.

"Lee, I'm so sorry about this." Ms. Crow turned to leave the Medical Wing.

Mr. Mendenkov had vanished. Laylea had been able to see both doorways. He didn't go back into ST. He didn't follow Fenn and Gorse into the infirmary. He'd just disappeared.

Ms. Crow took Laylea to the library. "I know I should put you to bed, but I don't think you'll sleep. If you need a book, write it down and I'll get it for you." She set a piece of scrap paper and a display pencil from the old-time card catalogue on the floor by her front desk. "If you stay here, I'll let you know what's going on with KC."

She started to head behind the counter but stopped as if she had something more to say. She looked back down at Laylea and then walked around and pushed into the protected texts room.

Laylea wasn't about to sit there and do nothing. She didn't have any proof. Telling Gorse wouldn't matter if she did. Maybe she could show it to all the students. But no, they all thought she was mentally disabled due to the sligh nut fudge. She had to get the proof out of the school to someone who could do something about it. Maybe KC could help her get ahold of the Enforcer. He'd have to do something. It was kind of right in his name.

Step one, though, was still saving her friend.

She stood up and turned to the doors. They burst open and she was bowled over by a skinny black cat and a Hispanic girl with wild hair. Oscar and KC rolled her and then dashed to the row that led to their bright nook. When she didn't move, Oscar came back and threatened to grab Laylea by the neck. He had a dark blue jumpsuit tied around his middle. It tripped him up enough that she easily bounded out of his way. She leapt onto a chair, up to the table and hurled herself at Oscar's back. He rolled out of the way, swatting her toward the bright nook as he did. She ran. The cat laid chase.

Laylea ducked under the French chair while Oscar leapt over it. If she wasn't sure he was playing or herding, KC made it clear. The girl dove on Laylea and cuddled the hell out of her. She ducked as if something were being thrown at her and flash shifted to white wolf and back to fully-dressed girl.

"I'm so jealous." Laylea hadn't even noticed herself shift. But her state of undress made her complaint more poignant.

"Here," Oscar tossed her the jumpsuit KC had dropped at the library entrance when she first tackled Laylea. "We found it in the alcove."

He unwrapped the other from about his waist and stepped into it before he climbed over the French chair.

KC knelt on the bench seat. "What did you do to me?"

Laylea sat beside her. She kept her eyes focused on buttoning up her jumpsuit. "I'm sorry. I thought if I put you to sleep you'd be safer."

"Not that. I get that. Makes sense for a certain value of nothing-you-could-really-do-to-keep-me-from-Fenn." She looked over at the French chair, though Oscar had sat on the bench on Laylea's other side. "I mean I can see things I've never seen before."

"And I can see them if I touch her." Oscar reached around Laylea to take KC's hand. He joined her in looking at the back of the French chair. "Like the bird."

"That's Dizzy." Laylea felt such a sense of relief that she could talk about the raven. "She can write but she won't. All she's told me is her name."

"Why can we see her?" KC asked.

Laylea squinted at the back of the chair. "I can't."

Oscar scoffed. "But you're looking right at her."

"That's where she always hangs when we're back here. She's the one who showed me this nook in the first place." She grabbed their clasped hands and not only could she see Dizzy but she also lost the eerie sense of calm that had settled on her. "The lizard foot from my collar is charmed to protect me from magic. I guess it works on anyone."

"There's no such thing as magic." Oscar couldn't finish the sentence with a straight face.

Laylea dug in KC's shoe.

"Stop it! You know I'm ticklish. That's why I wear shoes. Hey, where did Dizzy go?"

Laylea held up Sher's sneaky gift. "Without it, the intake room would be a very hard place to want to leave." She looked between the two who were still goggling at the back of the chair. "How did you get out of ST?"

KC pulled herself together first. "Durrah put me down in a leather chair. I was trying to figure out where the bird came from. Then he sat Oscar in another and I saw Oscar's face. I screamed. He looked dead. Happy. But dead."

"I was on a mountain overlooking the most gorgeous veldt. I could have run for days if I felt like it. You're right. I didn't want to leave. Durrah and KC didn't even exist anymore." He looked like he wanted to go back.

"All I saw was a room with rich-people chairs and medical equipment. Durrah spun around when I screamed. He tried to strap me down. I remembered you knocking me out. When I woke up, this bird I thought you'd made up was haunting me. Then it looked like Oscar was dead. There was no way I was going to let anybody trap me anywhere. But Durrah wouldn't let me go. Kept talking in Latin, too. So, I kicked him where my dad taught me."

"That is so not nice," Oscar said.

KC raised one eyebrow at him. "I have three brothers. I learned effective, not nice."

"It worked," Oscar admitted. "Durrah was on his knees when she pulled me out of my veldt. The raven," he corrected himself with a nod at the bird, "Dizzy drove us out of there. I thought she was attacking so I shifted to defend us but as soon as we got into the lobby, she pecked at the door until KC opened it."

"I locked the inner door first," KC grinned.

"By slamming my paw against the palm reader." Oscar massaged his shoulder.

"I didn't see the one on the floor," she retorted. "Then Dizzy led us here. She took us a roundabout way, but at top speed. Are you okay?"

Laylea realized they didn't have much time before the faculty would be looking for KC and Oscar. As much as she wanted to celebrate having her friends back, she knew they had to get to work. "Dizzy, can you stand guard for us?"

The raven croaked at her and flew away down the row.

"I know I've been acting crazy and I'm sorry. But I overheard Dr. Fenn earlier and then Dean Gorse just confirmed it, in front of Ms. Crow and Mendenkov." She took a breath. What would she do if they still didn't believe her? "They're selling student medical information to someone outside the school."

"Not to mention they're messing with our brains in there," Oscar growled.

"If my intake information gets out there, someone at—"

KC interrupted her, "a big scary place will figure out it's you and they'll come steal you away."

"They'll come do medical experiments on all of us." Laylea corrected her.

"Oscar, if we get the proof to your dad, can he help?" KC asked.

Oscar was already shaking his head but he said, "Yeah, I might be able to convince him to take it to the council."

KC said, "I can get it to the Enforcer."

"I thought you said you never want to meet the Enforcer."

"*You* never want to meet the Enforcer. He's my godfather."

Oscar blanched.

KC stood. "Can you get to Morioka, Lee?"

"Yeah. You believe me?" Laylea stood too.

"Yeah." KC shuffled her feet. "Sorry I doubted you."

"It's okay," Laylea said. "Someone's charmed this place to keep everyone calm."

Oscar scoffed, "Except Jase."

"And Emerald," KC added.

"And Merrilynne. How do we get proof?" Laylea asked.

"I need to get into the iso-tower booth."

"That server room in the ST lobby?"

"Yes. I should be able to trace log-ons and downloads showing that the information isn't secure and that Dr. Fenn has accessed it. I can also look for a record of the kinds of tests they're doing on students. I'm not sure how we prove that he's selling them. If he messaged the buyer, I could probably find a record of it on his personal drive."

Oscar stood and tugged on KC's twin ponytails. "I think all we have to prove is that he accessed the files. The ST data is isolated by an order from the council. They'll have to investigate why he downloaded them."

"Then let's go." KC headed for the French chair. "Pardon me, Dizzy."

Laylea reminded her, "She's keeping watch."

"Right." KC frowned. "Think your mom could make some lizard feet for us too?"

"KC, how are we gonna collect the data?" Oscar asked.

"On the dibs drives in my charmband. I can carry a drive in my pockets. Laylea can put one in her collar. And you'll look very pretty with my charmband on your paw."

Oscar looked at Laylea and then pointedly at KC's arm.

"Oh shit, my charmband is in storage."

"And so is my collar."

"And we have no idea where storage is." Oscar pointed out.

"Not true." Laylea handed the lizard foot to KC. As soon as she let it go, she felt her house key calling to her. "I can find it."

CHARACTERS

- **Adele Lagat** - *see Lagat, Adele*
- **Adrien Denier** - *see Denier, Adrien*
- **Ahanu** - student, thunderbird, Mer dorm
- **Ali** - student, hawk, Mer dorm
- **Amal** - brownie, co-owner of Brown's Resale, member of Team Wyrdos
- **Bailey Hillen** - grad student, witch, Laylea's brother, aka Bailey Woodford
- **Barrett, Elan** - sociology teacher, wolf
- **Bayard** - Laylea's biological brother, dog
- **Benniker** - zoo guard, wolf
- **Benny McBride Greene**- student, turtle, Sphinx dorm
- **Bertram Gorse** - *see Gorse, Bertram*
- **Beth** - aka Jukebox Beth, former regular at The Office
- **Bianchi, Enrico** - music teacher, wolf
- **Big Mo** - student, maned wolf, Centaur dorm, aka Maurice Braga
- **Brenda Samborsky** - student, works in Executive Wing, python, Mer dorm
- **Brian** - student, gorilla, Sphinx dorm

- **Britny** - student, goat
- **Caliban Meillissene** - student, linden shifter, Mer dorm
- **Carrie Marshall** - student, wolf, Mer dorm
- **Chad** - receptionist at surveyor's office, Laylea's contact
- **Chef Tod** - LPSS chef, Shetland pony
- **Chloe Serra** - student, moose, Sphinx dorm
- **Clark Hillen** - former conditioned force soldier, pilot, Laylea's adopted father
- **Conner Stone** - student, wolf, Mer dorm
- **Correnti, Toni** - shop teacher
- **Crow, Elizabeth** - librarian, counselor, Raven shifter, aka Lizzy
- **Davis Rucker** - childhood neighbor of Laylea and Bailey, lost a leg
- **Dee Morton** - homicide detective, banshee, member of Team Wyrdos
- **Denier, Adrien** - Council Enforcer, wolf, KC's godfather
- **Dizzy** - raven, invisible to most people
- **Diejuste** - voudon loa riding Jane Delphine, member of Team Wyrdos
- **DJ Delcampo** - Daniel Joaquin, wolf, KC's brother
- **Dove Betts**- student, tiger, Mer dorm, twin to Reggie
- **Drouillard, Jean-François** - shifter historian, French, hummingbird
- **Durrah, David** - LPSS doctor, head of special testing
- **Durant, Felzer** - client of Laylea's, stock analyst
- **Dustin Huono** - student, wolf, Sphinx dorm
- **Emerald** - student, singer, selkie, Sphinx dorm
- **Fenn, Sidney** - school doctor, gorilla
- **Grandpa Delcampo** - dean of Montana Shifter School, wolf, self-declared Alpha of the Americas, KC's great grandfather, aka Luis
- **Griffin DeGee** - student, gryphon, Sphinx dorm, aka Griff
- **Gorse, Bertram** - dean of LPSS, Lipizzaner

- **Harper Pemberton** - student, rhesus monkey, Centaur dorm
- **Jase Batka** - student, wolf, Sphinx dorm, grandson of the Detroit Alpha
- **Jay Doe** - recovering Conditioned Force soldier, Laylea's "uncle"
- **Jeannie Nellwin** - doctor, Kyle's wife, KJ's mother
- **Josh** - Laylea's biological brother, dog
- **Julia Jimenez** - student, wolf, Sphinx
- **Junior Leo** - apartment manager, boogeyman, member of Team Wyrdos
- **Kadota** - student, orangutan, Centaur dorm
- **Kara** - student, Centaur dorm, dating Reggie
- **KC Dells** - student, wolf pretending to be a coyote, aka Karly Carlotta Delcampo
- **KJ Nellwin** - Jeannie and Kyle's kid
- **Kyle Nellwin** - homicide detective, vampire, believed by some to be dead, Jeannie's husband
- **Lagat, Adele** - shifting teacher, pigeon
- **Laylea Hillen** - student, dog, Mer dorm, member of Team Wyrdos, aka Lee Woodford
- **Lee Woodford** - see *Laylea Hillen*
- **Lucio** - brownie, co-owner of Brown's Resale, member of Team Wyrdos
- **Luke, Oliver** - councilmember, leopard, Oscar's father
- **Madam Fan Hu** - Laylea and Bailey's landlady
- **Madame** - French teacher, spider
- **Mendenkov, Rex** - gym and health teacher, wolf
- **Merrilynne** - student, koi, Mer dorm
- **Milly** - dancer, student, mouse, Mer dorm
- **Milo** - Laylea's biological brother, dog
- **Morioka, Yaksha** - Captain of Chicago PD 44 division, demon, dragon, member of Team Wyrdos
- **Murph** - student, cheetah, Sphinx dorm
- **Ned Biggerson** - knitter, The Office regular

- **Nemo** - a canine neighbor of Laylea's and Bailey's, true German shepherd
- **Onioka** - Yaksha Morioka's mate, demon
- **Orin Morton** - co-owner of Brown's Resale, brownie, Dee's brother, member of Team Wyrdos
- **Oscar Luke** - student, leopard (black panther), Sphinx dorm
- **Patrick DelValle** - student, wolf, LPSS student alpha, Sphinx dorm
- **Peter** - student, fox, Mer dorm
- **Raederie Rivers** - student, selkie, Sphinx dorm
- **Reggie Betts** - student, tiger, Centaur dorm, twin to Dove, dating Kara, aka Reginald
- **Rhea** - Laylea's biological mother, dog
- **Rhemy** - Laylea's biological brother, dog
- **Rico Stanis** - author of the *Ten Percent Plan*, fox
- **Riva** - student, sloth, Centaur dorm
- **Roger** - former student, friend of Durrah's, victim of the Chicago Fire
- **Sanna Luke** - artist, leopard (black panther), N addict, Oscar's mother
- **Sean** - former student, friend of Durrah's, victim of the Chicago Fire
- **Seb** - bartender at The Office
- **Sher Hillen** - doctor, witch, Laylea's mother, aka Katherine Coogan
- **Sue** - neighbor of Laylea and Bailey
- **Theresa** - student, lion, Centaur dorm
- **Toby** - bear in Lincoln Park Zoo
- **Vaughn Howe** - student, wolf, Sphinx dorm
- **Walter Bowman** - Consortium therianthologist, Laylea's biological father, true-human
- **Wanda Bargo** - LPSS administration, elephant
- **Woodford** - Laylea's brother, killed by the Consortium, true dog
- **Yaksha Morioka** - see *Morioka, Yaksha*

34

Not a one of them thought it was a good idea to go back to the Medical Wing. But that's where the key led them, so they traipsed that way anyhow with Dizzy flying ahead to keep watch. Since KC held the lizard, she was the only one who could see the raven. Her whispered reports had them ducking into classrooms and down hallways the entire way to the alcove.

There were only two doors in the alcove. The Infirmary and ST. Laylea walked right past them. The draw of the key pulled her straight to the Medical Wing clothes closet. It wanted to pull her into the clothes closet. They searched through every cubby but couldn't find any kind of secret stash or hidden compartment. The whole time they searched, they each kept looking over their shoulders for any of the many faculty who must be searching for them. Each time they saw nothing. Except KC who saw Dizzy watching around the bend.

They'd stopped worrying about being caught and started worrying that they would never find storage when Big Mo slid open the infirmary door. Oscar dropped behind the couch, Laylea fell as her body shifted in shock, and KC just held a far-too-big jumpsuit up against her. Big Mo didn't even look their way. He limped on down the corridor, around the corner, and out of sight.

Laylea barked. She'd found a dark spot on the ground that matched the palm locks by their pods in the dorm. She stepped on it. Nothing happened. But, of course, she'd never been paw printed. Oscar crawled over to place his hand on the dark square.

Click.

One side of the shelves released from the wall. Laylea squeezed through with KC and Oscar hot on her heels. The thin tunnel behind the shelves had no light trough. A sliver of light from the alcove drew a line on the tunnel wall, but that was it except for a distant, flickering glow far ahead. Together, they crept along the rapidly shrinking tunnel. The ceiling brushed KC's head by the time they reached a wall with a four-foot tall opening. Laylea had to leap up to get through it.

The other side opened into a deep cave with hundreds of cubbies carved into the walls. Only two of the standing lamps around the room were lit. Laylea smelled gas. This part of the school was so old, it had no electric light. Trunks and suitcases and KC's stuffed backpack sat on the ground with other scattered and stacked cardboard boxes.

In the middle of it all, Rex Mendenkov stood rifling through a cubby, wearing Oscar's snare-snap hoodie.

In hindsight, they might have tried hiding until Mendenkov left, but Oscar didn't think it through before he yelled, "Hey, that's mine."

Mendenkov spun. He dropped a wallet and handful of jewelry. He was going for his armpadd when Laylea spotted his treasured White Sox hat sitting on an ancient-smelling trunk. She ran for it. The Phys Ed teacher saw where she was going a second too late. He had no hope of catching her in the tight tunnel but he chased her anyway.

Laylea bounded out of the shelves and careened around the blind corner leaving the Medical Wing before it occurred to her that she should give him a chance so he'd keep chasing her and not go back to the storage cave. She doubled back and ran right past him as he took the corner. She rebounded off the wall with twice the speed she'd had going in. Mendenkov threw himself at her and missed by a mile.

She led him through hallways she'd discovered her first week in LPSS when she'd gotten lost every day, several times a day. She avoided the more popular evening gathering areas, Musicians Row, the Theatre District, Gaming Central, and led him back to his home court, bursting through the door to the Jungle inches ahead of his grasping hands. She didn't see the Linden roots weaving across the main path until she was rolling through them. But she found her feet and swerved off the path.

She leapt over boulders and using the moss-covered logs piled up everywhere, vaulted herself into the crook of an old tree to rest a minute and catch her breath. Mendenkov doubled over right inside the door. When he could straighten up, Laylea saw the evil smirk that filled his face. He peeled off Oscar's hoodie and shoved it into an empty cubby. He pulled his Bears jersey over his head in that one-handed yank boys use.

Then he tapped his armpadd and gasped out, "Secure Field doors."

Clicking echoed through the Fields, quiet sounds from afar as bolts slid home.

Mendenkov never looked behind himself as he continued undressing and placing his clothing carefully into one cubby. Laylea let him hear her tumble out of her leafy bower but then aimed for moss to muffle her paws. She dashed across the path, hearing his roar as the Phys Ed teacher shifted into his wolf form. It took him two bounds to reach her resting tree but by that time she was rolling in the fishy mud at the edge of the river. She crawled under a twisting pattern of roots and slipped into the water beside a swirling bundle of leaves and twigs and debris.

The current was stronger than she'd expected. She'd planned to paddle to the far bank and climb out still here in the Jungle, but the river gave a fig for her plans. It dragged her, sometimes head up, mostly muzzle under the water through the Jungle, past the mountain wall and underground for ten meters before she popped back up, gasping for breath, in Farms. The current eddied around the wide bends that collected water in rivulets and directed it towards the various gardens before it dipped back underground for yards before popping up into the next watering hole. Laylea banged off the banks and spun through the bends. She didn't once catch enough breath before being dragged under.

Reeds, cattails, and bamboo shoots crowded the fourth pool. Laylea grabbed at these, slowing until she was able to sink her teeth into a bitter reed. She half-swam, half-scrambled to the bank and dragged herself far from the shore before she risked stopping to cough the water from her lungs. Mendenkov's howl rang off the transparent ceiling. Even now, it surprised Laylea that the people walking around in the Conservatory up there couldn't hear him. She waited for him to howl again before she coughed up more water. He was moving swiftly. Too swiftly to track her in this dim starlight. He was trying to frighten her.

And if she was honest, it was working.

She had to find a way out of the Fields. The river eventually ran all the way around back to the Jungles. But she didn't think she had the guts to dive back into that. She squatted at the edge of the elderberry rows and emptied her bladder onto soft soil where it wouldn't make much noise. She risked a dash back across the path, then belly-crawled as far into the shallows as she dared, covering herself in mud again. Then she slunk slowly to the end of the nearest bridge and waited.

It wasn't long before Mendenkov appeared on the far side of the bridge, sniffing fiercely as he loped along. He was a lanky wolf. One ear had a chunk missing and while he was a general mix of browns, the limp fur on his tail was all black, not the most attractive wolf she'd ever seen. He'd sniffed nearly halfway across the bridge before he caught the scent.

Laylea shut her eyes and envisioned rich soil. She conjured the thick, black, forgettable scent of invisibility and imagined cloaking herself with it. It wasn't exactly any kind of magic Sher had taught Bailey, but it calmed her heart. And it worked.

Mendenkov tripped right past her in his rush to the elderberry bushes. The instant his tail cleared her airspace, Laylea padded low and soft across the bridge and ran hell bent for leather to the Jungles.

She didn't imagine Mendenkov would be fooled for long and he was back on her tail even faster than she expected. She leapt over logs and bounded up boulders to leap from tree to tree and soar down into impossible landings on moss-covered slopes, through tangles of roots to the main entrance to the Fields.

Mendenkov howled in triumph, she guessed to remind her that the doors were all bolted, in case she'd forgotten. She hadn't. He just hadn't seen Caliban grow a root through the doorway after he came in. The door hadn't shut, so the door hadn't bolted. If you listened very closely with your animal senses, you could hear the buzzing as the door tried to complete its mechanical duty.

Caliban raised her roots to let Laylea race by without slowing. When Laylea fell into the corridor, the door fell shut, bolt slamming home at last. The boom was followed by a plinking of something small and metal bouncing off the cobbled wall.

Kyle's cursed mortice key lay at her paws. The key that would use anyone to get it closer to Onioka's prison had escaped from storage. Had Mendenkov dropped it? Laylea hesitated to pick it up. Would it let her go back to KC and Oscar or would it pull her outside?

It was better that she take it. She knew the key's dangers. She knew she'd have to fight it. Better she risk her own weakness than leave it for someone who'd have no idea what horrors this key could unleash. She scooped the key and its chain up in her teeth.

The mortice key niggled at her but so did her far away house key. She set her mind to Bailey's magic and let it pull her to her friends. With no Dizzy to keep watch, Laylea made a slower way back to the Medical Wing. But people so rarely looked down. She kept walking, confidently, and nobody stopped her. The alcove was empty. She wouldn't have noticed the gap between the shelves and the wall if she hadn't been looking for it. But the house key had moved. It pulled her to the right hand door. The ST door that could only be opened with thumbs.

Laylea didn't dare bark. She didn't know who was on the other side of that door with her house key. Maybe there was another way. She trotted over to the closet and ran down into the storage cave again. She started to sniff through the lower cubbies, not sure what she hoped to find hidden amongst the abandoned belongings of pre-phoenix shifter kids. Whatever treasures were there, the key didn't give her peace to find it.

She followed the pull deeper into the cave, down an alley she hadn't seen before. She passed rows and rows of cubbies like the school had expected to have thousands of students instead of just under three hundred. If she hadn't had magic dragging her along, she would never have found the large doggy door that led out of the cold storage cave and into a disturbingly warm and dark room smelling of artificial flowers and death.

Before her eyes even adjusted she knew she was in the ST intake room. A chair had been shoved against the dog door, but Laylea only needed a few inches of clearance to get in. She didn't even notice the chair until she trotted out from under it. She caught her bearings and ran under the curtain and nosed open the door to the lobby. She had to scrabble at the crack to get it started, but it slid easily after that.

The lobby was empty. The key pulled her to the glass wall of the server room, the iso-tower booth as KC had called it. Oscar popped out from behind a stack of servers.

"You scared us," he mouthed through the glass.

She tilted her head at him, her own heart pounding.

He opened the door to let her in and did a complicated gesture with his hand against the palm reader when he closed it.

"Seals it," he explained. "Nobody else can get in until I leave."

KC appeared from the back of the small room. "Lee! I can't hack it. It's bio-protected."

"Which means we need Fenn's thumbprint and blood match," Oscar explained like he'd always had this information. Though from KC's expression, Laylea guessed he'd just learned it seconds ago.

"I've got one more workaround to try. Give her her collar, Oscar." KC typed like a madwoman on a raised access padd.

Oscar led Laylea to the far side of the tower where her collar hung from some highly technical plastic thingie extending from one of the server racks. "We took everything in the box. Just a house key and a roll of dibs drives? If there was anything else, my money's on Mendenkov having it now.

If he was right, it was Laylea's money on Mendenkov. So much for her ghost-hunting cash. She spit the mortice key out of her mouth and nosed it at Oscar's foot.

"Sure." He unzipped the second pocket and tucked the cursed key in. His eyes caught on something else in there. Was she going to have to explain why she kept the sligh nut fudge? Because she really didn't know.

It wasn't the fudge. Oscar pulled his mother's red note from her collar. "I threw this away."

Laylea held his gaze. It was a note from his mother and she would have prized such a thing above a never-ending book. So she'd rescued it and flattened it out and carried it with her. Just in case he ever wanted it.

Oscar couldn't seem to find the words he wanted.

"Guyseses!" KC hissed with cautious glee. Her fingers never stopped typing.

Oscar tucked the note back into Laylea's collar and zipped it up. He wiped his eyes as he stood, though Laylea couldn't hear it in his voice. "We in?"

"Si, mis amigos." KC inhaled sharply. "Oh my phoenix. I've got it, all the download records and log-ins. I'm gonna save a screenshot first. Whoa, this is—"

The keypad sparked. Quick as a snake, KC smacked her charmband and the dibs drives off the interface. She snatched her hands away just before a clear tube slammed shut around the tower. Alarms squealed and bright red lights flashed in the chamber.

A calm, pleasant female voice intoned, "You have violated council-sanctioned security procedures. Please wait for the proper authorities. You have violated council-sanctioned security procedures. Please wait for the proper authorities."

35

Oscar bolted for the door. KC caught the back of his jumpsuit and pulled him back just as they heard voices in the hallway.

He hissed, "We have to get out before they get in."

She hissed back, "Not that way," and dragged him between two servers. "See that slice in the carpet? Lift it."

Oscar looked at KC like she might have sligh nut poisoning. Laylea scraped the carpet back with her paws to reveal a wooden floor with a notch cut out just big enough for a human hand. Laylea hopped aside. Oscar fit his fingers into the notch and pulled up. A rectangular section of floor tilted up, revealing a staircase leading down into darkness.

"We've done dark, mysterious stairs before," Oscar said. "Nothing to it." But he didn't move.

Until KC kicked him in the back. "Pick up Laylea and go. I've got to get my charmband."

Laylea did not like the few seconds that KC was out of sight but she couldn't do much except hold as still as possible under Oscar's arm. They were four steps down when the door to the lobby slammed against the wall and they heard Fenn, Gorse, and Durrah rush in. Seconds later KC pretty much dove through the trapdoor. She reached up outside it to hold the carpet on as she pulled the door shut behind her.

Then the three were trapped in the dark again. KC put one hand on Oscar's shoulder and they made their way down, step by step.

Only eight dusty, disintegrating steps later, they hit the bottom. Mendenkov couldn't have stood upright down here. Their eyes adjusted to the darkness a little, but Laylea didn't feel safe moving.

"Whoa." KC's voice echoed. "You guys see that weird glow everywhere?"

"I can't see anything anywhere," Oscar replied.

Laylea barked. KC moved her hand to touch Oscar's hand on Laylea's chest.

"Magic," KC breathed the word.

"There's no such thing as magic." Oscar said it again and snorted.

The low room stretched on as far as Laylea could see, in every direction. She couldn't see too far though, because a ten-foot-round cement column rose from floor to ceiling every ten feet. In every direction. Residual magic coated every surface; ceiling, floor, columns, the stairs. It was like someone had wanted it to be visible.

"Okay. We appear to be beneath our subterranean school," Oscar observed. "Which way do we go?"

"I vote away from here." KC headed away from the stairs.

Oscar tugged her in a different direction. "Let's go to the library. If any other room has access to this, it'd be the library."

"The library is this way." KC turned back in her direction.

Oscar shook his head. "No. It's this way."

Laylea was still trying to reorient herself to the iso-tower booth. She had no idea which way the library was.

KC came back. "Really?"

"I'm a cat." Oscar preened. "I always know where I am."

They headed north.

Just as the unchanging landscape threatened to destroy even Oscar's self-touted navigation skills, they saw blue light ahead. As they got closer they saw that the lights were pools; some enormous, others just a few meters across. Each pool of water was encased in a net of sparkling light.

KC stepped up to one of the pools. When she let go of Oscar and Laylea, the lights disappeared and all they could see were uneven columns of water rising to the ceiling. KC reached out and touched the water. She pushed through, into the column, and drew her hand back wet.

Oscar inched up next to her and reached out his hand. The pool shocked him. Laylea felt the electric jolt to the tip of her tail. KC took his hand.

"Okay, try now," she said.

"I don't want to."

"Oh? Are you a werechicken?"

Oscar glared at her, already wincing as he made his hand reach for the water. This time, it slid through.

"Great." KC dried her hand on her hair. "I know how we're getting back upstairs—well, up one level at least."

"I think it would be a better idea to find another staircase." Oscar tried to walk away.

"I think we should get up there, get some copies of this screenshot, and get out of the school before all three of us are thrown into ST."

Laylea growled.

"Right, or worse," KC agreed.

She prepped to jump up into the water.

"Hold on," Oscar pulled her back. "There's a koi pond in Jungles. The Jungles door is closest to the library."

"You can find the koi pond?" KC asked, clearly doubting.

"I'm a cat," he repeated.

"Right. You're a cat." KC let him lead the way among the pools and the columns. "You don't want to go up through the pools because you're afraid of water."

Oscar glared at her over Laylea's head. "I'm not afraid of water." A few minutes later he added, "I just don't like getting wet."

They found the river. It rushed silently through the underground. Laylea shivered. All that water was pretty when you weren't being dragged along at its whim. At places light shone through but then shadow would cover the river at other places.

Laylea barked as they passed another dark section.

"We're in Farms." Oscar brushed the ceiling with one hand.

KC poked her head up into the river. "Oh, and this is where the river goes under the gardens." Her hair dripped. "Why can't we see the roots of all the plants?"

The roof glowed with the same visual magic as every other surface. Laylea would bet both her keys that the roots reached that barrier and turned aside just as they would if they hit stone in the real world.

It disturbed her that she was no longer thinking of this as the real world.

She barked and leaned out of Oscar's arms in the direction she thought the Jungles lay. It was easier to navigate with the familiar river running alongside them and they moved a little faster.

"What do we do if we run into Merrilynne?" Oscar asked.

She was the only koi he knew by name. The other two tended to keep to themselves. They were brother and sister and seemed much more the quiet, wise type she'd expect fish to be. Although there was clearly some wisdom in Merrilynne's unshakeable distrust of wolves. Laylea looked up at KC and revised her assessment. Merrilynne didn't like the wolves across the board. She didn't talk to Carrie, not even in the sad-little-sister way that many of the older Mer adopted with the stuttering wolf. Would she treat KC differently if she knew the coyote line was just an act?

"Here, take Lee." Oscar handed Laylea over to KC. "Think that lizard will let us breathe underwater?"

KC laughed. Laylea sang out. She approved the handoff. She hadn't entirely gotten over her battle with the river yet.

Oscar took KC's hand. "Just don't let go of my hand until I'm all the way through."

"I won't let go until you do." KC held Laylea tightly against her chest.

Laylea had to consciously relax her claws. Both Laylea the dog and

Laylea the human knew that digging into KC's chest would be bad. She chanted at her racing heart. *I will not kill another soul today.* With all the magic flowing through this underground, maybe the water could hear her. She sang out a war cry and sent her mental chant at the water. *Our lives are in your hands and you must not throw them away.*

"Deep breath on three," KC said. "Ready?"

Oscar and Laylea nodded.

"One."

KC and Oscar stepped right up to the edge of the water.

"Two." They bent their knees.

"Three."

They all sucked in air and before Laylea was quite ready, KC leaped up into the water, Oscar right beside her. They sliced upwards and as soon as Oscar let go, KC reached up to stroke. Pulling and kicking against the water, she dragged them towards the dim light far above.

They broke the surface long before Laylea expected them to. It was so startling, she almost forgot to breathe. The sound of Oscar sucking in air reminded her. She grabbed at the oxygen and found herself free to swim on her own.

Oscar reached the shore first. KC pushed Laylea to help her reach the shallows before she stood.

"Come on, there are towels in the cubbies." She struck out through the foliage.

"Hey!" Oscar hissed.

KC stopped. "So you're a little wet. Suck it up, kitten. We made it!"

Oscar pointed. "The cubbies are that way."

KC swiveled to the right direction. Laylea bounded after her, happy to be alive. Oscar sluiced water from his hair. He was probably regretting the long-sleeve jumpsuit.

They found dry jumpsuits and after KC changed her Keds, she tucked the lizard, still dripping wet, into the new shoes. She took a towel with her and dried her hair as they tried to casually walk the short distance to the library.

Oscar cracked the In door. Laylea slipped through. Ms. Crow

wasn't behind her counter and no other faculty lay in wait for the three. She barked.

"Nook?" KC asked as she headed that way. She popped a deskpadd out of a table without even stopping. The two girls sitting there looked up and blushed.

"Hi, Oscar."

"Hey, Milly."

"Hi, Oscar." Brenda imitated Milly.

"Bren."

Oscar and Laylea hustled to catch up with KC. She slowed in the stacks to make Oscar palm the padd and then sped up again. When Laylea reached the nook, KC had set the padd on the bench and was rubbing her charmband in the dry section of her towel even as she swiped and typed one-handed.

"We might be able to print and send it through Oscar's contacts to get the image to his mother. She's also more likely to believe us than anyone else."

"If she's sober." Oscar tossed an extra jumpsuit into the nook.

Laylea tilted her head at the faded 1930's suit. It wasn't his style at all. Then he threw the book. She dodged and fell against the French chair, catching an elaborately carved leg in the small of her human back.

"You're welcome." Oscar kept his back turned until she'd pulled the jumpsuit on.

"Shit, shit, shit." KC had set each of her three dibs drives on the padd.

Oscar crawled over the chair to her side. "What? The dunking destroyed the drives?"

"No. The screenshot never copied over. I must have done something wrong." She punched her thigh.

"Or you're still a genius and the security system worked." Laylea crawled up onto the bench on her other side. "Clearly, there are more people in on this than just Dr. Fenn. Maybe you can find something on the faculty server."

"I'm on the faculty server. That's why I used Oscar's log-in. I'd have to read through all of everybody's emails to find anything. It's impossible." KC pulled her legs up to her chest and buried her face in her knees. "Go away, Dizzy."

Laylea looked around. She didn't see the raven anywhere. She put a hand on KC's neck and Dizzy appeared on her own lap. The raven was nipping at KC's pant legs and croaking. Oscar pulled the book he'd thrown into his lap and started flipping through it, looking for something.

"It's okay, KC. We'll figure something out." Laylea didn't know what. "Maybe we can get some kids to remember what happened to them in ST. That'd be something."

Even as she suggested it, she thought of how Sher hadn't been able to restore any of Clark's memories. Sher was a world-class witch and geneticist and the one who'd stolen his memories in the first place. If she couldn't fix it, what hope did they have?

"Hey, maybe it's not a bad thing." Oscar held the book up to defend himself when they turned on him. "Not the selling our private info thing. But, look, ST was started to figure out how to cure the depression so many shifters suffered living underground. Maybe sharing all this shifter medical data could help researchers find a cure for other things, like N addiction."

Laylea choked. "That's not what they'll use it for."

"They stole that medical data." KC hissed at him. "There's nothing in the admissions forms that say you're gonna be tied down and experimented on. I don't care what they use the info for, the way they're getting it is wrong."

"You haven't seen what addiction is like." Oscar flipped a page so hard it ripped.

"I've seen plenty of awful things, rich boy. Most of them a result of people not caring about other people's privacy. They'll mess with us."

"How does it hurt anyone to know more about how shifters work?"

"Because." Laylea tore the book from Oscar's hands. She stood to throw it into the stacks. "Then they'll want to take us apart. They'll want to cut us open and see the data first hand and try to recreate it and attach pieces of me and pieces of you to someone like Jase or Mendenkov."

"Don't you make fun of me." KC jumped up and pushed Laylea. "I'm not joking."

Oscar pulled KC away. "Wow, you really don't do well with sligh nut poisoning, Lee."

KC shoved him away from her. "If you don't want to help, just run back to your wolf buddies.

"I'm not hallucinating!" Laylea yelled, not caring what the other kids in the library thought. "That's what I'm hiding from!"

"What!?" KC turned away from Laylea. "What do you want, Dizzy?"

The cushioned seat they had just been sitting on flipped off and crashed to the floor.

36

KC grabbed Oscar and Laylea's hands. They all watched Dizzy hop into the hollow bench. She snatched up a beakfull of something, which finally muted her raucous croaks. It took her two tries to hop up to the edge of the bench and dump a variety of drives on the carpets. There were old-fashioned thumb drives, power drives, penny drives, and some dibs.

KC dove for the padd. But it had been flung against the stone wall when Dizzy opened her hiding place and lay cracked and unusable on the comfy pillows. While KC tried inserting a variety of drives, she said, "I think Dizzy wants you to put the lid back on." She glanced up. "How is that not hurting your face, Oscar?"

Oscar fit the seat back on the bench. Laylea noticed he didn't peek inside as he did.

"This isn't going to work. It doesn't even have a slot for the thumb or power drives."

The pile of drives slid and vanished except for a few that fell onto the floor. Laylea picked them up and followed KC and Oscar past the French chair. Some kids looked up as they passed other nooks and the central study tables. Milly giggled, but nobody said anything.

Oscar hesitated when KC sprinted to the far side of the counter.

She didn't even notice. The drives scattered on the low side of the counter holding Ms. Crow's deskpadd and Laylea grabbed onto one of KC's ponytails just so she didn't keep freaking out when things moved on their own.

KC had already tried her palm on the padd. She grabbed Oscar and dragged him closer to try his palm, but Dizzy flapped between them. Laylea had to duck out of her way. The bird tugged out a keyboard tray and flipped the Dvorak board on it. A torn fortune cookie fortune had been taped to the bottom. Ms. Crow had written her password below the printed words *You will find that you seek.*

KC peered down. "She uses a manual backup?"

The raven croaked.

KC swiped to a password screen and typed DIZ7Y.

She set one of the dibs drives on the padd. The screen didn't change.

"Dumb dumb dumb." KC grabbed the drive and bent to set it on the primary CPU under the counter.

The padd lit up. Lines of gibberish scrolled up the screen. KC stopped breathing. She swiped the dibs drive and grabbed another drive from the counter. It took her two tries to slip the old technology into the proper slot. More gibberish. Different gibberish. This was deep green lettering on a green background and it flashed through screens as KC tapped the padd.

"Oh, my phoenix," she breathed, grabbing the oldest-looking drive. She stuck the USB end into the CPU extender. "Oh, my god."

This time scanned images of handwritten forms appeared. Charts with blood pressure, pulse, temperature, something called contractual response. She tapped and the next sheet offered more details in a crabbed script. She tapped through several pages before they realized these were full medical charts from the turn of the last century.

"Stop." Oscar leaned in. "Adele Lagat. Is that our Adele Lagat?"

They looked at him blankly.

"Oh, that's right. Neither of you are in a real shifting class yet." He reached over KC to scroll back in the record.

The upper right corner of the third page featured an oval portrait of a girl with an enormous bow in her hair and fierce eyes. KC tapped through thirteen pages of records for Adele Lagat. The last page ended with the word *continued.*

KC typed and the records were replaced with technical gobbledygook.

"Someone has been collecting these records for a very long time and they've been really good at hiding their tracks." She shook her head. "I don't see how the council or the Enforcers haven't heard about this."

Dizzy suddenly launched from the counter. She soared over to perch on the light trough beside the doors. KC flipped around. She ducked down to grab the flash and power drives and then unzipped Laylea's collar. She shoved half the drives in the collar and half in her pockets before she turned back to slap a dibs drive into her charmband.

"Zip up. Oscar, you grab the rest. We have to let everyone know."

Dizzy croaked. She soared back and tapped on the padd as the In door cracked open.

Ms. Crow's voice carried from the hallway. "I promise you, Sir. I will let you know if I find them. Of course, of course, it's awful. You go check on Rex."

Oscar ducked down. Laylea waited for KC to finish cleaning up her tracks and log out of the system. The three duckwalked to the far end of the counter. There was no way they could get to the doors without being seen. Ms. Crow was still talking to whoever was outside with her. There was no way to tell where she'd go when she came into the library and if she caught them, she could lock down the room and it would all be over. There was no way for them to win.

KC unzipped Laylea's collar again. "I'll distract her. You go that way. Stay behind the counter." She swallowed the last of the sligh nut fudge before Laylea had any idea what she had planned.

She and Oscar hissed "No," at the same time. But it was too late. She wrenched the charmband off her arm and shoved it at Oscar then dove out beyond the counter and threw up over at least four antique area rugs.

Ms. Crow burst through the door. They heard her inhale sharply and rush past the counter. She didn't say a word until she was at KC's side. "What did they do?"

Oscar tried to drag Laylea away on the far side of the counter. But Laylea wouldn't go until she'd fished the blue plastic bottle out of her collar. She tossed it, only turning to run with Oscar after she saw it hit KC's foot.

They peeked around the far end of the counter to see KC doubled over her knees, Ms. Crow hovering over her with the blue bottle in her hand.

"Where did you get this? Who gave this to you?" Ms. Crow was completely distracted. She didn't notice the Out door open.

Once in the corridor, Oscar took the lead. He and Laylea tore through the school, bouncing off turns and nearly bowling over every other student they encountered. Only Mr. Bianchi saw them, and he ducked back into Musician Central to get out of their way. They tried to run faster after that.

The dining hall intersection was tricky, but they only knocked over a few kids on their way by. They saw nobody outside the Sphinx corridor. Then they saw the tunnel. Or the wall where the tunnel was supposed to be. The corridor ended. The stone walls curved and came together where the tunnel entrance had been before. Laylea slowed but Oscar didn't stop until he slapped his palm against the stone. A small square glowed and he tapped in a rhythm.

"Come on." He reached for her. "They're on our heels."

Just then Laylea heard the footsteps, too. Far behind them, but gaining quickly. She took his hand. He stepped into the stone wall.

Sparks flew off the walls and ceiling all around them. Oscar was kicked back and for the second time in an hour she felt a shock through his body. They fell hard. She shifted to dog and right back to human. Oscar couldn't heal so easily.

"They changed the code." He swore and pushed himself up, going for the palm lock again. "Okay, Lee. There's another way but we're only gonna have two seconds to get through and then you'll only get one chance at the next two gates before they lock down. You remember how to pass the other gates?"

She thought back to what Patrick had yelled at each archway. "Second gate, Second form."

"Right. And?"

"You must be in your natural state to get through the third gate."

"Good. Let's go." Oscar palmed the plate again. When it glowed he looked at her to make sure she was ready. "Right on my heels."

She nodded, ready to run. He tapped the square four times evenly. Then threw himself at the stone barrier. Laylea was so hyped, she flew by him. She was ten feet into the glowing, jewel-encrusted tunnel before she realized he wasn't with her. She heard a humming, zapping noise and spun back to see the gate sizzling. Oscar was trapped in the golden sparks. His body seized up and he shifted to leopard. Then the leopard's tail snapped straight and he shifted back to human.

Laylea ran to him. "Oscar!"

"Don't!" he screamed, his voice thick with pain. "Don't touch me. Go!"

"Oscar, I can't leave you like this."

"Might be worse in ST. This is teamwork."

Tears poured down Laylea's face. "I can't get through the next gates. I can't shift."

Leopard Oscar yowled. Fierce claws extended from his paws and he scraped KC's charmband down to his forearm. Laylea screamed and fell back as he shifted in an explosion of sparks.

"You shift every night for bed." He pulled the charmband over his hand and threw it clear of the magical sizzle. "Trust you, Lee."

She wrestled the charmband up past her elbow and would have argued more, but she saw Mendenkov running down the final corridor followed by others. Oscar followed her gaze.

He turned back to her and his scream, "Go!" turned into a yowl.

She ran.

37

Second gate, Second form. Second gate, Second form.

She'd only get one shot at the gate. When they'd come through the night of the bonfire she'd trotted through all three gates in her dog form. Everyone else had shifted to animal form for the second gate and then back to human for the third. But Laylea had been carrying the lizard foot then. She wasn't protected from the magic now. And, deep inside, she just didn't believe she was a were-dog. She'd been born a puppy. For eleven years she'd lived as a puppy. For more than eighty percent of her life she'd been a dog. How could she consider that her secondary form?

Voices echoed behind her. They'd reached Oscar. The gate was only steps away now and she had to make a choice. If she chose wrong, then KC was suffering sligh nut poisoning for nothing. Oscar had electrocuted himself for nothing. Dr. Durrah would wipe their memories and go on putting shifter info out there, including hers and it would only be a matter of time before the Consortium found her and invaded the school.

She unbuttoned the top few buttons of her jumpsuit so she could wriggle out more easily if she shifted. Once upon a time she'd thought thumbs were the answer to every problem. She'd dreamed of having thumbs so she could open doors and pick out books on her own, so she'd be able to fly the plane and set up a tent. Now that she had them, she knew they weren't all that. She liked them, sure. But they still didn't feel right to her. None of this human-self felt right to her.

Oscar was right. She shifted at night to go to sleep. If she didn't, she shifted to dog in her sleep. What sense would it make for her to shift to her secondary form while unconscious? Wouldn't her body prefer its primary form?

"Double tap it with your full palm!" a male voice echoed down the tunnel.

The crackling hum of the force field went quiet for a bare instant. When it came back up, it was joined by running footsteps. She had to choose. She ran.

She passed the second gate unbuttoning a fifth button with her human thumbs. She dropped as soon as she was through, slipping out of the billowing jumpsuit without pausing. Her paws tore up the dirt and she gained speed through the third gate.

Her haunches took the brunt of the hit when she slid out into the molded-cement cave entrance in the primate house. A half-dozen humans turned to stare when she dashed out and ran smack into the glass exit doors. She looked up at the nearest, a young man with a thick beard and a nearly empty glass of champagne.

She barked and pawed at the door.

"Where did you come from?" He asked, but he also opened the door.

A gentleman inviting an old lady to enter ahead of him held open the second set of doors. Laylea dashed between their legs and raced down the path by the outdoor gorilla playground.

Fenn was too close behind her and people were stopping to point at her as she passed. You'd think nobody had ever seen an animal at the zoo before. She'd have to find someplace to hide, and she'd have to get there without being seen.

"Dessert is served in the DeGee Pavilion." Laylea dashed by a man ringing a giant hand bell, herding folks northwards. "Dessert is served in the DeGee Pavilion." He didn't even notice her.

She remembered passing a lake on the way to the bear enclosure on the night of the bonfire, a lake surrounded with trees and bushes and plenty of places to hide. She sniffed the air for water and remembered how close they were to Lake Michigan. But she could smell the difference. The little zoo lake was closer and had the scent of life. She aimed for it.

Even though it was late, dozens of people roamed the zoo. A jazz band had set up on a wide lawn area and she passed a tablecloth-covered card table with snacks and champagne. A zoo employee at this stand shouted as she ran by. Then took up the chase. She wore a fashionable dark-blue jumpsuit. Laylea might have been able to pass for an employee if she'd come into the zoo as a human. But she'd left her uniform at the second gate and couldn't go back for it now.

She ducked through some trees and barely noticed as she passed into a chained-off area of orange lilies. She stopped to take stock when she reached the edge of the water. The zookeeper had lost sight of her and the flamingoes ahead were all asleep, each beak tucked under a wing. The far shore was sandy and open, but far down the lagoon, on the far side of a quaint bridge, Laylea spotted a rocky bank shaded by boxelders. She picked her way along the bank, fording through the lagoon when she had to until she reached the bridge. From there she could see a cave high up in the rocky face of the opposite shore and she dove into the water.

Two minutes later, she was tucked into the dark recesses of a cave big enough for just a couple of humans to picnic in, as evidenced by a blanket-covered basket in the corner. Nobody had yelled so she was pretty certain she hadn't been seen. Should she wait until everyone was gone, when she'd be free to find an exit unseen? Or should she try to get out of the zoo and run to The Office as quickly as possible?

A shadow crossed the cave entrance. Laylea ducked. And shifted. Her head knocked against the picnic basket. She didn't even have time to hope the shadow hadn't heard. It flew through the entrance and dove for her head. She batted at it, trying to get by to run out of the cave. She would definitely be spotted by staff and guests as a human splashing through the lily lagoon, but she had to get the information out.

The creature flew away from her towards the starlight and then back in, chittering. Laylea had heard that sound before. She focused on seeing the figure rather than fighting it, which was made easier when it landed on the handle of the basket.

It was Kyle. Unless Dr. Fenn also shifted into a bat. How could she be sure? She'd only seen Kyle the bat twice. The first time he'd just fallen on her head and the second he was flying away after stranding her with the cursed mortise key. The key, she realized, was the way to be sure.

She wrapped the picnic blanket around herself and tucked it in place. Then she pulled the key out of her collar and held it up. The bat leapt at it. He smacked the key with a wing and tangled his head in the chain. Definitely Kyle.

And he gave her an idea. She unwrapped the chain and stuffed it and the key back into her collar. She had to hold Kyle to keep him from diving at her collar.

"Kyle, you need to get these drives to Morioka. The students are in danger."

The elastic charmband weighed his head down for an instant but when he leapt into the air, the three quarter-sized dibs drives balanced nicely around his neck. He clicked and screeched at her as he darted around the small cave, diving for her head more than once.

"Right. You can't go to Morioka. You're a demon and she'd destroy you." Laylea screamed her frustration. "I need help!"

A flash of light filled the cave. Laylea heard the bracelet snap. She saw it fly into the air and then Kyle's hand snatched it. He stuck it in his pocket.

"Why didn't you say so?" He pulled a pen from his shirt pocket and handed it to her. "Write a note. I'll get it to Seb at The Office."

"Do you have paper?" She couldn't cry now. No matter how relieved she was, she had to keep it together.

"You're very needy this evening, Lee."

Kyle searched his pockets but Laylea pulled the red note from her collar before he found anything. She scribbled out *Morioka,* and froze. What could she write? Would Morioka understand what the data meant? Keeping the school secret was important to the captain. It was the most important thing. So she couldn't just say 'school's in danger.' Was there anything she could say? She could state the basic truth.

She wrote, *I need help.*

Morioka knew where she was. She just had to hope the demon trusted her.

She added, *Please come. Lee.* Then folded the note and handed it and the pen back to Kyle. He put them both in a pocket.

Before he could shift, she asked, "Did you kill Benniker?"

Kyle squinted. "Who?"

"The security guard. That night we saw you."

"Sorry, that was a dumb question."

"It's important, Kyle. You promised me."

"My question was stupid. Not yours," he said. "The guard ran. He got picked up outside the zoo by a trio of werewolves from the pack who chased you that night Junior got shot. I messed them up pretty good, but just to keep them from hurting you. I didn't drink from any of them."

Laylea must not have looked convinced.

"I have plenty of bloodcicles left in the freezer, Lee. Don't worry."

"But you've been hanging out here."

"Not all the time. Just when I need to be close to the key or I'll go mad." His eyes strayed to her collar and he snapped a rubber band on his wrist. "Lee, I have never killed anyone who wasn't already dead." He meant the vampire who'd turned him. "I shot a guy in the line of duty once, but he survived. I keep my promises."

"Promise you'll get those drives to Seb?"

"I'll get them to Morioka."

Laylea looked up sharply.

He held her gaze. "I promise. Now shut your eyes."

She did. He flashed and the bat circled Laylea once before heading for fresh air. A gust of wind blew Laylea back. She opened her eyes to see a buzzard attacking Kyle just outside the cave. She ran toward them.

"Don't hurt him!" She flailed at the bird.

The buzzard smacked her with a wing and in a spark, a man's hand was squeezing her wrist. She gasped.

"I'm not going to hurt it, girl. I'm going to hurt you."

Putting word to deed, Dr. Durrah threw Laylea against the wall of the cave.

38

In a feat of physical prowess she would have sworn she only possessed in dog form, Laylea spun and got her hands up before she hit the cave wall. Her hands bled where she scraped them but she could handle that pain. Clearly. Because when she couldn't she shifted.

"Give me the charmband, Lee." Dr. Durrah towered over her. "We saw Oscar throw it to you."

Laylea couldn't respond. She couldn't think of anything to say. Dr. Durrah was intense. But he was kind. Was he still following Fenn's orders?

"Give it to me," he repeated, "or I'll have to hurt you."

Laylea found her words. "I'm not giving it to you."

Durrah tilted his head. He looked down at the ring on his right hand. "I had friends like yours once. We were inseparable. I wasn't planning to be a doctor. That was Sean. He wanted to save the world. Roger was going into finance. I was interested in mechanics. LPSS was a real school in those days, packed with students, teachers for every subject. Parents were encouraged to get involved. My dad took my whole mechanical engineering class out of school one day to meet a real live train conductor. We went down to the stockyards.

"I saw how thumpers treat animals that day." The doctor trailed off, caught up in the memory.

Laylea rolled to her knees. She thought she could dash for the entrance.

Durrah came back to himself. He slammed a hand into her throat to help her stand.

"Sean and Roger met the phoenix that day." He eased his grip but kept his knuckles under her chin. "I would have died for them. Would you die for KC and Oscar? If you give me the charmband, I'll let them live. KC and Oscar." He added this like she might think he meant Sean and Roger. "I'll have to wipe their minds, but they can start over and live long, productive lives if you wish it. Just give me the charmband."

Laylea didn't miss his inference that he wasn't going to let *her* live. "Why?"

"So I can make a million dollars and leave this school and open a private lab with huge windows and skylights. A lab where I will be in charge, where nobody tells me what to do, where I can figure out why some of us live so very long while others die so young."

That didn't sound like a horrible dream. It just seemed like he needed money and had found a horrible way to go about getting it.

"What happens to the information you sell, though? Do you know what they're using it for?" she asked.

"I don't care. It doesn't matter as long as I get to leave those tombs."

"What if it's being used to," she tried to recall what she'd learned in history, "to create the next Ten Percent Plan? What if they're using your research to kill us before you even get a chance to build your lab? What if they're building a new phoenix?"

Durrah caught his breath. He believed what she was saying was possible. She saw it in his haunted eyes.

Then he slammed the breath out of her.

"No. The phoenix is frozen. They're using it to make us happier."

Laylea heard chittering clicks and hoped it was the blood rushing past her ears as she slowly passed out. But then she saw Kyle buzz by Durrah's head. The doctor released her.

He shifted and grabbed Kyle's head with a claw in one move. The huge buzzard flung the bat at Laylea.

Kyle slammed into her chest. The buzzard tried to grab him back and missed. The force of his swipe ripped three gashes in her chest. Laylea felt his claws scrape against her ribs. She grabbed the buzzard's wing and screamed at Kyle to fly away. Then the pain in her chest was replaced by a flash deep in her heart and she fell to four paws. Sound and sensation washed back over her as her brain, hands, and ribs healed instantly.

The relief was temporary.

Durrah the buzzard sank his claws into her fur and wrenched her into the air. He soared out of the cave and over the zoo. Laylea flailed. She didn't fight too hard because as much as it hurt, she didn't want to fall. It looked like a long way down to those happy, drinking people.

Kyle followed. He darted at Durrah's head and away so quickly the buzzard snapped at empty air. Kyle flitted around Laylea, picked at her fur with his tiny claws until Durrah smacked him down with a wing.

Kyle floundered down onto a roof planted with flowers and vines, recovered, and zipped up at them again.

Laylea howled at him. He was their only chance. He had to go. He chittered back. She realized that he wasn't going to leave until she was safe. He was one of those shifters that didn't keep all his wits in animal form. Yet the bat was as fiercely loyal as human Kyle, or vampire Kyle.

If she wanted to save the school, Laylea was going to have to save herself. But how?

First she had to get to the ground. She was the only one in this chase without wings. They were flying towards the forested end of the zoo. If she could get Durrah to drop her over the trees, she might not be hurt so badly. She'd fallen pretty well when Ali dropped her in the Jungles during their Wilding. She remembered that Ali had dropped her because she shifted. As a human, she was too heavy for a bird, even an enormous bird, to carry.

Laylea found the trigger inside her. She called on the magic Sher had taught her and the truth she'd learned in the tunnel. She reached for her second self. She wished for thumbs. She thought of using those thumbs to strangle the buzzard. The burn trickled into her torso all at once and like the phoenix who had killed all of young David Durrah's friends, Laylea the twelve-pound dog burned up only to be reborn as one hundred pounds of Laylea the human.

Durrah lost altitude. But he didn't lose his grip. Laylea reached up to pry his claws from her flesh. She got one claw out. Her feet brushed the tree tops. Durrah fell lower. She looked up and saw Kyle battering the buzzard's eyes.

Then Kyle was soaring away and a huge black figure leaped from the ground to swipe the bird from the air. The second set of talons ripped through her flesh.

Laylea screamed as she fell. "Go, Kyle! Go!"

A thick, furry arm broke her fall but she rolled into the depressed bear's chest and bounced off. Her eyes focused on his floppy white ear until she hit the molded-cement boulder and everything went black.

39

Hooves woke Laylea. She felt the vibration of four-legged pacing nearby and smelled horse mixed with eggs, veggies, and fresh bread. Her stomach growled and she twitched her tail off her nose so she could smell more.

"Chef, you didn't have to deliver," Ms. Crow whispered.

Chef Tod whinnied a denial.

"And fresh ice packs. Thank you."

Laylea heard a snuffling sound.

Ms. Crow replied, "Oscar is recovering nicely. Though his leopard is nearly bald. Such a sad tail. He's pretty sore all over and a few burns are going to require close attention for the next few days. We have to keep him calm to reduce further damage to his heart. But he hasn't had any seizures in about six hours."

"I bet food would help with all of that." Oscar sounded a lot better than Ms. Crow had described. He also didn't sound muffled like Ms. Crow. Laylea moved her chin in his direction and found that she'd been lying on her side, on a warm, fabric ice pack. Just moving made her head spin. She didn't dare open her eyes.

Chef Tod snuffled again and the vibration of his pawing made Laylea realize she was lying on the ground, surrounded by fabric.

"No, Lee hasn't woken yet. Sydney says there's nothing broken and no bleeding on her brain. All we can do is keep icing and wait."

That was strange, because it felt like her head was split in two and breathing was not so pleasant, either. As soon as she thought of breathing, she yawned. The squeak and tiny yelp echoed woodenly around the small space she'd been tucked into.

"Lee."

Laylea opened her eyes to see KC kneeling in a square of dim light. She yawned again.

KC yawned back even as she tried to say, "She's awake."

She leaned back and repeated herself then reached out to rub Laylea's birthmark. "How are you feeling? You won't believe what's been going on."

"Careful." Ms. Crow knelt beside KC.

Laylea liked the gentle vibrations of Chef Tod's hooves as he left the library. She focused on that instead of on the violent pulsing in her head.

"How are you feeling, Lee? You've had us so worried." Ms. Crow slipped the old ice pack out of the nest.

Laylea stretched and took stock of her head, her ribs, her attention hog of a left hip, and a strange pain at the base of her tail and up through her lower spine. She remembered hitting the bear's boulder but she thought she'd been human then. So why did she hurt all over as a dog? Why did her right paw sting? She licked it instinctively and hissed. A deep slice ran from between her toes almost all the way back to her elbow. She whimpered.

"Here." Ms. Crow set a flexible ice pack on the arm. "Dr. Fenn didn't wrap it in case you shifted. He didn't want to cut off circulation in your hand. Oh, I should get him."

Laylea was more concerned with how she'd been cut than with the treatment plan. She was also a little concerned with why she hadn't shifted as soon as she'd regained consciousness. Sure, it made sense that she didn't shift when she didn't feel the pain, but now she was definitely feeling some pain. As happy as she was to be a dog, she'd be okay with thumbs for the split second it would take to shift, heal, and shift back. Like she'd done at the first gate.

If only she had the ability to shift at will. But if she had the ability to shift at will, Morioka never would have pressed her into LPSS in the first place, and she wouldn't have gotten dropped by a buzzard into a bear's cage.

Her stomach growled. She growled back. KC laughed. Ms. Crow frowned.

"I'm sorry, Lee, but we can't give you anything to eat until Dr. Fenn approves."

She barked.

Ms. Crow misunderstood. She laughed. "Okay, I will go get him. He's in ST so I can't message him." She turned away. "Can you take care of both of them for a minute, KC?"

"Of course." She didn't bother to swallow before answering.

"You should be in the infirmary, Lee, but Sydney said we had to eliminate stress and he said you hated the infirmary. Since Oscar wouldn't settle unless you were in sight, we couldn't put you in your pod. KC said you were happiest here." Ms. Crow blushed. "Was she right?"

Laylea barked. She'd been pretty sure they were in the library and this confirmed it. But why had they put her in a box filled with uniforms?

When Ms. Crow backed away, Laylea realized they'd tucked her under Ms. Crow's rolltop desk. She could see Oscar sitting up on a cot with KC. Both were eating burritos. Laylea really wanted one of those.

The librarian fussed over Oscar until KC reminded her Dr. Fenn would want to know Lee was awake.

KC finished her food while Ms. Crow left. Laylea crawled out until she was on the edge of the jumpsuit nest. She sang out at Oscar, who waved.

"Can't get off the cot," he yelled. "It's linked to Fenn's armpadd. He'll come back and bite my head off again and you heard Ms. Crow, no stress."

KC held up a hose attached to Oscar's arm. "Plus, fluids."

Laylea would have given her wounded left paw for a pencil and paper. She had so many questions starting with why Dr. Fenn was still doctoring and why they were okay with it.

Luckily KC was a bit psychic. "You're probably wondering why we're all pro-Fenn."

Laylea tried to bark an approximation of *ya think?*

"Fenn knew about Durrah's deal. And he saved Oscar from turning into a fried kitty or," KC petted Oscar's face, "worse of a fried kitty."

Oscar kicked her off his cot. "He's been writing the council for years. They kept saying they'd schedule a hearing to look into setting up a committee to consider investigating the accusations. But nothing ever happened."

She wondered how much Oscar's dad knew about it. She'd bet Oscar was wondering the same thing.

KC collected his trash and tossed it in the compactor. "Fenn ingratiated himself with Durrah so he could pick the students going to ST."

"Except the wolves," Oscar added.

"Except all the wolves had to go. But otherwise, he was picking kids he thought could handle it." KC peeled back a bandage on Oscar's back and applied a noxious ointment.

"Ow," Oscar tried to swat at her, but he winced and gave up after one swipe. "He really didn't want you in there after he misdiagnosed the sligh nut poisoning."

"Misdiagnosed?" KC huffed. "I told him it was sligh nut. He didn't listen."

"He's an adult."

The kids all nodded. Laylea yelped as the motion sent her head spinning.

"Hey." KC settled on the carpets outside Laylea's den. "Why haven't you shifted?" she asked. "Doesn't that heal you?"

Laylea raised her eyebrows at her friend. Oscar voiced her thoughts perfectly. "Hey KC, remember why Lee was pressed?"

"Oh yeah, I forget you're not pretending like me. But you had to shift to get through the gates. How'd you manage that?"

"Think quick!" Oscar yelled and a small brown and yellow object sailed over KC's shoulder right at Laylea's face.

She banged her head on the low roof of the den as the object hit her human stomach. He'd thrown her collar. "Ow."

"Idiot!" KC helped Laylea crawl out from under Ms. Crow's desk.

"No, it's okay." Laylea said. "My head feels better than it did."

She wasn't about to let Oscar feel guilty after he electrocuted himself to let her get out of the school. The thought flipped her stomach. She half-crawled to the cot to hug him. Then she turned and hugged KC.

"You're okay?" She looked KC up and down.

"Yeah. Ms. Crow helped me take the antidote right away. I'm fine. No hallucinations."

"Good." She took both their hands and squeezed. "Now tell me what happened! Was Fenn with Mendenkov in the corridor?"

"No." Oscar's forehead crinkled as he searched his memory. "It was Durrah with him. And some other faculty. One of them shut the gate down. But only for a second. Just long enough for Durrah to go after you. Then they turned it on again."

Laylea gasped.

"I wasn't entirely conscious by that point but I thought I was dead for sure. A whole bunch of kids showed up and the teachers were telling them there was nothing they could do. But Big Mo pushed through the crowd and offered his crutch. Mendenkov said it was too dangerous to get that close. Mo didn't listen. He tried to whack me out of the gate. Then Benny said that the gate would probably short out if enough people rushed it."

"That doesn't sound right," Laylea said.

"Well, it worked. Don't ask me how. Benny was still explaining when Emerald and Ali led the charge. A dozen kids rushed the archway and the gate came down. The energy transferred to a closed system of me and several others but the teachers skirted around us and ran for the second gate. Most of the kids waited until Caliban reached her branches in and separated us. By that point, Fenn had arrived. He shifted into a silverback gorilla and hefted me like I weighed nothing, according to Milly."

Oscar started coughing. KC was right there with the mouthpiece to a camelback.

"Meanwhile," she said, "the depressed bear was defending you from Mendenkov like you were his cub. He had Durrah on the ground and kept dragging him along to stay between you and anyone who tried to come near. Dean Gorse pulled a real gun. He was going to shoot and risk hitting you. But Ms. Davies hit him square in the glutes with a tranq before the dean could get a bead on the bear."

"She shot Dean Gorse?" Laylea laughed in spite of her better instincts.

"No, the bear. Might have been better if she'd shot Gorse. Mendenkov grabbed up Dr. Durrah and Gorse snatched you. They kept saying they had to get you both to ST to assess your injuries. Ali said they never mentioned the infirmary. Gorse was saying to stay away because you were unstable but everyone could see you weren't even conscious. And he wasn't holding you like he was worried about your injuries. They'd made it as far as those stupid wolf statues when your buddy, Captain Morioka soared in."

"What?" That was too fast. Kyle could never have gotten the message to her that quickly, not going through Seb.

"She was full dragon in the sky and shifted with cuffs in her hands. Thanked Mendenkov for capturing Durrah and while she handcuffed the good doctor, she spread a wing to stop Gorse from getting away with you. The cops showed up without any sirens. One of them checked you over, then handed you off to Mr. Bianchi on Morioka's orders. She even sent that cop to check on Toby."

"The depressed bear is okay?"

"Yes," Oscar answered. "But Ms. Lagat is unhappy he had to be tranqed twice thanks to faculty incompetence. Came into the infirmary to have words with Dr. Fenn about it. He may have brought me here more to get out of that conversation than to lower our stress levels."

"ST is shut down," KC jumped back in. "Morioka's orders. Dr. Fenn is getting everybody out now."

"Is Durrah going to jail?"

"Unclear," Oscar said. "Morioka is going to order—"

"Request," KC corrected.

"Request the Enforcer investigate what was going on in Special Testing and where Durrah was selling the info. So you'd think she'd give them Durrah. But Ali said the cops were booking him for possession, trespassing, and endangerment of a sentient creature."

"So he's not coming back here."

"No. He's never coming back here." KC confirmed.

"ST is shut down, the bad guy was taken away by a man-eating demonic dragon, and you're gonna be okay?" She looked to Oscar.

"Yeah. It looks that way."

"So, it's safe for me to take a nap?"

Oscar and KC smiled.

KC said. "You should both take a nap." She dashed over and fluffed the uniform nest. "Here."

She turned back with Laylea's collar. Laylea tried to reach for it and realized she'd shifted on her way back to the desk.

"A little tired?" KC fixed the collar around Laylea's neck and attached it. "I sewed the lizard foot back on."

Laylea licked her friend's nose. She stumbled into the knee nook under Ms. Crow's desk, circled three times counterclockwise, twice clockwise and collapsed. Her ribs didn't hurt anymore and her head had stopped throbbing. She licked her paw. No scratch, no blood.

"You done good, Fuzzface." Ms. Crow straightened her orange sweater.

Laylea hadn't heard her come back. She licked the hand that reached in to scritch her stomach. Ms. Crow adjusted the jumpsuits to create a divot by Laylea's feet.

"I'm proud of you." The librarian stood.

Laylea yawned. She stood and did a half-circle until she could see KC settling in her chair beside Oscar's cot. Seeing them reduced her stress. Doctor's orders.

She'd barely shut her eyes when a gust of air blew into the little den. Dizzy landed at the base of Mt. Jumpsuit. She rubbed her head against Laylea's and then climbed up into the divot Ms. Crow had made, tucked her beak under one wing, and went to sleep. Laylea rolled to her side and pushed all four paws against the bird. Then she sighed and passed out cold.

40

Three days later, Oscar was still rolling an IV stand about with him. He'd been allowed to return to Sphinx dorm but had to report to the infirmary every morning after breakfast. Every day he expected a letter from his father or mother about the incident. None came. He didn't say anything but Laylea and KC could see how much it worried him. His father was on the council. He had to know. They knew that Dean Gorse and Mr. Mendenkov had been called in to speak with the council. The dean had returned.

So, when Ms. Crow approached them at one of the study tables in the library with a note in her hand, all three expected it to be for Oscar.

With ST closed and Mr. Mendenkov on suspension, the library was more populated than usual. Laylea wanted to skip to any of the other study groups. Benny was tutoring Big Mo in geometry and it sounded like the injured wolf was finally catching on. Dove and Harper were flirting more than they were working on their Comparative Lit assignment with Carrie. Four wolves had been sitting in one of the pillow nooks with the selkie Raederie, talking mythology. One by one they'd shifted and Laylea wished she could join their cuddle and listen to Raederie tell ancient stories of gods.

But she was again trying to get a grip on shifter history. KC and Oscar had been trying to explain the whole twisted Ten Percent Plan war to her and how it intertwined with World War II. They were trying to explain how the devastation wrought by the phoenix had inspired Stanis to come up with the plan to fight back against the thumpers.

"His plan was to get the superpowers of the world to send all their young men to kill each other." Oscar told her. "He didn't count on the number of shifters who joined up to fight or the inter-shifter war that was instigated when his part in the devastation was discovered."

"Why aren't there more books on this?" Laylea spread out the vanity press books they'd gathered that covered the shifter role in the war directly. Every other bit of evidence came from reading the thumper volumes knowing some players were shifters but not necessarily which.

KC grimaced. "It's hard to hide books from thumpers so not much gets written down."

"The world learned that lesson in 1871. The Chicago shifters had thought we could be like Paris." Oscar flipped through the book by Jean-François Drouillard. "But the thumpers weren't having it. Ever since the phoenix, we've been on stricter rules than even Boston."

"Which is why the council should have been more concerned with Dr. Durrah selling our medical info outside of the school. What if he's selling it to thumpers?"

Both Oscar and KC looked horrified at the thought.

"No," KC said.

"No shifter would do that," Oscar echoed.

But they didn't know for sure. They couldn't. And they didn't know how often he had delivered the info to his buyers. She had to assume her intake exam was out there. They may have gotten rid of Durrah and shut down ST for the time being, but Laylea felt sure word of a weredog would get to Walter sooner or later. Even if it was later and Laylea herself was already dead, he'd find the whole school.

Unless she left him a more obvious clue somewhere else.

Dizzy croaked a warning and Laylea passed it on. The three shuffled the books under their schoolbooks and deskpadds. But it was only Ms. Crow, buttoning and unbuttoning the neck of her blue sweater as she approached their table.

All three held their breaths until Mr. Bianchi popped up beside her.

"Lee Woodford. I can't say I am at all happy about this but your family is sure to be overjoyed," he began.

Ms. Crow coughed and murmured, "Orphan," behind a hand.

"Oh." The music teacher deflated. "Well, where will she go?"

The top button of the blue sweater was in danger of being torn off as Ms. Crow kept her voice low. "We're not to concern ourselves with the students' upstairs lives."

Mr. Bianchi spluttered before he was able to say, "Sure, but she's so smart and I haven't even gotten her in class yet. I was going to suggest a private study after she settled in."

"Mr. Bianchi." Ms. Crow shushed him. "Lee, Captain Morioka has rescinded your incarceration."

"No!" Carrie yelled from the next table over. She slapped her hands over her mouth.

Laylea's mind leapt to the ways she could draw Walter away from the school. And she was halfway up to Oscar's house in her head before Mr. Bianchi jumped in with the addendum.

"However," he looked as hopeful as Ms. Crow looked unhappy. "The school charter requires every student to pass Testing before they may be permitted to leave. Ms. Lagat awaits you in the Testing facility."

"Oh," Carrie breathed out, "that's g… good."

"Carrie!" Dove hissed at the werewolf.

Big Mo laughed. "We'll watch your books," he said. "Since you'll be back in ten minutes."

Oscar and KC exchanged a look and gathered the books. "Can we come?"

"Yes," Ms. Crow put a hand on Laylea's shoulder to encourage her to get up. "You'd better. If Lee passes the shifting Test, she'll be escorted directly upstairs. I understand Captain Morioka is waiting at the seal pool."

Around the room, kids shouted, "See you later."

None of them said goodbye.

Mr. Bianchi and Ms. Crow escorted the three out of the library. In deference to Oscar's IV stand, they navigated the longer route through the corridors rather than cutting through the Fields to get to the nearly empty Testing hall. Dizzy joined them. Even though they couldn't see her, Oscar and KC had started holding doors open just a little bit longer than necessary, just in case. It was nice to know Dizzy wouldn't be totally alone when Laylea left. If she left. A small part of Laylea searched for kids she'd want to say goodbye to, just in case. But most of her agreed with Big Mo. She couldn't shift at will. Whatever had helped her in the tunnel, whether it was pressure or luck, it hadn't been skill. But KC and Oscar stuck close, like they had faith she'd pass.

"Alrighty, Lee. You wait here and I will go see if Ms. Lagat is ready." Mr. Bianchi patted her on the shoulder and hustled off to the middle Testing bay.

Ms. Crow faced her. "I'm very glad to have met you, Lee." She tortured the second button on her sweater. "If I get a note back from Detective Morton, where would you like me to forward it?"

Laylea stuttered, "I never gave you that note."

"Brian gave it to me." Ms. Crow said. "He said you left it in Biology. Should I not have sent it?"

"Thank you." Something lifted in her chest. Even if she didn't get out, Dee would look in on Oscar's mother. "That was really nice of him. If she replies, can you give the note to KC?"

"I will." Ms. Crow held her hand out. "Good luck."

They shook and Ms. Crow hurried out of the Testing hall. Dizzy followed her all the way to the door before she turned back to land on the precarious *Quiet, Please* sign.

Laylea turned to her friends. "I'd say goodbye but I don't think I'm going anywhere."

"Yeah, you are. You're going to see your brother and bust all the N dealers and go see Oscar's mom."

Oscar added, "Because we can't."

"No pressure." Laylea rolled her eyes.

KC hugged her. "You're gonna pass."

Laylea choked up. "I'm gonna miss you guys." She reached for her collar. "Hey, I'll leave you my lizard so you can see Dizzy."

"No." Oscar stopped her. "Your mom made that. Never give it up."

"Yeah, we'll see her again when you come back," KC said.

Laylea frowned. KC didn't seem to understand. "I'm not coming back."

"Yeah, you are."

Oscar stepped back and mouthed, "Sligh nut hallucinations."

Laylea laughed.

KC straightened. "Hey! I never made fun of you even though you were always talking about how Ms. Crow changed her sweater all the time. She only wears blue sweaters, Lee. Nobody else ever saw an orange one."

Oscar rolled his eyes. "Except when Benny won Wilding with it?"

"Oh, yeah."

"Excuse me." Caliban had slipped into the room without any of them noticing. "I heard you might be leaving, Lee."

"Captain Morioka is rewarding me for revealing Dr. Durrah."

"I will miss the nights you slept under my branches. I found it comforting to feel your breathing against my trunk."

"Thank you, Caliban. I'll miss you too."

The lanky girl wrapped two leafy branches around Laylea and whispered, "May you grow deep roots to find the water."

Laylea whispered back, "May your tail always have a reason to wag."

The door to the Testing hall banged open. Dizzy fluttered her wings as Ali, Merrilynne, and Brian burst in. Well, Ali and Merri burst in, Brian followed at a more measured pace. They each carried a stack of books like they'd run there from class.

Caliban stepped away to talk with Merrilynne.

"Captain!" Ali strode over and punched Laylea in the shoulder.

"We're not Wilding until the next *new* moon to throw off the hard noses."

Brian leaned in. "And so Carrie and Big Mo can join us."

"See if you can break some major shifter law by then, okay? I got faith in you, Captain." Ali wandered off to join Merrilynne harassing the few kids waiting to Test.

"I don't even know all the shifter laws," Laylea pointed out.

Brian bent over to hug her. "The only really big one is don't ever tell any non-shifters about us."

Laylea laughed, "Well, the only people I'd tell would be wyrdos themselves."

"No." Brian got serious, his eyes growing huge. "You really can't tell anyone."

KC reassured him. "It's okay, Brian. She was joking."

"Oh. Good." He nodded. "Here comes Mr. Bianchi."

"Hey, Brian," KC pushed him toward the Testing bays, "Can you stall him a second?"

"Sure."

KC grabbed Laylea into a hug. "If you do die soon, I just want you to know that you're the best friend I've ever had." She shot a guilty look at Oscar.

"I hang with wolves and rich kids," Oscar admitted. "I'm a jerk."

Laylea pulled him into the hug. "No, you're not. You're my friend."

His voice cracked, "I'll miss you, puppy."

KC threw her head back and howled. "Ahwoooo!"

All the kids around the room joined in. Even Dizzy croaked out an attempt. Laylea howled, too, even though she thought it was all a little silly. There was no way she was going to pass the shifting Test.

Mr. Bianchi clearly agreed. "Come with me, Lee. You can come back and howl some more after."

KC gave her a thumbs up.

Mr. Bianchi smiled encouragingly as he closed the door to the Testing bay. When Laylea saw Ms. Lagat sitting there, she forgot all about leaving or shifting.

She asked the old woman, "Is the bear okay? Ms. Crow said you were looking in on him."

The old woman took her glasses off and looked Laylea up and down. "You're worried about the bear after he tried to kill you?"

"I fell. It's not his fault. Is he okay?"

Ms. Lagat stared at her for another minute before she nodded.

"To the center of the room, please." She recrossed her legs and waited for Laylea to move in front of her. "Shifting at will is the most important skill a shifter needs to master in order to live in society. You will need to shift and shift back in order to pass."

Laylea took a deep breath. When Ms. Lagat raised her eyebrows, she nodded that she understood.

"When you're ready."

Laylea looked into herself. She thought if she could convince herself it was bedtime, she might shift.

But just then, a series of thuds sounded in the next room as if several someones had dropped a stack of books.

"Well done, Ms. Woodford."

41

Laylea stood outside The Office, shivering in her sundress and uggs, envisioning the chaotic scene inside when Morioka had dragged her away four months earlier. She couldn't avoid the guilt she felt seeing Junior bleeding out on the floor any more than she could avoid the bat hovering overhead.

She looked back to see Morioka parking her car far down the street, past the panaderia. The captain had refused to answer any questions about Dr. Durrah or the council. She hadn't said much at all on the car ride, other than being very clear about the consequences if Laylea told any non-shifters about LPSS.

Laylea glanced up at Kyle. He might know what happened to Durrah at least. "Go to the courtyard. I'll meet you there. Courtyard."

The bat did not leave.

"Shoo."

The Office door opened. Big band and the maddening scent of Seb's glög poured out with Ned, the bar's ubiquitous knitter. Laylea had never seen him standing before and she had to back away to get a good look. The man was a large block of muscle from his combat boots up to his shaggy beard. The only time she had seen him not knitting was when he'd donated his work-in-progress to be a pillow for Junior.

"Hi, Ned," she said. "Has Seb run out of glög?"

The man's voice was deep and it shook as he held one meaty paw out to her. "Welcome back, Lee." She had to move in close to take his hand and he lowered his voice to a nearly inaudible drawl when she did. "I don't remember anything bad happening to me in ST. I don't remember anything bad happening five times. Thank you."

Laylea couldn't think how to respond. Ned was a shifter? "Why are you leaving? The Office isn't The Office without you, Ned."

He took a deep breath. "I get upset easy and I'm still mad at Morioka for pressing you." He spoke softly, his Alabama drawl sounding sweet as elderberry pie. But a growl rolled deep in his throat under it all. "I left you something in your bed for your friend." He glanced across the street where Morioka was heading into the bakery and then up. "She's a kid. You carry your own weights." There was a pause like he was gonna say a name. But he didn't. He gave Laylea a short nod and lumbered down the street.

What did he know? She got the feeling he wasn't in the mood to be more expressive and since those were the most words she'd ever heard him put together, she figured she'd be grateful for that much.

"Thanks. I'll just go get it after I have some glög."

He laughed. One deep, growly *ha.*

She opened the door.

"Lee!" A crowd of regulars called out and a blanket of hands pulled her in just as she realized she had no toll for Beth and then that Beth wasn't collecting tolls anymore.

Someone had strung up two banners on the back wall. One reached all the way from the archway over to the third booth. It read *Congratulations on the Successful Completion of your Incarceration.* The other read *Welcome home, Lee.*

"Junior, she's here," Lucio called down the bar as he pulled her into a hug right over the spot where the boogeyman had been dying the last time she'd been here. "Welcome home, Lee. Did you learn to behave in juvie?"

"I heard they put her in super max," Orin pulled her away from Lucio and almost hugged her before Junior grabbed her by both shoulders.

"I'm so glad to see you, Lee. Morioka never stopped to think I might be worried about you. You weren't in the car. You never showed up here at the bar." He suffocated her against his chest and then pulled a rawhide out of his pocket and whispered. "I saved it. Only chewed on it a little that night."

Laylea took the rawhide. She kissed Junior on the cheek. "I *was* here. You were kinda busy."

"I'll show you the scar later," he promised.

Laylea hopped up onto a stool to see Seb. Fourteen lit candles and a match stuck out of a three-layer cake frosted white and decorated simply with black icing bars.

Several voices shouted, "Make a wish."

Diejuste hauled her tiny self up beside Laylea. "Hurry, girl. Before da place burns down."

She inhaled a huge breath of sweat and sugar and glög and blew out all but one candle. The brownies snapped and the last flame flickered out. The bar cheered.

"Now take that monstrosity off my bar." Seb set a hot cup in front of Laylea as he shooed everyone else away. "There are plates on Ned's table."

"Hey!" Laylea cheered up. "I'm getting my first glög?" She pulled the cup toward her and smelled the not normally disappointing aroma of Earl Gray an instant before Seb laughed at her.

"Prison hasn't aged you that much." He leaned in to be heard over the crowd. "Bailey had a night class or he'd have been here."

She wasn't surprised. "I'm gonna just go get something warmer to wear. I'll be back."

Seb had already turned back to his drinking customers.

Diejuste hopped off her stool. She hugged Laylea for the first time ever. "Take ya time. You know where to find us."

Her bed was right where she'd left it, tucked beside the closet door. The rusty-red corduroy looked so inviting she felt a shift burning up from her gut. She tamped it down. She couldn't rest yet. She picked up the tiny knit circlet laying in the middle of her bed. Plain black yarn knit tightly around a black elastic that fit comfortably around her wrist but stretched much wider. Its only feature was a small pouch just the perfect size for a cursed mortise key. Laylea pulled the key out of her collar. She tucked it in and shoved the chain in after.

Ned knew a lot more about what was going on than he let on.

She reached for a pair of sweats from her stash and noticed a second present from Ned. Neatly folded atop her sundresses was the cable-knit afghan he'd loaned to Junior.

Tears filled her heart. One spilled down her face. She had to breathe and remember that she'd just hugged Junior out front. He was fine. She hadn't killed him. She tucked Junior's rawhide in the blanket's folds, then changed into sweats, and ran out to the back courtyard. The pit held a low fire but no customers braved the cold. Laylea closed the door behind her and blocked it with the stone meant to hold it open.

She spoke to the dark corners of the courtyard. "Okay, buddy. Show yourself."

A flutter of wings and a flash by the alley exit revealed Kyle wearing a filthy set of third or fourth-hand clothes. He hovered by Orin's bicycle, peeking out into the alley and keeping an eye on the bar door.

"I'm incognito. What do you think?" he asked.

"I think you smell," Laylea grimaced, "really bad. And you're wearing your own shoes, which leave a pretty distinctive pattern. Why have you gone incognito?"

"Dee's been asking around since I stole a squad car to call Morioka to the zoo. She heard my voice."

That answered a lot of questions. It explained how Morioka and the cops had gotten there so quickly.

"I put your bracelet in the captain's car while she was playing cavalry, BTdub. Never needed your note." He pulled the red paper from his pocket and handed it over.

She tucked it into her collar, in the pocket behind her lizard foot. "How does Ned know about you?" she asked.

Kyle shot her a grin. "I don't know what you're talking about. I better get going before anybody comes looking for you."

He flashed, but Laylea was ready for him. She trapped the bat in both hands and wrestled Ned's knit necklace over Kyle's little head. It fit great. No telling how it would fare when he shifted but the key was not her problem anymore. She kissed Kyle on the head, threw him up into the air, and went back inside to find Dee.

Detective Dee Morton was more than happy to step out of the loud bar with Laylea. Laylea didn't really look her in the face until they were on the front sidewalk. When she did, she must have audibly sighed.

"Lee." Dee looked up and down the empty sidewalk. "You don't have to be afraid every time I look at you. You're fourteen years old, kid."

Laylea fingered her lizard foot and finally said it out loud. "The average lifespan of a twelve-pound terrier is thirteen to fifteen years."

Dee didn't laugh. She thought about it and frowned. "Come on. Let's go see Sanna."

"But, the party is for me."

Dee had already started down the street. She stopped. "Sanna Luke. Oscar's mom."

Laylea ran to catch up.

42

Dee pointed out the Luke's home as they passed by it, a gorgeous three-story brick home set back in the trees about two blocks from the lake in Evanston. She parked three blocks north and then led Laylea through side streets and trespassing through the neighbors' yards to a glass and stone greenhouse in the back. The windows that weren't covered with ivy had been painted red.

Dee knocked shave and a haircut.

"Nobody believes you went to juvie, kid," Dee told her as they waited. "I know where you were because Sanna thought I already knew. But Amal had hinted that he knew more than he'd say. He's been in Chicago since the World's Fair. I don't think the city has too many secrets from him. Diejuste isn't that easy to fool. Junior spent months trying to find you but he couldn't get to the right closet. He chatted with a lot of girls in real juvenile detention."

It was the first time Laylea realized that though LPSS was filled with clothes closets, none of them were in the dorm sleeping areas or even in the infirmary. People must sleep in classrooms sometimes but never in the corridors so Junior wouldn't be able to get in. Maybe the designers had known his dad.

"The others aren't sure where you were, but nobody bought the captain's story." Dee didn't wait for a reply. "Does your friend know his mom is addicted to N?"

Laylea sighed. "Still?"

"She tried, kid. Dealers sought her out. She tried to hide back here for a week but her husband wouldn't bring her food and as soon as she went to the main house, a dealer rang the bell. She can't get away from them."

The cracked wooden door slammed open. A thin black arm dragged Laylea inside. Dee followed and shut the door behind her.

The inside of the greenhouse had been strung with dozens of old-fashioned yellow bulbs, half of them burnt out. Plants thrived between easels and stacked canvasses. Taller plants wove through three clotheslines running the length of the room. The clotheslines had been tucked over easels and attached to the ceiling with string. Each one held too many red papers. Notecards, stationary, envelopes, origami birds and wolves and flowers, anything that could be made of paper hung drying from these lines. Surfaces were stacked with more of the red paper.

Each of the canvasses on the many easels and scattered around the room featured a black panther. Some were landscapes, some still lifes of the plants in front of them. Some more abstract pieces featured gravestones and moons. But every single one of them included an image of Oscar.

"Who are you?" The bony hand squeezed her arm. "You brought a stranger, Morton." She flung Laylea to the side to hiss at Dee. "Who is she? Who are you?"

Dee didn't even bother trying to get a word in. She let the tall, thin woman talk. Laylea got her free hand up to her collar. She managed to unzip it and pull out the paw print note.

"Mine." The woman dropped Laylea's arm. She reached for the red paper but drew back before she touched it.

"Oscar lets me carry it for him." Laylea offered it to the woman.

"Keep him safe." Sanna pushed the note against Laylea's chest. She had Oscar's fine bones and never-ending forehead. Her hair sprayed out in all directions despite an attempt to tame it into two braids. She patted the note and her dark brown eyes faded to a pale inhuman green as they lost focus. A tear fell from one. "Keep him away."

"Sanna."

The madwoman's eyes popped back to black when Dee demanded her attention.

The banshee looked into Sanna's face before handing her a wide plastic tub. "Use the lotion. Before and after."

Sanna nodded slowly. She set the tub on the floor at the base of an easel. Dee crouched to unlatch the container. She pushed on one side of the lid and it flipped open easily, shutting again when Dee lifted her fingers. It was simple enough for a leopard to open.

Sanna tested the tub. She stood, focused on the cemetery landscape half-finished on the easel. Her fingers brushed the black panther and smaller leopard crouched beside an ornate headstone.

"Go!" She spun so quickly, some of the red papers flew from their clothespins. "He's home. He can't see you. Go!"

She shoved Dee mercilessly to the door with one arm and wrapped the other around Laylea's waist, pushing her gently at the same time.

"Don't worry. We came the back way, the way you showed me." Dee reassured her. "I'll be watching you Thursday. Sanna, you're safe."

At the door, Sanna stared into Laylea's face as intently as Dee stared into hers. She reached up without looking and tore a red crane off a clothesline. Dozens of other papers fluttered to the ground. She tucked the bird into Laylea's hand and whispered, "A lizard foot for KC."

The next second she shoved them out of the greenhouse and slammed the door behind them. The door barely muffled the purring growl that followed.

There were lights on in the main house. Laylea thought she saw a figure pass by one of the dozens of windows on the second floor. Why did Oscar's dad let his wife live like that? Why wasn't he back here, helping her? Dee dragged her through the overgrown trees and the neighbors' yards. She led her east.

"The car's that way." Laylea pointed north when they were far enough away that it seemed okay to speak.

"The water's that way." Dee pointed and Laylea could see the glint of moonlight on the lake. "You know I can see further near water. I can see years out into the future."

Laylea nodded. "And you don't see any pallor around Sanna's face."

Dee shook her head. She caught Laylea's eyes. "Around yours either."

Laylea caught her breath.

Dee turned north. "Sanna's gonna help me track the dealers who approach her every time she leaves her house. Do you know why someone might want her addicted?"

Laylea turned her mind to that question rather than all her own. "Maybe it's something to do with what her husband does."

"What's he do?" Dee asked, naturally.

"I'm not allowed to tell you.

"So I need to follow him as well."

"I'm home. I can help. Maybe I can talk to Morioka about it."

Dee relented. "You want me to take you back to the party?"

"Think anybody would mind if I just went home?"

"Of course not. I'll drop you."

"I'm gonna run. I haven't—" She caught herself. Did saying she hadn't gotten much fresh air give too much away? How much did Dee already know? "I want to run."

"Yeah, I imagine it's easier to keep all your secrets when you're alone. You be safe." Dee headed north.

Laylea headed south. She assumed she'd shift and run home. But an hour later, her uggs were destroyed and her feet hated her. When she tripped over an abandoned bag of French fries and landed knee first on a beer bottle, she took it as a sign that the nearest bench was a bus stop with a metro card laying out as though waiting for her. The 97 pulled up seconds later and though the card was expired, the driver let her on anyway and gave her a napkin for her bleeding knee. Pain, loud noises, embarrassment when she missed her stop. But she didn't shift.

Lights were on in Madam Hu's apartment on the top floor and of course a blue glow emanated from her own window, which was cracked open. Bailey must be freezing. But he'd left her a way in. Laylea felt a sudden glow in her heart that had nothing to do with shifting. She pulled the charmed house key out of her collar and opened the door.

She had to shove to get it open. A pile of clothes lay in front of it. Papers and books and clothes were strewn everywhere in the apartment. She could smell the sheets from all the way over by the door, even over the dirty Tupperware in the kitchen. The dust buildup on the walls and desk and bookshelves wouldn't have been so noticeable if Bailey hadn't traced protective runes into it. Laylea turned to see he'd sketched a tripled sowelo on the door in what smelled like his own blood.

"Bails?"

Bailey spun. He didn't even notice the plastic container of Chow Mein that fell from his lap when he ran to her. Magic sang around him. Laylea felt it tingling through her whole body as he held her off the ground. She knew his Bailey Woodford appearance wasn't tall enough to lift her. When he set her down, she saw that he had shifted. He looked like Bailey Hillen now, the true Bailey. He looked her over like he expected her to have changed. When he spotted the blood on her knee, he brushed a hand over to heal it. Then he ran his fingers through her short hair. The tingle about him faded and blew away into the ether.

"Where have you been? Morioka gave me some bullshit about sending you to juvenile detention because you broke into some medical facility for drugs but the wyrdos said you got Junior shot. I've been lying to Mom and Dad so they wouldn't worry but where have you been?"

Laylea caught her breath. With all the things she'd been worrying about herself, she'd forgotten to worry about her parents, out hunting the Consortium.

"Are they okay? Have you heard from them?"

"I have a whole stack of letters for you to burn. Laylea, where have you been?"

Laylea had been thinking what to tell her brother. Morioka had threatened her with pressing again if she told anyone the truth. And before, she hadn't wanted to risk dying underground, never seeing her family again. But Dee said she wasn't dying. Dee had given her a whole stack of adoptionversaries to look forward to. Her parents weren't coming for them until they'd taken care of Walter at the very least. And they were going to take care of Walter. Her brother wasn't going anywhere as long as he had another decade of schooling to become the kind of doctor he wanted to be. The wyrdos could chase down the rest of the N production facilities and Morioka knew what it meant that N contained sligh nut. They didn't need Laylea.

If she wasn't dying this year, then Ned was right. She was just a kid.

"I was at school. There's a school full of shifter kids hidden under the Lincoln Park Zoo." She hugged Bailey. "But it's really good to be home. What the hell have you done to our apartment, you slob?"

Bailey looked around like he was seeing the mess for the first time.

He bent to scoop the Chow Mein into the Tupperware that had fallen from his lap and tossed it at the kitchen. The blue container made a hard left and landed beside a little city of suddenly cleaned and neatly stacked Tupperware. The counters gleamed. He pulled his stinky t-shirt off and flung it toward the chest of drawers which opened to admit all of the clean and folded clothing flying from the bed, the bathroom, and the back of the desk chair.

The runes glowed and sank into the walls and desk and counters before the dust disintegrated.

"Better?" he asked.

"It's a start."

Laylea went into the kitchen. She put the Chow Mein in the empty refrigerator, filled her water bowl, and poured herself some kibble. She returned to the main room, devouring a handful, to find Bailey physically snapping a clean top sheet onto the bed. He followed it with her favorite green woven blanket with satin edges.

She emptied her collar on Bailey's desk. The only clear space on the entire desk was her ashtray. She filled it with the red letter, her house key, the flash and power drives, and the still unopened roll of dibs drives.

"Hey, Lee." Bailey pulled a fake copy of Grimm's Faery Tales from the top of the bookshelf and extracted a handful of thick envelopes. She grabbed the homemade coffee can candle holder and met him at her dog bed. He ran two fingers up the wick to set it alight.

"I've got some work to do. Enjoy."

"Woof."

Laylea settled down and opened the first letter. Bailey had written the decoded version of the first page on the back of the second page and vice versa. But Laylea stared at Clark's handwriting for a long time before she read the translation.

Dear kids,

Burn this note. Fair Winds. We love you. Back at Uncle's. Did you read about the fire and flood in Montana? So did we. Worried about you. Must see you soon. Tell us more about how you're letting your baby sister hang out at a bar, B. Uncle has words for you. LG, you keeping him sane? Uncle has scritches for you. You must take care of each other until we can take up the job again. Sorry for the silence.

She'd barely begun the letter when Bailey spun back around. He fell out of the chair, to his knees, and crawled over to her. He'd done that a million times growing up but never once since they'd run to Chicago. He pressed his lips to her forehead and zerbetted her.

"I love you, Laylea."

"I love you too, Bailey."

He climbed into bed, fully clothed and held the sheets up. Laylea felt the burn in her gut. She blew out the candle just before every cell sparked and shifted into a small fawn-colored dog. She nosed the letters under the worn blanket in her dog bed and then jumped up with her brother. She circled once clockwise, four times counter-clockwise, then twice clockwise again.

"Just lie down, you weirdo." Bailey dropped the sheets on her head.

She cuddled into the crook of his belly and tucked her nose under his hand.

Maybe she'd drop in at Common Electronics to see KC's parents after she finished the letters tomorrow. Then she'd get Amal to fill her in on all the Wyrdos doings.

But for now, she was home, she was not dying, and she knew she was going back to shifter school.

CHARACTERS

- **Adele Lagat** - *see Lagat, Adele*
- **Adrien Denier** - *see Denier, Adrien*
- **Ahanu** - student, thunderbird, Mer dorm
- **Ali** - student, hawk, Mer dorm
- **Amal** - brownie, co-owner of Brown's Resale, member of Team Wyrdos
- **Bailey Hillen** - grad student, witch, Laylea's brother, aka Bailey Woodford
- **Barrett, Elan** - sociology teacher, wolf
- **Bayard** - Laylea's biological brother, dog
- **Benniker** - zoo guard, wolf
- **Benny McBride Greene**- student, turtle, Sphinx dorm
- **Bertram Gorse** - *see Gorse, Bertram*
- **Beth** - aka Jukebox Beth, former regular at The Office
- **Bianchi, Enrico** - music teacher, wolf
- **Big Mo** - student, maned wolf, Centaur dorm, aka Maurice Braga
- **Brenda Samborsky** - student, works in Executive Wing, python, Mer dorm
- **Brian** - student, gorilla, Sphinx dorm

- **Britny** - student, goat
- **Caliban Meillissene** - student, linden shifter, Mer dorm
- **Carrie Marshall** - student, wolf, Mer dorm
- **Chad** - Laylea's contact at surveyor's office, Laylea's contact
- **Chef Tod** - LPSS chef, Shetland pony
- **Chloe Serra** - student, moose, Sphinx dorm
- **Clark Hillen** - former Conditioned Force soldier, pilot, Laylea's adopted father
- **Conner Stone** - student, wolf, Mer dorm
- **Correnti, Toni** - shop teacher
- **Crow, Elizabeth** - librarian, counselor, Raven shifter, aka Lizzy
- **Davis Rucker** - childhood neighbor of Laylea and Bailey, lost a leg
- **Dee Morton** - homicide detective, banshee, member of Team Wyrdos
- **Denier, Adrien** - Council Enforcer, wolf, KC's godfather
- **Dizzy** - raven, invisible to most people
- **Diejuste** - voudon loa riding Jane Delphine, member of Team Wyrdos
- **DJ Delcampo** - Daniel Joaquin, wolf, KC's brother
- **Dove Betts**- student, tiger, Mer dorm, twin to Reggie
- **Drouillard, Jean-François** - shifter historian, French, hummingbird
- **Durrah, David** - LPSS doctor, head of special testing
- **Durant, Felzer** - client of Laylea's, stock analyst
- **Dustin Huono** - student, wolf, Sphinx dorm
- **Emerald** - student, singer, selkie, Sphinx dorm
- **Fenn, Sidney** - school doctor, gorilla
- **Gorse, Bertram** - dean of LPSS, Lipizzaner
- **Grandpa Delcampo** - dean of Montana Shifter School, wolf, self-declared Alpha of the Americas, KC's great grandfather, aka Luis
- **Griffin DeGee** - student, gryphon, Sphinx dorm, aka Griff

- **Harper Pemberton** - student, rhesus monkey, Centaur dorm
- **Jase Batka** - student, wolf, Sphinx dorm, grandson of the Detroit Alpha
- **Jay Doe** - recovering Conditioned Force soldier, Laylea's "uncle"
- **Jeannie Nellwin** - doctor, Kyle's wife, KJ's mother
- **Josh** - Laylea's biological brother, dog
- **Julia Jimenez** - student, wolf, Sphinx
- **Junior Leo** - apartment manager, boogeyman, member of Team Wyrdos
- **Kadota** - student, orangutan, Centaur dorm
- **Kara** - student, Centaur dorm, dating Reggie
- **KC Dells** - student, wolf pretending to be a coyote, aka Karly Carlotta Delcampo
- **KJ Nellwin** - Jeannie and Kyle's kid
- **Kyle Nellwin** - homicide detective, vampire, believed by some to be dead, Jeannie's husband
- **Lagat, Adele** - shifting teacher, pigeon
- **Laylea Hillen** - student, dog, Mer dorm, member of Team Wyrdos, aka Lee Woodford
- **Lee Woodford** - see *Laylea Hillen*
- **Lucio** - brownie, co-owner of Brown's Resale, member of Team Wyrdos
- **Luke, Oliver** - councilmember, leopard, Oscar's father
- **Madam Fan Hu** - Laylea and Bailey's landlady
- **Madame** - French teacher, spider
- **Mendenkov, Rex** - gym and health teacher, wolf
- **Merrilynne** - student, koi, Mer dorm
- **Milly** - dancer, student, mouse, Mer dorm
- **Milo** - Laylea's biological brother, dog
- **Morioka, Yaksha** - Captain of Chicago PD 44 division, demon, dragon, member of Team Wyrdos
- **Murph** - student, cheetah, Sphinx dorm
- **Ned Biggerson** - knitter, The Office regular

- **Nemo** - a canine neighbor of Laylea's and Bailey's, true German Shepherd
- **Onioka** - Yaksha Morioka's mate, demon
- **Orin Morton** - co-owner of Brown's Resale, brownie, Dee's brother, member of Team Wyrdos
- **Oscar Luke** - student, leopard (black panther), Sphinx dorm
- **Patrick DelValle** - student, wolf, LPSS student alpha, Sphinx dorm
- **Peter** - student, fox, Mer dorm
- **Raederie Rivers** - student, selkie, Sphinx dorm
- **Reggie Betts** - student, tiger, Centaur dorm, twin to Dove, dating Kara, aka Reginald
- **Rhea** - Laylea's biological mother, dog
- **Rhemy** - Laylea's biological brother, dog
- **Rico Stanis** - author of the *Ten Percent Plan,* fox
- **Riva** - student, sloth, Centaur dorm
- **Roger** - former student, friend of Durrah's, victim of the Chicago Fire
- **Sanna Luke** - artist, leopard (black panther), N addict, Oscar's mother
- **Sean** - former student, friend of Durrah's, victim of the Chicago Fire
- **Seb** - bartender at The Office
- **Sher Hillen** - doctor, witch, Laylea's mother, aka Katherine Coogan
- **Sue** - neighbor of Laylea and Bailey
- **Theresa** - student, lion, Centaur dorm
- **Toby** - bear in Lincoln Park Zoo
- **Vaughn Howe** - student, wolf, Sphinx dorm
- **Walter Bowman** - Consortium therianthologist, Laylea's biological father, true-human
- **Wanda Bargo** - LPSS administration, elephant
- **Woodford** - Laylea's brother, killed by the Consortium, true dog
- **Yaksha Morioka** - see *Morioka, Yaksha*

AFTERWORD

Thank you for reading *Shifter School.* I hope you had fun. If you did, please go to Amazon or Goodreads or your fabulous blog and write a quick review. Reviews are really important to an indie author.

Sign up at wyrdos.net to be the first to know all the latest on my books and audiobooks. I promise I won't inundate you with mail and I will not share your email with anyone. Just ask my sisters. I never share.

READ ON

If you want to know what happens next, read on! I give you: a teaser of *Shifter Ghost*!

SHIFTER GHOST

A WYRDOS UNIVERSE NOVEL

1

"Boomtown, Jeffers!" The captain of the opposing team bounced off a bench to high five the seven-foot-something white guy who'd just jammed the basketball in the hoop on his second try.

Laylea yawned, her long, pink puppy-dog tongue curling at the end. She should feel guilty that she'd been napping under that bench when she was supposed to be on guard. But, so far, nothing exciting had happened other than Jeffers making a basket.

Jeffers giggled, "Boomtown." He liked the word.

"Means you did good, Jeffers." The captain, a small, gangly kid, executed a complicated handshake with the big guy.

"I did good. Nicky, I did good." Jeffers kept his head down, watching in awe as his hands danced with his friend's.

"Yeah, you did good. Here, the taco truck is giving out free taquitos." Nicky led the way over to the Latino man in a spotless apron handing the fried treats around to the players and everyone else hanging out in the South Side Chicago neighborhood.

Laylea watched Nicky help Jeffers adjust his retro sports goggles on their way there. There was something odd about that.

Laylea blinked. The captain's footsteps hadn't woken her so much as the sound of both teams on the neighborhood court cheering for the big man with mirrored, single-lens goggles that hid everything but his grin.

She stretched all four legs out and curled her paws back in. Laylea was a twelve-pound, fawn-colored terrier. Under the bench was the perfect place for her to watch the pharmacy. Or it would have been, if she hadn't fallen asleep.

The smell of grass, el pastor, and sweaty humans seeped into Laylea's sleepy dog brain, reminding her that she was on a job and really shouldn't have taken the nap. She peeked out from under the park bench to see if anyone else on the stakeout had noticed. Feet pounded across the recycled rubber basketball court. Lucio waggled his fingers at her as he raced by in his three-hundred-dollar sneakers.

She peered out beyond the taco truck to see Orin grinning at her from where he was tuning up his bicycle. Damn. Still, Morioka and Dee, the final two members of their crew, probably hadn't seen her nap because they were ensconced in the fake service van with cameras focused on the pharmacy. Lucio had learned, through some of his more questionable contacts, that the pharmacy was a major delivery hub for the rapidly dwindling supply of N in town. According to Laylea's contact at the records office, the building was owned by a corporation owned by a guy named Gorshkov. They added the corporation to the list of different organizations that owned the many buildings they suspected were being used to create N.

N was a deadly drug. It made normal humans feel as powerful as shifters and they would do stupid things, like try to fly off buildings or race train cars. Wyrdos who took it either experienced a surge in their powers or lost them completely until the drug wore off. Many shifter addicts lost the ability to shift at all.

Laylea and her friends had teamed up to help keep the city safe from supernatural threats like the Mesozoic-era demon that had brought them all together. They'd trapped that demon in a magical box. Meanwhile the "good" Pre-Cambrian-era demon, the one who'd helped them trap her mate, was currently sitting in the OnSite Car Repair service van with Dee. Regardless of how they'd come together, or the many tragedies they'd prevented since, the scourge of N had become the team's primary focus. It was tearing the city apart and the police couldn't really fight the epidemic if they could never find the kingpin. And since the kingpin behind N was clearly a paranormal being, that made N a Team Wyrdos problem.

Thus, five of them watching the South Side pharmacy. Or, rather: three watching, one playing basketball, and one napping.

In Laylea's defense, it was a boring stakeout. This was a nice neighborhood. Dozens of people were out, enjoying one of the first temperate evenings of spring. Winter in Chicago was brutal, and these people seemed determined to break out of hibernation. They greeted each other, grabbed food from the taco truck, and watched the game as little kids up way past their bedtimes wrestled with the tiny jungle gym. Sure, the basketball players trash talked each other, but it was all in fun. And if anyone's language got too strong, the old lady leaning out her window would let them know.

Lucio, Laylea, Orin, Dee, and Captain Yaksha Morioka had arrived separately and were supposed to hang on the periphery, blend in, and keep an invisible eye on the enemy stronghold. Orin had flipped his bicycle over on the handlebars and was giving it a tuneup. Laylea, easily the queen of blending in—as she was a dog most of the time—wandered around at will, getting scratches from the neighbors and cleaning up abandoned food. She'd skipped the droppings around the taco truck. There was something off in the scent of the roasting meats.

Dee and Morioka ended up together in the OnSite Car Repair service van Dee had fixed up with surveillance equipment. Neither of them was very good at blending in. Not because they were wyrdos. Neither Dee nor Morioka was very good at looking like anything other than a cop.

Lucio, however, had done either the worst or best job at blending in when he'd joined the basketball game. The man's brown eyes sparkled with mischief at all times. They were on a stakeout, but he grinned at Laylea as the game tore past her hiding spot again.

Half the players carried taquitos in one hand as they ran. A girl in duct-taped boots stole the ball and the game turned around. Everyone's heads spun back in the other direction. Laylea stretched, waking up more. A guy's high-topped sneaker shot out. He tripped the girl in the duct-taped boots. High-tops stole the ball. Duct-taped boots went rolling into Jeffers. He fell into the grass right in front of Laylea's bench.

"Oof." For a moment, the big man's face scrunched like he was going to cry. Then Jeffers spotted Laylea and he beamed. He walked his fingers through the grass to her muzzle and giggled when she nudged his hand to get him to pet her. He wasn't hurt.

Beyond him, the cheater wasn't so lucky. His high-top's laces popped out of their neat bows and tangled up. In his spectacular fall, the guy missed the soft rubber of the court and the grass surrounding it, stumbling instead all the way to the torn-up street where he shaved flesh off of several limbs and almost got hit by a car. Other neighbors goggled at the impossibility of his fall. Laylea wasn't fazed. That was just the sort of thing that happened when you behaved badly around brownies. She guessed it was Orin who had handled the karma, since Lucio's eyes were focused on Jeffers and Laylea.

Few players saw the cheater go down. Like Lucio, most of them watched the man laying full out in front of Laylea. Nobody was trash talking anymore. All the tough guy voices turned gentle as they called out.

"You okay, Jeffers?"

"He okay?"

"Jeffers, my man, you got to get up. We can't win without you."

"Hey, Jeffers!" Nicky, walking like he'd grown six inches in the last day and a half, trotted over to the big guy. "What you got there?"

Jeffers ran his hand over Laylea's head as gently as if she were a glass figurine. He took a moment to glance back at his friend, still beaming brighter than when everyone had feted him for making a basket. "Nicky. Kitty."

Despite the unintended insult, Laylea crawled closer so the guy could pet more than just her head. As she got near him, she saw that his grin was that of a kid, even though Jeffers appeared to be in his twenties. He smelled muskier than your average American man, too. Another odd primate scent wafted down from Nicky, along with the off-putting scent of the taquito in his mouth. Neither one of them was completely human.

As Jeffers turned away from Nicky, the late evening sun hit the single lens of his retro sports goggles at exactly the right angle. Laylea saw beyond the reflective surface. Her jaw dropped in a canine grin. She'd thought the glass was too shaded for an evening game, but now she understood. The goggles were his disguise. Jeffers was a cyclops. She was extra impressed that he had gotten the ball in the hoop at all with no depth perception.

He kept petting her gently, whispering that weird "pspspspsps" thing that cats melted over until Nicky crouched beside him and explained, "That's a puppy, man. You say 'who's a good boy? Who's a good boy?'"

Lucio laughed over their shoulders. "Yeah. Who's a good boy?" Unseen by the others, he gestured at himself.

Jeffers changed his murmur to, "Puppy puppy puppy puppy," and kept petting her like he was accustomed to breaking things. Laylea licked his hand. Jeffers sucked in a breath and didn't exhale. His face glowed with joy.

"Come on, Jeffers. Let's get back to the game, man." Nicky checked the man's goggles to be sure they were in place as he pulled him away from Laylea. She sniffed, but didn't recognize Nicky's scent. She'd never run into his kind of wyrdo before.

Jeffers cradled his hand against his body while Lucio and Nicky led him back to the game. Nicky took the opportunity to shovel the last of his taquito into his mouth. Lucio turned him down when he offered him another taquito, from his pocket.

Jeffers took it. Before he shoved the whole thing in his mouth, he whispered, "Who's a good boy?"

Nicky and Lucio both chuckled.

"You are, Jeffers. You're a good boy," Lucio assured him. He added, "Lee's a girl."

Laylea's friends knew her as Lee Woodford because Laylea Hillen was in hiding. Unlike Jeffers, she didn't have to hide *what* she was, only who she was, because all her close friends were wyrdos. Just like Jeffers and Nicky, they were supernatural creatures making their way in the modern world of Chicago.

The boys returned to the game, everyone hurrying to swallow the last of the free fried food. Laylea returned to watching the pharmacy, the surveillance van, and Orin. The sun inevitably dipped behind the roofs of the close-packed apartment buildings, and darkness fell over the pools of streetlight not quite illuminating the whole court.

The pleasant evening was turned on its head as the world grew darker. The pharmacy door opened with a quiet tinkling of bells, followed by the rattle of many guns being cocked at once. The game ground to a halt as several players started fighting each other. Jeffers tore the net from the backboard as the girl with duct-taped boots slammed the basketball into the ground so hard it exploded.

Dee burst from the service van and raced for the court.

Testosterone flooded Laylea's senses, sending her hackles up. A particularly strong and familiar musk dragged her attention to Jeffers' not-so-small-anymore friend. He'd shifted into an ape. Something clicked in her brain as the gunmen from the pharmacy beelined for the taco truck. She finally identified the off-putting smell in the roasting el pastor smoke that had been bugging her all evening. It was N.

The complimentary taquitos the truck's owner had passed around to the basketball players had been laced with N.

By wild chance, or, as the brownies would insist, well-deserved karma, the wyrdos had come out to get proof against the pharmacy on the very night that a rival dealer had chosen to steal their customers away. And Laylea had fallen asleep in the middle of it instead of using her preternatural senses and saving all those neighborhood kids from being dosed.

Or shot.

Guns appeared in the taco truck's service window, and she felt more than heard as the truck's electric engine purred to life. All the drug dealers had to do was drive away to escape the cops. Laylea couldn't let that happen. It was her fault they'd succeeded in drugging everybody there. She scrambled to her paws and tore across the grass. In seconds, she was under the truck. A cable brushed along her raised hackles. She spun, bared her teeth, and latched onto it. Green salsa spurted from the punctures. Laylea blinked and tried to push the spiciness out of her mouth with her long tongue. She leapt for another cable. This time, the fluid that spurted out made her eyes roll up into the back of her head. She worried at the holes, throwing her head back and forth to widen the punctures until the greasy, black stuff poured out onto her face. She stumbled back and gagged, blowing air out of her nose to clear it.

A low whine rose in volume and pitch. The truck shifted above her. At the same moment, she felt the burning in her gut that often preceded a shift to her human form. The wheels around her started rolling. She would be seen. She couldn't be seen shifting. She couldn't let the truck get away.

In a panic, Laylea flailed out with her claws at the cables and hoses she saw all around her through the burning pain of brake fluid in her eyes. She stumbled along, staying with the truck as it rolled into the street. Liquids spurted out, drenching her fur in salsa, power steering fluid, pico de gallo, coolant, and a coppery substance she feared was liquified N. Finally, her claws reached a wire that sparked and incited a small explosion when she sliced it. The hum of the engine died, and the truck coasted to a halt.

She couldn't hear the gunfight, but muzzle flashes lit up her limited view from under the truck. Her ears buzzed with static and some kind of high-pitched wailing. She smelled burning fur. A snazzy pair of hand-painted Chuck Taylor high-tops approached, limned in gunfire. When Orin's bright green eyes appeared, his face crinkled with fear, she realized that the wailing was her. The burn in her eyes, on her fur, and in her mouth shifted to a fire in her belly. The fire spread like a flash throughout her body. In that instant, just as Orin got a grip on her neck, Laylea changed form.

And she healed. As her muzzle flattened into a human face and her legs lengthened into a small teenager's appendages, her paws changed to hands. Hands that gripped an electrical wire just as foolishly as her claws had. Orin's scream joined hers as both shook in the grip of the great god Electricity. Laylea shifted to dog, to human, and back again. She didn't know how many times she shifted, but she was never able to shake either Orin or the live wire.

The flashing lights of gunfire and the blue wash of city lighting suddenly blacked out. Laylea cried out for her parents. She cried out for Bailey and for the friends she'd made at Lincoln Park Shifter School and would never see again. An instant before she would have fulfilled her long-standing fear that she would die before age fifteen, the wire was pulled from her human hand. The taco truck flipped on its side, revealing her to the open sky.

"Puppy hurt!" Jeffers' voice rang over all other sounds.

Laylea's body instantly shifted her to dog to heal the internal burns. Her nose wrinkled at the sharp, terrifying testosterone wafting off of the cyclops. His eyeshade askew, the big man stood swinging an electrical pole at the shooters who had tumbled out of the toppled truck.

"Puppy's safe, Jeffers," Orin reassured the cyclops, scooping Laylea out of the lake of auto and taco fluids. "I've got the puppy. You go home now. Go home, Jeffers."

Orin didn't wait for Jeffers to comply. Laylea watched over his shoulder as Orin raced away from the chaos. Jeffers tossed his pole onto a pile of park benches, car parts, the basketball hoop, backboard, and pole all nested together in a small, but solid, wall rising between the armed pharmacists on one side and the taco truck terrorists on the other. Morioka had joined Dee in covering the gunmen with her service pistol. The bigger guys laughed at the little Asian woman, and all raised their guns.

The last thing Laylea saw as Orin tossed her in his bicycle basket was Lucio running in between the two cops and the many criminals. She howled at the uncountable gun barrels pointed at him.

"It's okay, Laylea. You know he's a brownie. It will be okay." Orin chanted the words in rhythm with the pedals going up and down as they raced north, away from the approaching sirens.

2

The next day started like a perfectly normal day. By nightfall, everything had changed.

When Orin dropped Laylea off at home after the disaster at the basketball game, she slipped in through the cracked window, since even though she remembered her apartment key she couldn't really use it without thumbs. Bailey wasn't home. She assumed he was at the library. He was always at the library. He took his premed studies pretty seriously.

When she woke, his backpack was on his desk chair, but Bailey wasn't in the apartment. She wanted to race to The Office to find out how many drug dealers Dee and Morioka had arrested, but it was unlikely anybody would be there this early. So, instead, she hopped onto the cushioned barstool beside the bed, bounced from the stool to the makeshift headboard, and up to the window where she could wriggle out into the crawlspace under the front porch. From there, she trotted out to the lawn to find the perfect place to take care of business.

Laylea didn't know it was her fifteenth birthday. If she had, she would not have been wasting her time searching for the right place to relieve herself.

By all accounts, a twelve-pound terrier could be expected to live twelve to fifteen years. Dee, the banshee who could see if a person was going to die soon, had told her she was safe. Still, the day would have gone differently if Laylea had known she'd reached her expected expiration date.

Instead, she was mincing through the snow-covered patches of grass in front of the three-flat, searching for a place to pee that wouldn't offend Nemo or Luna, but would remind Tippy that the house was Laylea's territory. Laylea didn't know where Tippy lived, but she knew the large fawn terrier didn't live in the three-flat. Their landlady, Madame Hu, and her teenaged granddaughter took up the top floor, Stan kept to himself on the main floor, and she and Bailey rented the tiny garden apartment. Still, Tippy's scent was everywhere around the converted three-flat, more than could be justified by the times she and Laylea hung out on the front porch.

Laylea's tail flipped up as the terrier in question came bounding around the Prairie Style Greystone on the corner. Tippy's face markings were as white as the snow falling from the bushes she brushed against. Laylea herself had a white diamond brightening the fawn-colored fur over her eyes. It faded to a pale birthmark on her human face. Tippy's diamond covered most of one side of her face.

Laylea's tail went into overdrive as her brother Bailey, in his ancient sneakers, tore around the corner, hard on Tippy's heels. Laylea scratched aside a little snow and peed over some uppity male dog's mark near the elm tree in the front yard. Then she bounded over to sing at her favorite human. She approved his new morning runs. Bailey tended to be a little overly focused on his studies and in a bit of denial of his particular abilities, magical and physical, but Laylea knew that he was just trying to find the answers that would keep him from ever hurting anybody again. She understood. There was a price that came with knowing that you were different—in his case, with knowing that you were possibly all-powerful.

The running was good. It gave him endorphins and made him get out of his brain for a little while every day. He'd made it a habit while she was gone last summer, condemned to attend the coolest high school in the universe, the Lincoln Park Shifter School.

Bailey paused to stretch out his calves against the first step leading up to the porch. He kissed the top of Laylea's head as he did. "I ran into Nemo and Brandy three blocks over. The chemo must finally be working if she's able to go on long walks again."

Laylea trilled at him in response. Brandy was Nemo's human.

"I thought that would make you happy. You're a good girl, Tippy. Go home. Go home, Tippy."

Tippy ignored him. She rolled in the grass before tearing down the alley beside their three-flat.

Bailey backed away from the porch and hopped down the steps to the door leading into their garden apartment. "Brandy said that Madame Hu has been helping her with the vet bills. Did you know that?"

Laylea barked in the negative. She hadn't known.

"Hey." Bailey held her up to eye level and looked at her sternly. "You have your key?"

She nipped his nose and dropped her jaw in a doggy grin. She used to forget it all the time. But he'd laid a spell on her key so she would always know where it was. She kept it in her collar, the one item of clothing specially designed so that she wouldn't lose it when she shifted between forms. Unlike typical dog collars, Laylea's was wide, with two zippered pockets spaced between cleverly hidden elastic bands that could expand when she was human and contract when she was a terrier.

Bailey laughed—again—and chewed on one of her ears like her fur brothers used to do before their birth mother had hidden them all. Out in the street, a garbage truck dropped a dumpster with a chaotic clanging. A spark of hot pain flashed in her gut, and Laylea suddenly felt the icy cold of the winter air on her bare, human skin. Bailey shoved the door open with her body and dropped her inside the apartment, listening with his preternatural senses for anyone who might have seen her shift. The laughter was gone.

"Lee. That's not safe." He scolded her in a tone colder than the wind as he slammed the door shut.

He stepped over her and stormed over to the galley kitchen as she sorted out her long, awkward legs and brushed short, dirty-blonde hair out of her eyes, struggling to get some control over her facile human tongue as she always did when she shifted. "Sorry, Bails. I am getting better."

He grunted in return and drained a glass of water. Then, without changing out of his sweaty running gear, Bailey plopped himself into his desk chair and woke the three screens covered in data and medical displays that looked like broken down sections of DNA. So, that moment of filial love was over.

Laylea's eyes caught on the envelope sitting in a homemade clay ashtray at the back edge of the desk. The ashtray had been a gift from their friend Kyle's daughter before Kyle had died. Anything in the ashtray belonged to Laylea. The envelope held their rent for April. Bailey had praised her when she put the envelope in there right after paying March rent. He didn't know that she'd saved up enough to pay the next six months. Which reminded her...

She rolled over to face the bottom shelf of their bookcase. A worn copy of Jack London's *Call of the Wild* was tucked in with other classic titles that Bailey would never read again. She flipped it open and pulled rolls of hundred-dollar bills from the hollowed-out compartment inside. She stuffed the cash in her collar, one roll in each pocket, and forced the zippers shut. The collar pushed uncomfortably against her throat. Hopefully, she wouldn't have to wear it that way for long.

She grabbed a pair of sweats and a sweatshirt reading "Go Cobs" from under the bed and wriggled into them. What with not having mastered shifting, Laylea didn't waste much time with fancy clothes she was guaranteed to lose out on the streets of Chicago. Misprinted tourist fare was her winter uniform, a sundress in summer. She had stashes of clothes hidden all over the city. There weren't a lot of size-one homeless, so she hadn't lost many of them.

Laylea pulled herself to her feet and dashed out the door, yelling over her shoulder at Bailey, "Be right back."

She paused just a second, expecting him to respond, "Don't forget your key." He didn't say a thing. Her brother was already brain-deep in his research. He'd never notice she was gone.

Which was one reason she was in charge of the rent. They couldn't set up a direct debit like most people because Bailey didn't want to risk opening a bank account, even with his fake identity. He had the papers. He'd used them to get into college. He said that was different. He trusted the school to keep their information private. So, Laylea paid their rent monthly, in cash. Their parents used to send money, but they hadn't written in a while.

She sighed as she swung around the railing from the cement stairs to the wooden stairs leading up to the porch. Their mother was a witch and their father was a super soldier. Bailey said they were fine, just being cautious. Laylea mostly tried to stay busy to keep from worrying.

She fished the enchanted key from her collar to open the front door. It wouldn't work on Stan or Madame Hu's doors. They had keys that worked on the front door and their own apartment doors. Laylea would love to know how that worked. She stared at the key as she bounced toward the stairs, trying to imagine how three different keys could open the same lock.

She was so caught up in her thoughts that she almost jumped into their landlady's lap. There on the fourth step up, Madame Hu sat quietly, a giggle on her theatrically-painted face.

Laylea screamed.

"Good morning, Wai-Sun." The giggle dribbled from Madame Hu's Kohl-lined eyes into her voice. "Coming to see me?"

"Yes, ma'am." Laylea stumbled on the words as she focused on tamping down the fire in her belly. A surprise like that would once have made her shift with no chance to stop it. She took it as a huge improvement that she hadn't just dropped into a pile of fur and poorly printed sportswear. "Are you okay? Why are you sitting here?"

Laylea wasn't accustomed to seeing older people sitting on the floor. She wondered if stairs counted as the floor and decided they did.

Madame Hu slid over and patted the step with her wrinkled hand. "I haven't seen Mr. Stan in several weeks, and he has been suspiciously reasonable in his recent email complaints. I was hoping to catch him on his way to work."

"He hasn't been running his trains as much since I got home." Laylea thought about it and realized that she hadn't seen the grumpy old guy in the flesh since then, either. It had been nearly six months with no slurred insults or weak kicks at her for merely standing near his path.

She sat beside Madame Hu and pulled her knees up to her chest. "As long as you're in concerned-for-your-tenants mode, I was wondering if you could let me pay you the rent in advance?"

"For April? I suppose that would be okay. Are you going away again?"

"No, I don't think so. I just..." She futzed with the zipper on her collar. "Ghost hunting has been booming this winter, and we've got a lot of cash in our apartment." It wasn't just ghost hunting, but she couldn't exactly tell Madame Hu about all the supernatural mysteries that she solved. Humans didn't know about the creatures that surrounded them. But most of them either believed in ghosts or understood that others did. It was a safe subject.

"I'm worried about getting robbed with Bailey so busy and focused all the time. He never remembers to pay the rent, right? So, I was hoping that you could take the next, say, six months of rent, since you have a bank account where it would be safe." She blurted the request while picking at the pink and blue bear cub printed on her sweatpants.

Madame Hu was silent for too long. Laylea glanced up to see the landlady examining her. She grinned reflexively. Her smile fell as she took in the worry in the old woman's eyes.

Slowly, Madame Hu shook her head. "I can't do that, Ms. Lee. Money is a delicate thing."

"My friend, Amal, says it's evil."

"He's not wrong. It can do evil things to people. But think of it this way, Wai-Sun." She took a deep breath and let it all out in a rush before continuing. "If you give me all this money and then Mr. Bailey becomes injured, you will feel horrible, coming to me to beg for your money back. A good girl doesn't beg, does she?"

Laylea shook her head silently. She had been raised as a dog for the first eleven years of her life. There was no higher calling than to be a Good Girl. "No, but Bailey doesn't pay attention to what's going on around him. If someone broke in, it could be very bad." Bad, in that Bailey would react out of instinct, and his magic could bring the house down on top of all their heads. Money, or a lack thereof, would be the least of their worries, in that case.

"Mr. Bailey's focus is admirable. He will learn what he has set his mind to. However, one of life's sneakier lessons is that what we need to learn is often quite different from what we think we need to learn. Your rent is low because you and Mr. Bailey help me with maintenance issues, yes?"

Laylea drew her brows together and tilted her head. "Yes, Madame Hu. Have we missed your calls?"

"No." Madame Hu smiled. "The fault is mine. Knowing how busy you both are, I have not called for you. I make you this promise: Fan will knock on your door more often, looking for Mr. Bailey's assistance. It will increase traffic to your door, as well as break into his unhealthy focus. And force him to interact with other humans," she added, guessing at Laylea's true concern.

"Thanks, Madame Hu." Laylea stood. "I understand."

"There are ways for a minor to open a bank account, you know."

Sure there were. It required a parent's signature and a social security card, birth certificate, or other proof that you existed. A dog license was hardly going to impress the banks. "Thanks, Madame Hu. I'll look into that." She started toward the front door and then glanced over at Stan's apartment. With a quick grimace at the landlady, she dashed over and pounded on his door. "Hey Stan! That pesky dog is peeing on your car!"

There was no response from the other side of the door.

She shrugged at Madame Hu. "I'd say he's at work already."

"Ah, well." Madame Hu accepted Laylea's help to get to standing.

"Thank you, Wai-Sun." She took hold of the the railing and started up the stairs as Laylea slouched to the front door. "I guess Fan will have to start knocking on Stan's door, as well."

"Yes, ma'am." Laylea was already deep into her own thoughts again. She had to do something about the money.

"Ha!"

Laylea stopped with the front door open, frozen by Madame Hu's sharp laugh.

The old woman smiled at her. "You have my permission to tell Mr. Bailey that I just compared him to Stan. If that doesn't shame him into being more social, I don't know what will." The old lady didn't wait for her response before heading up the carpeted stairwell to her own door.

ALSO BY GWENDOLYN DRUYOR

WYRDOS Urban Fantasy Series

WereHuman 1: The Witch's Daughter

WereHuman 2: The Warrior's Son

WereHuman 3: The Hunter's Heir

WereHuman 4: The Wizard's Mutt

Voices of Reason (AVAILABLE FREE TO NEWSLETTER SUBSCRIBERS)

Shifter Ghost

Shifter Witch

Shifter Moon

Free Wishes

Dee

Laylea

Junior

Doug vs. The Boogeyman(EXCLUSIVE TO MY NEWSLETTER)

MOBIOUS' QUEST Fantasy Series

Geoffrey's Queen

Hardt's Tale

This is a work of fiction. All concepts, characters and events portrayed in this book are fiction and any resemblance to real people or events is a damn shame.

First Edition, March, 2018

LCCN 2017919015 |
Print ISBN 978-1-948421-01-0|
Ebook ISBN 978-1-948421-00-3 |
audiobook ISBN 978-1-948421-02-7

Editing by My Two Cents Editing

Published in the United States of America.

Wyrdos.net

www.ingramcontent.com/pod-product-compliance
Lightning Source LLC
Chambersburg PA
CBHW071053250626
47159CB00002B/460

* 9 7 8 1 9 4 8 4 2 1 0 1 0 *